AFFETON

*An historical novel about the French invasion
of the Isle of Wight in the fourteenth century*

AFFETON

*An historical novel about the French invasion
of the Isle of Wight in the fourteenth century*

Keith Dyer

ATHENA PRESS
LONDON

AFFETON
*An historical novel about the French invasion
of the Isle of Wight in the fourteenth century*
Copyright © Keith Dyer 2007

All Rights Reserved

No part of this book may be reproduced in any form
by photocopying or by any electronic or mechanical means,
including information storage or retrieval systems,
without permission in writing from both the copyright
owner and the publisher of this book.

ISBN 1 84748 177 9
ISBN 978 1 84748 177 1

First Published 2007 by
ATHENA PRESS
Queen's House, 2 Holly Road
Twickenham TW1 4EG
United Kingdom

Printed for Athena Press

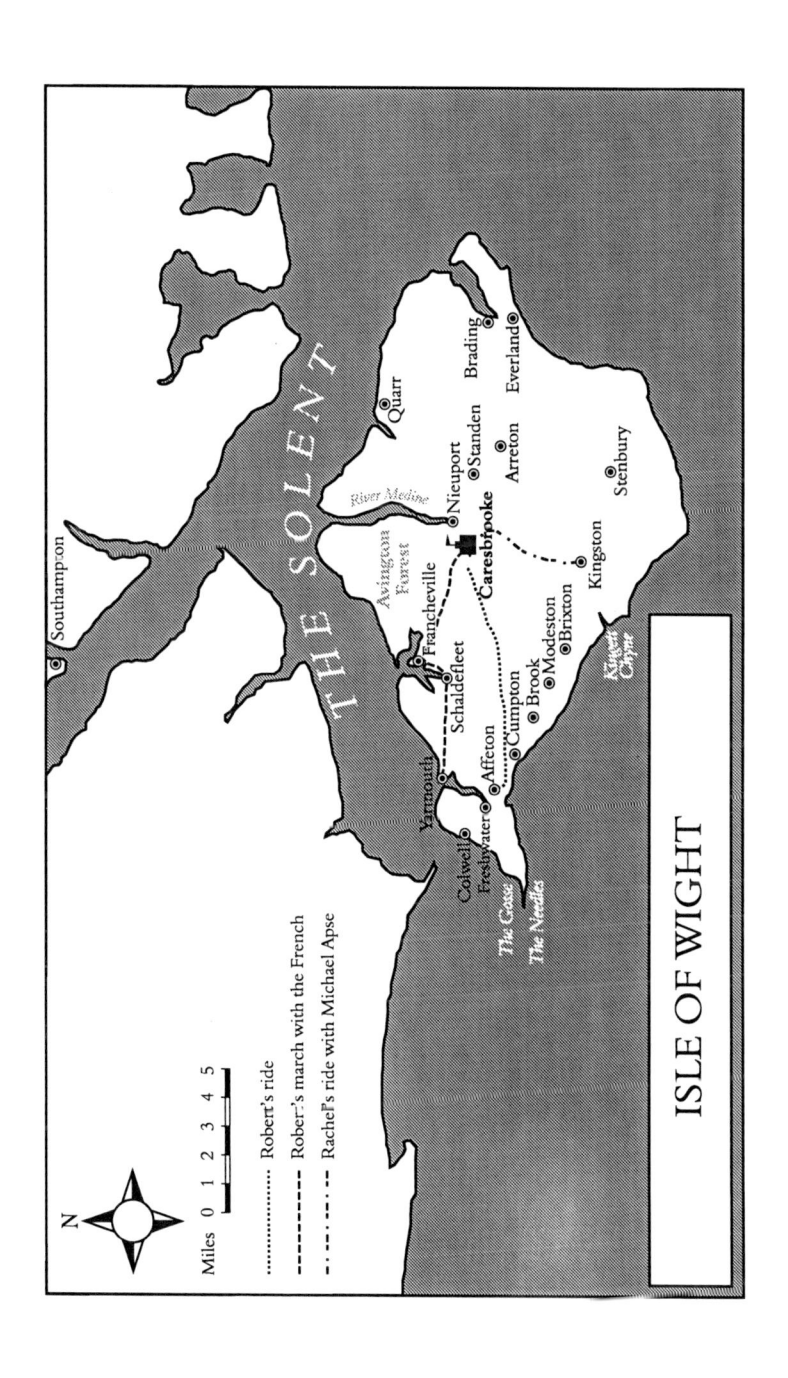

ISLE OF WIGHT

This book is dedicated to my wife Jane and my children, Georgia, Steven, Tim and Fran, for their interest and support

26 June 1377

Afternoon

The pony was out of breath. The pull up the steep slope of the downs with the young rider on her back was hard work. Being a strong and fit hobby she was used to both the rider and the path, but it was hot. The summer afternoon was sultry and still. It was five days after midsummer's day in the year of Our Lord 1377, the fiftieth one in the long and turbulent reign of the warring Edward III.

The rider eased back on the reins and the pony slowed thankfully to a stop. He pulled the pony half round so that its back was a level seat and, with his hand on the pony's hot and sweaty hindquarters, he looked over his shoulder at the view unfolding to his left. He could feel the first puffs of wind cooling his sweaty forehead and he anticipated the relief of the afternoon breeze from the sea as he reached the crest of the hill.

'Not much further, Bess,' he said aloud, giving her neck a fond pat, 'and then we can rest.' He urged the pony on with a gentle tensing of his thighs and knees and a flick of his hands on the reins. They were not too far from the top and the slope was gradually easing, becoming gentler with each pace. The sound of the pony's hooves was soft and muffled on the short thick turf. With a flutter, a skylark rose in front of them and went soaring away into the blue, singing his sweet hymn of joy.

At the top of the downs the rider swung off the pony onto the grass and sat looking northwards down the slope at the view, the sun warm on his back. The pony grazed contentedly nearby, her reins hitched over her neck, and the sweat steamed and gradually dried on her withers. The breeze whispered gently through the grass, bringing the scented smell of flowers and herbs, and the sound of seagulls screaming around their nests on the cliffs only a few furlongs to the south. Bees droned by, heavy with pollen, and

26 June 1377

little blue butterflies danced among the equally blue harebells, the purple knapweed and the yellow birdsfoot trefoil. Though the skylark's song could be heard, it was invisible in the clear blue sky, which contained only a few wisps of ragged white mare's tail clouds.

The rider was nearly six feet tall, so that he generally stood above his fellows who seldom reached a span less. He was rather slimmer than average but was sinewy and surprisingly strong, with the lean and supple frame to be expected of a young man of twenty-three. His shoulder-length light-brown hair was blowing across his widely spaced grey-blue eyes, his whole complexion revealing Saxon ancestry. Despite the three centuries since the invasion of William, Duke of Normandy, the differences between the blond and blue-eyed Saxon natives and the darker, brown-eyed Norman conquerors were still noticeable, and taken as a mark of class. However, in this case there was no hint of the serf in his appearance, nor in the firm mouth and determined chin. Though an Islander born and bred, and not so lowly born either, his character had been strengthened during the time he spent in Gascony and Normandy in service of his lord. Clean but worn brown trousers and a loose shirt was all he needed this day, but there was a coat and a blanket in the roll tied behind the saddle, for it would be tomorrow before he returned home, and who knew what the weather might bring. His main concession to the important task he had was the fine new pair of boots on his feet, though they felt strange as he had become much more accustomed to sandals of late. His name was Robert de Affeton.

Behind him the downs gradually sloped away towards the steep white chalk cliffs and the sea below, where the sun sparkled and the restless blue shimmered all the way to the horizon. To the west, the crest of the downs sloped towards the curved bay of Freshwater Gate. White cliffs and tall pinnacles and stacks guarded each end of the cove, with cool, dark, damp caves eroded into the base of the cliffs – caves where Robert, as a youth, had waded at low tide searching in the rock pools for shells, shrimp and crabs. The back of the curving bay was fringed by a steep beach of rounded flint pebbles where, in winter, the storm waves roared, flinging spume high, and making the stones rattle and groan. During gales the waves would rush right up the beach and spill over into the marshes beyond. Sometimes he could even hear the rhythmic pounding roar while the wind moaned and rattled around his house at night. Beyond the bay the tall white cliffs stretched for miles past the crest of High Down and on, to end in the sea stacks and rocks of the Needles and the Gosse, forming the western end of the Isle of Wight.

The downs were dotted with dark green and yellow clumps of furze amongst which moved the white shapes of the sheep tended by the villeins who farmed most of his father's land. Nearby, Robert could see the fat shape of Samuel, the oldest of the shepherds, leaning on his stick. Samuel had been a second father and a great friend to Robert when he was young. He used to take Robert to see the badgers' set in the woods below, taught him to catch fish in the river and showed him the best places for reaching the seagulls' eggs on the cliff ledges. With Samuel's help Robert had discovered the lore of the woodlands and hillsides, could move silently up to the conies and stand still enough for deer to almost graze at his feet.

Below the stretch of the downs where Robert sat was an undulating landscape of trees and fields, copses and woods, stretching away for several miles, much of which he would one day inherit. From one of the nearer clumps of trees rose a lazy column of blue smoke, drawing a vertical line in the clear summer air. There was no breeze down there in the shelter of the hills. Robert guessed that Marion, Samuel's wife, was lighting the fire to cook the evening meal, and he could hear someone chopping wood. In the middle distance he could see the thatched roof of his own home, Affeton Manor, built by his ancestors decades before, but where, now, his father lay on his sickbed.

Just beyond the manor was the silvery streak of the Ere River, otherwise more often now known as the River Yar, and this stretched northwards towards the Solent. The tide was high, the mudflats were covered and the fringing reed beds were sticking out into the water. Around the high-tide mark the overarching branches of the fringing trees were dipping their leaves in. Several small boats were also visible. The fishermen were probably setting traps in the creeks to catch fish stranded as the tide ebbed, or they

26 June 1377

were catching oysters. They would have come from the town of Eremue, now more commonly called Yarmouth, that sat low on the sand spit on the east side of the river mouth. Warm though the day was, Robert could see smoke rising over the town, and the squat towers of the two churches reached above the roofs of the houses. He could see in his mind's eye the bustle of the town, the noise and the smells, particularly those coming from the fish drying, or being smoked, in the special huts near the beach.

On the western side of the river mouth the golden sand spit of the duver separated the open Solent from the salt marshes and reed beds behind. Many times he had searched in the dunes for terns' eggs, and even now he could see a wheeling cloud of white wings as someone disturbed the nesting birds.

Beyond the town was the wide strip of the Solent separating the Island from the mainland. It was only about two miles wide, but this was enough to allow life to go unhindered by the strife that often afflicted the mainland.

A windhover came swinging along the side of the down, light on graceful wings, to hang quivering and almost motionless before darting off again. Robert watched it without wonder, as his mind had slipped into contemplation of the future for the island he loved. He brooded on the fears and discontent that distance and the warm summer air was hiding. From this distance the Island had the appearance of peace and prosperity, but a closer look at the fields would show some untended, with crops unsown, and others with crops grown over with unharrowed weeds; crops that would not be worth harvesting. Hedges were overgrown and if one were to walk along the footpaths, many cottages would be seen empty and decaying, with thatch falling in and walls full of holes caused by the rain. Robert was used to this desolation of the land; it had begun before his birth with the arrival of the Black Death from the Low Countries in 1349.

At first the Isle of Wight had remained untouched while the disease raged on the mainland, killing indiscriminately without favour: young and old, rich and poor. People alive and well in the morning could be dead by nightfall, black and bloated. For a while it was hoped that the Island would escape, and the Warden of the Island issued statutes preventing any contact with the mainland. But people smuggled across the water eventually brought in the disease and the Island suffered just the same. Robert's father had told him of whole families that had died and been left to rot, denied a Christian burial because others were afraid to go near them. Their neighbours had set fire to the cottages to try to stop the horror spreading, thereby forming funeral pyres over which a priest, or a travelling friar, if there was one still alive, would say a few words. Passers-by, seeing the deserted ruins, would cross themselves fervently in hope of protection, and hurry on. Eventually the disease burnt itself out. But every few years since then outbreaks had recurred, one of which took Robert's mother when he was but five years old. As a consequence, the total population of the Island was now reduced to just over 7,000.

In addition, the continuing war with France had laid the Island open to raids, and many had fled to the mainland to escape the marauders. Parliament had tried to stop this by giving the Warden of the Island the power to seize the lands and belongings of those who left. Even so, many did leave. As further incentives to stay, exemption was granted from jury service at Southampton and remission from many of the king's taxes. These privileges and immunities even caused some overners, the Island's word for those who came from over the water, to settle on the Island. Newcomers did not always fit in, with their strange ways, dialects and ideas. Nevertheless, they were welcome if they helped to defend the Island.

As a further incentive, the Islanders were excused service in the armies raised by the king to fight the war, provided they spent forty days a year helping to defend the Island. Despite this, when he was but fourteen years old, Robert's father had sent him to be a page, and later a squire in the army raised by the Lord of the Island, Edmund, Earl of Rutland and Duke of York. The Duke was fifth son of Edward III, and brother to the Black Prince and John of Gaunt, the Duke of Lancaster. Though he was a high-born and powerful master, he had never actually set foot on the Island. This was not unusual: if a lord was absent from the centre of power, this created all sorts of dangerous intrigues that might lose him the king's favour, which conferred both power and wealth.

26 June 1377

Squires served their lord in many ways – there were squires of the body, squires of the pantry and of the wines. They prepared their master's arms and armour, and looked after his needs, just as a servant would. In addition, they received training in the ways of chivalry and war, and were taught skills with the sword, the bow, and the horse. During battle they acted as protectors of their lord's goods, as messengers and servants, carrying their lord's banner into battle, and afterwards grooming his chargers. As their skill and age advanced they would have to fight, and eventually could become leaders of battalions of the army, on the way to becoming knights themselves. If they showed enough skill and daring, they might even be knighted by the king on the battlefield – the ultimate honour.

Robert had served for several years and had campaigned in Gascony and Normandy, often in the forces commanded by the Black Prince himself, that most lordly and brave of men. He had gone on raids, the chevauchée, that penetrated far into enemy territory, had fought skirmishes, laid waste to towns and villages, and plundered valuables and hostages. He had become an adept fighter with sword and bow, was no mean horseman and an accomplished jouster. He had also become a good French speaker, a skill required of the lordly classes; but the ordinary people largely did not understand French. Few on the Island spoke French, and unless he persisted in using it his new language would become distinctly rusty in time.

He was assured that he would have progressed to become a knight himself, except his father had become severely crippled and had petitioned the Duke for Robert's release to return and take over running of the Affeton estates. The Duke had granted this reluctantly, for he had taken a liking to the lad, but the campaigning was producing less and less booty, and one fewer retainer made a small but useful saving on the demands of the war chest. Robert had been back on the Island now for almost a year and he had easily settled back into the slow and placid way of life, without missing greatly the stress and excitement of war. How long this could go on would be for time to tell. Only occasionally did he feel that life might be passing him by, with experiences and adventures unlived. But then he would think over the adventures he had had, and was satisfied that they had been enough for a lifetime, and decided it was about time he settled down and ensured the survival of his inheritance.

Since he had returned Robert had been able to share his experiences with his father, Sir Roger de Affeton, who had also served in the wars in France, and had taken part in the battle of Poitiers the year after Robert was born. Many times Sir Roger had relived that battle when Robert was young, enthralling him with descriptions of how, despite the fact that they were outnumbered by at least two to one, the English longbowmen broke the French charge. Also, how the French King John and his fourteen-year-old son, Philippe, were both captured and imprisoned, and how the king's magnificent silver salt cellar was picked up on the battlefield by a group of archers who presented it to the Black Prince – they had been well rewarded. These tales had whetted Robert's appetite so that when the time came he had been excited when it was suggested he became a page and be part of the English army. He had never regretted it.

In those days Robert had been in awe of his father, who was so large, so strong and so glamorous. Now, Sir Roger was crippled by a wasting disease, which the herbalists and blood-letters could not cure. At first, even though in considerable pain, he could ride a horse around the estate to oversee the workers, and play his part in making sure the Island was well governed and defended. But as the pain became worse he could do less and less, until now he lay abed getting weaker by the month. As a consequence, almost all the duties of the lord of the manor of Affeton were now falling on Robert's slim shoulders, though Sir Roger was always able to give sound and experienced advice. Day-to-day management of the estates was left almost entirely to Robert, and of late his father had even told him to preside over the manorial court, and make judgements when there were breaches of laws and disputes. Not that Robert minded the duties; he enjoyed being trusted to carry things on and learn by his mistakes, and he especially felt he had to care for the villeins who depended on the estate. As a consequence of his care they generally respected him and considered him a good lord and master.

Robert had also taken his father's place in the council that organised defence of the Island. In that respect, one duty he had was to act as vintner, second-in-command to Adam de Cumpton who was lord of the neighbouring estates, and who was one of the lords of the West Medine. This meant that Robert was responsible for the enlistment, equipping, and victualling of the locally raised militia from Cumpton, and the neighbouring manors of Affeton and Freshwater. That very night he and Adam de Cumpton had to attend a meeting at Caresbrooke Castle, together with the other lords of the Island, to discuss with the Captain of the Island the disposition of the militia and organise the watch on the coasts for enemy raiders. This was in response to rumours that the French were preparing to launch new raids because of a weakening in the strength of the English army.

Thought of this brought Robert out of his reverie, and he jumped to his feet, for he had a good dozen miles to ride eastwards along the downs to reach the castle. He whistled to the pony, which had moved towards more succulent grazing some way away. Her ears pricked up and she slowly walked towards him, whinnying and snuffling softly. With a bound Robert leapt into the saddle, caught up the reins, dug his heels in, and they were off, pounding across the open downs, scattering the sheep and chasing their own fleeing shadows.

Two hours later Robert reined in on the downs above Caresbrooke. Both he and the pony were blowing hard, exhilarated by the ride on the springy downland turf. The only thing he had had to look out for was avoiding the occasional coney hole. He didn't want the pony to put a foot in one, to throw him off and break his leg, or even his neck, as had happened to one of his uncles not long before. But the pony had a good eye for a safe footing, and the track along the downs was easy to follow, firm and well travelled. Initially they had to go further uphill from where he had been sitting until they reached the crest of Affeton Down. Then there were a succession of chalk downs separated by steep wooded valleys. These valleys were the easy routes connecting the low land on either side of the central ridge of the downs that extended from one end of the Island to the other. The sea on their right-hand side gradually receded and a broad expanse of lower land became visible, stretching away to the south, where the coast became obscured by a further stretch of downs capped by St Catherine's Down.

At the crests of many of the downs they galloped past tumuli, places shunned at night by the local people, who believed them evil because of the strange lights and noises reputed to occur around them. Many said ancient warriors walked out of their graves in the darkness and woe betides anyone who should meet them face to face; they would be turned to stone. There were standing stones nearby that were supposed to come alive at night to testify to that truth. But during the day there were no such fears, and the way was faster than having to tread the winding paths through the woods and fields lower down. The downs were unbroken by hedges or woods, except in the valleys, and a fast hobby or pony could make good time.

Before Robert was the deep green tree-lined valley of Caresbrooke. To the left the square tower and large thatched roof of the church of St Mary peeped over the trees. To the right, and across the valley, was the steep conical mound surmounted by imposing grey battlements of Caresbrooke Castle and topped by the ancient keep constructed centuries before in the time of William the Conqueror. The banner flying from the pole showed that the captain of the Island, and constable of the castle, Sir Hugh Tyrril, was in residence. Lower down were the twin towers of the gatehouse with their conical roofs, and the grey curtain walls leading away around the keep, enclosing a bailey of just under two acres. This was Robert's destination. However, he still had to go down through the trees, cross the stream and ride up the lane to the castle.

He urged the sweating pony on. They entered the beech woods, cool and still, and the thick soft leaf mould and moss deadened their hoof beats. The woods were quiet, apart from the twittering of tits and chaffinches. The early evening sunlight dappled through the leaves, and midges danced in the sunbeams. Where the trees had fallen and gaps occurred in the tree cover, grass spread and deer browsed, only for the lawn to disappear as the trees grew and branches closed overhead. The grey and silver trunks of the soaring beech trees stood like frozen armoured

26 June 1377

warriors, caped in moss on their northern side. Platforms of white and brown fungus spread at the older trees' feet, advertising their approaching downfall. Beneath the dark canopy there was no undergrowth, only a soft carpet of last year's leaves. Low branches swept down across the track; Robert ducked low in the saddle and left the pony to pick its way, as hidden surface roots could catch the unwary. All that was needed was occasional pressure from his knees to keep the pony going in the right general direction.

As they skirted the edge of the village a pack of barking dogs appeared, snapping and snarling at the pony's heels. Groups like this always roved around the villages. But they quickly lost interest in the solitary rider once they had voiced their warning to the neighbourhood and could content themselves that they had frightened him off.

Robert crossed the track leading down the valley from Shorwell without seeing anyone, and descended to the stream, the Cares Brook, which murmured its way from pond to pond and into the large millpond to the left. The cool, shady, leaf-dipped millpond, clear, limpid and still was refreshingly inviting. Robert slid off and knelt on the bank while the pony reached down into its own reflection to drink. He plunged his arms elbow-deep and held his breath while the cold struck through and refreshed his tired muscles. He would have liked to take off his clothes and jump in, but contented himself with leaning further over and quickly shovelling water over his face and head. Then as he leaned back on his haunches, and stretched, a cold trickle crept down between his shoulder blades, making him shiver. Rubbing himself dry with his hands and wiping his face with his sleeve, he looked at his reflection in the water and combed his fingers through his hair. He was just about to rise off his knees when a malicious face appeared beside his in the water. He felt a violent shove in the back that sent him sprawling in the pool.

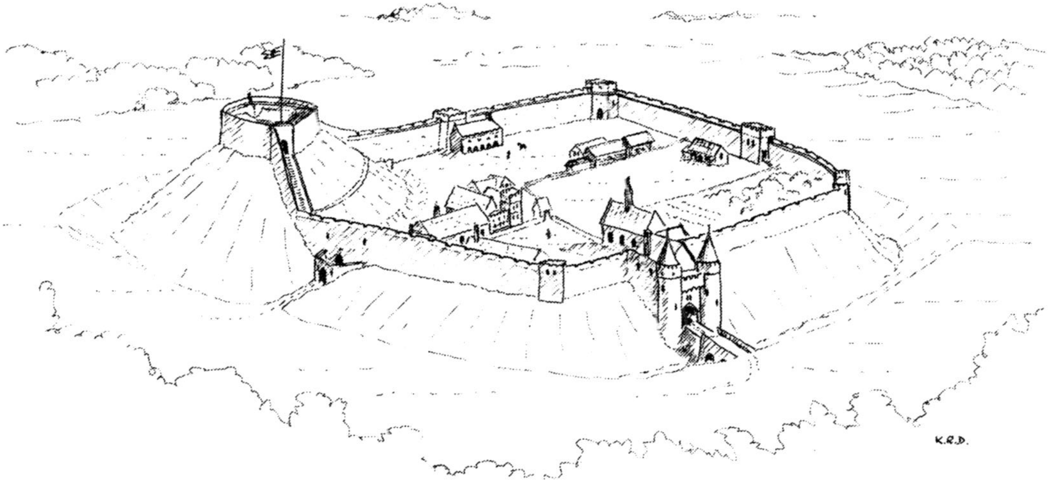

Caresbrooke Castle

26 June 1377

Evening

On his hands and knees in the water, Robert spluttered, and anger cut through the shock welling up inside him. He could feel the cold water now penetrating through all his clothes and filling his boots. He rose to his feet, the water cascading from him. He rubbed his eyes to clear them and turned to confront his attacker. As soon as he recognised him, his heart sank and his anger became an icy disdain. Before him on the bank stood a short, squat man, who only came up to Robert's shoulder in height, but who was almost twice as broad and obviously as strong as a bull. Though huge, there was not an ounce of fat on him. Large, spade-like hands on the end of immense thick arms reached down beside the tops of the thigh boots that encased his straddled legs. Inside a leather jacket his massive torso was exposed between the folds of a linen shirt. It was covered with thick black curly hair. His head seemed to grow straight from his shoulders, his neck being so short. His hair was long, black and greasy. Bushy black eyebrows almost hid the small black button eyes, and a wide mouth surrounded by a stubble-covered chin framed a nose that had been broken so often it was almost non-existent. The mouth was wide open and from it came a braying laugh that sounded more like the cawing of a crow. Robert knew him. He was Michael Apse, the steward of John de Kingston.

Behind him, sitting on a black horse and swathed in a black cloak, sat his lord, John de Kingston himself. He was an equally formidable man, but more from his imposing presence than from size. Nevertheless, he was also large and strong, though developing some slackness around the waist with approaching middle age and easy living. He had piercing brown eyes, bushy black eyebrows and a long straight nose, all set in an angular face, with a wide jaw and prominent cheekbones. He had a sinister appearance, which was heightened by a distinctive white streak in his dark but greying hair, running from the peak of his forehead to over his right ear. A sneer curled his thin upper lip. Though Robert had seen him in the meetings of the defence council, they had never exchanged more than a perfunctory word. By reputation John de Kingston was a thoroughly unpleasant man.

Robert wasn't sure whether it was de Kingston who had instigated the attack on him, or Michael Apse himself, and he was never to know. One thing he was certain of was that de Kingston was making no attempt to curb his steward's actions.

De Kingston was of Norman descent and was the lord of the manor bearing his name, which was situated a few miles southwest of Caresbrooke, near the coast. He owned much land in the neighbourhood. He had only lived on the Island for a few years, being one of the overners attracted by the cheap land and low taxes. He had bought his estates and title from the Crown after the entire family of the ancestral lord had perished from the plague. He had not attempted to make himself popular with the local folk and seemed to have the ability to create trouble wherever he went. This was exacerbated by the fact that he was one of the King's Justices and had to try felons, robbers and runaway serfs, and impose laws both good and bad. The way in which he administered this justice was arbitrary and was done with little mercy, and little attempt to understand the local conditions and practices. Consequently he had upset both the gentry and the peasants.

In particular he had a longstanding grievance against Peter de Heyno over what he saw as a significant insult. De Kingston had been out hunting in a party, which included de Heyno, not long after he had taken up residence. A stag had been put up on de Heyno land in Stenbury and they had chased it for many exhilarating miles until it came to a stand, exhausted on de Kingston's land. In the chase they had crossed several properties, but it was de Heyno's stag and it was his privilege to shoot the final arrow. However, de Kingston thought otherwise. He argued that as the chase had ended on his land it was his deer, and he should have the kill. Nevertheless de Heyno had loosed the first arrow, which hit the deer just behind the shoulder and pierced its heart. It was dead within seconds. De Heyno was the owner of a very splendid crossbow that he had inherited from his father. It was inlaid with fine silver, and in his youth he had practised and practised until he was one of the best crossbowmen on the Island. De Kingston was livid and was unconsoled by de Heyno generously saying that he was welcome to take the carcass. Ever since then there had been very tense moments at the defence council meetings, which de Heyno also had to attend.

Two years before, Peter had married Robert's elder sister, Rebecca, and it was possible that de Kingston considered Robert should share blame for his grievance. Robert had been looking forward to seeing his brother-in-law that evening. They would have much to talk of, once the business of the evening was over, for Rebecca was seven months gone with their first child.

'Well then, my lord de Affeton, you should be thankful for being so readily refreshed,' said the steward Apse.

Robert kept his temper. He knew that the only way to respond was with sarcasm, otherwise they would come to blows; he was the underdog, and would lose the impossible argument. Rather than addressing the man directly, he spoke to Apse's master, making it plain that he considered the steward a servant.

'Good afternoon, Lord John. I thank you for your timely appearance. The perfume of the clean spring water is better than many other smells in these woods.' Robert clambered, dripping, out of the water and was pleased to see a flush of anger rising on the steward's face. He could also see the discomfort of three other villeins, who had appeared out of the trees behind their lord. They glanced anxiously at him, trying to judge his mood.

'I trust that we will be able to drink a cup to your continued very good health this evening in the company of our other friends,' Robert added with a sneer, well aware that de Kingston was not popular with the other lords, who might well decline to honour such a toast.

Upon this, Apse started forward with outstretched hands, obviously bent on pushing Robert back in the water. Struggle as he might, Robert was no match for the huge strength of his adversary. He was propelled back towards the pool, but he was determined that he wouldn't get a second wetting unaccompanied and kept a firm grip on the other's jacket. Together they teetered on the bank, each struggling for a firm foothold to tip the other in.

'Ah! My Lord John and our young friend Affeton. A lively dance you seem to be enjoying. May I join you to enjoy the outcome?' This lazily spoken comment cut through their struggles, and the steward released his hold on Robert and took a step backwards.

The newcomer towered over them from the back of his tall grey stallion. This was the Lord of Knighton, Theobald de Gorges, Warden of the Island, the second most powerful man on the Island after Sir Hugh Tyrril. He was obviously also on his way to the council. Notorious beyond the Island and well loved by all who knew him (apart, that is, from de Kingston, now uncomfortable under his steady gaze). De Gorges, though now well into late middle age, sat his horse better than many a younger man. He had inherited his famous father's spirit – it was apparent in the set of his chin and in his clear steady gaze. He was tall and grey-headed, with a long grey beard, and had a real aura of authority. His father, Sir Theobald Russel, had also been popularly elected as Warden of the Island and had gallantly led the people against the French raiders in 1340 when they had landed at St Helen's Point. Sir Theobald had been fatally wounded in the fight, but the Islanders, inspired by his leadership, had driven the French back to their boats. De Gorges was an old friend and contemporary of Robert's father, to the extent that Robert thought of him as an uncle, and in return he treated Robert like a nephew.

'Come, Robert lad. Let's be off to the castle,' de Gorges said. ' 'Tis getting late and I'm sure we will be supping before the council meeting. Anyway, you need to dry out before you catch a fever.' Turning to de Kingston, he added, 'I think you would be wise to be rather more comradely to our people, since we depend on each other these difficult days. There are many more pressing problems than petty squabbling amongst ourselves.'

De Kingston grunted a non-committal reply and gave a rather sardonic inclination of his head towards de Gorges, before turning to his followers. 'Enough of this tomfoolery, Steward,' he

26 June 1377

said. 'There will be many more opportunities to enjoy yourself in good time.' He spurred his horse on, splashed through the stream and started the climb up the slope on the other side. His henchmen hurried along behind.

Robert squelched across to where his pony was standing, head down, on the edge of the glade. Sitting on a fallen tree trunk, he took off his boots one at a time and poured out a stream of water from each. He was annoyed that they had been spoiled the first time he had worn them.

'I am very glad you came by when you did, sire, for I feel that I was going to get the worst of the encounter,' he said with relief as he mounted.

De Gorges gave him a hearty slap on the back and asked how Robert had run foul of de Kingston. Robert told him of the quarrel with de Heyno.

'You must keep clear of that blackguard Apse,' said de Gorges. 'He likes a joke, but only when it is at someone else's expense. Make him the butt of it and he'll turn as black as thunder and like as not try to crush you with one blow of his fist. Never be alone with him, that's my advice. Many people have learnt that to their cost. De Kingston doesn't ever try to curb his vile humour and, in fact, I think he probably uses the man to achieve his own ends. But he will meet his match someday, I'll be bound, and I hope that he will then be trimmed down to size – it would ease many of our troubles, and give a lot of people a great deal of pleasure.'

Robert nodded. 'I've heard tales of him and of de Kingston from many people. Peter has told me about the disagreement that he has had with de Kingston, but when he is at our meetings he has been reasonable, and helpful, though he has a cutting tongue.'

'Aye, 'tis true, Robert, but 'tis possibly only a facade put on for the benefit of appearances. It doesn't fool most people of course. Sir Hugh is as wise to him as any, but he is a powerful landowner, is a King's Justice, and has some influential friends. He and his tenants are essential to the defence of our island, so we must put on a good face and wheedle him along our way. There is a limit to what people will put up with, though, and I think that we will have to endure some more spite at the meeting before we get him to agree to the organisational arrangements to be discussed this night. Still, enough of this! Let us proceed before we appear too tardy and miss the supper.'

So saying, de Gorges led the way across the stream and together they worked their way through the gathering gloom of the woods and up towards the castle.

Ten minutes later they drew rein on the rutted track in front of the castle gates. The twin grey drum towers on either side of the gateway made an imposing and impregnable defence. The towers were capped by peaked conical spires with banners hanging motionless in the still evening air. Above the gate itself ran a castellated walkway, and a sentry stood peering through the embrasures. From where he stood there was a good view of the castle approaches; enough to give warning to lower the portcullis and raise the drawbridge if there was any prospect of danger.

The wooden drawbridge was already lowered for the evening's visitors, and they trotted across it, their horses' hooves drumming on the old oak boards and echoing from the walls above. The moat beneath was not filled with water, as was customary elsewhere, because the castle was on the top of the hill, but it was thick with thorn bushes and sharpened stakes. If attackers tried to force a way through they would have a painful time, as well as being exposed to a hail of arrows and other missiles from above.

The sound of their hoof beats changed as they clattered onto the cobbles beneath the echoing archway. As they passed under the arch Robert looked up at the portcullis that was half lowered down the worn channels that testified to years of use. The sharp iron spikes at the bottom of it were only a couple of feet above their heads, and they involuntarily ducked as they passed beneath. There were also two other portcullises, but they were fully raised. Behind them, hanging on strong recessed hinges, hung huge gates of massive oak planks at least half a foot thick, studded with large nails and strapped with thick iron fastenings. Both were open.

Once inside the cobbled courtyard they had to stop outside the guardroom on the right-hand side to present their names to the sergeant on sentry duty. With a curt salute he gestured them

26 June 1377

on and shouted to ostlers to come and take their horses away to the stables on the far side of the bailey.

Within the castle, the evening air was still warm as the walls gave back the heat of the daytime sun. Blue smoke wreathed around them from the open fires of the soldiers cooking their evening meals. All was noise, activity and smells; there were about a hundred soldiers garrisoned in the castle. The ostlers came running out to hold the horses' heads while they dismounted.

As they crossed the courtyard, Robert looked around, catching a glimpse of Michael Apse talking to two of the soldiers. To their right was the chapel of St Nicholas, while in front was the well house and grouped close under the walls were a number of buildings inhabited by Sir Hugh Tyrril and his retainers. The great hall was in the centre, built against the castle wall, and flanked by the various chambers of the residence. They were large, solid buildings with roofs of mossy reed thatch in which many sparrows lived. The walls were built of rough grey weathered greensand and chalk, relieved by small pointed windows, heavily leaded with thick glass, from which shone welcoming multicoloured lights. From inside came the murmur of voices and the occasional burst of laughter.

De Gorges hammered on the door of the great hall then, tipping the latch, he swung the heavily nailed door open. Stooping beneath the low door lintel, he led the way into the passageway separating the hall on the right from the kitchens and private chambers on the left. Their arrival in the hall was greeted by a chorus of shouts from the assembled men.

Though he had been there several times before, Robert never ceased to be impressed by the room. It was all of sixty strides long and forty wide. At one end was a wide fireplace set into the wall, with a large blackened beam head-high above it. On the hearth a fire topped by two large logs was flaming up the chimney, casting flickering lights and shadows over floor and walls. Puffs of smoke spilled out of the chimney and rose silently up into the roof to hang motionless in the gloom of the already smoke-blackened rafters. Along the side they had entered were two deep-set lancet windows with wide window shelves providing seats. On the opposite side were several small arched doorways, across which curtains of rust-coloured woven wool were hanging. These separated off small chambers set deep in the castle walls, each one being provided with a narrow slit window to the outside through which an archer could shoot if the castle was besieged. These were the sleeping rooms for visitors. In the far corner was the door to the small private chapel of St Peter, built a hundred years before. All around the hall were rushlights thrust into holes in the walls, and these gave additional flickering light, smoke and smell. The floor was flagged with worn, uneven stones strewn with rushes. In the centre of the room was an enormous table, old and scarred, surrounded by benches and stools, and covered with hides and skins. At either end of the table were chairs with arms and high backs carved with coats of arms. The table was laid with a long linen cloth, which was rapidly disappearing under dishes and trays of food being brought in by pages through the door from the kitchens. This was to be the reresoper, the late evening meal. It was only on special occasions that a meal was taken so late, as normally supper would be eaten before dark in order to avoid the expense of having to use valuable tallow candles. This evening was such an occasion.

There was already a group of a dozen and a half men standing near the fire, and a few more still to come. To external appearances they were a motley collection. But Robert knew them all as the lords of the Island, each one a powerful and wealthy landowner. In order to protect their land and the Island from raids of the hostile French they had grouped together in mutual defence to organise watchers on the coast, who would raise the alarm by firing the beacons. Besides this they organised their tenant farmers and villeins into companies of trained militia by holding archery and sword contests, as had been the law for many years. They provided regular stocks of food and weapons for the castle, to be held in case of emergency, which were added to those already provided at the King's expense.

The Island was divided into two parts, the East and the West Medine, separated by the Medine River that cut deep into the centre of the Island. The East Medine comprised five districts, of which Peter de Heyno commanded one: Theobald de Gorges, William Russel of Everland, John Urrey of East Standen, and the bailiffs of Nieuport, who had jurisdiction over the town, were the other commanders. In the West Medine there were four districts, John de Kingston, and Adam de Cumpton being two of the commanders, and the Lord of Brook and the Lord of Modeston, Thomas Chyke were the others.

Each lord had their vintner in attendance. In addition there were a few others present, such as the Abbot of Quarr, who had considerable land and who contributed taxes to the Island's defence. They knew each other well, though there was considerable rivalry and distrust between some of them. They had met many times over the last few years as Edward, the king, had grown older and the strength and resolve of the English forces in France had weakened. This resulted in the ever-present threat of invasion increasing considerably.

A gruskyn of wine diluted with water was thrust into Robert's hand and he was enveloped in the throng. He was by far the youngest there, and as such was always the butt of their teasing. Peter de Heyno put his brotherly hand on Robert's arm, but withdrew it quickly when he felt that his clothes were wet.

'You are very wet, Robert. Have you been swimming fully clothed, eh? I think there must be a good tale behind this,' he said. 'What has happened?'

Peter was of the same height as Robert, but dark-haired with a strong chin, broad cheeks and a nose badly broken in a fall from his horse when he was young. He was smiling and always good-humoured, and it took a great deal to upset Peter. Indeed, Robert had never seen him lose his temper. He was a few years older than Robert, and they had become firm friends at Peter's marriage.

'Methinks a wench must have pushed him into a stream to cool his ardour,' said the portly Sir John Lisle with a laugh. He had adjoining estates to de Kingston, and acted as his vintner.

'You'd be wrong in your thoughts, my lord. His horse stumbled in the brook and unseated him. I saw it myself, and nearly fell off my horse and joined him by laughing so well,' cut in de Gorges in an attempt to avoid Robert further embarrassment.

As he said this he looked straight at de Kingston, who simply flicked an eyebrow, showing no discomfort.

'Come over here to the fire, my lad, and dry out.'

The sepulchral voice came from a tall gaunt figure with a large beak-like nose, long moustaches and thinning grey hair, who leant against the fireside with his elbow on the mantelshelf. His sparse hair accentuated the paleness of his skin and his prominent cheekbones made him appear deathly thin and skull-like. However, his looks belied his strength and stamina. This was Sir Hugh Tyrril, the constable of the castle and captain of the Island, responsible only to the King for the safety of the Island and the inhabitants. He and de Gorges had to work closely together, as the latter had charge of the justice and the raising of taxes on the Island, much of which supported the defence.

'How is your father these days?' Sir Hugh asked of Robert, as the others turned to their own conversations.

'As well as ever, I thank you, sire. He sends his best wishes and regrets for not being able to attend. He chaffs hard at his inability to see to his business and get about as he used to.' Robert was grateful not to be the centre of attention any more.

'Aye! Well that is to be expected with a man who was so active. I remember the many fine deer hunts we had, and the skirmishes too in France and at Poitiers, where we stood together. Those were good days. Nevertheless, he is lucky to have someone like you to look after the estates.'

Sir Hugh pulled himself away from his memories and turned to a short man on his left. 'Have you had any more villeins take to the woods of late, Standen?' he asked.

'No, sire,' relied John Urrey, lord of East Standen, a small, hunched untidy man in greasy clothes with pockmarked face, who had the habit of always rubbing his hands together as if they were cold.

'They seem fairly settled at the moment, though there would have been more trouble if Parliament had increased taxes last February. So far we haven't done too badly; only six people have left to escape their villeinage. I can't afford to pay for their services on my desmesne because the wages they are demanding are too high. Why, I hear that franklins and lords of the manor in some parts are having to pay fourpence and even sixpence an acre just for reaping.'

26 June 1377

Traditionally serfs, or villeins, owed many days of service to their lords. This left them little time to tend their own acres on which they and their families depended. By agreement with their master they could remit the service by supplying produce or goods, but the system was becoming highly resented by the villeins.

'Aye, 'tis true,' broke in another. 'But the work they get from payment is better than that from villeins who only do it because they have to. Though the villeins once did the ploughing with their own horses or oxen, we now have to supply the teams of horses and bear the cost of keeping them over the winter. The work may be better, but we need to make extra hay for the winter fodder, so it all ends up much the same in the end.'

'That's why many are turning the fields that used to be arable land into pasture, and are increasing their flocks of sheep. Sheep are less trouble than continual ploughing, sowing and reaping. And the wool we produce is fetching a fair price at the moment, though not as much as it would if we could only get it safely to the markets of Flanders, Ghent and Bruges. The French and Castilians are so strong at sea now that few of our merchant ships can get through to those ports.'

'Things could be worse though,' said Sir Hugh. 'If the good Parliament hadn't managed to force the Duke of Lancaster's hand, then Richard Lyons would still be extorting all the customs dues and inflating prices to ridiculous levels.'

'But, as it is, much of that has been reversed since then,' broke in de Gorges.

Richard Lyons had been given the right by the King, much to the resentment of many, to set the export duty on goods, especially wool, going overseas out of the main ports. It had made him very wealthy. The duty had increased the prices so much that it had resulted in a strong contraband trade, but much of that was being pirated by the foreign ships. So the wool merchants either had to pay the dues, or run the risk of losing everything to the pirates.

'We've heard about the goings-on in Parliament from de Gorges who, as you know, was one of our shire members. I'm hoping that he'll tell us about this new session while we eat,' said Sir Hugh.

Other conversations had ceased and all were grouped round the fire listening to these exchanges; the topic was close to all of their interests.

'I will indeed,' said Theobald de Gorges. 'I have some very strange and interesting stories to tell you about the session of Parliament I attended last February. I haven't been home from London more than a fortnight, but I am sure you have heard the main facts before, no doubt...'

'But you must fill in the details,' demanded Sir Hugh. 'Let us sit and eat, and perhaps good food will put a less gloomy aspect on what we will hear.'

So saying, he led them to the table and took the big high-backed chair at the head. The others took the benches on either side. Robert slid in beside Peter de Heyno.

Opposite them was Adam de Cumpton, and Robert acknowledged him with a bow of the head. De Cumpton was a middle-aged bachelor, a very severe man, rotund and balding, known for his complete lack of humour. Robert was always careful to be very deferential to him and to be serious in any remarks he addressed to him. As they were neighbours, de Cumpton and Robert's father had many interests in common, and they had had to develop a workable relationship between each other, but it was a very uneasy one because they were such totally different characters.

Silence fell as one of Sir Hugh's squires brought in the magnificent salt cellar that was the customary centrepiece of the table. Salt was a valued and necessary addition to the meal, the perquisit of the lord to distribute. The pages then brought round baked slices of the two-day-old bread that formed the trenchers off which they would eat, since there were not enough wooden platters for everyone. Each person had a napkin and a spoon, and a mazer to drink from, and a large newly baked loaf. Pitchers of ale were brought to quench their thirst, as water was avoided whenever possible because of the risk of catching the bloody flux. Nevertheless, water was the main drink of the very poor. It was generally drunk with wine, but since wine was not normally imported in the summer it often ran out or turned sour before the new supplies arrived from Gascony in the autumn. However,

26 June 1377

some of the higher quality 'wine of the reck' had arrived in May, and this is what they had been drinking before the meal.

There was a discreet cough and all fell silent as the Abbot rose to say grace and bless the meal they were about to eat. Then the pages circulated round the table with bowls of water, and they all rinsed their hands to wash off the dirt of their travel, drying their hands on the napkins. The alms dish was put on the table, and on it was placed a loaf and a portion of all the other dishes, before it was carried out for the poor and sick. The carver then proceeded to cut the bread for Sir Hugh, and this was the signal for everyone else to start their meal.

Robert and Peter drew their knives. Robert grabbed a loaf and hacked off two chunks of bread, while Peter ladled spoonfuls of thick broth onto their trenchers. As was customary, the serious business of eating was dealt with before conversation. The potage was made from meat liquor with herbs, oatmeal and salt, and was both tasty and nutritious. Then there was meat, venison, mutton and beef, hacked into small lumps. Chicken, pheasant and rabbit were cut into pieces, and the meat stripped off the bones by the mouthful. Dishes of boiled lettuce and cabbage, leeks and peas appeared, and various sorts of fish, both fresh and wind-dried stockfish. Hands stretched across the table and grasped the ale jugs and food off the servers, though with gentility because it was a time of very fastidious manners.

Two long grey shadows rose from the rushes in the corner and came towards the table. They were Sir Hugh's wolfhounds. They slunk under the table to search for dropped scraps. Since all of the scraps were placed in special voiders, there was little for them. However, some bones were surreptitiously dropped, and the hounds pounced on them, growling ferociously. The pages stepped carefully over them as they took empty dishes away and brought refilled ones back to the table. These contained fruit, though it was still too early in the year for the best fruit, and jellies and wafers, a batter fried with cheese or honey.

Eventually, one by one the men loosened their waistbands, sat back, wiped the congealed fat from their mouths and beards and washed the grease from their fingers in the bowls of water the pages brought round. The Abbot of Quarr said the grace of

Evening

thanksgiving while they reverently bent their heads, and suppressed their belches. The pages then carried the reversion, the remnants of the meal, away for themselves and the cooks and other servants to eat.

'Fill the cups again,' shouted Sir Hugh, wiping his moustache, for all the pages were disappearing quickly so they might eat before the food became cold.

There was a general scraping of the benches as more comfortable positions were sought and legs were stretched out. Several of the lords left the table briefly to find the garderobe where they could relieve themselves.

'Now, de Gorges, let's hear the details of the events in London.'

Theobald de Gorges took a gulp from his goblet and cleared his throat as he gathered his thoughts.

'As you all know,' he said, 'the only reason that Parliament is ever called is the need for fresh taxes to continue the war in France, and we have to agree them. Though we may hedge such agreement with laws that we may believe are necessary for the running of the country, they can always be reversed by the King afterwards. He is open to being persuaded by the Privy Council and by his descendents. As he grows older, their influence seems to be growing.

'There are many different factions in both houses of Parliament. The Lords are in competition for power, influence and favours from the King, and in many ways the Commons is a reflection of the same thing. Most of the elected members owe their position to some faction or other, and are bound to support their benefactor.

'There are basically four main groups. Since the Black Prince died last year the influence of his brother, John of Gaunt, the Duke of Lancaster, has grown considerably. He now has many more supporters. One of his main complaints is against the Church, its wealth and power. The Church is also represented, since the bishops are all members of the House of Lords, and there are frequent disagreements between these two groups. Also there are a number of lords in opposition to Lancaster, and these are the generally faithful, and favoured, supporters of the old

26 June 1377

King; the Earl of March is one of them. Then there are a number of members whose main purpose is to improve the governance of the country, and decrease the misuse of taxes. These tend to be more numerous in the Commons. However, our voices tend to get swamped by the other interests, as not many get elected for more than one Parliament. The House of Lords is even more a battleground of personal interests and ambition.

'As you know, there is little support for the war. Everyone is saying we should leave France to the French. You may remember that before we voted on the taxes in the last Parliament we managed, with the help of the Lords, to pass some good and helpful laws. We tried to remove those who had been mismanaging the affairs of state, to get rid of the worst corruption and ensure the money collected in taxes was spent honestly. John of Gaunt was the main problem, with his desire for money, influence and power, but even so, many people share his arguments for reforming the Church, making it return to its religious roots, making it more accountable and making it pay taxes on the same basis as the rest of us.'

At this the Abbott of Quarr looked disapproving, but de Gorges continued. 'We thought that we'd won when he said that he would correct the abuses of power, and Richard Lyons was arrested and imprisoned, and the King's mistress, Alice Perrers, was prosecuted and had to leave court. However, just as soon as the Parliament had voted the taxes that were demanded, and was dissolved, the King declared it to be no Parliament and all of the laws we'd made were cancelled, the Speaker, Peter de la Mare, was arrested and imprisoned, Lyons was freed and Alice Perrers returned to court. It seemed that Lancaster had regained his influence after all. At least when the Black Prince died last July, his son Richard was proclaimed heir, and not John of Gaunt himself. For that we have to be thankful!

'This session of Parliament was entirely different from the last, which is now being called the "Good Parliament". This time there were only eight of us who'd been in the previous one. Normally there is a pretty high turnover of representatives between parliaments, especially of knights of the shire, but this time there were only eight, which was extraordinarily low. There were rumours that the elections had been tampered with by John of Gaunt and his followers, so that in some shires even though the sheriff had proposed candidates, no election had been held. Consequently, this Parliament had a completely different tone from last year's, with most people being supporters of John of Gaunt, or at least owing him some sort of allegiance.'

He took another drink before continuing.

'Anyway, this time it was Richard, even though he is only ten years old, who opened the first parliamentary session on 27 January, which was held in the Painted Chamber at Westminster Abbey. The first thing that happened was that Sir Thomas Hungerford from Wiltshire, who is the Duke's steward, was elected Speaker. The last Speaker, Peter de le Mare, is still imprisoned in Nottingham Castle without any prospect of a trial. He was absolutely fearless in insisting that the reforms be met before the taxes would be agreed. Of course, some of us protested that he should be released but there was nothing we could do, as we were completely outvoted. When we were asked by the Chancellor to agree the taxes for the coming year, we in the Commons tried to use the same trick as last time and got the same lords to sit in with us when we withdrew into the Chapter House to discuss the bill. Only this time it didn't work. Instead of the lords providing enough backing for us to refuse agreement until our other grievances had been settled, it seemed they were now mainly on the Duke's side. Lord Percy was the main person leading the refusal last time, but now he had switched sides. He had been bought off by being made king's marshal, mainly, it is thought, because of the Duke's influence with the King. So we couldn't do anything, and everything that was suggested by these lords was accepted. We, the old members, were very annoyed.'

De Gorges was really warming to his task now that the memories were revived and the heat of his righteous anger rekindled.

'There is a poet, one John Gower, who is going round the country blaming the state of society on the failure of the knighthood to do their duty. He says that the knights with their misdeeds, together with their squires – some going off to make wars, others staying at home, proud and covetous – are the

26 June 1377

evildoers. Those who fight in wars do so often for the wrong reasons, while those who stay at home are valiant only in courts where they conquer with their tongues, rather than their swords. When they do fight it is in support of other people's quarrels, or to oppress poorer neighbours. These "hedgerow knights" will never besiege a castle; they unfurl their banners only in a safe place, where no wound is to be feared. The knights at court are rife with lechery, luxury, adultery, incest and pride, not the chivalry of the old days.' There was a murmur of agreement round the table and a general shaking of heads at this.

'If that is the general feeling, it is not surprising that the countryside is so uneasy and the serfs so rebellious. I think that there will be an uprising against the court soon if something fundamental is not done,' said Sir Hugh. De Kingston scowled in agreement with the sentiment of the quotation of John Gower.

'However,' went on de Gorges, 'it so happened, that the Church Convocation started at St Paul's on 3 February, beneath that splendid spire with the golden ball and the huge cross. They also had to agree the taxes that they would pay. Sudbury, the Primate, is basically a humble and peaceful man, but Courtenay, the Bishop of London, who is related to the Duke of Devonshire, is stronger and they refused to agree the taxes the Church had to pay until their grievances had been settled – just as we had wanted to do. Their first grievance was that William de Wykeham, the Bishop of Winchester, had been deprived of his see and was being hounded all round the country. Though he was supposed to be at the Convocation, the Duke's men had prevented him from coming. So the Convocation refused agreement until he was allowed to come. When at last he did arrive, they then insisted on John Wycliffe answering to a charge of heresy, because he had been preaching for confiscation of Church property. He thinks the Church is far too rich and too many people take holy orders not because of belief, but for the sake of the riches and the easy life they can lead. This is why he is one of the Duke's main spokesmen. The Duke wants to see the power of the Church reduced, and must think that he will be able to share in the spoils if the property was confiscated. This was the point when the fun really started.'

'Rightly so, too,' said the Abbot of Quarr. 'It is heretical to speak against God's house and his ordained ministers. Wycliffe should be punished.'

Everyone else shifted uncomfortably, for they agreed in some measure with the sentiments of those who agitated for reform of the Church and curbing of their worst excesses, but they were reluctant to say so in public.

Sir Hugh held up his hand to prevent further disagreement upsetting the discourse, and gestured to de Gorges to continue.

'It was eventually agreed that Wycliffe should appear before the bishops at St Paul's on 19 February to answer these charges of heresy. We succeeded in having the sitting of Parliament postponed for that day, despite the fact that the Duke of Lancaster and his allies were trying to push through a bill, introduced in the King's name. This was aimed to take the government of London from the mayor and cease to make it politically independent. They wanted to put it in the hands of the King's Marshal, none other than Lord Percy himself.

'The King really is too old to see the trouble that the Duke of Lancaster and his followers are causing. As he gets older everyone is out to line their own pockets and they twist him round their little fingers. I suppose the old man must dote on his fourth son, the Duke, now that the oldest, the Black Prince is dead,' de Gorges said sorrowfully. 'After all, he is rather like his father was when he was younger.'

'Why would they want to get authority over London, though?' asked John Urrey. 'It is far too large with too many different factions to be manageable. It would be a continual headache.'

'Ah!' said de Gorges. 'London has been opposing the Duke at every turn. Being independent, wealthy and influential, the burgesses of London must be a big obstacle if they oppose you, but a big asset if they are on your side. Percy himself was the instigator of this bill, together with Thomas of Woodstock who is another younger brother of Lancaster. They probably just wanted a share of the wealth – as if they weren't rich enough already.

'As you might guess, the city was in a ferment and a huge mob crowded the whole length of the aisle of the church. They all wanted to see what would happen to Wycliffe, the man who had

26 June 1377

expressed John of Gaunt's policy of disowning the Church of its property. Of course, the crowd sympathised with his sentiments, but I think that distrust and hatred of the Duke was stronger on this occasion.

'I'd been able to get a good position by one of the pillars so that I could see and hear all that went on, though it was so noisy that it was often difficult to hear. The bishops were assembled behind the altar of the Lady Chapel talking among themselves when Wycliffe appeared at the door of the cathedral. He was followed by four friars from Oxford, each of a different order judging by the colour of their habits. They were to be his witnesses. By his side was the Duke himself and just in front of them strode Percy, the King's Marshal. With his sheathed sword he was pushing everyone back to make room. Bishop Courtenay was standing in the aisle waiting for them to arrive. He went purple at this affront to the Church and said that he'd have never admitted them had he known they would behave in such a discourteous and irreligious manner. The Duke answered that they'd do as they pleased whether he liked it or not. This caused uproar, as you might guess.

'They walked straight through to the Lady Chapel, and everyone who could followed. Luckily I managed to get in. In the chapel all the other bishops of the Convocation were waiting. Primate Sudbury was sitting nervously, and was obviously uncomfortable, in the centre behind a large table. The Duke and Percy took chairs for themselves, and Percy told Wycliffe to sit down as it could take a long time. This was too much for Courtenay who told the prisoner to stand during his trial. The two lords swore he should sit, and Courtenay insisted he should stand. At this Percy lost his temper and said that he would bring down the pride of all the bishops, and that Courtenay had better not look to his parents – the Earl and Countess of Devon – for any help. At this the Bishop said he placed his trust in God who would be his protector.

'This exchange had set the crowd shouting and they made a rush at the Duke and fights broke out between them and the Duke's guards. The Duke and Percy pushed their way out of the cathedral, taking a rather dazed Wycliffe with them, and everything was confusion. Then all the notables left, and only the burgesses, citizens and apprentices of the city remained. That evening all the alehouses were full of argument and a number of troublemakers were trying to stir up some sort of rebellion, and get the people to take matters into their own hands.

'Even greater things happened next day because it came out that Percy had assumed the powers of a magistrate by arresting one of the people who attacked him and had locked him up. When the leading citizens heard this they took up arms, broke into Percy's house, released the prisoner and made a bonfire of the stocks in the street. I heard that they even looked under the beds for Percy, and if they'd found him I am sure they would have killed him, whatever the consequences. The mob was really out of control for they then went to the Duke's house, the Savoy, intending to burn it down. On the way they caught a priest who was silly enough to revile Peter de la Mare as a traitor. They set upon him and beat him to death. By this time Courtenay had appeared and argued some sense into them, and managed to break up the mob before they reached the Savoy. Instead, they paraded the streets to try to find some of the Duke's supporters, but they'd hidden their caps in their sleeves to avoid being recognised. There is a shop in Cheapside that the Duke patronises, and his armorial shield hung over the door. I heard they tore it down and put it back upside down as a warning to him and his followers.'

'What had happened to the Duke and Percy during all this, Theobald?' asked Sir Hugh, while de Gorges emptied his goblet. 'They must have been keeping out of the way somewhere else.'

'Ah! Apparently, the Duke and Lord Percy were dining together when they were warned of the approaching crowd. They got away across the river to Kennington Palace before the mob reached Percy's house. Ironically, they took refuge with the Black Prince's wife, and stayed there until things simmered down. The city elders sent a deputation to the King to complain about the attack on their liberties. The King received them well enough and promised their liberties would be respected, and the Duke gave way and was forced to withdraw the bill about taking over the city of London. But the King was not well and it seems that since then the Duke has re-established his position against the Londoners.

26 June 1377

Just before I left London I heard that the King had deprived the Mayor and sheriffs of their offices.

'What will happen when the King dies, as he is sure to soon, one can only hazard. It will depend on how much power the Duke can gain over the boy Richard, his nephew. All in all there seems to be nothing but contests for power and government of the country. The wars with France take a very poor second place, and the general population suffers.'

Sir Hugh, who had been gazing dejectedly at the cup between his hands while listening looked up, banged the table and said, 'A toast – to law, order and reason.'

Everyone stood and raised their goblets. 'The King, law, order and reason!' they chorused as they drank deeply. 'And death to the French,' added de Kingston, and the goblets were raised again.

'Did Parliament do anything about the labourers' unrest and the wages they're demanding?' asked de Kingston once they were seated, returning to the previously aired topic.

'Oh yes,' said de Gorges. 'A statute was passed that ordered a special commission of Justices of the Peace to hear cases the Lords put up against any offenders, and to punish them. If I remember rightly, it went something like this: "Complaint has been made by the lords of the manor, as well as men of the Holy Church, that the villeins on their estates affirm themselves to be quite and utterly discharged of all manner of serfage due of their persons, as well as their tenures, and will not suffer any distress or other justice to be made upon them; but do menace the ministers and their lords of life and limb, and gather themselves in great riots and agree by such confederacy that everyone shall aid each other to resist their lords with strong hand: and much other harm they do and evil example to others to begin riots, so that if remedy be not imposed on the rebels, greater mischief may spring through the realm." '

De Kingston broke in. 'Sounds like this commission won't do much good, though. The single villeins take to the woods in attempts to remain free. The others are so damned surly that the work they do is no good anyway. In my opinion the only way to stop this rebellion is to beat them and teach them who their rightful masters are. It only needs an example to be made of a few for the rest to fall into line.'

He was in a position to carry out this threat, since as the King's Justice he had to try those serfs who ran away from their duties. If they were caught within four days they were fined by the manorial court and sent back to work. If they were free for a year and a day they were then free men. Between those times the punishment was at the discretion of justices, such as de Kingston. His judgements were harsh. Some escapees were put in the stocks and whipped, others were branded on their foreheads with the letter 'F', for falsity. Nevertheless, those harshly punished remained poor workers and still tried to run away. Many of the other lords had tried to persuade de Kingston to be more lenient so that the serfs would not be so resentful afterwards, but without success.

'But that only incenses them more,' said Peter. 'Can't you see? Why not pay them a fair wage for a day's fair work on your demesne, as I do. They work better and feel freer. They each have their own parcel of land which they can feed themselves from, and they can send excess produce to market. Then they will not want to leave for somewhere else where conditions may actually be worse anyway. If they do leave, their lands are forfeit so that you do not lose everything. We then would not have any responsibility for them or their families if the harvest were poor.' Peter was one of the more progressive-thinking of the landowners, and he had very little unrest on his estates as a consequence.

'Sometimes it's even worth selling them their freedom and some land,' added William Russel. 'They are not so likely to leave land that is theirs and which they've paid for. The only problem is that few have the money to buy the land.'

De Kingston huffed angrily. 'It is not right that they should be paid! They are villeins. It is their duty to work and pay obeisance to their lords, and it is our right to expect it. Too many don't worry about land anyway. They run to the mainland for fear of attack from the French – either that or they move into the towns, or somewhere with more fertile land. A good bailiff and a set of good dogs to catch them soon brings them to their senses. Let them all go free and I'd have to look after my own sheep and plough my own land. Catch me doing that!'

26 June 1377

'Might be a good change from hunting all the time, not only hares, but poachers, and then bringing them to court. Why, you lose more of your villeins by hanging than you did by the plague,' Peter stated with a mischievous grin, though he immediately regretted his impetuous taunt.

De Kingston, with a curse, threw the contents of his goblet at Peter, who ducked. The wine hit Robert on the side of his head. He put up his hand to wipe his eyes clear and felt the warmness of the wine prickling his hair as it trickled down his neck. Peter was on his feet, pulling his sword from its scabbard, but Robert caught his elbow to restrain him and others crowded round to keep the two dissenters apart. Though Peter tried to get free, he was not letting his temper get the better of him. Robert moved towards de Kingston to demand an apology. But before he could say anything, Sir Hugh pushed in front of him and confronted them.

'Lord,' he said with a dark scowl to Peter, 'your taunts are insulting and inappropriate here. You must apologise.' Then he turned to de Kingston with a sardonic sneer. 'Your shortness of temper and inability to take a jest betrays you. We must not brawl in the style of the villeins that you revile. You and de Heyno should apologise, or settle this in the way of knights. Would you prefer a tilting match, a joust...? Choose your way.'

De Kingston flushed and, breathing heavily, paused to gather his wits. 'I believe you profess to be something of an archer,' he said to Peter. 'I've a mind to test your ability, but with longbows, not crossbows.' Few could beat Peter with a crossbow, but with a longbow de Kingston was thought to be at least his equal. It would be an interestingly even contest.

'I would be happy to withdraw my remarks that have caused you upset, but if you wish to settle it as a matter of honour in a contest of skill, that would suit me well,' replied Peter. He sounded rather pleased, for he was sure he could win and be vindicated. 'Two ends to the butts at 200 paces. And I wager ten marks on the result.' This was a total of twelve arrows each, six arrows either way along the range, to even out advantages of wind. They would then split a sheaf of two dozen arrows between them, so that there was no apparent advantage through differences in the arrow shafts or fletching. The winner would then be considered the most skilful.

De Kingston looked satisfied, nodded his head and rubbed his hands together, saying, 'Agreed! And I'll double your wager.'

'Come now, my lords,' broke in Sir Hugh. 'Let us put these differences aside and carry out the business we assembled for. The hour is late and we have a lot to do.'

They acquiesced and turned back to the table, setting upright the overturned benches. Spaces were cleared on the table for writing, and they prepared to sit down.

At that moment there was the sound of galloping hooves on the cobbles outside and of shouts. A fraction later the door burst open and into the room, with eyes screwed up and blinking against the light and the smoky air, ran a youth, followed by a rather distraught guard. The lad was out of breath, having obviously ridden hard. Robert recollected having seen him as an apprentice to one of the burgesses in Nieuport. The newcomer glanced round until he saw Sir Hugh at the head of the table, and fell to one knee. Sir Hugh was just about to remonstrate with him for his bad manners in not seeking audience properly announced, when he burst out.

'My lord, the news has just come: the King... the King is dead.'

A stunned silence fell and the boy, to cover his embarrassment, stood, looked around and rattled off all the details he knew.

'I beg your pardon, sire. A messenger has just arrived from Southampton. I heard him speaking in the butter market in Nieuport, and my master thought you should know straight away. The King died of a stroke on 21 June at Shene. Richard is being proclaimed king, and is to be crowned on 16 July. The Duke of Lancaster is reconciled with the Earl of March and our Bishop of Winchester—'

'Cease, boy, cease!' shouted Sir Hugh. 'Let us catch up. The 21st. That's five days ago. Now, slowly. You say the Duke is reconciled with March, his old rival.'

'Yes, sire. It was the day after the King's death. The Duke of Lancaster, the Earl of March and William of Wykeham were present at the ceremony of the seals, whatever that is...'

26 June 1377

'That is when the Privy Seal and the other official seals of the dead king are presented to the new king, King Richard,' broke in de Gorges knowingly. 'Go on, lad.'

'Yes, sire. As this was happening, a deputation arrived from London to swear allegiance to the new king. Richard made them and the Duke agree to peace. The Duke then embraced the deputation one by one. Also one of the King's first actions was to send an order out to release Peter de la Mare from Nottingham Castle. It is also reported that Alice Perrers took the rings off the late king's fingers and left him with a priest to die. That's all the messenger said, sire.'

'You have done well, my boy. Here's something for your trouble.' Sir Hugh tossed him a silver penny and the boy, covered in confusion and muttering his thanks, backed towards the still-open door and fled, clutching the anticipated coin.

The lords looked at each other in amazement. The silence broke and a clamour of comment started. There wasn't much sorrow that Edward III's long reign had come to an end. In the early days things had gone very well for England. The wars with France had been successful, there had been plenty of booty and trade and everyone, even the lowliest serfs, had profited, despite the problems caused by the Black Death. But as he grew older much had slipped from the King's grasp, especially after his wife, Phillipa of Hainult died in 1369. In the war, the guerrilla tactics of the French king, Charles V, had succeeded and more and more taxes had to be raised to carry on the conflict, in which no one had very much interest. Trade had suffered and the standard of living had decreased. There was much intrigue at court and the King's opinion had become swayed by the Duke of Lancaster, especially after the Black Prince's death. Now the whole country would be hoping that King Richard would change things.

Theobald de Gorges stood up with his goblet in his hand saying, 'My Lords, a toast. To the King! Long live the King!'

They all chorused this, thinking that only a few minutes before they had been toasting a different king. They were all too excited by the news to sit down again and crowded round the fire, immediately discussing the possibilities provided by King Richard's accession.

Robert could hear de Gorges saying, 'The boy is only ten years old; the government will have to be in the hands of a council, which, I presume will have to be elected by the old King Edward's council. What will happen will depend on whether Lancaster has as much weight with them as he had with Edward. Personally, considering what happened when I was in London, I don't think he will have much support. He will have to be seen to show loyalty to the young king, otherwise it would become an open conflict, or even civil war. Richard is well known to favour March and Courtenay, as his father did and as his mother still does. The Duke of Lancaster was too jealous of the Black Prince, and continually scheming against his influence, to be in favour with his wife.'

Adam de Cumpton leant across and asked, 'What do you think will happen with the war with the French now, Sir Hugh?'

Sir Hugh spread his hands wide and shrugged his shoulders. 'It can't be much worse, can it? The Channel isn't safe for us any more, with the now combined French and Castilian fleets being so strong. Our possessions in Aquitaine are only a fraction of what they were, and all we have left is Calais, Bordeaux and the land held by the Duke of Burgundy. But it's possible that we might now get the money spent on the war that's raised in taxes for it, instead of it lining the merchants' pockets. However, my feeling is that when Charles V of France hears of Edward's death, he will sanction some immediate raids. They seemed to have a healthy respect for Edward in the past, even after his claws became sheathed, but now they will probably take advantage of the uncertainty and try to strike while our leaders are distracted with other things, such as protecting their positions at home. We will have to look to our defences immediately, for, after all, it is only two or three days' sailing for the French to reach us.'

De Kingston laughed. 'But they were fought off in 1340. They'd be fools to come again.'

'Would it be so foolish? They've raided five times in the last forty years. They managed to sack Southampton, and since then the plague has taken some of the best of our men. The war has claimed others, and England is not well defended now, especially by sea. Political squabbles have taken the attention of those in

26 June 1377

power away from these important issues, certainly those that are more important to us. When you consider it, we on the Island are both very exposed and very vulnerable. As far as the mainland is concerned we hardly exist. We ought to apply to Southampton for extra reinforcements. We have the seventy-six men-at-arms sent by the Earl of Devon, to which we can add about nine companies of our own trained militia, each of one hundred men. But it will take a day or two to mobilise them in the event of emergency. All would, of course, be under my command, as Constable of the Castle,' said Sir Hugh. 'However, as Warden, de Gorges, together with the Abbot of Quarr, can authorise raising of more militia and more victuals for the troops.'

De Gorges turned to Sir Hugh. 'Out of a population of just over 7,000 I'm not sure that there are more able-bodied men that we could enlist, unless we take the old men and youths. Do you agree with me, Sir Hugh, that we should prepare and stock the castle for a siege? After all, it is the only real refuge on the Island,' he said. 'How long do you think we could hold out for if we had to?'

Sir Hugh leant on the table. 'At the moment we could stand about two weeks, but there are only about one hundred men here. If the militia were called out we would need much more.'

He ticked off on his fingers. 'Ten tuns of wine, a hundred quarters of malt, fifty quarters of beans and peas, one hundred quarters of oats, with salt, eggs, chickens and other things, such as wood. We have plenty of water in the deep well; all we need is men on the treadmill to draw it. But remember that the castle fell to a siege in Steven's reign because the well in the keep ran dry – that was when Earl Baldwin was besieged here in 1136. What we also need for defence are hobblers, men mounted and lightly armed to provide a mobile force in addition to the pikes, swords and bows of our local militia. Then we could perhaps prevent any raiders landing, or defeat them as soon as they do. It might be possible to get some sent across from Southampton.'

He looked across at de Gorges, who interrupted saying, 'Besides that, it is important to tighten up on the coast watchers and make sure the beacons are stocked with wood and dry tinder. We have the regular beacon of La Wyrde – the watch – at High

Hat, the highest point on the southern downs. Then there is the chantry on St Catherine's Down, and that is manned all the time by the hermit, when the weather is good enough for him to see the sea; being over 700 feet up means that it is in the clouds much of the time. Also there are those at Chaledone, Atherfelde and at Apuldercame, Smeredone and Schencling. Covering the west and east entrances to the Solent are Hetdone and Puttoksdone. The manors in which they lie have a duty to provide dry kindling at all times and have someone on watch during daylight hours who can give warning if a fleet is sighted. It need only be a shepherd, but someone who can light the beacon if it is needed. At the moment we have the Island split into nine districts, and each lord has to provide eighty trained and armed men ready at a moment's notice. Would it be possible for everyone to increase that to one hundred? If there is any trouble in arming them I am sure the castle armoury should be able to help,' he added, looking at Sir Hugh.

'That's right,' replied Sir Hugh. 'We are well stocked with bows and arrows. We have a few poleaxes and glaives, and some short swords and bucklers, but no harness to spare.'

'Does everyone agree that we must increase the numbers of militia and supplies?' asked de Gorges. They all nodded their assent, even de Kingston.

'Right then! We must settle the details of contributions, communication and assembly.'

Their voices murmured on as they discussed ways and means. The fire died away to glowing embers and the rush lights flickered and grew dim. Eventually Sir Hugh rose with a yawn saying, 'Well, I think that's about it. We'll carry out those agreed actions within the month. We'll meet then and see if there is more that needs to be done, and we should know if our request for more troops from the mainland has been agreed. By then there may be more news about how our new king will conduct the war. I'm going to bed, but you gentlemen may stay if you like. You know your way around. I bid you all goodnight!' He walked over to the door, taking de Gorges by the arm, and they went out in deep conversation towards his private quarters.

De Kingston moved round the table and confronted Peter and Robert as they rose. 'Well, you young puppy,' he said to Peter, 'we

26 June 1377

haven't yet fixed a time and a place for our match. Seeing as it'll be your defeat, you may as well choose.'

Peter looked enquiringly at Robert and replied, 'I disagree with you as to the outcome, but time will tell. There is an archery competition on the second day of the fair held in Francheville on the Feast of St Mary Magdalene. That makes it 22 July, almost a month from now. I will be there and Robert here will be my second.' Robert nodded.

'Suits me very well!' said de Kingston. 'John Urrey of East Standen will second me. Next month! Hah!' He swung on his heels and, sweeping his cloak about him, strode to the door and slammed it behind him. A few seconds later his hoarse voice could be heard shouting for his mount. Then the sound of the hooves of his and his retainer's horses echoed within the battlements as they clattered out of the courtyard. He was obviously setting out to ride back to his estates that evening.

Robert and Peter looked at each other grinning, then, following the example of some others who were not occupying the cubicles, flung some skins on to the rushes, which they heaped up by the dying fire. Wrapping themselves in their cloaks, they lay down to sleep. However, it was an hour or more before they ceased quietly talking.

FRANCHEVILLE

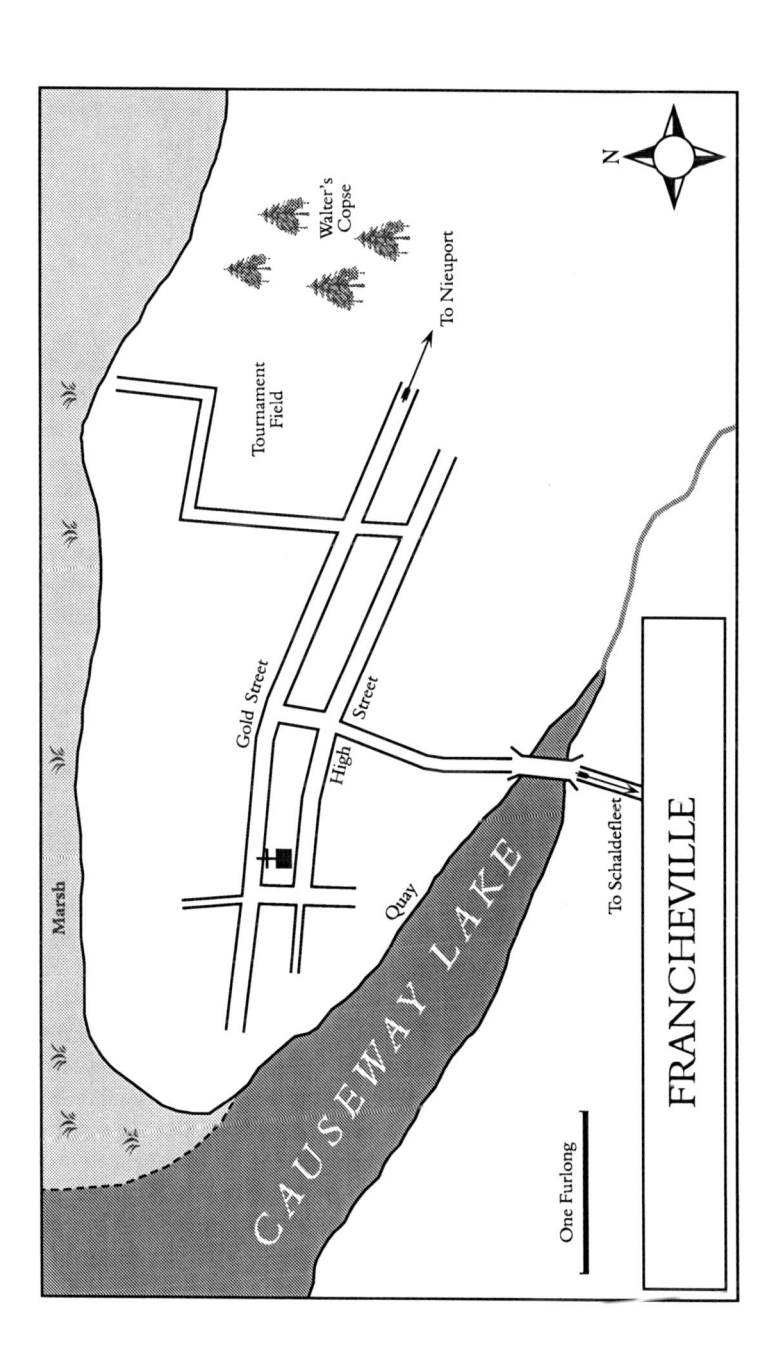

Marsh

CAUSEWAY LAKE

Walter's Copse

Tournament Field

Gold Street

High Street

Quay

To Nieuport

To Schaldefleet

One Furlong

N

22 July 1377

Morning

The rays of the sun streaming in through the window onto his face woke Robert from a dream in which he had been fighting off John de Kingston. He was sweating and breathing hard, and it was with some relief that he realised where he was.

He yawned, stretched and lay back in comfortable relaxation. The straw sticking through his palliasse prickled his back and he wriggled to get rid of the irritation. A succession of idle thoughts roamed through his brain as he tried to wipe the dream from his mind. He gradually awoke fully. Excitement and anticipation swept over him when he remembered that it was 22 July, the Feast of St Mary Magdalene. He had been at the fair the day before for the first day, but was unable to stay overnight with his cousin as invited, because he had to return home to care for his father. Luckily his pony knew the way home unaided as Robert had been half-asleep most of the time. Today he had to ride to Francheville again and act as second to Peter in his contest with de Kingston. Maybe that's why he had dreamed what he had.

The banging of pots and pans in the kitchen below made him realise that he was very hungry and enticed him to scramble out of bed and leave his comfortable nest. He threw wide the shutters and stood there enjoying the cool breeze playing on his naked body. It promised to be a fine day. The sky was blue and a few slowly moving clouds reflected white in the sunshine. He could hear the seagulls call down by the estuary and a cockerel crowed nearby. The smell of freshly baked bread and cooking meat wafted in, sharpening his appetite and making his mouth water in anticipation. He was late. He must hurry before breakfast was all eaten or thrown to the chickens. He bent down and picked up the shirt that he had thrown to snuff out the candle last thing the night before. He put it on and reached for his breeches that were

Morning

hanging over the back of a chair. Pulling them on, he went down the stairs into the hall. He little knew just how eventful the day was going to be.

The house was a simple but imposing building, large and low, nestling comfortably into the trees. The walls were of chalk blocks quarried out of the downs a mile or so away. On the outside the whiteness had weathered into grey, but the courses or horizontal layers of hard black flints gave a pleasantly dark decoration. Overhead the roof was thatched with reeds gathered from the banks of the nearby River Yar, and tunnelled by noisy chattering sparrows that bickered with each other incessantly.

The shape of the house was traditional for a manor house. It was composed of a central hall, where all of the meals were eaten, and where the business of the estates and life in general was carried on. This lofty room stretched up into the smoke-blackened rafters, black from when the fire had originally been in the centre of the room. However, Robert had recently persuaded his father to install a chimney, a recent development, so that now the smoke did not always sting their eyes and sear their throats. Robert had often wondered whether the smoke had contributed to his father's illness, as he had always had a bad cough. Long windows gave light to the hall, and the Affeton family were wealthy enough for there to be glass in them. The sun shone through, casting brightly coloured pathways of light over the table, the benches, the rush-covered floor and the tapestry on the far wall. Against the wall was a rack containing a pair of pikestaffs, several longbows and quivers full of arrows. His father's harness, nowadays often called 'armour', was hung beside the rack. Though it was many years since it had been worn, and it was unlikely Sir Roger would ever wear it again, it was kept bright and shining by one of the pages. Separated from the hall by a passageway were the buttery, the wardrobe and various storerooms, with the bedrooms above; altogether a compact and convenient arrangement.

Robert walked through the passage and out into the courtyard and the fresh air. The cool and the mists of night had already gone, except in the shadows, and the warmth of early morning predicted a hot day to come. On one side of the yard was a long,

22 July 1377

low building where the big plough horses and the smaller sturdy hobbies were stabled. A couple of men moved around preparing for the day's work in the fields. They bowed their heads and uttered greetings to Robert and he greeted them in return.

The other side of the yard was a series of sheds containing hay and straw, and pens for the pigs and calves. Chickens clucked and fluttered around searching for insects, grain and scraps, and getting under everyone's feet. In the middle was a pump and trough, surrounded by wet and uneven flagstones. Robert thrust his head beneath the spout and pumped vigorously until a stream of cold clear water poured over him. He gasped with the shock, but it cleared his head of last night's ale, of which he had drunk too much. Then rubbing the water from his eyes he stumbled into the kitchen to grope for a cloth to dry himself with.

'Come on you lazy lay-abed! Your breakfast has been ready for hours. I thought you'd be up and off before now, but I suppose you were out carousing, as usual.'

Robert wiped the water from his face and looked at the large form of Alice, standing with her feet firmly apart and her hands on her ample hips, scolding him. Because Alice had effectively taken the place of Robert's mother when she had died, there was no deference in her attitude towards him. She had washed him, cleaned him and held him tightly when he had bad dreams. She kept the house in order, and looked after Robert and his father, at the same time as bringing up her own family. She was always cheerful and smiling, cooking, sweeping or washing, and spoiling Robert, and she considered him the same as one of her own lads.

She and the maid, who was her helper, baked fresh bread every day, and on the third or fourth day would throw away the old stale ale and brew some more, enough for the household and the outside workers. Baking and brewing were continual occupations, so that she was always busy, but she never seemed to tire or get any older. Robert could not imagine life without her.

'Now, Alice, don't go on so. I don't think I would have woken now, but for the noise you've been making down here,' he said fondly.

He dodged out of the way of Alice's playfully swinging hand, picked up a ladle and started to play at fencing with her, while the maid giggled in the background.

Morning

She laughed at him and said, 'Enough of your silly foolery. Come and eat before the day is gone.'

Robert put the ladle down and collapsed onto a bench at the table. Alice put a plate before him piled high with slices of freshly smoked ham, with two poached eggs on top and a big chunk of bread beside. Robert picked up a knife, cut the bread, still warm, soft and deliciously fragrant, and thrust it at the eggs until they broke and the orange-yellow yolk spilled over the ham. He stuffed the dripping bread into his mouth with satisfaction.

'Today should be a grand day, Alice,' he said between mouthfuls. 'I have to be at Francheville before noon to second Peter at the archery contest against John de Kingston. I'm sure most of the Island will be there to see it. Yesterday there seemed to be no other topic of conversation. There are rumours that de Kingston has wagered considerable money on the result. Also there's the tilting tournament between the East and West Medine, for which Peter de Heyno has to mount as captain of the East Medine. It is possible that I might have to join in the joust too. Compared with today, the other days of the fair will be rather ordinary.'

'Ordinary for you, Master Robert, maybe. But for us folks it is something we look forward to all year. We can hear some news of the mainland, and meet our friends and relations from other parts of the Wight. Besides, there is so much that's unusual to see. There are jugglers, tumblers, preachers, strange animals, cloth and trinkets to buy. All sorts of things.' Her eyes were glowing and her normally ruddy cheeks were flushed even redder as she bounced up and down with excitement.

'Yes! And you'll talk of nothing else all year. You'll be remembering so hard that your pies will burn in the oven, as they did last year.'

'More of that, my lad, and I'll see you don't get any, burnt or not!' And she flounced out, puffed up with imaginary indignation, saying as she went, 'I'll be going as soon as you've eaten, and my man has got the horse ready.' Then she turned back to add affectionately, 'Now, you will take care in that tilting tourney if you do have to take part. 'Tis mighty dangerous, and I couldn't bear you getting hurt. What would we do if you came home with a broken arm or leg? And while you are there please ask Lord de Heyno to convey our best wishes to Mistress Rebecca in her confinement.'

'Of course I will act as messenger for you,' said Robert contritely. 'It will please my sister to know she is not forgotten. She is always asking after you. And don't you worry about me, Alice. I'm very good at avoiding the lance, for I'm a coward at heart! Anyway, I am not sure that I will have to mount for it, for I am not in the West Medine team as yet.'

Robert finished his meal, and putting his platter, knife and spoon in the wooden tub with the other crockery he went to the door. He shouted across the yard, 'William, make sure Bess is brushed well and tie up her mane and tail with ribbons,' before he realised that this request was entirely unnecessary – it would have been done already.

'Aye, sir,' came the curt reply from the stables, followed by some mutterings about frills and fancies. William was husband to Alice, and though he grumbled and cursed, Robert reckoned that he doted on Alice, and his bad temper was put on to provide a foil for her sunny nature. Together they were the backbone of the household. After a few contests with them, Timothy, the bailiff, who should have been second to the master, had given up and now left them alone, confident that they would do everything required of them, and more.

Robert smiled, and went upstairs to see his father. He knocked on the door of the solar, formerly the family room, but now his father's bedroom and living quarters, for he seldom could come downstairs. Hearing no answer, he went in. The shutters were still closed and the room was gloomy, only chinks of light shining through the gaps and knotholes. The air carried the stale smell of sickness. Sir Roger had eaten some breakfast and was sitting up in bed, leaning against the carved bedhead, almost lost in the wide pillows. The counterpane was pulled up around him. He looked weak and drawn. His eyes were closed and his nightcap was half over one eye. Robert thought that it was time to waken him and remind him that he was going to the fair again. He crossed to the window and opened the shutters. Sunlight streamed in across the room, setting all the dust motes dancing, and bringing out the warm brown of the floorboards and the bright colours in the counterpane and the tapestry on the wall. His father stirred.

'Good morning, Father,' said Robert. 'How are you feeling today? Better, I hope?'

Sir Roger fumbled his way to wakefulness. 'Good morning, Robert, my boy. I did feel somewhat easier before I breakfasted...' The old man coughed. 'I may even be able to get up for a while later.'

'You must not do too much, because I am going to the fair at Francheville again today and Alice also will be there. But William and Timothy will be here, should you want anything. They will look in on you occasionally.'

'Yes, I know. Alice told me. She always makes sure that I am provided for, so you've no need to worry.' He coughed again, a long racking cough, and panted for breath afterwards.

'You will be seeing Peter there, I am sure. Find out from him how Rebecca is and give him this letter for her.' With a shaking hand, he held out a folded piece of paper. 'I hope that she'll have an easy time and give me my first grandson, when her birthtime comes. They must come and visit just as soon as they can.'

He paused wearily for breath before going on. 'I hope the arrows fly true for Peter and that he wins against de Kingston. He is a devious man, from all I hear. Do not trust that he will be honest. Peter is a good bowman, but there are many tricks that can be used to spoil the flight of an arrow to the target.'

Sir Roger then asked how the crops were looking, as he was concerned about the possibility of blight getting on the wheat. This was a topic that had been discussed for several days running; he had little to do during the day but lie and worry about unlikely or trivial things. He advised Robert what would need to be done if the signs of blight appeared. Despite his being ill, Sir Roger's mind was still very active and Robert relied on his wisdom and experience, learning so that he could take over when the time came that his father was too weak to care. After a few minutes Robert took his leave by embracing his father, and took the breakfast tray downstairs to the kitchen where the kitchen maid was cleaning up.

He then went into the wardrobe to change into some clothing more appropriate to the occasion. He rifled through the clothes in

22 July 1377

one of the cupboards and selected a pair of stout breeches, a fine lawn shirt with lace at the cuffs and collar, and a short light-brown cotte with red stitching, fastened by a broad leather belt. He disliked the modern fashion of ankle-length overgarments and long pointed shoes, and capes with liripipe hoods that hung down to the ground at the back, which were often worn in the towns – they were totally impractical for the countryside; they wouldn't be comfortable for a hard day's work in the fields or for riding. He dressed and put into a saddlebag a heaume, which was a light helmet, and a quilted tunic called a gambeson. These would be enough protection if he was called upon to take part in the tourney.

He picked up the bag and went out to the courtyard. In the stables he found William putting the saddle on Bess. The hobby looked sleek and skittish, ready for the ride, even though she had been ridden miles the day before. As Robert rode her every day around the manor, or to the downs to look at the sheep, or into the village, she was fit and clear-eyed, stamping and ready to go. The pony snuffled a welcome to her master. William took the bag and tied it to the saddle, then he stooped to give Robert a leg-up.

'Thanks, William,' Robert said as he wriggled into a comfortable riding position. 'I have left father cosy in bed, though he says he may get up later. Keep an eye on him, will you? All being well I should be back by nightfall, though if I eat at my cousin's it may be morning.'

'Of course, sire. All will be safe with me. I wish you success at the fair, and I hope Lord de Heyno wins the contest,' William replied. 'And, if it please you, my lord, look to my Alice, and keep her from chattering too long with her sisters.'

Laughing, Robert gathered his reins, waved his hand, and with a click of his tongue urged the pony on across the yard. As they went round the end of the building the full scene opened before him. The meadows near the house were interspersed with huge oak trees and sloped gradually down towards the silver water of the river. Robert rode down to the edge of the reeds and the track just above the strand line of flotsam, left behind where the spring tide reached when the wind was in the west. The tide was out; the smell of the mud and seaweed was strong as it dried in the sun and he could hear the mournful piping of the curlews and clacking of the oystercatchers.

The track turned northwards along a line of osiers, and followed the shore just above the line of flotsam. A little way along the track divided. To the left it crossed the causeway and a short bridge to the village of Freshwater. On the far side of the estuary the track climbed steeply up the short hill, where the stubby tower of All Saints Church peeped over the trees.

However, he took the right-hand track that kept on along the water's edge, gradually curving round towards the east. Far across the calm and shimmering water to his left he could see the distant reflections of the trees and houses of Yarmouth. At a second fork the left-hand track led to Yarmouth, but they took the right-hand track that led away from the creek and into the woods towards Thorley and Ningwood, to Schaldefleet, to Francheville and to the fair.

About an hour later Robert and a still-fresh Bess came out of the woods into the fields surrounding the small village of Schaldefleet. The broad, squat tower of the old church showed above a clump of trees, but the village itself was hidden below in the narrow valley of the Caul Bourne stream. The village stood at the head of a shallow creek, where the tide gave way to the little stream that provided the villagers with water and powered the mill to grind their corn.

Several tracks converged on the village, and the bridge across the point at which the stream became the tidal creek. Peasants, cottars, villeins, yeomen and franklins, with their women and children, walking, on horseback and in carts were all moving in the same direction towards the bridge, for the road to Francheville lay on the far side. The carts were piled high with vegetables or contained wicker baskets of squawking chickens and squealing pigs, tethered by their feet. Pennies and marks, closely hoarded over the year were carefully buttoned into purses so that the people could buy the necessities as well as the luxuries they craved. They were all heading to the fair and were in high good humour, calling to friends and relations whom they may not have seen since the last year's fair. They were in their best clothes, clean and bright. Many of them knew Robert and acknowledged

22 July 1377

him with a salute, or a brief word, but they were all keen to press on quickly.

As they passed the church some quickly darted inside to say a short prayer and ask for a blessing. The church had formed a refuge from the marauding French for their ancestors, who had hidden in the thick-walled tower, and respect for its sanctuary lay deep in their tales and traditions. Some also took their children in to marvel at the window in the south aisle showing the arms and crest of Isabella de Fortibus. A century before, this formidable woman had owned the whole Island. But she had sold it to Edward I on her deathbed, in order to better protect her people. She was widely revered as a consequence. Some visitors also paused before the carved sepulchral slab over the grave of Pagan Trenchard, a famous knight of the parish, about whom legendary tales were told to keep the children amused in the winter evenings.

Bess walked slowly down the street, weaving her way through the throng. On either side were simple buildings. These had wattle walls woven from the hazel branches coppiced in the woods, covered with mud from the creeks, mixed with horse hair. They all had roofs thatched with reeds from the saltings. They were an excellent design, being cheap to construct, cool in summer and warm in winter, even though they were also home to hosts of insects and spiders. Barking, snapping dogs worried at the heels of every passer-by and the whole village was in a ferment of excitement. They crossed the narrow stone bridge, which was only just wide enough for a single cart. To the left stretched the narrow creek leading out to the sea. A few small fishing boats were hauled out on the mud, and nets were hanging out to dry. The smell of the mud mixed with that of dead and rotting fish and seaweed gave the air a particular pungency.

Robert felt the excitement beginning to infect him too, and he quickened his pace. He urged Bess on and they broke into a trot up the hill on the eastern side of the stream. After a couple of furlongs they reached the junction where a road went off to Nieuport, and south to the village of Caulborne, and on the left hand another went north to Francheville. Even more crowds coming from the south now joined the way. Robert turned left and became part of the moving human stream.

Morning

'Robert! Robert!' a voice called. He eased on the reins and the pony slowed to a comfortable walk. Looking behind him, he saw Peter de Heyno cantering up, hair flying and his horse beginning to blow. They hadn't met during the month since the council at the castle, and had a lot to talk about.

'Well met, Robert,' Peter said breathlessly as they started to trot along the road side by side. 'How are you and Sir Roger? I wanted to see you before we reached the town, because you must join in the tilting tourney. The West Medine team is one man short. The Lord of Brook has a touch of gout and cannot put a foot to the ground. He asked me to find a substitute and present him to de Kingston, the captain of the team. I hope you have your clothes in that bag,' he added, gesturing to the bag on Robert's saddle.

Robert nodded. 'We are both well, and father sends his best sentiments to you and I have a letter to Rebecca from him. How is she? I hope that everything is progressing normally.'

'Yes, all is well with her, except she is getting very tired, especially in the heat, and her ankles swell so that she cannot stand for too long,' Peter assured him.

'I thank the Lord that she is fit,' said Robert. Then answering Peter's other question, 'You are lucky that I do have a heaume and a gambeson with me. I put them in just in case. But I only have this hobby. I shall need a fresh horse for the tourney, so that Bess here can get me home tonight.' He patted her neck affectionately.

'Don't worry,' Peter replied. 'My men are coming along behind with fresh mounts, some extra clothing and the lances.'

Robert skirted around a pair of oxen being driven along by a small lad wielding a short switch. 'It seems I have no choice but to say yes then,' he laughed. 'What time is it to start? For your contest with de Kingston must be this afternoon, with the other archery contests.'

'De Kingston will be riding in the tourney as well, so the archery will have to be after the tilting. I think they will both be in the afternoon.'

They trotted down past the farm of Fleetlands and the fields and pastures on either side became marshy, eventually giving way to reedbeds and saltings, soft and muddy, covered with water at

22 July 1377

each high tide. The track now ran along a raised causeway that separated marshes on the right-hand side from the wide Causeway Lake on the left, on the far side of which were the quays of the town. Round the bend and out of sight was the narrow channel out into to the sea. The middle of the causeway was cut by a narrow culvert, crossed by a wooden bridge. Water poured through the gap on each tide to flood the marshes, and on the ebbing tide fishermen slung nets across it to catch fish that came in to feed on the weed and the muddy worms.

The people walking had to stand aside to let the riders pass, their horses' hooves thudding on the planking. As they reached land again, the track broadened and rose towards the town, which was built on a broad spit of land between two arms of the estuary. Founded in 1256 by the Bishop of Winchester, it was laid out in a grid pattern with seventy-three burgage holders. The inhabitants held parcels of land and had been granted a numbers of freedoms, which had led to it being called Francheville (Freetown). It had developed into a very important town, and a centre of trade. The estuary supported a healthy oyster fishery, much of the produce of which went to Southampton wrapped in wet weed, and there was a good fishery in the Solent. The fish was dried in the sun and the wind, or salted, the salt being evaporated from the seawater in ponds within the marshes, or made by boiling the water. The anchorage could safely harbour many ships, and they carried a regular trade across to the mainland. Oysters, fish, salt, wool and grain went to the mainland towns and wine, cloth, leather and other goods came back. Several of the local merchants had become very rich from this trade. It was they who organised the fair, for they made money out of that too. Robert's maternal grandfather had been one of the foremost merchants in Francheville, and he still had relations living in the town whom he had arranged to stable Bess with during the fair.

Robert and Peter threaded their way up the hill through the throngs of merry people and entered the High Street. This ran westwards along the spit towards the church, eventually leading down to the quay, the stores and warehouses and the fish-drying huts. On either side of the road were houses, orchards and burgage lands, and further houses, buildings and warehouses

Morning

stretched down to the water on the left-hand side. Small lanes and alleyways went off to the right from the High Street to join Gold Street, which ran parallel to it on the northern side.

Robert reined in before an imposing set of gates behind which could be seen a solid stone house, one of the few stone buildings in the town. He slid off the pony's back, saying, 'This is my cousin's house, and his grooms will look after the horses. I am to dine here this evening before returning home. Do you want to come in, Peter?'

'No, thank you,' said Peter. 'I must find my men and make sure the horses are safely tethered and watered at the tourney ground. I will see you there later. You should be able to find my tent; the steward will know where I am.' With a wave of the hand, he turned and rode eastwards.

Peter went in through the gates and round the back of the house to the stables, where he found Walter, the old ostler. Apparently his cousin was out around the town on his business at that moment, so Robert decided he would spend time looking around the fair, and left a message that he would return for his bag later and would be back for supper in the evening.

He then walked out into the High Street and towards the centre of the village. The road was lined with stalls and carts piled high with vegetables and fruits, eggs, herbs, meats, pies and bread. There was all manner of livestock for sale: fish, fresh and dried, meat, tar, salt. There was local and mainland produce: pots, cloth and silk, silverware and pretty baubles, and there were weavers, haberdashers, smiths, woodworkers and many others that Robert could not get near enough to see. The air was alive with shouts of dealers calling their wares and the people haggling over purchases. Herrings were being sold, six for a penny; oysters four pence a bushel; finches ten a penny and thrushes three for tuppence.

A thicker crowd further along the street attracted Robert's attention and he elbowed his way nearer, brushing eager vendors aside. In deference to his obvious stature and authority the crowd let him through with murmurs of acknowledgement. From the middle of the crowd came the sound of a flute playing a jig and there was a chorus of gasps of amazement, and cries from children. Robert peered over the heads of those closest in and beheld a strange sight. A wizened midget, playing a whistle, and dressed in red-and-yellow clothes was cavorting in front of a huge brown bear, which was attached to its master by a collar and chain. The bear was standing on its hind legs, its front legs held out in front for balance while it jigged from side to side in time with the music. Its mouth was open as far as the thick leather muzzle allowed and sharp yellow teeth showed behind the snarling lips. The red tongue dripped foaming saliva, which flicked over the audience as the bear waved its head, and the beast snorted foetid breaths reeking of rotting flesh. Every now and then the music faltered as the midget bent down and picked up a coin flung from the crowd, most of whom had never seen such a frightening creature. Robert watched for a little while, then tossed a coin of his own before elbowing his way back out of the press of people.

He went into a side street to get into Gold Street, but the crowd was even worse there, with people going in both directions, jostling against each other and being squeezed against the walls on either side. Suddenly a woman's scream rang out above the general hubbub. 'Help! Thief! Thief! Cutpurse!'

Robert looked in the direction of the cry and was nearly pushed to the ground as a man cannoned into him clutching a richly embroidered purse.

'My purse! A robber has taken my purse!'

Robert's hand shot out and grabbed the man's wrist and, though the robber struggled, the grip was of iron. Robert twisted the other's hand up behind his back and the robber's pockmarked face screwed up in pain. Despite this, he still wriggled and twisted.

'Oh, sire! That is the thief. See, he has my purse in his hand. I thank you indeed, sire.'

The voice was full of relief and soon the woman appeared in front of him. She had an oval face, a pure complexion and eyes the colour of the sky. A firm, determined chin showed a woman of character, Robert decided, but full red lips showed gentleness and the possibility of inner passion. She must have been almost the same age as Robert, and came up to the level of his eyes in height. She was cloaked and hooded in a rather dishevelled light grey cape, even though the day was warm; wisps of corn-coloured hair escaped from beneath the hood. At a first glance she seemed dressed in poor fashion, but a closer look revealed that beneath the shabby cloak were clothes of rich cloth and fine weave. Obviously she had wealth and taste, but was trying to be inconspicuous in the crowd.

Robert took all this in at a glance and, as she raised her eyes to meet his, he felt his pulse quicken and his heart pound. He had never seen a girl the equal of this before.

A sudden violent blow to his stomach knocked the breath out of him and he doubled over, gasping – the thief had taken advantage of his momentary relaxation. With a violent twist, the cutpurse broke free and disappeared into the surrounding crowd. Several tried to stop him, but he was gone. Robert gasped for breath as the girl bent and picked her purse from the ground where it had dropped in the struggle.

'I trust that you are not hurt, gallant sire,' she said.

The soft and lilting voice charmed his ears. He fought to draw breath so that he could reply, though the thought crossed his mind that his breathlessness may not be entirely the result of the elbow in his stomach.

'I will survive, my lady,' he gasped. ' 'Tis only an injury to my pride. I should have kept a firmer hold on him. But you, did he hurt you?' he asked solicitously.

'No, I am all right, thank you kindly. He cut through the strap of the purse. See!' She drew back the cloak and showed him the severed leather thongs hanging from her belt. In doing so he saw her fine white cotton surcoat and the jewelled belt around her slim waist. He sensed the full curves beneath, straining at the thin cloth. An unaccustomed thrill came over him, and a stirring in his loins. Who was she, he wondered, and where did she come from? He must find out more! He cast a surreptitious glance at her hands. There were no rings. God be thanked – she was not spoken for.

'Your surcoat is cut here too,' he gestured to a slit in the material, catching a glimpse of her fine white thigh beneath. 'The thief must have been very close to cutting you.'

'But he didn't,' she said defiantly. She threw her hands up.

22 July 1377

'Oh, this crowd is too intense! Would you please escort me out of it?' She looked at him beseechingly.

He took her arm. 'With the greatest of pleasure,' he replied gallantly, with a slight bow, and steered her down towards Gold Street. When they gained the slightly less crowded, broader street, he turned to her.

'It is not safe for a woman to be unescorted in such a crowd. There are always thieves, cutpurses and criminals to take advantage of the weak and vulnerable,' he told her.

Her eyes flashed and her cheeks flushed. She stamped her foot. 'I am not weak and vulnerable! That is just what my father says. Why can't I do anything by myself without interference?' She calmed down and added in explanation. 'That is why I set out to lose the rest of the family. I wanted to look round by myself.'

Robert thought she was even more beautiful in her anger, and he cursed himself for the unthinking implication of what he had said. 'If you wish to be alone, I will bid you good day,' he said with a courtly bow.

'No! I didn't mean it like that. Please stay with me. I mean that I wanted to meet other people and... Oh dear! I...' she ended in blushing confusion.

Robert smiled and congratulated himself on the fact that she had broken away from her family, otherwise they might never have met. 'Well, my lady, in that case I feel that it is my duty to remain with you and ensure your safety until you regain your family.' But then, hopefully, he added, 'But until then, shall we enjoy ourselves by looking around together?'

Her eyes sparkled with mischief as they looked into his, and she smiled her agreement. 'You may call me Rachel. "My lady" is much too formal. And you, I believe, must be Robert de Affeton. My father has spoken of you.'

Robert was astounded that she should know of him. 'That is my name, Rachel, but I feel at odds calling you by your given name on first meeting, without a formal introduction.'

'Don't be, Robert. It's the privilege you have gained for saving me from that thief. You will learn my ancestry soon enough.'

She smiled frankly at him and Robert's heart sang. Never had he met a young woman he understood so well, so quickly, and felt so comfortable with. Always before, he had been tongue-tied and confused, not knowing what to say. He had always found young and eligible women difficult to talk to, but with Rachel it seemed different. It was almost as if she could see into his soul. He liked the feeling.

To cover his confusion, he looked for something to give him diversion from the thoughts invading his mind, and to give her a new experience and amusement. Hearing a shout nearby, he guided her towards it, saying, 'Shall we see what is going on over there?' She nodded agreement, with a smile and a dimple on her cheek.

A large crowd was grouped around a man standing precariously on an upturned barrel. He was a tonsured friar, almost as thin as a skeleton, which was unusual for a friar who were popularly believed to live well on what they managed to wheedle out of the people. He was dressed in a rough brown habit drawn in at the waist by a length of knotted rope. His black eyes burned with a fanatical, unblinking stare, which switched from one person to the next, roving the crowd. His thin voice held the fervour of a zealot, and berated and whipped emotion into his audience.

Robert turned to a man on one side and asked who the friar was. 'Ah! 'Tis John Ball, sire. A wandering preacher who says he's freshly come from London.'

Robert raised his eyebrows in surprise and turned and whispered to Rachel. 'I've heard of this man John Ball before. It is said that he preaches sedition, trying to get the peasants to resist the manor lords by refusing to carry out their demesne duties or pay their dues. He's caused a lot of trouble in some parts, but I don't think he'll get much support here – most men are now effectively freemen and are pretty content. But John de Kingston had better watch out if his villeins hear this!' Robert laughed.

Rachel glanced sharply at him and whispered back, 'Sh! Keep quiet and then we may hear what he is saying.'

'When Adam delved and Eve span, who then was a gentleman?' The friar paused to let the thought sink in. 'My good friends,' he said, leaning forward as if to confide in his audience, 'things cannot go well in England, nor ever will, until everything is held in common, when there shall be neither vassel nor lord

22 July 1377

and all distinctions are levelled, when the lords shall be no more masters than ourselves.

'How ill they have used us?' He hit his fist into his open palm, and his voice strengthened. 'And for what reasons do they thus hold us in bondage? Are we not all descended from the same parents, Adam and Eve? And what can they show, or what reasons give, why they should be more masters than ourselves, except perhaps for us to labour and work for them to spend. They are clothed in velvet and rich things, ornamented with ermine and other furs, while we are forced to wear poor cloth. They have handsome seats and manors when we must have the wind and rain in our labours in the fields. We are called slaves and if we do not perform our services we are beaten. But it is from our labour they have the wherewithal to support their pomp.'

'Seize that man,' shouted a voice from the other side of the crowd. 'Any more of this and you'll be beaten some more. Seize him and lock him up for preaching sedition.'

The whole crowd looked round to see who was speaking. Looking fierce and shaking his fist at the friar was de Kingston. His face was pale with anger as he and Michael Apse tried to push their way forward to reach the speaker. The peasants in front of them muttered to each other and hindered their progress by turning this way and that, sticking their arms out, and simply turning their backs on them. Apse started to beleague the peasants around him with a stick, and it looked as if the crowd might turn against him.

Rachel tugged at Robert's jerkin and said in a rather frightened voice, 'Please, Robert, can we go somewhere else? I don't like this.' Her little pink tongue flicked nervously round her lips, and she put her hand up to the hood of her cape, to cover her face. She seemed to be seeking to keep Robert between herself and the newcomers.

Robert was contrite. 'Of course! I'm sorry. I should have realised that it was unwise to stop here; there was the risk of trouble occurring.' So saying, he led her out of the crowd and they passed further down the street, leaving the uproar behind.

Rachel's face was pale and strained, and Robert suggested that they find somewhere to sit down for a while. She protested that all was well, and that she would rather carry on walking until they were away from the disturbance. Robert smiled reassuringly at her and some yards further on he stopped in front of an ale seller. He bought a cup of the clear, refreshing liquid. Once she had sipped half the cup the colour came back to her face and the sparkle to her eye.

Robert also bought some sweetmeats and some fruit and they shared those too. He took a scrap of linen from his pocket so that they could wipe their hands, sticky with the juice. Handing it back to him, Rachel squeezed his hand thankfully, at the same time looking at him coquettishly out of the corners of her eyes. Robert's fingers tingled with the soft warmth of her skin. Then they were content to saunter down the road through the crowd, feeling a thrill each time their hands touched.

Further on there was another group of people. Peering over their heads, Robert was able to see a ballad singer who was playing softly on a small harp and telling a story. Straining his ears he could make out the gist of the tale, which he related to Rachel who stood by his side. He was somewhat distracted by her close presence as she relaxed. Also when he leant to whisper in her ear the faint perfume of her hair and the muskiness of her skin made him short of breath. He had never found his desire so potently aroused. He had to make a conscious effort to concentrate on the minstrel.

The tale was about the recent triumphal entry of the uncrowned King Richard II into the capital. The minstrel went on to tell of the glories of the coronation the following morning, and the banquet in Westminster Hall afterwards. The number of people invited to the feast was so great that the Duke of Lancaster and Henry Percy had to ride up and down the hall to make room for the servants with the dishes to reach the tables. Outside, the gardens and paths were lit with torches, and the fountains played with wine. The new king invited all his subjects in to drink from them, and many scenes of drunkenness, revelry and debauchery resulted. The minstrel then recounted that four new earls had been created during the evening following the banquet, the foremost being Henry Percy who was made Earl of

22 July 1377

Northumberland. This fact caused quite a buzz of conversation round the audience because they knew of the conflicts there had been before Edward died. Seeing that the narrative was coming to an end, Robert led Rachel out of the crowd.

'Well that's interesting,' he commented. 'I wonder whether making Percy the Earl of Northumberland will mean he will be a favourite with the new king.'

'It may be a sweetmeat to keep him quiet and stop him being troublesome,' said Rachel, much to Robert's surprise. Though some women had knowledge of politics and of state affairs, generally, he thought to himself, they had nothing more in their minds than clothes and idle gossip.

'Oh yes, Robert. You may look surprised, but my father had me well schooled, and I can read and write, and calculate numbers. I'm sure I'm quite unusual,' she laughed. Robert could only agree, but changed the subject because he felt she was teasing him. Though he enjoyed it, he wasn't sure enough of his ground to respond in kind.

'I think we should start towards the tourney area as I have to take part in the tilting competition this afternoon,' he said, to cover his confusion.

They walked eastwards down the street and on their way they had their nuncheons, buying a penny loaf of good manchet bread from one vendor, half a roasted coney for tuppence from another, and some more ale from a huckster, together with sweetmeats and fruit.

Robert found himself more and more entranced by this slim and graceful young woman, who was obviously well bred and brought up; she had no pretensions and a healthy appetite. She was open, alive and interested in all that was going on around her, in contrast to the feather-brained young women of her class that Robert had met before. Though he probed gently he still could not find out any more of her background; his hints and questions were cleverly deflected. But this seemed to be the only thing she was defensive about: she told him of her childhood in Essex and that she had recently been living with an aunt in London. She seemed to know many of the notable people there but, unlike Robert, few on the Island. He often acknowledged a person here or there as they passed, and occasionally he would stop for a word or two with particular people. All the time he was aware that their interest was more in his companion than in himself, perhaps because of lack of a chaperone. Nevertheless, their conversation was light-hearted and their laughter merry as they strolled along. On the way they collected Robert's bag with the clothes he needed for the afternoon.

The games, events and tournaments were an essential part of the fair, and had been for centuries. They lasted for the three days of the fair and were held on a stretch of common land of several dozen acres to the east of the town. There the townsfolk normally grazed their sheep and goats, and tethered their cows. The common was bounded by fields and by woodland, called Walter's Copse, which extended further east towards the dense Avington Forest. Today the ground was thronged with a noisy crowd. Many a man carried a bow and a quiver full of arrows slung on a baldric across his back: as they were obliged by law to practise and become good marksmen as part of their dues to their lords and to the king, this would be a visible demonstration of this duty. Years ago serfs owed their liege lord a number of days each year that could be called upon whenever he needed. Now that there were greater freedoms it was expected and accepted that such an army would be paid. The law meant that there was always a trained and disciplined army that could be called upon at times of war or dispute. The archers would be part of the local militia, and required to defend the Island should the need arise. Good prizes were to be won, and honour too, at the contests that afternoon, and the winners would be able to boast for the rest of the year about their skill.

Groups of horses were being led through the crowds towards the gaily flagged tents, where small enclosures provided temporary stabling. Women and children sat around on the grass eating food they had brought with them. Small children ran around barefoot shouting and playing, and mangy dogs prowled around searching for scraps. The early afternoon heat caused the air to shimmer in the distance. Dust clouds arose from the horses' hooves. A blind beggar hesitatingly made his way through the crowd, thrusting forward his bowl and crying for alms. People moved out of his way, but some put in the odd coin, together with a mumbled blessing.

Rachel took a kerchief from her purse and held it to her nose to ward off the dust and smells, but looked around her with interest rather than distaste. Robert led the way towards the tents where the contestants in the joust were to be found, and he looked for the red and green of Peter's tent.

Surrounding the tents was a barrier of wooden hurdles erected as an enclosure for the competitors. Inside they could see many people dressed in finer clothes even than theirs. The entrance was on the other side, so Robert turned and, much to her astonishment, swept Rachel up in his arms, lifted her over the barrier, and dropped her lightly on the other side. He then vaulted over it himself. She put a hand on his arm to steady him, tilted her head back and looked deeply into his eyes. He felt that she could see right into the depths of his innermost being, and was enveloped by a sense of oneness with her, as if he could see far into the future, with a calm satisfaction and a spirit that felt complete and whole for the first time. He felt the message he was giving was being returned in kind. A blush started mounting her cheeks and filled them as the glory of dawn fills the skies. Her eyes dipped under his gaze; she was clearly overwhelmed by her feelings. He forced himself to break the spell.

'Well, Rachel, I must go and prepare myself for the tourney, and after that I have to second Peter de Heyno, my brother-in-law, in an archery contest against de Kingston.' She looked up sharply, appearing slightly flustered. 'Would you like to join my aunt? I see her over there.'

'No, Robert, I must look for my family,' she said with determination. 'They are bound to be here and will be wondering where I have got to.' She put a hand on his arm. 'God will watch over you in your tournament, I am sure. You will do well. I'll be watching.' With a smile, she turned and was gone.

She had left so quickly, and Robert had wanted to ask her if he could visit her family, have a formal introduction and permission to see her again. Then at least they could have the chance to get to know each other better and make sure their feelings were true and not just a momentary passion. He scowled, puzzled and perplexed. He was determined to find out who she was and where she lived.

There came a hearty slap on his back. 'So that's what you have be doing! No wonder you wanted to be alone, to sneak off for an illicit rendezvous. Who is she anyway?' Robert's reverie was broken by Peter, who came laughing from behind.

'Truly,' sighed Robert, 'I know only that her name is Rachel, and she had only come to the Island recently. I wish I knew more. It was only by chance we met: a thief picked her purse and I caught him. She wouldn't say who she was, but she must come from a wealthy family, for her clothes are good, and she's well educated.'

'Upon my word, you've come to know quite a lot, for merely catching a thief. And yet you don't know her surname. Odd that! Very odd! Still, we haven't time to waste in speculation; come and prepare for the tilt.'

22 July 1377

Afternoon

Taking Robert's arm, Peter led him towards a squat, round tent, quartered with red and green, on top of which flew Peter's banner, a red hawk on a green background. Even though they were to be in different teams the tilt was a friendly competition: any injuries were accidental and the rules were fairly relaxed – the teams could even share or exchange horses and accoutrements.

They would be tilting at the quintain, which was the way a knight would gain experience and reputation before he graduated to the more dangerous events. Had they been jousting it would have been a different matter: in a joust two riders with lances rode in direct conflict, with the intent of unhorsing one another. Even though the lance tips had guards on them, injuries were frequent.

In some of the biggest tournaments there would be several riders jousting at the same time, and that could end up with a melee, a free-for-all with other weapons – swords, axes or clubs – where each team tried to beat the others into submission. The victors from a tournament of that sort would gain rich prizes and great honour, with their names being known far and wide. However, such jousts often led to mortal injury, something no one wanted at this time – trained men were too valuable to waste.

Robert had seen some big and very bloody contests when he was a squire but he had never been entrusted with the honour of taking part in a major joust, though he was experienced at the tilt, had jousted in minor affairs and had carried sword and lance through many bloody skirmishes while in Gascony. Indeed there were still nights when he would wake in a sweat after reliving some of the battles. He had been lucky to survive only lightly wounded.

Inside the tent the light was diffuse – the sun shone through the coloured walls – and it was warm and airless. Peter opened a large leather bag and drew out his tournament clothing. Both of them stripped off their fine shirts and put on thicker vestments on top of which they donned their gambesons, quilted padded tunics which would take the brunt of any impact they might have to endure. In war, gambesons were a good defence against arrows: not entirely stopping them, but at least reducing their penetration. When worn together with chain mail they gave reasonable protection in battle, though a crossbow bolt could go straight through if fired from close quarters. Robert had seen knights in France wearing plate armour instead, thick sheets of iron riveted and jointed, covering all of the vital areas. That was a better defence against bolts, but chain mail was still most used in England. Over his gambeson Peter wore a thick armless leather cotte quartered in red and green, which would leave his arms free to move. Robert did not have a cotte with him, but was sure that he would be cooler as a consequence. They both picked up their heaumes, Peter's being topped with red and green plumes, and thick leather gauntlets completed their protection. Apparently, Peter had already informed de Kingston of the substitution in his team and though he had not liked it there was no time for him to arrange anything different.

Together Peter and Robert walked towards the end of the tiltyard. There the pages and squires were holding the horses of all the contestants, who were standing talking or nervously checking their mounts and saddle girths.

The tiltyard was a good 300 paces long, and forty wide. Along the western side was a raised platform with benches and cushions for the gentry, the lords, gentlemen, esquires and burgesses with their ladies, who were moving into their places, conversing with their neighbours and making wagers on the forthcoming events. They had their backs to the afternoon sun, and were shaded by a large red-and-white striped awning. This was open at back and front to funnel the cooling breeze through. On top, banners fluttered gaily. On the other side of the greensward, the common folk were gathering behind a barrier of hurdles; they had the sun in their eyes and the bare green turf to sit on.

In the centre of the yard the quintain had been erected. It was a scaffold-like arrangement from which hung a dummy stuffed with wool, with a large shield attached to its front. The dummy simulated an opposing knight and was suspended about six feet above the ground: just the right height to be a target for a horseman with a lance. At the other end of the crossbar was a similar but smaller suspended bag, except this was filled with sand, to balance the target. The galloping lancer had to aim for the shield. If he hit it, he needed to be going fast enough to avoid being struck by the sandbag as it swung round, since this could easily unhorse him. The shield was divided into a series of coloured sectors, or honour points. Points were awarded for a strike on the shield, with the highest marks for hits on the sectors in the middle of the shield, and successively less in the other sectors. The three sectors across the top were the dexter, middle and sinister chief points. The honour, fess and nombril points were across the middle, and across below them the base points, again dexter, middle and sinister. In a joust or in a battle, a hit in the centre three points would probably unhorse the opponent, or penetrate his shield. One to the chief or base would stand a good chance of being deflected, and were therefore rated lower. Each contestant in turn would tilt at full gallop at the quintain, which was set up so that it swung gently, to better mimic a real riding opponent and to increase the degree of skill required for a hit. All the contestants were naturally hoping for first-time clean hits in the centre points, whereas the spectators were hoping for misses and possible unhorsing, and much entertainment and excitement at the expense of their lords. Some were still making wagers on the outcome.

A start was about to be made, and the marshal called the two captains to ride out with him. The eyes of the crowd now focused on the proceedings in front of them, and a hush descended. Peter hurriedly mounted the pony held for him by a page and grabbed his lance. De Kingston, the other captain, was already mounted on a black courser prancing about in the entrance to the arena. He was well accoutred with a tall, black plume on his helm, and a red velvet jupon emblazoned with a black crow covering his hauberk, a coat of chain mail that almost reached down to his knees. On either side of the marshal they rode down the arena, plumes nodding and accoutrements jingling. They reined in before the platform and stood quietly, with the pennons fluttering gaily at the tips of their upright lances. As Warden of the Island, Theobald de Gorges was the pre-eminent lord present to whom the contestants had to pay respect, and it was to him and his lady that the captains dipped their lances. Though he was one of the lords of the East Medine, de Gorges could give no special favours, and he acknowledged both of the captains equally.

The marshal in loud voice introduced the captains, named the teams, and outlined the rules. At each name there was a flurry of applause. John Urrey was one who would be riding with Peter for the East Medine. For the West Medine there was John de Kingston, Thomas Chyke of Modeston, Thomas Langford of Chale and, as the last-minute substitute, Robert.

Each team member would have three tilts at the quintain, and the teams with the greatest number of marks would be declared winners. A clean strike in the honour, fess and nombril points would score ten marks, the middle chief point eight, the left and right chief points six, and all the base points four. The marshal produced a coin to toss to determine which team would ride first. De Kingston called and won the choice, but demanded the other team tilt first. Whether this gave them an advantage or not remained to be seen.

While this was going on Robert was not really following the proceedings. He was more intent on trying to see whether Rachel was on the platform, but to his disappointment he couldn't see her from his oblique vantage point.

The introductory formalities over, the captains trotted back to the holding ring, and nominated the order of tilt in their teams. Robert had to tilt third, as he was reasonably experienced. De Kingston was to tilt last for the West Medine, as was customary for the captain. Similarly, Peter de Heyno would go last for the East Medine.

The first contestant, John Urrey, donned his heaume, gathered up his reins in his left hand and was handed the light wooden lance by an attendant. The lances were all sixteen feet long and, to save weight, were hollow. Their tips were blunted, so they wouldn't stick in the shield and break. Nevertheless they were awkward to handle and control on a galloping, bouncing horse. He started forward with the lance held straight up, out of harm's way, but when well clear of the holding ring tucked the butt in under his right armpit, and lowered the tip so that it was pointed across the horse, in front of the saddle. He approached the quintain correctly, keeping it on his left side.

He kicked the horse forward into a gallop and adjusted the position of the lance to point it at the target. He held it steady and horizontal with his right elbow, controlling the horse with the knees and the left hand on the reins. Thundering across the sward, he struggled to keep the horse on a straight line, and the tip of the lance wavered. With a crash, it hit the target in the nombril point and the quintain swung round violently, throwing the sack in a wide arc. The horse pulled off towards the right immediately on impact, as it had been trained to do, and by leaning that way too the rider managed to avoid being struck by the swinging sack. Ten points, and a good start for the East Medine. There was a burst of shouts and applause from both sides of the lists. The attendants ran out, caught hold of the quintain, lined it up for the next rider and stopped it swinging too violently.

The next rider was obviously not very experienced; he looked pale and apprehensive. He found it difficult to control his steed and missed completely, and failed to score, much to the dismay of one group of supporters and the delight of the other. He then had to ride the length of the list back to the start, enduring catcalls and the ignominy of failure. The third competitor was so intent on hitting the target that he rode too slowly. Peter shouted at him to push the horse on, but though he hit the shield fair and square, he failed to avoid the swinging bag. It hit him on the left shoulder, knocked his heaume off, almost unhorsing him. Nevertheless he scored six points as, according to the marshal, he had hit the dexter chief point.

Then came Peter's turn. He grinned at Robert, put on his heaume, hefted the lance and trotted out into the lists. After a few yards he urged the horse into a gallop, and rapidly closed with the quintain. At the last moment when they were almost on the target the horse threw up its head and skipped a step. Something had spooked it: a fluttering kerchief, or maybe a bright reflection. The tip of Peter's lance described a wild arc as he tried to keep it on line and hit the target, and by some lucky chance he managed to hit the shield a glancing blow at the base. He returned to the enclosure cursing his unpredictable mount. The East Medine had scored twenty points, and it was now the turn of the West Medine.

The first rider, Thomas Chyke, successfully obtained a hit directly in the centre of the shield, for a good ten points. Thomas Langford also had a good hit for a score of eight, but failed to avoid the bag which hit him right in the middle of the back. He was knocked forward over the horse's neck, lost his stirrups and his balance, and slowly slid down the horse's withers, falling head over heels to the ground. The crowd was delighted and shouted howls of derision, but when Chyke got a little shakily to his feet and waved that he was all right, there was a chorus of cheers and applause. He picked up his lance while his horse, which was running free round the arena, was caught up, and he limped back to the collecting ring.

Now it was Robert's turn. He felt sick with apprehension, but knew that the feeling would go as soon as he started. He put his heaume on his head and immediately the noise of the crowd became distorted by the metal. All he could hear was a muffled roaring sound, rather like the sound a seashell makes to the ear. He stuck his heels into the pony's flanks and it catapulted forward. Frantically he tried to rein it back and slow it down, for it was going too fast to control properly. But it was galloping as straight as a die in the right direction. Giving the pony its head, he concentrated on lining up the tip of the lance with the target and keeping it there. It seemed only seconds before he was up to the target, hitting it square in the middle. His lance shattered upon impact: the wood splintered and he felt a stinging blow as a piece flew up and hit him in the face. Luckily the metal projection covering his nose took the main force of the blow. He felt rather than heard the bag swing past his ear, and then he was in the clear. Throwing the stump of his lance to one side he gathered up the reins that had slipped from his grasp, pulled the horse to a trot, and turned to go back to the enclosure.

It was then that he caught sight of Rachel sitting on the platform. She had taken her cloak off and her fair hair was shining in the sunlight. Her hand was covering her mouth and her eyes were wide. Robert inclined his head in a slight bow. She lowered her hand and gave him a slight wave and a smile tinged with relief. It looked as if she had been holding her breath all the while he was tilting. Robert rode back to the enclosure, his heart singing with success, but with an increasingly throbbing ache on his right cheekbone. He took off his gauntlet and felt the swelling lump. A sharp prickle caused him to draw a quick breath – there must be a splinter embedded in the skin. He dismounted just as de Kingston went thundering down the list. He scored an easy, clean, first-time hit for maximum points.

So, the first round was over, and the West Medine led by a good total of thirty-eight points to the East Medine's twenty. There was a short rest while everyone looked to their mounts and caught breath. Peter came across to Robert to look at his injury.

'You did well, Robert. Are you hurt?'

'I think there is a splinter in my cheek here,' said Robert with a grimace touching the point where it hurt. 'Can you pull it out for me?'

'Yes, I can see it. It's in quite deep, though. Hold still while I get it out.' Peter took off his gloves and pulled out his knife. He put the blade behind the exposed end of the splinter to press against and to help grip it with a fingernail. With a sharp intake of breath Robert squeezed his eyes shut. After a couple of tries, the splinter came out. It was a good two inches long and had gone in quite deeply. Robert squeezed gently around the wound to make sure there were no small pieces left in, and to help the blood cleanse it, then held a cloth to it to wipe away the blood until it coagulated.

In the second round, one of the East Medine was unhorsed, and another of the West broke a lance and failed to score. Peter and de Kingston both had clear hits, but Robert was troubled by slight double vision in his right eye caused by the blow. As a result he only managed to score a four. At the end of the round the East was still in the lead but only by sixty points to fifty-four. Everything rested on the last round, and the difference could easily be made up with one ill-judged tilt. All of the horses and riders were tired and they were likely to be slower and more erratic. Shoulders were aching from the strain of the weight of the lance, and the wrench of the impact. Hearts were pounding and the pulsing veins affected the judgement of speed and distance. The scores were bound to worsen. The marshal called for the third round to commence, not giving them much chance to relax and recover.

John Urrey, the first rider in for the East Medine, had been unhorsed in the previous round, and tried to make sure of success by spurring his horse hard – a bit too hard, by all accounts, and he held the lance a bit too high, ending up just catching the upper edge of the shield for six marks. The second rider was determined to make up for the poor showing in the first round, though he had improved somewhat in the second. He was very pleased to get a ten, and came out of the arena grinning broadly. Likewise, the third rider, having had some verbal instruction from Peter, succeeded in a hit in the sinister chief point, for six marks. It was then the captain's final turn.

Despite its previous exercise, Peter's horse was still prancing and being very skittish. As he galloped towards the quintain the horse was pulling hard towards the right, and Peter had to move his lance tip further and further away from the line of movement, at the same time as trying to get the horse to keep to the line. Just at the last moment the horse responded and veered sharply to the left. By a supreme effort Peter brought the lance round to hit the target at a base point, but he was off balance and the bag swung round and hit him, pushing him even further. His left foot slipped out of the stirrup, and as if in slow motion the horse gradually fell over on its right side, its legs thrashing and eyes staring. There was a gasp from the crowd, most of whom jumped to their feet with concern. The horse struggled, snorting and wild-eyed, to its feet, leaving the crumpled and motionless form of Peter lying on the grass. Immediately two brown-jerkined squires ran on from the sidelines. One of them ran after the horse that was beginning to trot back to the safety of the enclosure, and caught it up. The other hurried towards the injured rider.

Together with a number of others, Robert ran across to help his fallen friend, but by the time he got there Peter had taken off his heaume and was struggling to sit up. He looked pale, dazed and weak. He lay back down on the ground, clutching his head

22 July 1377

and moaning softly. Robert slipped off his gambeson, put it under Peter's head and loosened his jerkin so that his friend could breathe more easily.

'Peter! Can you hear me? Are you hurt? What is wrong?' pleaded Robert.

Peter moaned again. 'Oh! My head hurts. Where am I?' He rolled over and retched, and then lapsed into unconsciousness again.

'I think he must be concussed. He's had a great blow on the head,' said another man who had rushed over, gesturing to the rapidly growing bump on his temple. 'He had better be carried into the shade of a tent.' He signalled for a stretcher, to find that two of Peter's men were already carrying up a hurdle pulled out of the surrounding barriers. Peter was gently lifted on to it and the two men picked it up and started carrying it towards the tents.

Robert wanted to accompany them, but the competition had to be completed and the marshal told him to return to the enclosure so that it could proceed. The custom always was that the tournament should be finished, notwithstanding injury to the contestants. Peter had to obey.

When he got there he found de Kingston joyful that the opposing team had only scored eighty points. This gave the West Medine a good chance of winning, as they only had to get twenty-one to win from the four tilts in the last round.

The first man in was Thomas Chyke. He was obviously tired and could hardly keep his lance horizontal. De Kingston gave the horse a hard slap on the rump to get it moving, and it started thundering down the list. There was a groan from the crowd as he almost missed, just tipping the dexter chief point for six marks. De Kingston punched his gloved hand into the palm of the other and swore loudly. The second man managed successfully to strike a base point for four marks, and he was unhorsed by the quintain. However, he was lucky not to be hurt, though he ruefully rubbed his backside as he hobbled up.

Robert groaned as he realised it was his turn. He could not afford to make any mistakes. To win now, himself and de Kingston needed to score eleven between them. If one of them scored a maximum, the other simply had to obtain a strike somewhere. As he was remounting he suddenly realised that he was not wearing his protecting gambeson; it had gone off with Peter to the tents. There was no time now to go and get it. He would have to take the risk. Just then, de Kingston walked across to where Robert paused wondering whether to earn the marshal's displeasure by waiting for a groom to fetch it. He had something in his hand and had a half-smile on his face.

'Here, lad! You had better wear this,' he said, handing his own gambeson up to Robert. 'Take care to get a clear hit.'

Robert was surprised and grateful for this unexpected gesture. 'Thank you, sire,' he said.

He put it on and glanced quickly towards where Rachel was sitting. She was watching him intently and gave a small encouraging wave. He donned his heaume, saluted briefly to her and the crowd, lowered the lance and spurred the horse towards the dummy. His face was set and his eyes were focused on the target approaching so rapidly. He didn't hear the encouraging shouts of the crowd. Beneath him he could feel the horse pounding along, and he held it on a straight course with his knees, the reins resting loosely in his left hand. The horse veered slightly to the left, but he corrected it with a slight pressure from his right knee, and a movement of the reins towards the right. The lance tip hit the shield fair and square, though a little high, and he managed to avoid the swinging bag. He let out a heavy sigh of relief, for he had scored eight. The crowd cheered wildly. He raised his lance into the air, turned and saluted to the waving crowd. It all now depended on de Kingston. A scoring strike of any value would ensure that West Medine were the winners.

De Kingston looked grim and tense, his mouth a hard line. He put on his helmet, the black plumes nodding, and took his lance from his page. He saluted the crowd, who cheered, though more out of sheer excitement rather than any regard for the man. He forced his horse on and leaned forward as if with urgency to reach the target. His lance struck the target with a clang, and the bag swung wildly by his ear as he charged past. He had scored six, but he flung the lance to one side, and with triumph he tore off his heaume. He raised a gauntleted hand to the crowd, smiling with pleasure at the victory. The crowd was cheering, though there

22 July 1377

were one or two subdued jeers and catcalls, which raised a brief scowl on de Kingston's face. He rode up to the enclosure and called for the rest of the team to ride with him on a victory circuit of the lists. All four of them cantered up the front of the platform, their heads bare, their heaumes in their hands, and their excited mounts snorting, stamping and prancing. All of the ladies were waving their coloured handkerchiefs, the men standing and clapping. Some were not so pleased that they had lost their wagers, nevertheless, they were not complaining at such an even and exciting contest. For the peasants it would be something to talk about for many long days and dark evenings.

Back at the enclosure de Kingston gruffly thanked the team with a curt, 'Well done.' He dismounted and was immediately surrounded by a throng of supporters. Robert slipped off his horse, elated to have been the top scorer for his team in the final round. He thrust the reins into the hands of one of Peter's men and hurried over to the tent to find out how his friend was.

Peter lay pale and still on a horse blanket on the ground. It looked as if he was asleep but as Robert bent over him his eyes opened and he said weakly, 'Ah, Robert. How did the tourney go? Did the East Medine win?' He struggled to sit up.

'No, Peter, I am afraid to say that the West won by three points. But how are you? Are you feeling any better?'

'My head hurts still, and I can only see you vaguely. It looks as if there are two of you. I don't think I will be able to draw bow against de Kingston today.'

Robert was pleased that Peter's memory seemed to be clear. He thought it was a good indication that the blow to his head wouldn't have lasting effects. 'Don't worry, Peter. I will settle the contest with de Kingston. I'll try and postpone it to another day when you have fully recovered. Meanwhile you had better lie quiet and I will arrange for a cart to take you home.'

'No, Robert,' Peter replied. 'I think I'll be able to ride home in a little while. Just let me be and I'll recover sufficiently.'

At that moment the flap of the tent opened and Rachel stepped in. Robert's heart leapt and Peter stirred with surprise.

'Hello, Robert! Do you mind if I come in? You did well in the tilting. It was so exciting. But how badly were you hurt?' She peered closely at Robert's face, inspecting the wound the splinter had made. She gently touched the swelling, but seemed satisfied that it was not going to be mortal.

'I think that you'd better wash it and put a cold compress on it to bring the swelling down. You are going to have a lovely black eye for a day or two,' she surmised.

She then turned to Peter, and curtseyed to him on being introduced by Robert. 'You were lucky not to be more badly hurt,' she said teasingly. 'You will have to give that horse some more schooling so that he doesn't shy away from the quintain so badly.' As she was saying this she knelt beside him and put her hand to his forehead. 'Does it hurt here?' she asked. He grunted a reply and closed his eyes in pain.

'I know a cure that will help with the pain. I saw a herb seller in the town and I think he should have what I need.' She looked at Robert who was watching with interest. 'My aunt was well versed in herbalism and taught me many remedies. Some people called her a witch, but she only did good deeds. What he needs is some willow bark and peppermint oil. I'll go and purchase some. Will you stay here with him? Just keep him quiet. I'll be back shortly.' She turned to leave as Robert at last found his tongue.

'Peter is not fit to enter the archery contest he is supposed to have later with de Kingston. I have to find him to postpone it before it is too late. But I will make sure one of Peter's men is here with him.'

Frowning briefly, Rachel caught Robert's hand and gave it a squeeze, but then gave Peter a quick smile and gracefully swept out.

Robert was entranced by her gentle competence and her forthright manner. He thought that she would have the ability to wind anyone, particularly men, round her little finger. Following her out, he saw her disappear with another woman into the crowd on their way to the town. He looked around for one of Peter's men, and found a page tending to the horses.

'Look to your master for a while; I have to make some arrangements. A lady has just gone for some medicines for him; she will be back shortly.'

'Aye, sire,' the page answered, 'I'll make sure he wants for nothing.' He rushed to serve his master.

22 July 1377

Robert turned and started searching through the crowd for de Kingston or one of his men. After almost completing a circuit of the lists he found de Kingston drinking a cup of wine outside John Urrey's tent. Seeing him, de Kingston immediately guessed the reason for Robert's appearance and smiled sardonically. 'Well now, Robert Affeton, I suppose you have come to say that your brother-in-law cannot stand in the archery contest. At least he has a good excuse for not being beaten in the butts, as he was at the lists. Will he be fit enough to give me satisfaction?' he added, as he glanced around his seated companions, almost as if he was playing to impress them.

Robert suppressed his impulse to reply in kind. 'Sire,' he said, 'my brother-in-law has been badly shaken in the fall and is concussed. He cannot yet stand unaided. It would be unfair to force him to a competition that you would have no real honour in winning. Can I request that you agree a postponement till a future time?' Then, on the spur of the moment he rashly offered, 'If you still desire a contest today, I was nominated as second to Peter and I will claim the right to stand in his stead.'

De Kingston appeared to consider the challenge for a moment and looked Robert up and down, as if appraising his worth. 'That seems to be very fair,' he said in a rather different and much more agreeable tone of voice. 'I will draw bow against you today, as his substitute, but reserve the right to meet him later.' Then, with a half-laugh, he said, 'We cannot disappoint the crowd, can we? We will meet in half an hour at the butts, where it shall be decided.' On Robert's nod of agreement, he turned away with a grunt of satisfaction and called for a servant.

Robert now had to find a bow and arrows and have a few quick practice shots at the butts beforehand. He hurried back to Peter's tent to see if he could borrow a bow from one of his men. Rachel had returned and was kneeling by Peter, smoothing some fresh-smelling ointments into his forehead while the page looked on. Peter was looking distinctly better; his eyes had lost the glazed, out-of-focus look and he had more colour to his cheeks. He looked as if he was enjoying Rachel's ministrations.

'I found de Kingston,' Robert said. 'He was happy to postpone your contest, but as your second I had to offer to stand in your stead. He accepted and I could not refuse, even though I am nowhere near as good a shot as you, Peter. Now I must find a bow and go to the butts to practise. Are any of your villeins taking part in the archery contests? Can I borrow a bow?'

Rachel looked up, apparently startled. Peter tried struggling to his feet. However, he fell back with a groan. 'I wish I wasn't so groggy, Robert,' he said. 'I don't think I could go through with it now. But there will be no dishonour if you do get beaten. After all, his disagreement is with me, not you. The page here will find my bow; you can use that.'

With a slight smile and a wink he added, to Rachel, 'Why don't you go with him? I'll be all right here with my page, and I'll try to come down to the butts a little later when the ointment takes effect and I feel better.'

Rachel rose, looked at Robert, smiled and nodded. 'I really ought to find my maid, Sarah... but I'm sure she is very happy looking at the young men. She will not miss me too much for a while longer, I'll be bound. Come then, Robert, for the more time you have to practise, the better.' Then she turned back to Peter. 'The ointment should begin to take effect soon. You'll probably be able to stand and walk then, but take it steadily and don't overexert yourself.'

Robert held the tent flap open for her, and they stood outside waiting for the page to return with the bow. Rachel looked rather pensive and after a slight hesitation opened her mouth to speak, but the page appeared before she could say what was on her mind. A flicker of dismay crossed her face.

'Sire, I am not sure which bow you will need, but I have brought the two that were in the cart.' The page held out a large crossbow and a longbow. The former was Peter's famed bow with which it was said he could dint a silver penny at seventy yards. The wooden stock was dark brown with age and use, and this was accentuated by the bright silver embossing. The bow had to be cranked with a handle to draw or span it and the short iron-tipped bolt, or quarrel, was then placed against the drawn string. The stock was held to the shoulder so that the archer could sight along the bolt and it was fired by a trigger that released the string. In good hands the crossbow was very accurate, could penetrate chain

22 July 1377

mail, and even light armour, but it was slow to cock so that the rate of firing was poor.

On the other hand, the longbow could be fired at twelve arrows a minute, but it didn't reach as far and was not as accurate at distance. It was the preferred weapon of the English, and had been the means of victory in many wars and battles against the French, who had been for the most part armed with the crossbow.

'I think that we will be using the longbow today,' Robert said, reaching for it. He also took a handful of arrows. 'Look after your master well, and make sure he stays quiet.'

'Yes, sire, and good luck. May St Sebastian smile on you,' said the page, calling down the blessings of the patron saint of archers.

Robert and Rachel walked down to the lists that had now been turned into an archery arena, with the targets set up in butts at both ends, and markers at set distances away from them for the various competitions. Some archers were already in action and there was an almost continuous *swish* of arrows being released. They arced across the blue sky, making a noise rather like flights of birds passing overhead, or the sighing of the wind in the trees.

The practice butts were set up further over towards the woods and away from the town. They quickly went that way and Robert found a spare target, handed Rachel the arrows, and proceeded to string the bow. It was a good bow of yew, termed 'painted' because it was well seasoned and varnished to keep in the natural oils and maintain the essential suppleness. Robert pressed the end of the bow against the inside of his right foot. With his right hand he pulled the centre of the bow towards him, while pushing the top end away with his left, thus bending the bow. At the same time he slid his left hand up the bow, gradually working the end of the string towards the nock at the top end. In this way the strain was evenly distributed and the bottom tip was not forced against the ground. As the bow was over six feet long, it took quite an effort. He slipped the loop of the string over the nock in the horn tip of the bow, and slowly released the tension. As he drew his leg out of the bow there was a sudden snap and the string broke. Robert cursed inwardly and frowned. Just his luck!

Now he would have to borrow a bow from someone else, for there was not time to get another string.

Rachel's voice came from behind him. 'Don't worry, Robert. I can get you another longbow. One of my father's men is shooting over there. I'm sure he'll lend you his. There he is, just drawing his bow.' She gestured towards a thickset man a half a dozen places away. He drew the bow until the flight of the arrow touched his right ear, then raised it, estimating the trajectory, and released the arrow with a twang. It soared away towards the butts. Robert didn't watch to see where it hit for he was looking intently at the man's face. It was familiar somehow, but he couldn't place where he had seen it before.

Rachel touched Robert's hand and moved across to where the other man stood pulling another arrow from his quiver. 'Stephen,' she called. The man turned, and when he saw them his weatherbeaten face broke into a good-natured grin, showing a line of surprisingly white teeth.

'Good afternoon, Mistress Rachel,' he said, his hand touching his forelock. 'Is there something I can do for you?'

'Yes, Stephen, there is. Robert de Affeton here requires a bow for a tournament shortly this afternoon, as the string on his has just broken. Would it be possible to borrow yours?'

'Of course,' he replied. 'I don't mind, but I can see the master may not be too happy if he comes to hear about it.'

'He's not to know. Anyway, you wouldn't tell him, would you?' Rachel looked at him beseechingly.

Stephen gave in, and without another word handed Robert the bow. Robert was puzzled by the implications of the exchange of words. There was some mystery and hidden meaning behind what was said, but he dismissed the thoughts, as he had to concentrate on the immediate problem. He weighed the bow in his hand and felt the smoothness and strength of the curves in the yew. He then checked the fistmele, the distance from the string to the belly of the bow, a distance that ideally should be equal to the width of fist and erect thumb.

Robert was impressed by the quality of the bow. 'It is very well balanced and strung. You have looked after it well, Stephen; it must be quite old.'

22 July 1377

'Aye, sire! It was my father's. He used it at the battle of Poitiers when he was in the wars with the Black Prince. He bequeathed it to me when he died. I have been offered many marks for it, but I'll never sell,' he said proudly. 'With a fore-hand shaft the arrow will carry a good 300 feet.' A fore-hand shaft was an arrow aimed no higher than the eye could sight along. To go further meant raising the fore hand higher, obscuring the target and losing accuracy.

Robert took an arrow from Rachel and nocked it on to the string. The other two stood back, watching closely. The yard-long arrow, sometimes called a 'grey goose wing', was iron-tipped and fletched with goose feathers bound with green silk. In the right hands it could penetrate a three-inch-thick oak door. He curled the first and second fingers of his right hand round the string to draw it, with the arrow between them. Tensing his shoulder and back muscles he pulled the bow open with both arms, almost as if he was going to step into it. His left arm locked and he pulled the arrow back until the string was against his chin. He thought that he must be exerting at least sixty pounds of pull on the bow, and he couldn't hold it for long. Looking along the arrow past his left hand he could see the butts with the straw-stuffed target covered with a cloth painted with brightly coloured concentric rings. He raised his left arm until he judged the arc of the trajectory should carry the arrow to the target, and when he loosed it, it zipped as it sped away, just visible against the sky. It started to dip towards the target when Robert noticed that it was beginning to carry slightly towards the right. It struck the ground just to the right of the target.

A grunt came from Stephen. 'A fine shot for length, sire. But there is a bit more breeze than one would suspect, for we are protected here. Do you see how the trees over there are moving now?' He gestured to the tall trees on the edge of Walter's Copse, stirring in beginnings of the light afternoon breeze. 'Aim to the left by half the target width, I suggest.'

Robert took another arrow, and allowed for the wind the amount that Stephen had suggested. This time the arrow sped straight to the target and stuck quivering just outside the gold. Rachel clapped her hands with glee and Stephen nodded approvingly.

'A few more like that and I'd have the measure even of Peter,' said Robert cheerily.

'I've seldom seen better with an unfamiliar bow,' said Stephen, 'but I think you ought to shoot more to get the feel of the bow properly.'

He proffered another shaft, and Robert smiled at Rachel as he took it. She looked into his eyes and her cheeks dimpled. Robert felt a strange elation and a great desire to gain honour in her esteem by performing well. He strung the arrow and drew the bow a third time, taking careful note of the wind. The arrow again just clipped the inner. With these efforts Robert said he was satisfied, and Stephen strode away to the butts to retrieve the arrows.

Rachel stepped in front of Robert, who was leaning on the bow memorising the actions he had just gone through so that he could repeat them later. Tipping her head back slightly she looked up at him. Her eyes were sparkling and her lips were slightly parted, showing even, white teeth, and a dimple appeared on her right cheek. Robert stood dumbfounded, his eyes wide with amazement as he fought against the desire to kiss her. She took his hands and held them firmly between hers.

'I must go and find my maid before she gets into mischief, and I expect my father will be wondering where I am. But before I go, I must explain something...' But, before she could start John Urrey came up to say that the tournament would take place in about ten minutes in the main arena, following a quarterstaff match. Rachel looked downcast at not being able to finish her explanation, muttered quietly under her breath and slipped away through the crowd. John Urrey also turned and hurried off.

Stephen returned with half a dozen arrows in his fist and looked at Robert with a rather odd expression on his face. Robert wondered whether he had seen what Rachel had done.

'Here, sire,' he said with a slight inclination of his head. 'These should be enough for further practising, if you have time. Good luck in your tournament.'

Robert thanked him, and started moving towards the main arena. He thought of the touch of Rachel's hands. Did her heart leap in the way his had? Did she feel the same excitement and anticipation? He hoped so.

At the main arena the quarterstaff match was just about to begin. Robert stood to watch, since there was little else he could do until it was over. The marshal introduced the match, which was a challenge between the Island champion, Michael Apse and the champion from Southampton, an equally tough-looking man called Thomas Shirley. He had a cauliflower ear and his nose was twisted to one side, obviously broken in a previous match, and he had a luxuriant ginger-tinged beard. They were very well matched in terms of both height and weight. They were both dressed in rough breeches, and leather jerkins that left their arms bare and free. Likewise their feet were bare so that their toes could dig in and help them from slipping. The prize was a purse of twenty marks – as much as a man could earn in a year, as well as honour and reputation as champion.

There were few rules to this sort of combat, the objective being to beat your opponent unconscious, or into submission, by blows about the head and body. The weapon was one that the peasants would easily cut out of the nearest copse, a thick staff about six-feet long, generally of ash, hard yet supple, with the side shoots trimmed so that a man's hands could smoothly slide along it to change grip.

The two men faced each other in the middle of a square of about twenty feet that had been marked out, and within which they had to stay. The marshal introduced them to the crowd, the supporters cheering their own man and jeering the other one. He then reminded the pair of the few rules: no headbutting, eye gouging or punching. Then he left the ring.

The two men crouched about six feet apart, both with legs straddled, their staffs gripped across their bodies, their hands about a yard apart. Faces fierce with concentration, they stared into each other's eyes, waiting for the flicker that would betray movement a fraction before it began. They started warily circling, feinting and weaving. After what seemed a few minutes the impatient crowd catcalled and shouted for them to get on with it. Then there was a flurry of action. A left hand slid down the staff so that a blow could be aimed at the head. A quick movement and the opposing quarterstaff took the blow, and a riposte was made, again to be countered. The air was filled with the crash and clatter of wood against wood, and the grunts of effort. Michael Apse drove hard with his staff flailing to right and left, forcing his opponent back towards the edge of the square. But Shirley was experienced. He dropped onto one knee and suddenly took a scything blow at Apse's legs; Apse took a heavy blow on his thigh. He retreated to the middle. Shirley had taken a blow on his knuckles, which were dripping blood onto the ground. He took a second to wipe them on his breeches, before coming forward again. Another rain of blows, defence and counter from both men ended when Apse took a hit on the side of his head that sent him reeling; his guard came up again before any further damage was done. Both men were breathing hard through their clenched teeth. Sweat ran from their brows and darkened their jerkins.

Another attack: this time it was Shirley who suffered a blow on his neck, but he only shook his head and came barging in again with his staff swinging to force Apse to his knees. The overner swung a tremendous two-handed blow at Apse while he was trying to regain his feet, but it was met by a solid defence that split one end of Shirley's staff. Reversing it quickly, he tried again to break down Apse's defences and succeeded in striking the Islander again on the side of the head, this time causing a cut which started blood running down his face.

Apse was both tough and brave: he sprang to his feet and responded with rapid succession of blows that were blocked, each blow ending with splinters flying from his opponent's staff. With a cry of triumph, Michael Apse rained more blows on his opponent. Shirley was dodging them now rather than blocking them because of the state of his staff. He twisted and turned to avoid the blows but he took several on his shoulders and upper arms, and became slower by the second. He was desperately trying to grasp Apse's staff as it hit him, with the aim of wrenching it out of the other's grip, but without success. Eventually Apse scored a blow to Shirley's head that sent him reeling, at which he raised his arm in submission.

The marshal shouted to stop the contest and raised Apse's arm as the victor. The crowd roared its appreciation of the contest.

22 July 1377

Apse, with a broad smile on his face, immediately turned to his opponent and embraced him. They pounded each other's backs enthusiastically. There was no animosity between them, as they were old adversaries – apparently Shirley had won last time they met. Once the prize money had been handed over they both went off with linked arms to the town to spend some of it on some good wine or ale. No doubt on the following morning they wouldn't know whether their aching heads were because of the blows they had received or the drink. In the background, de Kingston smiled with satisfaction.

With the quarterstaff contest over, the arena was now clear for the rest of the archery. More contestants were assembling around Robert for the next shoot, when the herald interrupted and announced that John de Kingston would be shooting against Robert de Affeton in a special challenge match. De Kingston shouldered his way out of the crowd, and he and Urrey walked across to where Robert stood idly rubbing the wound on his cheek.

'My principal requires that you, as challenger, should draw first. You will shoot two ends of six arrows each, and the winner to be the top score. In the case of a draw, a further two arrows will decide,' John Urrey said, while de Kingston stood to one side with his arms folded.

'I have no second, but I accept,' Robert replied.

He felt very isolated, as he had no immediate supporters or friends there to encourage him. Peter was not to be seen and Rachel was nowhere in sight. De Kingston, on the other hand, had a number of people with him who formed a semicircle behind the two of them. Robert tried to clear his mind and concentrate his attention on doing as well as he had at the practice butts. They walked up to where the marshal stood at the end of the lists.

The marshal took the linen wrapper off a new sheaf of arrows and handed a dozen each to de Kingston and to Robert. Robert took off his gambeson, laid it on the ground and inspected the arrows. They were expensive barrelled arrows, tapering from the fletching to the point, and true in flight. Choosing the one that he thought appeared straightest, he put the others carefully on his gambeson. He had a quick glance around. On the platform he saw movement where Rachel and Sarah were helping Peter to find a seat. He took comfort from their presence. Now he knew where she was, and that Peter was recovering, he felt more at ease and relaxed. He felt that fate would now determine the outcome of the match.

He turned with his back to the platform and placed his feet in line with the target, which was almost a furlong off to the left. He nocked the first arrow into the string between his curved fingers. The crowd fell quiet, waiting with bated breath as he carefully gauged the distance, angle and wind strength. He drew the bow to its fullest extent, with the string touching the tip of his nose and his chin, and his right hand tucked beneath his chin. He could feel the strain pulling at the muscles in his shoulders. He paused a fraction, sighting along the arrow at the target, raised the bow to the angle he thought would make the arrow reach the target, and then let go the shaft. The string twanged and the arrow soared away with a hiss. It curved upwards slightly, but the trajectory was very flat at this distance. It then plummeted downwards, striking close to the red inner on the right-hand side. The judge in the butts, however, signalled seven points, and there was a burst of applause. The arrow must have just grazed the inner circle after all.

Robert was satisfied, but thought that the wind might be increasing. He ran his fingers through his hair, and decided to allow a little more off to the left for the next arrow. He surmised correctly and the next shaft struck the gold, the bull's eye, for the full nine points. A shout went up from the peasants massed behind the hurdles on the right, with more restrained applause from the gentry under the awning on the platform. It was obvious that the peasants had adopted Robert as their champion for this contest and were willing him to win. He felt a surge of exhilaration. Perhaps it was going to be his day after all. Nevertheless the tension of the people around and behind him was almost tangible. Robert realised that he was sweating profusely, and it was running down into his eyes. He bent and took out a cloth to wipe his face, trying to quell the trembling in his knees.

22 July 1377

His third arrow was not so good. A blue – five points. The tension was making his shooting erratic. He took a few seconds to draw a deep breath and to calm his pounding heart. Again he ran his fingers through his hair, and rubbed his forehead with his fingertips. The fourth arrow struck beside the second in the gold. The cheering was tumultuous. Robert was beginning to feel elated; his confidence grew.

As he picked up his fifth arrow he glanced across to de Kingston, who had a worried scowl on his face. The fifth arrow struck the blue again. Thirty-five points so far. One more good shot and he'd be satisfied that he'd done his best on this end. It was another gold, for a total of forty-four points, with three bull's eyes. Robert was highly satisfied with dropping only ten points out of the possible fifty-four, and he stepped back with a satisfied smile.

De Kingston stepped forward and drew his bow smoothly, quickly shooting off six arrows in succession without waiting for the judge to call out where they found their mark. The crowd murmured the scores as the arrows struck home, and totalled them up. Three golds, two reds and a blue – forty-six. A lead of two. There were muted cheers for de Kingston who smiled grimly. Robert wondered whether this was lucky consequence of bravado or a true reflection of his shooting ability.

Now was the time for the reverse shoot, so the whole group trekked up to the other end of the lists while the targets were checked. They now had the wind in their faces, blowing from right to left across the line of flight. They were also facing the platform as they drew bow, with the sun in their eyes. Again, Robert had to shoot first.

There was a movement in the crowd behind him and Rachel appeared. Just at that moment de Kingston turned to speak to one of his friends and caught sight of her.

'Daughter!' he roared. 'Where in God's name have you been all the day? Off gallivanting, I suppose. I thought you were in the care of your aunt, but she says she hasn't seen much of you. So much for the London manners you've been taught.'

Robert nearly dropped his bow. Rachel de Kingston, thought Robert. Daughter of that man. No wonder she was so reticent about her family name! Stephen the bowman – of course, he is one of Kingston's men. He was with Michael Apse and de Kingston at the Cares Brook when I was pushed in the stream. I knew I'd seen him before. These thoughts flashed through Robert's mind as he stood there, bemused, looking at her. He felt betrayed, just as if the bottom had dropped out of his world. 'Had she deceived him on purpose?'

'Father,' she said crossly. 'I am no longer a girl who needs you to provide a guard me for every second of the day. I have been well looked after.' She shot a glance at Robert. 'Anyway, I have come to tell you that a messenger has come saying that mother is not well. She desires that we return as soon as we can.'

She went and stood by her father's side, where she looked appealingly at Robert, as if trying subconsciously to tell him something.

Robert had a horrible sinking feeling in the pit of his stomach and his ears burned as he felt a blush of confusion rising to his cheeks. Had he made a fool of himself? He turned away and fumbled his arrow into the string. The wind was getting stronger all the time, but his hands were trembling with the anger and frustration of disappointment, and he scarcely noticed. He raised the bow and tried to concentrate on the target. Twice he raised and lowered the bow before he felt calm enough to loose the arrow. It curved away, and Robert could see it gradually being swept off course by the wind. It just clipped the right-hand edge of the target. A black outer! Robert's shoulders slumped with despair. A bad start to the last round. He ground his teeth with determination. I'll show her I don't care, he thought to himself as he wiped his sweating palms on his breeches.

He grabbed the next arrow and nocked it into the string. A couple of deep breaths and he felt calmer, almost detached, as if he were outside himself watching the contest as a dispassionate observer. That arrow scored a red, and the next a gold. Robert began to feel better, recovering his poise. The last three shots comprised two more gold bulls and a red inner. Forty-four points – the same as the first round. Under the circumstances a very creditable performance, though no one would ever know the effort it cost him.

22 July 1377

De Kingston stepped forward with a half-smile on his face. 'Do you acknowledge me the victor yet, de Affeton?' he sneered ungraciously.

A spark of spirit was still left in Robert's turbulent mind, and he snapped a retort.

'Only when you have bettered my score. There's many a slip.'

De Kingston smiled, stuck five arrows in the ground and strung the first one into the bow. With legs straddled he drew the arrow back. Robert could feel Rachel's gaze on him, but it took a great effort of will not to look at her. He felt her sweet appearance might entrap him again. Even so, he was aware of her presence in a most peculiar way.

The bow twanged and Robert opened his eyes to watch the arrow soaring towards the target, plunging into the gold. He didn't really care now. He knew he'd be beaten and this made him more angry against de Kingston and his daughter. Perhaps she purposely appeared at the last in order to put him off, he thought unjustly. That would have been a masterly stroke!

A red inner this time. Robert perked up a bit and de Kingston scowled. The wind was increasing, the flags on the platform standing out stiffly. A large black thundercloud had come up behind them and now cut out the sun. It seemed cold all of a sudden, as if it would rain shortly.

Another bull's eye, and de Kingston was lucky to get it, the way the wind was gusting. Robert smiled. Perhaps all was not yet lost! The fourth arrow went soaring straight for another bull's eye, but struck one of the arrows already there, and was deflected. It struck the target, but did not stick in. No points. Robert was elated. He might still actually win. De Kingston only had to drop two points and he would lose. That would be poetic justice, he thought.

De Kingston waited for a lull in the wind. With the bow drawn the tension on the arms was extreme, and no man could hold it for long without the muscles trembling. He lowered the bow, shrugging his shoulders to relax them. A lull appeared in the wind and he quickly raised the bow and loosed the arrow – another gold. He smiled in relief, and looked at Robert with satisfaction. Another gold with the last arrow and he would win; a red, and he would lose. The trees were starting to lash again in the wind. He would have to hurry before the next gust came. He drew and released in one smooth movement. The crowd roared – it was a gold. De Kingston had won by a single point.

He turned away in triumph to salute his supporters in the crowd. Rachel hurried over to her father and whispered something in his ear. He obviously disagreed with what she said. She stamped her foot, said something more and nodded fiercely at him. With a resigned expression he came over to Robert, and very graciously said, 'I consider honour is satisfied. You have been an able opponent. I will not be calling on de Heyno further. I am grateful we do not have to shoot more, otherwise the wind would be the victor rather than one of us.' He held out his hand and Robert, flabbergasted, shook it. This was a side of de Kingston that Robert had never thought existed. De Kingston's grip was hard, as if he were testing Robert again, but Robert responded in kind, squeezing the hand in his. Perhaps he could come to respect the man.

'I agree, sire. It was an enjoyable contest and you were unlucky with that deflected arrow. I hope that your lady recovers quickly from her ailment,' Robert replied, relieved that it was all over and that he hadn't disgraced himself. De Kingston acknowledged the sympathetic comment with an inclination of the head and a slight smile.

When the crowd realised what had happened they cheered and clapped before they moved away to find shelter from the rain that was beginning to spot the dry ground. Though Robert had lost to de Kingston, he had not been beaten mentally. He knew that if he had not been distracted in such an unfortunate way he could have won. He got the impression that de Kingston realised this, even though he couldn't know the reason for Robert's discomfort.

De Kingston turned away saying, 'Come, daughter, we must prepare to return home.' He put his arm round Rachel, guiding her away to the shelter of his tent. Rachel smiled over her shoulder at Robert, but he was still confused about her intentions and the role she had played in the archery match.

He turned away without any acknowledgement, picked up the bow and made his way to Peter's tent, the rain now falling freely on his bare head. Peter was there, having returned from the platform. He looked much better, with something like normal colour in his cheeks.

'Well done, Robert,' he said. 'You did well, and except for the poor arrow at the beginning of the second end, I thought you had him beaten. What happened?'

'I'm so annoyed with myself. Just before that shaft Rachel appeared with a message. It turned out that she is de Kingston's daughter. It knocked me sideways for a moment and I couldn't concentrate. How can someone like him have a daughter who is so beautiful, open, warm and friendly? I find it hard to believe.'

'She's certainly very unlike him. I must say she is a very sweet girl. I like her. Perhaps she takes after her mother rather than him. I have never met Lady de Kingston, though I hear that she spends most of her time in her gardens. She doesn't travel very much.'

'But did you see what he did after the contest? He came over to me, offered me his hand and said that honour was satisfied, and that you wouldn't be bothered with further challenges,' said Robert, feeling the he had discharged his duty to Peter. Then changing the subject, 'Are you recovered enough to travel home without me, or shall I come with you?'

'I don't think you need to do that. I'm sure I'll be all right,' replied Peter. 'I have a number of other things I must do first. I have instructions from Rebecca to buy some necessaries for the baby. You won't want to be involved in that.' He laughed. 'I feel much better; Rachel's ointment has worked wonders. My page will make sure I get home in one piece but I think that I'll forego tomorrow's festivities and go back to Rebecca. She may need me. I'll rest tomorrow at home.'

Robert nodded his head approvingly. 'I am to dine with my cousin James today, and then I too will ride home to make sure father is safe. But first I have to find Stephen, de Kingston's man, and return this bow. The string on your bow broke and Rachel asked one of her father's men to lend me his. It's a fine bow and I must return it, for he values it very highly. I'll come back before you leave.'

Outside, Robert found the rain had stopped, not really having wetted the ground and the sky had cleared. He was unsure where to find Stephen but started towards the practice arena where they had met. The afternoon was growing old; the sun was dipping towards the downs in the west, and the shadows were lengthening. The last of the day's contests were just finishing and most of the people were beginning to drift back to the town for the evening festivities, or to find their way home before dark. The practice area was empty except for a couple of scavenging dogs and a beggar searching through the rubbish. The butts had been stored away for the night, for they would be used again the following day, the last of the festival. Robert realised that the most likely place to find the man now was around de Kingston's tents. He turned and started back, looking morosely at the ground and kicking at bits of rubbish. When he looked up he saw Rachel coming towards him.

'Robert!' she said breathlessly. 'I'm so glad I've found you. I went to the tent and you weren't there. Peter de Heyno said that you were looking for Stephen to return the bow, and I guessed you might come here.' She was flushed and excited. She stopped in front of him and placed a hand on his arm. 'Please do not think badly of me. At first I didn't want you to know who I was, in case it turned you against me. It's not that I am ashamed of my father, I love him dearly, but he can be very difficult and off-putting and has upset so many people. I tried several times to tell you, after I knew you well enough to be sure that you wouldn't mind, but we kept on being interrupted. Please forgive me. I didn't mean to spoil your last end. I could have died when I saw the look on your face. I wanted to get close enough to see properly and I was going to keep the message about Mother until afterwards, but Father saw me first.'

She looked so sorrowful in her pleading that Robert found relief sweeping over him. So he really had been right in his first impressions: she was not like her father, but was lovely and desirable, sweet and innocent. He wanted more than anything to get to know her better.

'Rachel, my dearest,' he said with relief, 'don't worry. It was a shock at the time, and I thought that it might have been all part of some plan, your knowing who I was without me saying, and you not saying who you were. But I believe our meeting was truly preordained and we weren't to know what would happen later. I see that now. Anyway, de Kingston wouldn't need to plot to get the better of someone like me,' he said modestly. 'How did you know who I was?'

'I guessed who you were: my father described you once, and after that I questioned others. After he spoke of you, for some reason, I have always had a peculiar feeling that I needed to meet you, and to get to know you, and now I have all I want is the opportunity to get to know you better. You may think me very forward, but I have always spoken my mind. I suppose that comes from being my father's daughter,' she added ruefully with a small grin.

Robert was amazed at what she said. He had never met anyone so open, honest and forthright, without being in any way brazen. She obviously knew precisely what she wanted and was determined to get her own way. He felt he was being swept along on a rushing stream and was losing control, but for some reason he didn't mind. He welcomed her intrusion into his life, and knew that it would never be the same again. He wanted to make sure she remained in his life – at least until he knew her better.

'But you are so different from your father. Don't you argue with one another?' asked Robert cautiously.

'Oh yes,' she replied. 'When I was small it was terrible. We had the most terrific rows, and I used to run away and hide. That is why he sent me to London to an aunt, and had a tutor try to educate me in the correct graces for a young lady, but I also learned many other things. It is very different now I've grown up. I can persuade him, if I use my womanly wiles, and I've discovered he is really very kind and generous inside. But he doesn't show that side of his nature to most people. He has a short temper, and I wonder whether it's related to the bad headaches he frequently has. I keep on trying to change the way he acts, but it's very difficult. Unfortunately, Mother doesn't help a great deal. She's borne the brunt of his temper for years, and now doesn't stand up to him as she used to.'

'What do you think his response would be if I asked if I could visit you at Kingston Manor? I want to court you properly and I cannot see how we would be able to meet again otherwise.'

Afternoon

'At the moment I don't think he'd allow it. You will have to let me work on him slowly and persuade him that he should be more welcoming to his neighbours. I don't think any of them have ever feasted in our house. However,' she said archly, 'that doesn't mean that we couldn't meet. I often ride out by myself. We could arrange to be in the same place, by accident, one day. No one need know.' She gave him a sidelong glance and an encouraging smile, hoping that he wouldn't be offended or put off by her presumption.

Robert was relieved that there was some way of developing their relationship without the formal need to confront and be polite to de Kingston, or run the gauntlet of his ire. After a brief pause for thought, he said, 'Shall we meet then at Kingett Chyne? It is a lovely spot, and away from prying eyes. I've been there many times. It's only about three miles from your manor, and I can easily ride there in a couple of hours. Do you think that you could get there without raising any suspicion?'

Rachel, in turn, thought for a moment. 'I'm sure I could. It would be best if it were times when my father was away from home on business. As he is a magistrate, one of the King's Justices, he is frequently in Nieuport on Wednesday and Thursday attending the court. I'm sure I could meet you next Wednesday in the forenoon, and Kingett Chyne will be easy to reach. If I cannot get there I will either get Sarah to be there or leave a message for you in some obvious place.'

Then with a resigned sigh she said, 'I must go now, for my father will be looking for me to leave for home. We will not be here tomorrow.'

'I too must go, for I have to dine with my cousin in the town. Then I have to return home to see to my father. He's mostly bedridden and cannot be left too long unattended. God speed next week; I'll be looking forward to it. I hope nothing will stop us meeting. Fate has certainly smiled on me today, and I feel that some interesting new turns of destiny have been unveiled.'

Robert was being almost as open about his feelings as she, and knew that the rest of the week would be tedious until the time of their tryst. He put his hands on Rachel's shoulders to look her straight in the face, but he suddenly found his arms around her,

22 July 1377

and her face pressing against his chest. He could hear her breath coming quickly and feel her heart beating against him. He could feel his legs trembling and his loins beginning to stir. He was really enjoying the experience and wanted it to continue, but by mutual consent they drew apart. They would have to keep their feelings in check for the time being. They parted then and went their separate ways, both with a light step and singing hearts, she taking the bow for Stephen.

AFFETON AND THE SURROUNDING AREA

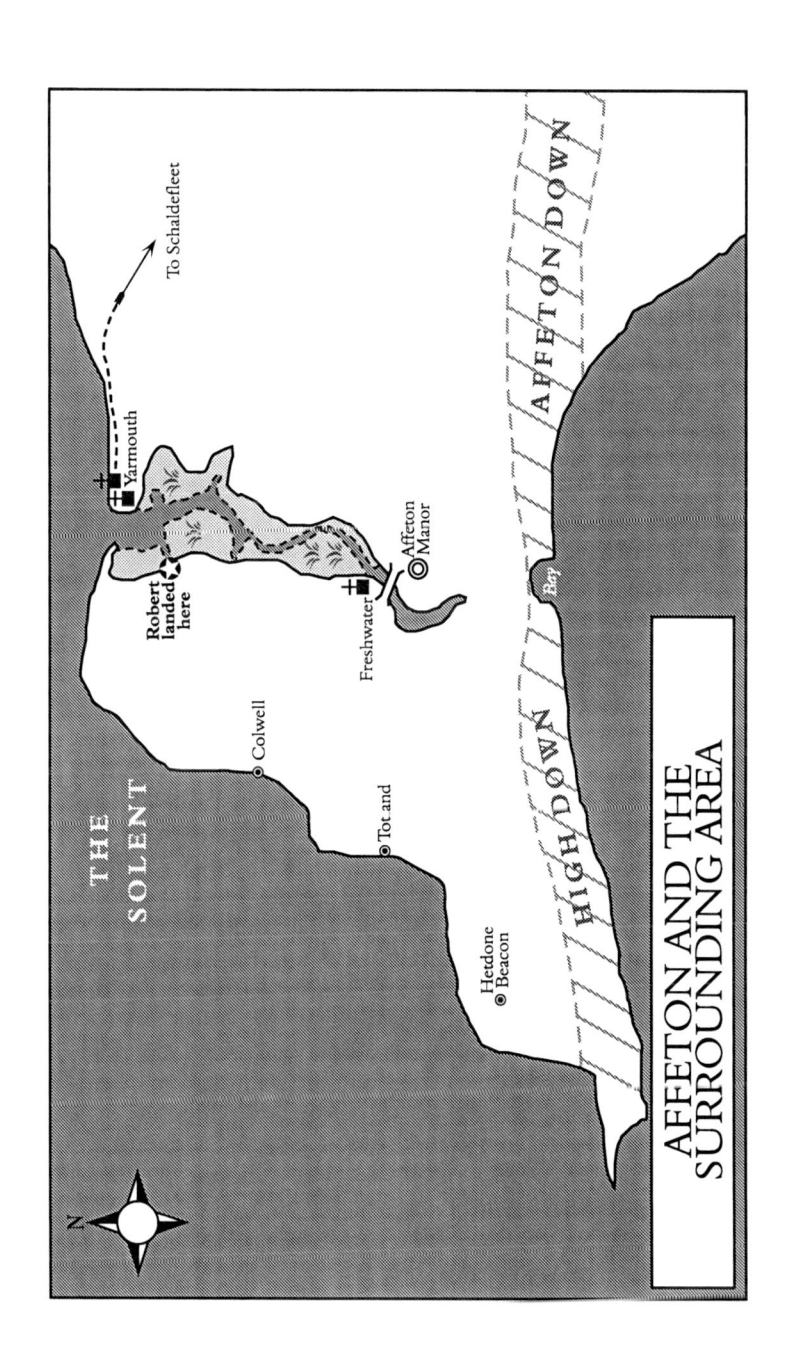

THE SOLENT

To Schaldefleet

Yarmouth

Robert landed here

Colwell

Freshwater

Affeton Manor

Tot and

Bay

Hetdone Beacon

HIGH DOWN

AFFETON DOWN

N

21 August 1377

Afternoon

The afternoon was hot and sultry; thunder had been threatening all day. Little thunder flies were irritatingly crawling over any exposed skin, and fleas were very active, so that scratching was hard to resist. Robert was presiding over the manorial court that was held every six weeks in the main hall of Affeton Manor. As his father's substitute, and effectively lord of the manor, he had to settle disputes and pass judgement on his tenant's duties.

He was finding it hard to concentrate. He had drunk rather too much ale at noon, and felt sleepy and bored. At times he was oblivious to his surroundings, yet he should have been paying strict attention so that he could be fair in his treatment of the complaints brought before him. He sat in the chair at one end of the hall, his elbow on the table, his head resting in his hand. To his left the open window looked out across the River Yar towards Freshwater. Dust was rising from a cart climbing the hill from the causeway towards the church. The sound of a barking dog wafted in on the slight breeze that stirred the wall hangings, but the movement of the air did not make the heat any less.

The proceedings were organised by Timothy, the steward and bailiff. The bailiff was the right-hand man of the lord of the manor; he looked after the estate when his master was away, ensured that the lands were farmed properly, and that the villeins fulfilled their duties in providing labour and their due share of produce. Timothy was small and upright, with fair hair, like his lord, blue eyes and with a weatherbeaten skin and a slow deliberate manner. Though the bailiff was shy and talked little, he was completely trustworthy. Sir Roger had depended much on him while Robert had been away at the wars, but Timothy had quite happily stepped back when Robert had returned.

Before them stood the reeve, who was the spokesman nominated by the peasants to keep an inventory of their work on the manor demesne and look after their interests. He was a small, smelly man who spoke with a whining nasal voice. His eyes shifted constantly, and he never looked anyone directly in the eye. Enormously long hairs grew from his nostrils, and he stroked them fondly, as if encouraging them to grow faster. Wafts of his dog-like odour spread around the room as he scratched incessantly. Despite being the peasants' representative, he was not popular, as he made sure that he profited from both the peasants and the lord of the manor. However, he could read and count; he could keep an infinite number of details in his mind and was a good wily speaker – all things the other peasants could not do. Robert distrusted him, but it was convenient to use the reeve to do some of the complicated things that either the bailiff or someone else would otherwise have to do, and this was why they depended on him. Consequently, both Robert and the bailiff kept a close watch on him to make sure of his honesty and curb his greatest excesses. Standing behind the reeve and lining the other three walls of the hall were yeomen, villeins and peasants, the plaintiffs, their friends and relations. In the heat they all shuffled, scratched and sweated.

The reeve was stating the case for settling an argument between two peasants who disputed the boundary between their parcels of land. They each had about twenty acres of land, which was enough for them to grow sufficient food for themselves and their families, with some produce left over for the market. As was common custom, adjoining strips of land were not marked by fences or hedges. Most peasants worked amicably together, helped each other at ploughing and harvest, and they settled disputes with a happy compromise. However, by pinching in the ploughing it was possible to gain a yard or two of the neighbour's strip. Likewise a similar gain could be made on harvesting by leaning over and sweeping the sickle wide. This had happened in the recent haymaking and the resulting argument had led to blows being exchanged. Robert suspected that both complainants were at it, that it was six of one and half a dozen of the other, but it was wise to let them have their say before passing judgement.

He allowed his mind to wander and it reverted to thoughts of Rachel. She was constantly on his mind and he had a curious

21 August 1377

emptiness when he wasn't with her. When he was with her he was filled with elation. He was sure that he was in love with her, except that he was not sure what love should feel like. Though he had heard tell of love before, it had always been an idealised state lauded by poets and minstrels, rather than the intense physical desire and longing that racked him. During the short month since the fair they had managed to meet twice, and this had focused and intensified his feelings.

The first time they met was the day they had arranged at the fair at Francheville. He had set out early in the morning, as it was a good two hours' ride to Kingett Chyne. Overnight rain had laid the dust and fringed each blade of grass with sparkling jewels. The rain had sharpened all of the scents and the air smelled sweet and musty in the morning sun. It was a day to charm the senses, heighten excitement and increase anticipation. Once he crested the downs behind the manor he could see far along the coast towards his goal. The steep white chalk cliffs deflected the gentle sea breeze, creating updrafts on which gulls hovered effortlessly, crying mournfully. Away to the south-east the coast took a wide sweep, the cliffs became lower and the sandstone and clay rocks changed their colour to soft browns and reds. The hot summer day and the calm sea belied the harshness of the coastline in winter. There were few trees, fields or cottages, and the land was poor, full of sedge and rush, boggy and salty. The farms, cottages and villages were further inland, nestling at the foot of the downs where there were streams for water, the fields were more fertile and the wind had lost some of its strength. There the trees could grow to full height without being sculpted and stunted. But the flat land was deceptive, for hidden to view were steep ravines down which streams tumbled to the shore. The chynes were anything up to a hundred feet deep, but gave access to the beaches for the fishermen and beachcombers.

Far away in the haze on the horizon rose the long stretch of St Catherine's Down, topped at the seaward, southern end by the hermitage and beacon erected as a penance by Walter de Godyton. A hermit kept the light burning there to warn ships of the treacherous headland below, though during storms and fogs it was lost in the clouds and couldn't be seen. Today Robert could easily make out the pimple-like tower set on the short turf of the down, which ended in towering gaunt yellow and grey cliffs from which landslips supplied rocks and tumbled screes spreading down to sea, and forming the headland of St Catherine's Point. The sea was always rough off the headland, especially when the tide was ebbing westwards against the wind. At those times it formed a death trap for ships, and many became wrecked on the coast between the point and the Needles. Each wreck was a joy and a profit to the villagers although they often risked their lives to help the seamen; many were the graves of the drowned sailors in the local churchyards.

Before Robert set out Sir Roger had been very curious as to where he was going and why, but Robert had evaded the questions, with the result that his father had drawn his own conclusions. Robert was very nervous. He was unsure whether Rachel would be there, and whether his memories of their encounter at the fair were true. Was she as beautiful as he remembered? Would she smile at him in the same way? He had to go; he was being drawn along by an invisible force. If he dallied she would arrive first and worry whether he was going to come. Perhaps he shouldn't appear too eager, so he made haste slowly, for he had set out in plenty of time.

He purposely took the footpath that followed the top of the cliff, even though that meant taking the occasional detour inland when he came to the chynes. He wanted to avoid the hamlets, villages and the people further inland. He didn't want gossip to spread if it could be avoided. It was amazing how people managed to put two and two together. Speculation was the food of gossips – normally to the detriment of those speculated upon. Nevertheless, there was always the risk of meeting a fisherman walking to his boat, but they were normally the least likely to say anything, being more concerned about the prospects of the weather, the dangers they faced and getting on with what they had to do.

The grass along the cliff edge was short and springy, the going was easy and he made good time. The sea to his right sparkled, and small waves broke on the beach with a continuous soothing rumble. During storms they would thunder on the gravel of the beaches, and even reached the cliffs, to erode big slices of rock that broke up and stained the breakers brown. The spray formed a fine salty mist that was blown inland to scorch the grass yellow and brown, and poison the land. The winds at such times made the coast bleak and wild and few people or animals were to be seen. The trees were stunted and bent as if they cowered beneath the wind, or had been trimmed with a giant's sword.

Robert had ventured here in the winter when the damp wind off the sea cut through his clothing like a knife, and the salt stung the lips and stiffened the hair. Then the whole landscape was coloured in shades of grey. The only living creatures were herds of half-wild cattle roaming unattended, at ease with the geese, snipe, woodcock and plover, and the seagulls wheeling, screaming and swooping along the beach, to fight over morsels. But today in the sunshine the harshness was softened, the greys were green and yellow. Pink thrift patterned the grass at the cliff edge, together with yellow buttercups and birdsfoot trefoil, and white waving ox-eye daisies and yellow flag irises grew further inland. Spiky marsh grass made thick tussocks where skylarks nested, and today they swung and fluttered high into the air with melodious trills. They helped to lift Robert's mood.

He kept himself well hidden from view as he passed the grange of Cumpton where Adam de Cumpton lived. He skirted around the villages of Brook and Brixton, and arrived at his destination about mid-morning, having not seen a soul.

Kingett Chyne cut deeply into the cliff before him and stretched about a mile inland. He could go no further without another long detour. Shading his eyes he looked keenly about, but there was no sign of Rachel, nor anyone else. No maid was there with a message of regret either. Robert felt somewhat relieved. He wiped his brow with a kerchief as he dismounted and sat on the warm turf at the cliff edge. The waves were soothing as he watched them tumbling against the shingle, they acted in tune with his mixed emotions. How long should he wait? He took a chunk of bread and cheese from his saddlebag and nibbled it to calm the gnawing feeling in his stomach, but then decided he didn't feel hungry after all.

In the near distance on the other side of the chyne he could see the beacon of Atherfelde. No one appeared to be attending to it, which made it of little use as a part of a warning network. He thought he had better mention it to Lord de Lisle, whose responsibility it was.

The chyne in front of him was at least fifty feet deep, full of uneven grassy mounds made from fallen rocks, overgrown with moss and grass, and with clumps of furze and small willow trees in the hollows. The red sandstone cliff had been etched by wind and rain into intricately written patterns of hollows, used by doves and martins for roosting and nesting. A small brook cascaded through the boulders in the bottom of the cleft and then disappeared into a small rank pool at the back of the beach. The tide line was strewn with branches and seaweed, and the occasional dead seabird or fish. Some gulls and shorebirds were foraging for small crabs and hoppers among the stones.

He stood up, beginning to feel disappointed that Rachel might not be coming, and looked inland, in the direction that she might come from. He reckoned that Kingston Manor must be over that particular small hill in the trees about three or four miles away. A movement attracted his roving eye – a horseman appeared about a mile away. The rider didn't move like a woman, sitting upright and manly. There was no flowing blonde hair, no flowing white dress. Robert moved into the shelter of a clump of bushes, but continued to watch the rider, disappointment beginning to creep further over him. Perhaps the rider came with a message from Rachel. The horseman disappeared into a dip in the land. He didn't reappear straight away, and Robert started to become curious. Something like five minutes passed without a sign of the horseman. Then an echoing call came from the chyne.

'Robert!'

He recognised the voice; his heart jumped and his breath came short. It was Rachel after all! She came round a bend in the chyne below him, walking and leading her horse along a faint track that Robert had not noticed. She looked up at him. She was dressed in a brown smock and hose, and her hair was tucked into a hood. In such garb it wasn't surprising that Robert had thought she was a man, though her slim and curvaceous figure would not fool anyone up close.

21 August 1377

'Robert, come down here where we won't be seen. There's a track about forty paces to your left.' The reverberations of her voice slurred the words into each other, and they went on rolling around the chasm walls after she finished. He waved in reply and went across to his pony, tethering it to a bush so that it would neither wander away nor eat so much that it couldn't be ridden home. He then went back to the chyne, and searched along the cliff edge. As Rachel said, there was a place where he could easily scramble down. With one hand against the cliff he slithered down the steep and slippery path. At one point his feet slid from under him and he ended up on his backside. Rachel's peal of laughter echoed from the cliffs. He stood up when he reached the bottom and, before he could turn round, Rachel was in his arms. They held each other close, and Rachel whispered into Robert's ear that she had feared that he wasn't going to come. They kissed, long and lingeringly, but then drew apart and he confessed that he too had worried the same of her. They both laughed; their fears suddenly seemed ridiculous. Hand in hand, they found a grassy patch in the sun where they could sit facing the sea.

For ages they sat and talked, sharing their childhood experiences, their lives, and their thoughts, gradually growing even closer in spirit. The electricity between them grew and grew, passing through their clasped hands. Alternately serious and lighthearted, they discovered how alike they were in many ways, but different enough to find excitement in each other's personalities. They had kissed some more, and Rachel's lips had parted against his, and her tongue had lightly explored his. Both struggled with their intense physical feelings, but by unspoken consent they didn't spoil things by going too quickly, both frightened that the other might be put off.

The pressure of Rachel's thigh and body against him as they lay on the grass stirred Robert in a way he had not experienced before. He had the urge to let his hands explore her body and its hidden joys, but he was afraid that she might think him too forward, and become upset. It was accepted that the peasant girls would lie on their backs in the haystack with their lovers, but Robert was sure her father would go berserk, seek to kill him and disown her if she were to do that too. It was going to be difficult enough to get her father to accept Robert as a suitor as it was, since he came from Saxon rather than Norman stock. Robert sensed a struggle also going on within her, and drew back, only to kiss her again later and start the struggle anew.

'Sire! That is the evidence.' Timothy interrupted his reverie and brought Robert back to the present with a start. 'Can we have your verdict?'

Robert had missed all the detail, but acting from sheer intuition said, 'I consider that the fault is equal and should be shared. Each contestant to be fined twopence, and bound over to be of good behaviour. I don't want to see either of you here before me on this matter again.' There was a general murmur of agreement from the assembled villeins, who knew better than any where the rights of the disagreement lay. The equivalent of half a day's labour was a just fine. Those plaintiffs moved away smiling in grim satisfaction; they considered honour was satisfied. Others took their place.

'The next case, sire, is that of John of Norton, who wishes to marry Mary of Colwell. They request your permission, and are prepared to pay the required sum of one shilling as merchet.'

Robert knew both of these youngsters. John was sturdy and slow-moving, but hard-working, dependable and conscientious. Mary was plump, jolly, and red-faced, and would make a good wife and mother. John would be well fed and Mary would get her way. They looked soulfully at each other as they stood before Robert, hoping that he would be beneficent, for without his permission they would have to run away in order to marry.

'Agreed, and may you be very happy,' said Robert. They both broke into smiles and were wreathed in happiness as they placed the money on the table before him. Robert could only take pleasure in their happiness and hope that it would be long-lasting. In many ways he envied them their simple joy, and the goodwill of their families. He made a mental note to send them a present for their life together – a good thick blanket for the winter nights would suffice; not that they would need one for a good while yet, as undoubtedly they would keep each other warm.

'The next case, sire,' the bailiff continued, looking with distaste at the reeve who was exploring a nostril with an index

21 August 1377

finger, 'is a petition from the fishermen about the oyster fishery.'

Half a dozen men shuffled forwards to explain their problem. Robert already knew about it, and had spoken to several of them, questioned their statements and weighed them against each other. The difficulty was that all fishermen thought they had the right to lift oysters from any part of the river, whereas the disposition of the rights belonged to Robert's father, as the river was part of the demesne. Robert thought it wise to let them present their grievance in the public court so that justice could be seen by all to be done.

The first started to explain about the conflict that had arisen between them, shifting nervously from one foot to the other. Robert drifted off again into his reverie.

He and Rachel had met again a week later. This time the weather was unseasonably cold and windy. Before Robert reached their trysting place, the rain had begun to drive in from the sea, hiding the coast with a moving veil of grey. St Catherine's Down had disappeared into sweeping clouds and mists of driving spray. The breaking waves galloped in from the sea, to break, foaming on the shore, where they made the gravel roar. The trees bent, writhing in the wind, branches straining, twigs and leaves being ripped off to whirl inland. Solitary gulls strained to make way against the wind, or turned to be quickly swept away. By keeping close to the cliff edge, Robert found the worst of the wind was deflected over his head and he made fairly good time, though he was rimed in salt and soaked through.

He was in despair, thinking that Rachel would not venture out in such weather, but she was there before him, crouched low behind a clump of willows in the bottom of the chyne, with a thick cloak wrapped round her. He almost missed seeing her from the top of the cliff but, as he slithered down the path, she stood up and rushed towards him. They embraced and she kissed the salt-laced raindrops that ran down his face. Her blonde hair had escaped from her hood and lay plastered across her brow and the chill wind had brought bright colour to her nose and cheeks. Robert thought she was even more beautiful like this. She shivered in his arms.

'We must find some shelter,' he said, 'otherwise we'll both be wet through and you will catch a fever.'

'I know just the place,' Rachel replied. 'A little way further up the chyne there is a small cave in the cliff that the fishermen have dug. They use it to store their nets and pots. No one will be there and it should at least be dry, if not warm.'

She took Robert by the hand, and they walked up the path along the bottom of the chyne, leading her horse. They rounded a bend, the walls of the chyne came closer and the floor narrowed. The wind on their backs strengthened and the rain became almost horizontal as the chyne walls funnelled the wind in. The little stream was now beginning to tumble and splash as the rain swelled its volume. Several times they had to jump it as the path crossed from one side to the other. Round a second bend there was a dark opening in the red sandstone of the left-hand wall. The sheltering cave was carved out of the living rock. The entrance was about six feet high and four feet broad and as they entered they saw that it opened out into a small, gloomy room-like cave. Inside the sound of the sea and the wind was reduced to a soft sighing. The floor was dry, the pink and yellow sand marked with old footprints. In one corner were the thick white ashes of a fire, circled with half-burnt driftwood. Nearby was a small pile of dry wood and a bundle of old dry grass and bracken. Smoke had blackened the roof and left a pungent tangy smell in the air, astringent on the nostrils. Obviously, the fishermen used it occasionally for refuge and for drying their wet fishing clothes. At the back was a larger pile of dry bracken, a few old lobster pots and some fishing nets.

Robert took off his cloak and spread it on the sand for them to sit on. Rachel took off her cloak too, and Robert spread that over the pile of wood to dry.

'It is a pity that we can't make a fire,' said Rachel ruefully.

'I think we might be able to,' Robert replied. 'The fishermen are unlikely to carry steel and flint around with them to light the fire. Perhaps they keep some here.'

He took a closer look around and discovered a ledge at head height at the back of the cave upon which was a small wooden box. When he opened it he exclaimed with delight, for there was

21 August 1377

all that they needed to light the fire: a flint, a piece of iron and some dry kindling. After a few minutes of striking the iron on the flint he managed to ignite some of the dry kindling and grass, and the beginnings of a welcome fire was glowing. They sat down on the remainder of the bracken in front of the growing flames. The smoke rose to the ceiling and then spilled out through the top of the doorway into the wind, which whistled eerily outside.

Rachel took Robert's hands in hers and looked searchingly into his eyes. 'My father's being very difficult,' she said with sadness in her eyes. 'He keeps asking me questions and saying it's about time that he started looking for a suitable husband for me again. He's done this before, but I have made it plain that I will not marry anyone he chooses. I want to be able to choose my own husband, someone I love. He has always given way in the past, but this time he seems more persistent.' Her eyes started to moisten, and she swallowed hard. 'I told my mother about you because she realised that I am meeting someone, but there is not much she can do to divert his purpose, though she is pressing him to be patient. I've tried to act normally, but it's difficult to sit and sew when I feel so fidgety and long for you. That is how my mother knew. She is worried about what father will do if he finds out. He might send me away again, and she doesn't want that to happen. I am sure she would never tell him, but we can't keep meeting in secret for long. Oh, Robert, what shall we do?' she sighed. 'I don't want to pressure you against your feelings, so if you don't want to meet me again I'll understand.'

'Rachel, I have been thinking of that too and it is about time that I asked your father formally for permission to pay court to you. I know I love you. I realise I have since the first sight of you. It would be impossible to part now we have found each other.'

Rachel broke into a wide, moist-eyed smile. 'I know I love you too. I have always been rather like my father in being very definite about my likes and dislikes, and quick to know my mind. He recognises that. You've been on my mind ever since the fair, and even before that I was avid for all information and gossip about you. Even though we had not met, I seemed to know instinctively that we were destined to be lovers. I just couldn't help myself. Perhaps it is God's will that we have been brought together. Fate may be the thread linking our lives, and destiny our friend,' she said, looking into the fire contemplatively.

Her face was lit by the flickering flames of the fire and sparks shone in her hair as she turned to him. His heart gave a surge as he squeezed her in his arms, and he felt her firm breasts pressing against him through her still-damp clothing. As they kissed, his hand slid round her and under her shirt. His fingertips tingled against the warm, soft skin and slowly crept upwards across her flat stomach to caress the delightful curves above. Rachel shifted even closer towards him, her hand went round his neck and twined in his hair. Her lips moved beneath his, and she moaned softly as she started trembling uncontrollably.

Robert snapped out of his daydream to hear the bailiff introducing the third of the fishermen.

'Enough,' Robert interjected. 'I have decided what needs to be done. To be fair to all of you, this coming season we will divide the river into sections, and lots will be drawn for the right to take from each. All fishermen will be included in the lottery, and there will be sections enough for everyone to have at least two. The draw will be held annually so that everyone will have a chance at the best areas. The bailiff will put in withies to mark out the sections. The draw will be held in a fortnight's time, before the fishing season starts, and the taxes will be divided in proportion.' He was sure that his father would approve this decision as it maintained the manor's income, yet it should please the fishermen – as much as they ever could be pleased.

Before Robert and Rachel had parted they agreed that he would visit Kingston Manor to speak to her father, and they decided on the date as being two days after the manorial court – the day after tomorrow! Rachel would have to speak to him to make sure that Robert was not rejected out-of-hand. They had left the cave with their hearts high with hope, though they had not discussed what they would do if her father refused. They had made a decision that would decide their future one way or the other. The rain had stopped and the sun was peeping through the clouds – a good omen, they hoped.

'That is all, sire,' said Timothy.

Robert rose gratefully, marking the end of the court. He then

21 August 1377

dismissed the assembled people who shuffled out of the room, glad to get away from the unaccustomed formality and back to their normal duties. The bailiff came over to where Robert stood looking out of the window.

'Sire, I would like you to look at the fish trap down by the mouth of the river. Because of recent movement of the sands a better place needs to be chosen for it. You know the ways of the fishing and could help select a new place.'

The trap was a particular interest of Robert's, because he had instigated its installation some years before. Since then it had supplied the manor regularly with fresh sea fish, supplementing the carp ponds behind the house, especially in the winter. It was true that just recently the catch had become rather erratic.

'If we go now we should be able to get there at low tide. On the way we can decide where the withies will need to be placed to divide the oyster beds into equal sections,' Robert said, glad to have a distraction from thinking of the ordeal facing him in two days' time at Kingston.

Together they left the hall and walked down to the small wooden jetty where the boats were tied up. Robert selected one of the larger ones so that they could take the fish trap on board, if it became necessary to move it. Since he felt that a stretch of hard exercise would help clear his head, he gestured to Timothy to take the stern seat, and picked up the oars. He sculled gently down the river, helped by the last of the ebb tide, and passed under the bridge in the causeway to Freshwater, acknowledging as they went the salutes of the village folk returning from the court. As they went they discussed the location of the oyster beds and agreed how to divide them into sections that should have equal fishing value. The bailiff knew the river so well that it would be easy for him to come out later with an assistant and mark the limits they decided upon.

After about a mile Robert looked over his shoulder and pulled in towards the left side of the river and into the small creek where the fish trap was located. The creek meandered through the exposed mudflats towards the reed beds near to the high-tide line. There it received the input of the small stream that flowed through the hamlet of Norton. The sides of the channel glistened wetly, and the wake of the boat made a gentle burbling against the mud. About halfway in, a line of stakes appeared on either side of the channel and these gradually converged towards the middle of the creek. During the ebb tide this barrier guided fish towards the trap, the top of which just showed above the water – except it wasn't in the deepest water in the middle of the creek, as it should have been. The bank on one side had eroded away and that on the other had built up, so that the fish could now escape at low tide out of one side of the trap. It was apparent it needed moving back to the deepest part of the channel, and the line of stakes needed filling in again.

Robert reckoned he and Timothy might as well do it between them straight away, though they would have to hurry, as the tide was now slack at low water and would soon begin to flood. They both knelt in the bottom of the boat to take hold of the trap. It was made out of willow wands woven into a cone-shaped basket, with a cylindrical end in which fish would be caught. The whole thing was covered in thin tendrils of green slime, and a skin of muddy brown sediment, and was difficult to catch hold of without poking the tips of their fingers through the holes. But between them they managed to undo the fastenings and slide it off the fixing stakes, one of which broke and drifted away.

As they lifted the dripping trap over the side a couple of good-sized flatfish tipped out and flapped into the boat around their feet – supper for the bailiff. Hand over hand, they pulled the boat along the stakes to the middle of the channel and placed the trap over the stakes into its new position. They then fastened it into place and weighted it so that it would not be lifted by the tide. All that remained was to replace the broken stake.

'If you drop me ashore, I'll cut a couple of new stakes,' said Robert as he leant over the side to rinse the mud off his hands.

The bailiff took the oars and manoeuvred the boat so that Robert could step ashore. It was muddy and Robert sank in it up to his ankles. The next step took him onto a clump of reeds and he picked his way across the flats from one clump to another, towards the trees above the high-tide line. A rush of wings startled him as a flock of redshank rose from their feeding place in a small gully, whistling shrilly in alarm.

21 August 1377

On reaching the trees he wiped the mud off his boots with a handful of grass, and relieved himself against a tree. Then he searched for a hazel grove that would provide some long, straight stakes. He found what he needed beside a footpath that ran along the shore not far above the high-tide line. Selecting a sapling of about the right thickness, he took his knife from his belt and began to hack it off close to the ground. He had cut about halfway through it when he heard the sound of hoof beats and a thrashing in the undergrowth. A horse and rider burst into view along the path. As soon as the rider saw Robert he pulled the horse to an abrupt halt. It was covered in lather, wild-eyed and breathing heavily. It had been ridden hard. Robert knew the rider as Thomas, a yeoman from Easton, beyond Freshwater.

'Thomas, what ails you?'

'Sire,' the rider shouted, 'the Noddies are here; the French raiders have come! I saw them coming into the Solent round the Needles. Many ships, all flying French banners. They were crammed with soldiers. I ride to warn Yarmouth.'

Robert's heart missed a beat. My God, he thought, we are all lost. 'Yes, Yarmouth must be warned,' he said, 'and messages sent to the other towns, as well as Caresbrooke Castle. You'd better come with me. I have a boat here and we can get across to Yarmouth quickly. If you ride up to the duver, you'd still have to get a boat to take you across to the town. It's quicker this way. I'll get my bailiff to take your horse and warn the castle.'

'I lit the warning beacon on Hetdone, and I warned Freshwater as I came through. Though how many will see the beacon now I don't know, because there is a sea mist coming in – that's why I didn't see them before,' the rider said as he slid off the tired horse, which stood dejectedly, head down, with its flanks heaving. Robert flicked the reins over a branch. The two men then squelched off across the mudflats as fast as they could.

As soon as they were close to the boat Robert shouted, 'Timothy, a French fleet is attacking. We must warn Yarmouth. You take the horse; you'll find it on the path in the trees. Go and warn my father and all at Affeton. Hide the valuables and take my father and the others to Caresbrooke Castle as quickly as you can. Use the back routes in case there are any French ashore already.

Warn everyone you see on the way to flee to the castle, but tell the militia to muster and come to help us defend Yarmouth and Francheville. We must go and help organise the defence of Yarmouth.'

'God be with you, sire, and God save us all!' The bailiff, looking horrified, scrambled out of the boat, crossing himself as he ran off to the trees. Robert and Thomas jumped in, Robert grabbed the oars, spun the boat round and started pulling hard down the creek and across the river to Yarmouth. There was a good mile to go, and Robert saved his breath for rowing. The sun shone off the water into his face; he started to sweat, and he paused to take off his shirt and let what breeze there was cool him down. The sun sparkled in the water spraying from the oars, making little rainbows in their wake.

On the way Thomas described what he had seen. There were many large ships, at least ten, coming in from the west round the Gosse and the Needles off the end of the Island. There may have been more ships hidden in the mist. Crammed to capacity, there could be several hundred men in each ship, even if they had horses. Consequently the fleet might contain upwards of a thousand men. It would be difficult to defend any of the towns against that number with such short warning. They could cause death and destruction.

As he rowed, Robert considered the different options for the probable French attack. At the moment the tide was only just beginning to flood and the attackers could only have started entering the Solent at the beginning of the flood tide. It would take some time for them to reach the Yar. He calculated that there was about an hour or so to either organise the defence of the town, or to evacuate everyone towards Caresbrooke. Which was it to be?

As they approached the town Robert glanced quickly over his shoulder. All seemed very normal. Smoke rose slowly from some of the houses, and people moved peacefully around them. The sun-bleached cob walls and thatched roofs blended harmoniously with the orchard trees and the sand of the beach. On the shore fishermen were mending their nets, or tending the fish drying on racks in the sun. The smell of seaweed and rotting fish hung

21 August 1377

heavily in the air. Women were washing clothes, with the inevitable scrabble of children around them throwing stones into the water. Some of the older children were employed throwing stones at the seagulls to keep them off the drying fish. Two small ships tied up at the quay were being unloaded. As the tide was still low they would not be able to put to sea to escape.

Once they were within hearing distance Thomas shakily stood up and started shouting that the French were coming. The boat wobbled dangerously. Some of the more quick-witted men immediately threw down their work and ran up the beach towards the houses to warn their families. Others just stood and stared. More people appeared from between the buildings, dogs started barking at the excitement, children shouted, and general panic was on the verge of breaking out. It was obvious that no one knew what to do.

Robert did a quick mental count of the able-bodied men likely to be in the town who could carry arms. He was depressed by the answer. There were probably about a hundred – not enough men to be able to put up any real resistance to the enemy, since weapons were so few. Yarmouth was fairly easy to defend from a land assault as it was built on the spit of land that partly enclosed the mouth of the river from the east. The spit was long and thin, and there were earthworks and defences across its narrowest point. The sea was on one side and marshes on the other. Nevertheless, a concerted attack from land and sea simultaneously would be bound to succeed against so few defenders and in the hour or so they had they couldn't do much to establish real defence. He realised that the best action was to evacuate the town and get everyone to either hide in the woods or hurry to Caresbrooke Castle for refuge – they would be safer there where the militia could be assembled and defence organised.

The boat grounded on the beach and Robert leapt out, hurriedly putting on his shirt. Thomas appeared beside him. They were quickly surrounded by a questioning throng all clamouring at once for information and obviously in need of a leader to tell them what to do.

Holding up his arms for silence Robert shouted over the din. 'Ten or a dozen French ships have entered the Solent. They will be here within the hour. There may be more. There will be too many for us to defend the town against without help. Go to your homes, all of you. Take food, drink and clothing and any weapons you have. Collect only as much as you can carry and go into the woods. Make your way to Caresbrooke for safety. The castle is being warned, but there is too little time for them to help us. We can do nothing to defend the town without the militia. Leave the town now, before it is too late.'

'You,' he said, pointing at a competent-looking young man, 'ride to the castle and warn them. Tell them that it is I, Robert of Affeton, who sent you. As you pass through Schaldefleet tell someone to warn Francheville.' The man immediately turned with a grunt of agreement, and sprinted off to find himself a mount.

Some of the quicker-witted people also turned and rushed away, shouting to the children as they went. These were followed by more, and eventually everyone was running with purpose, having been given definite orders and knowing what they had to do. Robert told Thomas to meet him by the boat in half an hour, so they could escape up the river, and then they followed the townsfolk to make sure no one was left in the town to the mercy of the enemy.

He spent the next half-hour going from street to street knocking on doors, peering into sheds and houses, darting down alleyways, and ordering everyone he met to leave. Thomas did the same in other parts of the town. The crowds of rushing people thinned until eventually there was no one. The hubbub diminished and town took on a deathly hush. Eventually the only noise was the sound of his own echoing footsteps. It seemed that everyone had followed his orders and left. Little was he to know that some were to return.

Robert ran to the northernmost limit of the town hard by the sea, close to the church of St John. He went down an alley to the beach and peered round the corner of the house to look westwards. He could see nothing yet of the French boats, though the trees on the headland on the other side of the river mouth hid all but the last two or three miles of the coast from view. To get a better view he climbed to the top of the church tower, but still could not see any ships. He retraced his steps to the boat and

21 August 1377

arrived out of breath and exhausted to find Thomas agitatedly waiting there.

'I was wondering where you had got to, sire,' he said with relief. 'All was so quiet I was on the point of leaving, thinking you may have left by the road. The tide is flooding hard now. We don't have much time.'

'Thank God, I think everyone has gone. Jump in quickly.' Robert pushed the craft off almost before Thomas had sat down. He clambered over the side as the boat moved away from the beach, picked up the oars, put them in the rowlocks, turned the boat, and started pulling hard for the opposite shore. He wanted to get out of sight as quickly as possible, and then make his way back to the manor to fetch a horse and follow his father to Caresbrooke. He also wanted to ensure that Rachel was safe. But his first duty was to see how many raiders there were – information on the strength of the invaders would be important to Sir Hugh, to the defence of the castle and the future of the Island.

It was now only a short bowshot to the reeds and Robert pulled as fast as he could. He hadn't realised that the wind was rising, the dancing wavelets slapping against the bow and slowing them down – fishermen often said that the wind rose with the tide. As he pulled on the oars Robert watched the scene before him over Thomas's shoulder: the quiet town, a few traces of smoke still rising from undamped fires, some dogs ranging along the beach. All looked very normal, except for the lack of people. Would the French think that it was deserted, or defended, with the inhabitants hiding in the houses ready to ambush the first ashore?

With a swish the boat entered the creek and the reeds hid them from view. Not a moment too soon, for sails topped by the oriflamme banner of France appeared above the sand dunes of the duver. Had the lookout up the mast seen them? Certainly those on deck couldn't have, as Robert himself couldn't yet see the deck. In the reeds they were safe, but they could see the mouth of the river and the town through the screen of waving fronds.

Robert shipped the oars and Thomas caught a handful of reeds to hold them steady. It seemed the whole world was holding its breath, waiting, except Robert who was panting hard after his efforts, with a pounding heart. The wind sighed softly through the reeds and the water gurgled as it spread across the mudflats. The mournful call of a curlew came from across the river, and a family of oystercatchers flew past piping shrilly.

The sails moved gradually along the spit until at the mouth the whole ship was revealed – a sturdy caravel, fast and sleek, its rail lined with soldiers. The sun glinted on their helmets and armour. They were dressed ready for combat. At the stern the tall castle was crowded with knights and crossbowmen. The vessel came up into the wind and stayed there, sails shaking, drifting gently eastwards on the tide. Two more ships appeared, then a further cluster of maybe a dozen. Was that all that Thomas had seen? They didn't stop, but drifted eastwards out of sight behind the town. Perhaps they were pressing on up the Solent with Francheville as their destination. On the other hand they might anchor and launch small boats for a raid on the town.

The two Islanders waited with bated breath to see whether the ships would return, or whether there would be some other sign of the French intentions. It would be dangerous to be seen in open water – a fast sailing boat could catch them. Robert also wondered whether Yarmouth was their target or not. After about five minutes, when Robert thought it might be safe to row out of the reeds and up the river, more sails appeared – just as many as in the first fleet. They too gradually passed out of sight to the east.

With shock in his voice he whispered to Thomas, 'This is not just a raiding force, it's big enough to be an invasion. You must have only seen part of the squadron. We must warn Sir Hugh at Caresbrooke that there are many more than we previously thought. If I put you ashore you must find a horse and ride to Caresbrooke and tell them. There should be hobbies at the manor – the bailiff won't have taken them all. If you're lucky you may get there before he leaves. I must see whether they attack the town. I'll stay here for a while and watch. Later, when it's dark, I'll row up to the manor and follow you. Make sure there is a horse left there for me. They shouldn't see me here, but I can see them. And what about your family? You will need to get them to safety too.'

'Yes, sire, I will do as you ask. At the moment my family are visiting my wife's parents at Chale. They should be safe there, I hope. I will go on there after I have delivered your message to the castle. Once the Noddies are ashore they will want to search for horses and loot the manors; you will need to be watchful if you only have that knife to defend yourself with.'

Robert carefully pulled the boat towards the shore using the reeds as handhold, and Thomas slid over the side once the water was knee-deep. 'God go with you,' Robert said as Thomas waded silently ashore. With a wave of the hand he was soon lost to view in the trees and thick undergrowth along the bank. All being well, he could be at the manor in half an hour and, given a good pony, at Caresbrooke within three.

Robert carefully manoeuvred the boat back almost to the edge of the reeds, and settled down to watch. His stomach was rumbling. It had been some while since he had eaten, and his mouth and throat were parched and dry. Oh well, he thought. It will be a good while yet before I can eat.' He stretched his legs to ease the cramp caused by the hard thwart on which he sat. The tension gradually lifted from Robert's body; everything was beginning to become normal again. A jumping fish plopped nearby, and a line of bubbles rising from the mud traced the water flowing landwards along the creek. The sun was now getting low and the shadows lengthened. Dark clouds were building up in the south, their tops tinged with golden sunlight. An elegant heron flew sedately by, head folded back on its neck and legs stretched out behind. It settled a short way away on a clump of reed, and peered intently into the water. Its head gradually moved forwards, the neck extending, and then the dagger-like beak plunged into the water to emerge with a silver eel wriggling and writhing. A quick toss of the head and the tasty morsel disappeared down the bird's gullet.

Robert fancied for himself a pot full of eels, with some fresh bread and butter. His mouth watered. Midges began dancing in swarms around his head, and he had to continually brush them away to stop them from biting his neck and face. He wondered again whether Rachel was safe. Kingston Manor was down near Chale, where Thomas's family were – a long way from this northern coast. It would be at least one day, probably more, before the enemy could penetrate that far. The news of the invasion should reach them sooner than that, and her father would be certain to get them all to Caresbrooke. He was comforted by this logical series of thoughts.

Robert's attention was attracted by a movement over by the town. What was it that he'd seen out of the corner of his eye? Had the French landed after all? He concentrated. The movement occurred again – between those two houses. Then a small figure appeared and trotted down the beach.

'Oh, no,' breathed Robert. 'The child must have been forgotten.'

A quick look showed there were no French ships visible, so without a second thought he picked up the oars and started to row across to rescue the child before it got captured, or worse. Every few strokes he glanced over his shoulder to make sure the child was still there. He was halfway across. Could he afford to shout? The child had turned away and was walking back towards the houses. Robert could hear it crying out. No point in shouting, the child would not be able to hear because of its own noise. By the time the boat grounded on the beach the child had gone. Cursing, Robert sprinted up the beach and between the nearest houses. No sign of the child. Up the alleyway he ran, and into the street. There the boy was, along on the right.

'Come here, lad,' he called as he ran towards the boy. The child turned towards him and Robert swept him up into his arms. The lad must have been about ten or eleven years old, but he was frightened by no one being at home, and by the silence and gathering twilight in the town. 'It's all right now, lad, I will look after you. How is it that you are all alone here?'

The boy sniffed back a tear. 'I went to sleep in a barn. When I woke up no one was at home. Where has everyone gone?'

Robert put him down, and took his hand, pulling him towards the boat. 'We must leave the town quickly. We are all in danger. The French have come. Everyone has left the town for safety. Your parents must have thought you were safe with friends or relations. You come with me and we'll find them,' he said comfortingly.

21 August 1377

They retreated down the alleyway that Robert had come up a minute or so before, and onto the beach. Robert stopped abruptly, for beside his boat there were now two more, and Frenchmen were clambering out of them. He turned quickly to retrace their steps back up the alley, hoping that they hadn't been seen.

'Those are Noddies,' he said to the lad. 'Where can we hide? Where is the barn that you were in?'

This time it was the boy's turn to lead. Despite his young age he was sensible and level-headed. Round several corners they went and into alleys of increasing narrowness. Within a few more seconds they crept through a rickety door into a hay barn. It was almost dark inside and full to the roof with new hay, smelling sweet and clean. No wonder the boy slept here, thought Robert. They clambered onto the top of the hay, the boy leading the way into a cosy hollow where he had already flattened the hay and made a comfortable nest.

'We will have to stay here until it is fully dark and hope they don't search too well. That should only be half an hour or so. Then we'll try to get the boat away up the river.' Robert hoped that the French would quickly find wine at one of the inns, or be more interested in looting, and not keep a good watch.

Through whispers Robert found out that the boy was called Harold, and that he was a fisherman's son. He looked wide-eyed when he found out that his rescuer was such an important person as the lord of the manor. The boy searched around in the hay and pulled out a number of apples he had hidden previously. He handed several of them to Robert, who was very grateful, and they both sat and quietly munched.

Obviously this was Harold's secret hideaway. They lay there in the hay as the twilight filtering through gaps in the wooden walls gradually faded. Occasional rustling in the hay betrayed the start of the nocturnal explorations of a mouse. They could hear frequent shouts and an occasional scream outside, and once the door opened. Robert put his finger to his lips as the lad gasped, but the men didn't hear and had no immediate interest in what the barn contained. The door slammed behind them. Robert held Harold in his arms, and the boy relaxed and went to sleep. Robert, however, lay there thinking, planning, and listening.

Eventually Robert thought that it was dark enough to cover their escape, and the noises from outside seemed far away. Thunder rumbled gently in the distance. Robert woke the boy and cautioned him to stay put while he went to reconnoitre. He cautiously opened the barn door a fraction and stood listening, trying to interpret the noises. There were shouts from near the quay and singing across the other side of the town, followed by crackling noises. It sounded as if they had set light to some of the buildings. But there seemed to be no noise from nearby. Maybe it would be safe to move now. He stepped outside to see a red glow beginning to light the sky behind the buildings opposite. They must have fired houses near St John's Church; it was in that direction. The enemy might all be involved with the fire, and he and Harold might be able to slip away unseen.

With a loud whisper he called Harold to come down and together they crept along the alley, keeping close in against the walls and in the darkness created by the overhanging thatch. The light coming from the burning buildings made it easier for them to see their way, but it also meant that they could be all the more easily seen. Harold started as a rat, fleeing from the fire, ran over his foot and scurried down the alley. Robert poked his head stealthily round the corner. No one was in sight, but there was a dark shadow lying against the wall further along the street. Robert paused to peer at the man. He was an Islander and had a huge sword cut down his face and across his neck, and was covered with blood. He was dead. Some of the townsfolk must have returned and resisted the invasion. With a sinking heart, Robert wondered how many others had been killed.

They pressed on quietly. On tiptoe they slipped into the alley leading back to the beach. Robert stepped over another body, and indicated to Harold to take care where he walked. He paused at the end where he could see across the beach towards the boats. His boat was still there, dark against the lighter sand, but there were several more beside it now. The French had really come in force.

He carefully leant forward to peer round the corner to left and to right. All seemed clear. Taking the boy's hand they started to run softly across the beach, their feet sighing gently in the sand.

21 August 1377

Not too fast, so as to not make too much noise – they were just dark flitting shadows. They reached the boat safely. Robert put the boy in, turned the boat round and started pushing on the stern. All of a sudden there was a shout from behind them and a violent blow struck Robert in his left shoulder, spinning him round. He fell on his hands and knees in the water. The intense pain made him gasp, but he dragged himself to his feet. The boat was sliding away from him. He tried vainly to reach it, stumbling, but he couldn't get in, the pain was beginning to blur his vision, his left side was feeling numb and his arm dangled lifeless. He pushed as hard as he could with his right hand, and shouted for the boy to row upstream and get away. He stood there swaying, watching the boy grab the oars and start pulling away. Thank goodness that, like all fishermen's sons, he knew how to row.

Robert slowly turned to face his attacker, a crossbow bolt through his shoulder. He staggered forward, thinking to delay them while Harold escaped, but his head bowed and he slowly sank to his knees. He could do no more. Waves of blackness swept over him, and then a blow on the head sent him into oblivion.

21 August 1377

Evening

Robert was vaguely aware of being picked up and carried across the beach. His shoulder hurt badly and the movement of the men carrying him sent waves of pain through him, so that even when he was eventually laid down he kept on drifting in and out of consciousness. How long this went on for he didn't know, but he later concluded that it must have been only a few minutes. When he came to properly he was indoors lying on a wooden trestle. He could feel the hard boards against his back, though his head was cushioned on something soft. Through half-closed eyelids he could see the roof of the shed, black and weathered, lit by the flickering of several candles and lamps. From the smell it was obviously one of the fish-drying sheds. His shoulder hurt, though he knew from experience that the worst was still to come when the numbness wore off.

He could sense a number of men around him, and several of them were talking together in French. Many of the knightly class and the gentry in England spoke French, partly because of their Norman heritage, and partly because of service in the perpetual wars in Gascony, but French was gradually being replaced by English, the language of the peasants. It was obvious that these were the French invaders. He could smell the heavy odour of garlic, mixed with that of wet salty clothing and faint whiffs of sea-sickness. He lay still and kept his breathing shallow and even, so that his captors would not realise he was conscious and listening. As he could understand and speak French he might hear something he could turn to his advantage. They were discussing him and his value to them.

'I think that we should kill him,' said one gruff voice. 'He will just be in the way.'

'No, Jacques, I disagree. He has all the appearance and bearing of a knight and his action in saving the boy speaks of knightly

21 August 1377

breeding. He will have value for ransom or for bargaining. Also he will probably know the disposition of the defences and the lie of the land, and could help to guide us.' This speaker had a more refined accent, and the intonation of a leader. 'We will keep him as our prisoner and when he awakens he will assist us in return for his life. In the meantime we must tend his wound; he must not bleed so much that he becomes too weak and of little use. Tell the barber to attend us here to take the bolt out of his shoulder and dress his wound.'

'Very well, sire,' the gruff voice replied.

There was a scraping of boots on the stone floor, and a burst of noise from outside as the door opened. At the same time as Jacques left, some more men came in. They brought with them the acrid smell of burning.

'The young man got away, seigneur. We got stuck on a mudbank and lost him in the dark. He obviously knows the creeks and channels well.'

Good for Harold, thought Robert. I knew he had sense and capability beyond his years. I hope that he manages to get to safety and tell others what has happened here.

'Never mind,' said the captain, 'he cannot do us any harm, for the countryside must have been alerted by now and know that we have arrived. The town is ours without a real fight; we have captured no one here, bar this knight. We have only encountered two small groups of peasants, and they have been killed. Perhaps it was this knight who gave the warning and organised the evacuation. He should know a lot that could be useful to us. But we must move quickly, before the damned English have time to organise defence of the other towns and villages. What valuables have we so far?'

'Sire, we have the plate and vestments from both of the churches, and the men are now going through the houses one at a time to find other valuables, as well as food and drink.'

It was not usual for churches to be violated, and their consecrated chalices, crosses and relics stolen, but there were always those who paid lip service to the restraints of religion and damnation in the life hereafter, when tempted by valuable loot.

Evening

'I ordered that the churches be left,' the seigneur barked. 'But it is too late to stop the sacrilege now. When we have finished going through the town, scouting parties can go to the neighbouring villages and manors to search for more valuables. Once the horses have all been unloaded, we will leave a garrison here, and I will lead the main force to rendezvous with de Mortagne and the battalion that should have landed at the port to the east of here. If they have met resistance, our help may be needed. How many extra horses have we found?'

Oh my Lord, thought Robert. So this is only part of the invasion! Talking of other battalions means there are many hundreds, and even thousands, of men more. They must have split their force and already attacked Francheville. I pray that the warning reached there in time for the people to flee.

'Seigneur, all of our horses have been landed, and are being fed and watered. When the townsfolk left they must have taken most of the horses with them. We have only found one old nag, two jennets, five donkeys and a few oxen.'

'There will probably be more in the farms nearby. Send out some platoons to scour the countryside and bring as many as they find, and meet us on the way to the next town, which I believe they call Francheville. A good joke that!' He laughed.

The door opened. 'Seigneur, you asked for me.' Another man entered, accompanied by further whiffs of acrid smoke.

'Yes, barber. This knight is injured. Take out the bolt and dress his wound, for he will accompany us as a hostage.'

Rough hands touched Robert's injured shoulder, causing him to groan. He opened his eyes and saw two heads bent over him. One was black-haired, dirty-faced and reeked of garlic and sweat, obviously the barber. The other had neat shoulder-length hair, clean and shining in the candlelight. He had a pointed brown beard and moustaches, clear brown eyes and a pale complexion. A richly embroidered silk kerchief flowed round his throat, and a surcoat emblazoned with a magnificent coat of arms covered his chest. Within the devices was a quarter containing a fleur-de-lys, signifying that the seigneur was of royal blood.

Robert immediately realised that the expedition must have been well planned and financed to involve such a powerful leader,

21 August 1377

and probably had the authority of the King of France himself. They would only be happy if they could succeed in returning with considerable booty and prestige, and surely reckoned to gain political advantage from the attack.

'Ah, our captive awakes,' the captain said. 'Perhaps he will tell us where the people have gone, and how many troops there are on the Island to oppose us.'

Robert struggled to sit up and, as he did, he considered for a moment how much, or how little, to tell them. If he refused to tell them anything they might just kill him immediately, or leave him behind. That would not help at all. On the other hand, by telling them things that they might know already, he could gain some of their trust, and learn more about their plans. Also, he could then tell them untruths; they would believe him, and he might be able to turn events to the advantage of the Islanders.

'Sire,' he said with an effort, and speaking in French, 'I see you are the leader and an honourable man. I will help you, but do not expect me to betray my own people.' He was surprised that his voice came out weak and shrill. It didn't sound like his voice at all.

The seigneur's eyebrow raised. He was surprised to hear Robert speaking French, and with a bow of his head replied, 'Bien, you can act as interpreter too, but if you try to betray me I will kill you with no hesitation. What is your name?'

'Robert de Affeton, sire,' he replied. 'And to whom am I speaking?'

'And where is this Affeton?'

'About one league south of here, sire, but you will find my people gone to refuge, and the valuables hidden.'

The seigneur's eyes narrowed and he gestured to the barber. The barber tore the sleeve away from around the bolt which had passed through Robert's shoulder, the flight sticking out of the back, and the point showing at the front. He grasped the shaft with both hands, and broke the flight end off. Robert gasped, but gritted his teeth to avoid showing the pain. Then with one hand on Robert's shoulder and the other gripping the shaft, the barber jerked the point free and pulled the remains of the bolt out. Robert's eyes misted over as he nearly lost consciousness again, but he was determined to show that the Islanders were tough. Blood flowed anew from the wound. The barber grunted that it seemed clean and was only a flesh wound, nevertheless, he poured a good measure of wine over it to cleanse it further, then he took a dagger from his belt and thrust it into the flame of one of the torches.

The seigneur had watched this without any emotion, and when it was clear that Robert was not going to faint away, he demanded, 'Now, Robert de Affeton, there is a town east of here. How big is it? Is it defended?'

Robert realised that the man was probably testing him; he might know the answers already. So he said, 'Francheville is a town of about 400 people and is undefended. However, they have been warned of your attack and will have gone for refuge.'

'And where is this refuge?' the captain questioned.

'The refuge is the castle of Caresbrooke. It is strong and well defended. You will not be able to storm that with any ease. They have provisions set by for many months of siege.'

'And how many soldiers are based there?'

Robert hesitated, so the seigneur leant across and twisted his injured shoulder. The wound bled afresh and the pain made Robert's head swim.

'There are about 1,900 militia and all the able-bodied men from the countryside, with ample arms,' Robert exaggerated. This caused the captain to pause, and he fell back a step and turned, stroking his beard, thinking.

The barber took the dagger from the flame, its tip glowing red hot and smoking. He approached Robert with it held in front of him. Robert closed his eyes, thinking that his time had come, and the truth was to be tortured from him. But instead, he was half-turned onto his right side, and the dagger was pressed against the wound, first at the front, and then on the back, to cauterise it. He couldn't help yelping in agony. There was a gush of blue smoke and the sickening smell of burning flesh. Robert descended into a black oblivion again.

★

21 August 1377

After he left Thomas and Robert in the boat, the bailiff returned to the path. The horse was nowhere to be seen – it must have slipped its tether and wandered off. Timothy searched through the trees and whistled, but couldn't find it. With resignation he started to run along the track towards Freshwater. He ran awhile until he was out of breath, and then walked until he had his breath back. Then he ran again. At this rate it took him about half an hour to cover the three miles to the village. He walked up the hill as far as the church, where he stopped briefly, went into the churchyard and looked over the wall towards Yarmouth, visible in the distance down the river. All seemed normal. There was no sign of anything untoward, but for a few sails just beyond the town in the Solent – a not unusual sight. At this distance in the haze he couldn't see whether there were any people about in the town, or not.

He continued into the village centre. There were only a few people along the dusty road and they were all busily loading belongings on the backs of horses and into carts. An old man loading a donkey told him that Thomas had warned them of the French invaders as he was passing through towards Yarmouth, and one young man had already ridden off to warn Caresbrooke Castle and the hamlets and villages on the way. Most of the peasants had already left and the last, including him and his family, were just about to go.

Relieved, Timothy turned and started for the manor. He ran down the steep track beside the church that led to the causeway. The tide was about half in, gradually covering the mudflats and slowly pushing the busy fringe of feeding wading birds towards the reeds. He could not see Yarmouth from this side, as it was hidden behind the hill. He would have to look from the Affeton side. The setting sun was hidden behind thick clouds and tall thunderheads that were massing to the south, their tops anvil-shaped and smeared by the winds. Rays of light shafted through gaps and lit the cloud edges with brilliant silver and gold. Underneath they were sombre dark grey, black and purple, ominous and threatening. At any other time Timothy would have stood and admired the beauty of the scene before hurrying to reach home before the storm set in.

Evening

As he strode across the causeway he wondered whether Robert and Thomas were still hiding in the reeds watching and waiting, or whether they were rowing back up the river towards him. Now he could see down the river towards Yarmouth far away to the left. The town still appeared to be quiet, but he couldn't see a boat approaching.

At the end of the causeway he turned right and approached the manor. All was silent. Exhausted, he entered the courtyard to find doors open and piles of clothing on the ground, a stool on its side, several buckets of water and hay scattered everywhere. The chickens were happily scratching around in the unaccustomed muddle. He called, but the only answer was his own voice echoing back from the walls and the startled squawking of the chickens.

He heard the sound of hoof beats and ducked for cover into one of the stables, fearing that the French might already be arriving. The rider appeared round the corner of the stables, and clattered to a halt on the cobbles, looking around him, appraising the situation. It was Thomas.

Thomas was grateful to have found his horse and caught up with Timothy and explained how he had left Robert behind to continue spying on the invaders, who were more numerous than they had originally thought. He was keen to press on quickly for the castle to pass on the news about the size of the French force, but was happy to delay for a few moments once he had heard that a message had already been taken there. Timothy wanted to be sure that Sir Roger and all of the other servants had left, and to hide any of the valuables they hadn't taken with them, or already hidden.

They rushed in through the kitchen where there was a confusion of pots and pans. Evidently Alice had been about to clear away the mess of dinner. Bowls were heaped in the tub for washing. There was a pile of scraps on the table, put ready to be thrown to the chickens. Smoke still curled from the fire where glowing embers remained, despite having been quickly doused with water. This room which was normally the heart of life of the manor, was so unusually quiet it was as if the pulse was dying.

In the gathering gloom they ran through the house checking in all the rooms, and up the stairs into Sir Roger's room. It was eerie in the half-light, with unaccustomed shadows, and the

21 August 1377

echoes mocked them in their fear. The master wasn't there; his bed had the covers thrown back and there were clothes strewn on the floor. They went down into the stables. The cart was gone, together with Robert's hobby, the two hackneys used for pulling the cart and several of the ponies. Obviously once the word had got to Affeton, William and Alice had organised the evacuation, and had left promptly.

However, Timothy saw that many of the valuables, the safety of which were his responsibility, had not been taken away or hidden. Hurriedly he gathered an old horse blanket from the stables and, with Thomas helping, went from room to room putting in it the best plate, the silver spoons and candlesticks, the salt cellar and the spice dishes. Tying them tightly into a firm bundle they carried it out to the carp ponds at the back of the manor, weighted the bundle with stones and threw it in.

Back in the hall they rolled up the best of the tapestries, hefted them over their shoulders and carried them outside. They covered the roll with canvas to protect it from rain, putting it in an old hollow tree behind the stables, much to the annoyance of the owl who lived there.

They then went into the kitchen to search for food and drink – both were famished after their exertions, and it was many hours since they had eaten. They found bread, some cheese, meat and ale. After quenching their thirst they ate some of the food immediately. The rest, together with a few bottles of wine, they put into saddlebags, as they didn't know when they would next be able to find a meal. This done, they saddled two fresh horses from one of the paddocks and put long reins on the others, and on Thomas's pony, so that they could all be led. Spare mounts would always be welcome at the castle, and they couldn't be left for the invaders. Nevertheless, they left one behind in the hope that Robert would come as he had said he would. Then, they mounted and set out to ride towards Schaldefleet on their way to the castle. It was now almost fully dark, and faint lightning, followed some time later by rumbles of thunder, flashed from behind them.

The first part of the route was the same as Robert had taken on the way to the fair at Francheville. Down along the river by the causeway they were horrified to see flames silhouetting some of the buildings in Yarmouth, lighting up rising billows of smoke and reflecting in the water. This spurred them to quicken their progress and they trotted quickly on. The moon was rising over the woods to the east and, by its light, it was relatively easy to pick their way along the path, though they looked with fear at the shadows of every thicket and clump of hazel.

A closer flash of lightning startled and momentarily blinded them. Some seconds later came a rumble of thunder from behind them. The storm was rapidly approaching, making the horses jittery and pull on the leading reigns. They bumped and kicked each other, their eyes staring and their nostrils flaring. Their progress slowed.

The flashes of lightning and claps of thunder came more frequently. After a mile or so, when they were still close to the water, Thomas paused and gestured the bailiff to stop also. He peered out across the water, saying softly, 'I thought I heard splashing over there, just like someone rowing.' But then there was silence. Perhaps it was his imagination.

They were on the point of moving on when the sound came again, only closer this time. Another flash of lightning illuminated the scene, and the reflected glare from the burning Yarmouth silhouetted an object moving in the creek.

'There, it is a boat. There, near that bank of reeds. Could it be the Lord de Affeton? It can't be the French. They wouldn't come this far up the river in the dark. Maybe it is someone else escaping from Yarmouth.'

They waited a while as the boat came nearer. The rower was small and weary, splashing at every pull on the oars, and sobbing with tiredness and fear.

'Over here. Come over here,' called Timothy. The splashing stopped as the rower looked round to where they stood. Another dozen or so strokes and the boat grounded on the gravel shore to be met by Thomas, who waded in and pulled it well up the beach. The rower shipped the oars and stood up. His shoulders were slumped and his eyes shone in the moonlight from the tears that streamed down his face, despite the determined set of his chin.

21 August 1377

'It's all right now, lad, you'll be safe with us,' Timothy said reassuringly, 'How come you are alone? This is my master's boat. Do you know what has happened to him?'

The boy blurted out his story, of how he had been forgotten in the town when everyone left, how he was rescued by Robert de Affeton, how they hid in a barn until dark, and how Robert was hit by a crossbow bolt while pushing him off from the beach.

'I hope he hasn't been killed,' Harold sobbed.

Timothy and Thomas were desolated to hear that Robert had been caught. There was nothing they could do, except push on to Caresbrooke as fast as they could to help the defenders. Robert's fate would have to wait until they could return with the militia.

They pulled the boat into the undergrowth and covered it as best they could with branches, making a mental note of where it was. Thomas then helped the boy on to the horse and mounted behind him. The lad calmed down when he had a hunk of bread and cheese to chew, and the strength and comfort of the yeoman's arms around him.

They set off again in the growing moonlight along the track towards Schaldefleet. The thunderstorm was almost overhead and the rain started. Very quickly they were wet through. The horses were very nervous; every flash of lightning caused them to jump, and the thunder made them snort and pull against the reins. The riders gave them their heads, so progress was now at a fast trot, with occasional periods of cantering. This was difficult because of the narrowness of the track.

Luckily they met no other people, and hoped that it was because everyone else was well on the way to safety. They didn't know that several families had heard them coming, thought they might be invaders, and taken to the woods on either side to avoid them, and let them pass.

As they progressed, they became aware of a faint pulsating red glow in the sky in front of them, as well as that over Yarmouth, now well behind them.

'That is the direction of Francheville. There must be fire there too,' said the bailiff. 'The French must have attacked both

Evening

towns at once. I think we should head south and avoid Schaldefleet. It will be too close to Francheville, and may be occupied by the French already.'

Thomas agreed and at the next opportunity they cut towards Caulbourne. From there they could take the Modeston road, climb on to the downs and take the track along its crest eastwards away from danger and towards the castle. There they should be safe from the French. However, they would continue to be exposed to the full force of the violent thunderstorm that seemed to be following them overhead.

★

Sir Hugh was sitting down to dine in the hall at Caresbrooke Castle. His brow was furrowed and his shoulders hunched. He was thinking about the Island's defences and was worried about the slow response to the agreement made at the meeting in June for extra men for the militia. The present troops were becoming restless and discontented. They were away from their homes and families and were dispirited, even though they were being paid generously – at the same rates as they would get if they were abroad at war. When nothing was happening it was difficult to maintain high morale and tight discipline for long periods, despite a regular routine of training and activity. Exercises, archery practice, marching, hand-to-hand fighting with sword and buckler, and with horses, kept the men's skills honed, but did little for their mental alertness. There was also the depressing routine drudgery of cleaning stables, fetching hay and water for the horses, and preparing meals for themselves. He had been forced to discipline four men for fighting. They were now languishing in the dungeons on a diet of bread and water, and with extra turns of treadmill duty. He hoped this would be an example to the rest.

He had no worries about the local militia; they would be called on when any threat appeared. They were already giving several days a week in rotation to their duties. Their morale was high because they saw their homes and families on a regular basis and could till their fields and look after their crops. But he

21 August 1377

wondered whether he could stand down some of the other troops and allow them, in rotation, periods of leave at home. With a letter of protection they would be guaranteed safe passage home and back, but there was no guarantee they would return. They would certainly be tempted to break their contracts by the wages available in the towns. Southampton in particular was always short of labour these days. Many of the troops came from there, or nearby, and might be seduced away by their friends and families from their agreed bonds of employment, even at the risk of being caught and punished.

He also dwelt on the state of the coffers. He had a certain annual income of money from the King's taxes to pay for defence of the castle and of the Island, but this came only intermittently from the mainland. He had to balance this against the essential expenditure on wages, armaments and victuals. In addition to this, the local landowners had to raise taxes to pay their part of the accounting. The problem Sir Hugh had to cope with was the escalating costs. The wages of general labourers had increased markedly over the last few years, because of the decline in the population since the plague epidemics. A skilled bowman was paid threepence a day, or sixpence if mounted, when he was expected to supply and feed his own mount. Now he could get the same for ploughing, without the danger. Nevertheless, there were always the younger sparks ready for glory and adventure, and who thought they could gain shares of booty, but there were not enough of those to fulfil all duties, especially for the tedium of home defence where there were no bonuses. In fact, some freemen were paying scutage, sums of money in lieu of them having to perform their service for their lords. This resulted in a further dearth of skilled fighting men. Sir Hugh wondered how long he would be able to keep a viable force operational for defence of the castle and of the Island. If peace lasted much longer he would lose men.

He was chewing on a tough piece of old beef and turning these things over in his mind when a page came bursting through the door.

'Sire,' he said breathlessly, 'there is a messenger arrived from Yarmouth saying that a French force is attacking.'

Evening

Sir Hugh leapt to his feet, and his chair fell backwards with a crash. 'Send him in. Send him in immediately!' he shouted.

A villein entered with his cap in his hand, covered in dust and dirt, travel-stained and tired. He was obviously overwhelmed by the surroundings. He had never been in such a large and splendid building, nor in the presence of such a high lord. He didn't know whether to bow, salute or kneel.

He stuttered 'My Lord, I have come from Yarmouth, where I live. Robert, lord of Affeton, came down the river to the town and ordered us to take our belonging and flee here to the castle for safety. He said that at least ten French ships had been sighted entering the west of the Solent. They came in under cover of a sea mist. I came quickly. The other villagers are coming behind.'

'At least ten ships, you say. A force of that size could certainly take Yarmouth, but would be no great threat to the castle, or to the Island.' Hugh stroked his beard thoughtfully. 'I am surprised that they are rash enough to risk venturing into our waters with that small a fleet. I wonder whether there are more of them than that.'

'That is as many as was said, sire. I have not seen them myself,' the peasant replied.

Sir Hugh strode to the door, and shouted for the sergeants of the militia companies to attend him immediately. He returned, set his chair upright, and sat down.

'No, stay,' he said, as the peasant made to leave, 'you can help us yet.'

There was a pounding of feet, and six sergeants rushed through the door, one still wiping traces of food from his chin, and another struggling into a jerkin. They glanced warily at the dishevelled villein standing next to Sir Hugh, wondering whether what they had heard outside from the guards of an invasion was correct.

Sir Hugh looked at them intently, marshalling his thoughts. 'There are reports of a force of French raiders threatening Yarmouth. All of the inhabitants have fled, and are likely to be on their way here. We are not sure of the strength, nor the intentions of the attackers. We must find out. Each of you will take three of your best men, those who can ride well and who know the paths

21 August 1377

and people of the Island, and reconnoitre. We need to know where the French are, how many men they have and as best as possible what their intentions are. As you go, warn the outlying farms and hamlets what is happening, and order any members of the local militia you meet to come here immediately. Their families should come too, at least until we know precisely what the situation is. Do not engage the enemy if you can avoid it. It is more important for me to know the facts, than for you to kill one or two Frenchmen and be killed yourselves.'

'You,' he pointed to the leftmost of the line, 'will go towards Yarmouth by way of Schaldefleet.

'You,' he pointed to the next, 'go to Francheville by way of Porchfield. Warn them, if they haven't been warned already. Tell them to come here for refuge, and wait to see whether the French land there.'

He directed the others to warn the burgesses of Nieuport, and the outlying districts to the south-west; to Shorwell, Brixton, Kingston and Chale, to the south; to Stenbury, Sandford and Rookley, and to the east; to warn the Abbot of Quarr and Theobald de Gorges at Knighton.

'All of you be sure that you return, or send messengers to me by dawn, so that we can send troops out and repel the damned Noddies,' he said earnestly. 'Have the rest of your men stand to, for we will have to bring in whatever extra supplies we can obtain from the neighbourhood, just in case we have to feed the people for a long time. Also the weapons must be brought from the stores and prepared for use.'

'Now go! And remember that the safety of the Island and our people are in your hands. I want no dead heroes; live soldiers are essential.'

With this, the men left. Sir Hugh turned to the villein from Yarmouth and asked him if he knew the whereabouts of Robert. He was concerned to hear that Robert was still in the town when everyone else was leaving, but consoled himself that Robert was sensible and had probably returned to his manor before reporting to the castle. He was not one inclined to rash actions.

Sir Hugh then dismissed the man and, following him out of the door, instructed the sergeant-at-arms to make sure his horse was seen to and to give him directions to quarters where he could make himself, his family and friends comfortable.

Outside the twilight was well advanced, and there was much shouting and confusion. In the courtyard torches had been set into holders and their light threw fantastic moving shadows on to the walls, as the soldiers moved into their platoons and scurried about the buildings. The sergeants formed the platoons into lines, picked out the few men to accompany them on the scouting and warning missions, and sent them away to collect their weapons and horses. Others were delegated duties around and within the castle.

When the men returned, each was leading a pony, had a bow slung across his back, and grasped either a home-made pavise or a mantlet shield. Short falchion swords swung from their belts. Quivers full with the regulation twenty-four arrows were slung about their shoulders on baldrics. The men's heads were protected by kettle hats. They looked determined, though a little nervous. This could be the test they had been training for, and they had mixed emotions – both excitement and trepidation. They mounted and one by one the platoons on their motley collection of steeds wheeled and filed out of the gate, cheered on by those left behind.

Sir Hugh paced the yard nervously, wondering whether his moves were the best that could be made, and how great a threat there was. Within a few minutes his mind was put at rest when a second messenger appeared, this time from Freshwater. He was leading his horse; it had gone lame in the frantic ride across the downs. He confirmed that the coast watcher had seen French ships and fired the beacon, though he was unable to say how many there were.

After a while a number of refugees began to arrive, tired and dispirited, but glad to have reached safety. Soon this trickle became a steady stream of people, on horses of all sizes and colours, some young and fat with the summer grass, others thin with old age and years of heavy toil in the fields. Oxen and some horses were pulling carts laden with children and animals, possessions and food. Women had babies in their arms, or children on their laps either asleep or wide-eyed from shock and

21 August 1377

tiredness. The sombre grey castle walls towered over them frightening them even more. Many had not even seen the castle before, let alone been inside it in the dark. Some men were walking, leading the tired horses and donkeys by the head, encouraging them up the steep cobblestone entry, others were riding, festooned with bows, arrows, swords and shields. All were solemn-faced and weary, but relieved and avid to share news and experiences.

Several soldiers were questioning the new arrivals, trying to gather as much information as they could: their names? Where they had come from? Had they seen any French? Did they know of others left behind?

Most arrivals came from Yarmouth, the area around the West Wight, and from the villages and hamlets those people had passed through. Then a few from Francheville came in, tired after their two-hour march. An appalled Sir Hugh was called over to hear their tale. Apparently they had had no warning of the invasion until the French fleet was sighted rounding Hamstead Point by some men fishing in the entrance to the river. The fishermen had thrown down their nets and immediately sailed in to warn the town. But not all of the townsfolk had managed to leave before the French landed. It was likely they had either been captured or killed. Those who had escaped had left everything except what was immediately to hand. They had no food or possessions. They had abandoned all their livestock, apart from their mounts. Their first thoughts were for their friends and neighbours who might not have escaped. No, they didn't know how many French boats there were or how many attackers – they hadn't had time to think of such things, but quite a number of townsfolk must have been killed.

The newcomers were directed to the area beyond the chapel where soldiers were erecting makeshift shelters from hurdles and covering them with thatched framework roofs. There they searched out friends and relations with whom they could share their worries and gain some comfort. The womenfolk were laying fires to cook, and some soldiers were passing round with bags of flour, peas, beans and dried meat for those with no food of their own. Others had bowls of water for the thirsty, drawn from the deep well on the edge of the courtyard over towards Sir Hugh's residence.

Sir Hugh realised that the attackers must be in considerable force to raid Yarmouth and Francheville at the same time. There must have been more than a dozen ships in the fleet. What next? he wondered. He crossed the courtyard to make a circuit of the sentries posted on the walls. He walked over to the foot of the steps near to the postern gate that led up to the keep.

Seventy-one steep steps climbed the side of the mound, on top of which the keep had been built in Norman times. The keep was the final refuge should the castle be overrun. A little way up the steps the curtain wall abutted the mound. There he could start a circuit of the walls. He started climbing. A shout came from the sentry on the walls of the keep a hundred or so feet above; Sir Hugh could see him outlined against the sky lit by the rising moon, pointing towards the west. Sir Hugh could not see anything from where he was, so he hurried up the steps two at a time to start with. By the time he reached the top he was puffing hard, and his knees were weak and trembling. He paused for a few seconds to catch his breath before tackling the last flight onto the walls. The sergeant in charge of the keep came to meet him.

'What is it?' Sir Hugh asked.

'Sire, there is a red glow in the sky to the west. It must be a fire.'

Sir Hugh ran the last few steps, and peered westwards. It was quite obvious from this height. Because of the downs he couldn't see the ground for more than a few miles, but the moon was strong enough to show up the clouds beyond. The lower parts of the clouds were tinged with red, a red that pulsated and gradually grew stronger as he watched. The clouds were also occasionally outlined by brilliant flashes of lightning, with ragged forks stabbing towards the ground. He couldn't see where they struck. Faint rumbles of thunder also came through the otherwise silent evening. He was now convinced that he was right. The French had come in force and the Island was isolated and alone.

★

21 August 1377

Robert came slowly back to consciousness. It must have only been a few minutes after his shoulder was cauterised. The hut was now empty, lit by a flickering torch thrust into a holder on the wall. His shoulder was throbbing, sore and painful. He pushed himself up and swung his legs over the edge of the trestle. His head swam. The dizziness made him feel sick.

He looked down at his shoulder. The tunic was torn and bloodstained right down to his waist. The bolt had passed through the fleshy part of his shoulder – painful but not serious. The wound was red and inflamed, covered with twisted and blackened flesh where the iron had sealed it. He flexed his fingers. They all moved, but felt rather numb. He was relieved they worked, except, he realised, he was unable to grip hard. He couldn't move his arm above the elbow, finding it was more comfortable to hold the upper arm tight against his side. Using his teeth and his good arm he tore the sleeve off his shirt and, knotting it, made a sling, which he slipped over his head to support the weight of the injured arm. That's better, he thought, and felt more cheerful.

He eased himself slowly off the trestle and stood rather uncertainly, leaning against it. He swallowed dryly, his tongue feeling furry and stiff. His legs felt like jelly, and his dizziness worsened. He wondered how much blood he'd lost. With slow, careful steps he crossed to the door, fighting all the way to keep in a straight line. As he might have guessed, it was bolted or barred on the outside. He pushed against it, but it didn't give. He walked round the walls, leaning on them occasionally for support. They were made of rough wooden planks, without windows, but with gaps between for the air to blow through to dry the fish. There was no way out other than the bolted door.

He returned to sit on the trestle to think and work out a way of either escaping and taking news to the castle, or of hindering the French plans. The French were obviously intending to return for him, since they had gone to the trouble of tending his wound and trying to prevent infection. He realised he was famished, and very thirsty. It must be some time since he had shared the apples with Harold. When had he eaten before that? In the forenoon before the manorial court, he realised. What ages ago that seemed.

Evening

There was no vestige of food in the room, apart from some fragments of smelly and brown wood-hard dried fish, which he couldn't bring himself to put in his mouth.

The torch began to gutter. It would not be long before it went out. A brilliant flash of lightning showed between the boards. He went across and peered out of one of the larger gaps. Further flashes dazzled his eyes, the forks spearing to the ground on the other side of the river. He crossed to the opposite wall and again peered through one of the gaps. On this side he could see a red glow from burning buildings on the other side of the town. There was a wall a few feet away, so that he could see little else. He put his ear to the gap and could hear the crackle and banging of the burning, as well as shouting and laughter. The French were relaxing in the aftermath of the invasion and were becoming drunk, either on excitement or on the wine and ale they had found. Robert groaned, thinking about the damage, the years of toil and labour invested by his people, and the lives that had been lost in Yarmouth. He wondered how many more losers there would be.

The door rattled, the bolts were drawn back and the seigneur entered, with a squire behind him. The squire was carrying an earthenware pot and a jug, which he put down on the trestle. He then went and stood guard beside the door. A mouth-watering smell came from the pot that evidently contained some sort of stew, and Robert guessed the jug held pilfered ale. Where they had obtained the stew from Robert could only guess – perhaps it was the anticipated meal of a fleeing villager.

The French seigneur gestured for him to eat and drink. While he hungrily ate Robert eyed the Frenchman and had a good look at him. The seigneur was an extremely imposing man, with an air of gentility and culture about him. He was tall, elegant, exquisitely dressed and with a lordly bearing – a man of obvious breeding and wealth. However, beneath the suave exterior Robert thought that he detected a steel-like resolve and a cold detachment. His magnificent unstained embroidered surcoat covered a cuirass of plate armour, and a sword with a jewelled pommel hung from his belt. In his right hand he carried a pair of velvet-and-leather gauntlets. He stroked his beard with his left as he, in

21 August 1377

turn, contemplated Robert. With food and drink inside him Robert felt renewed energy and hope return, though his arm was still painful.

The seigneur spoke in French. 'So, my young friend, you have recovered. Good! We will leave as soon as we can. We have got all we need here. It isn't a very rich town. There are few valuables, but we have food and drink to take with us. The moon is rising and the paths are clear. You will show us the way.' He paused to let his words sink in. 'You have two choices. You can give us your word not to escape, and you will be well treated. If not, you will be bound, and if you try any tricks we will put you to the sword. What is your answer?'

Robert realised that he really had no choice. 'You have my word that I will not attempt to escape. I will show you the tracks and answer your questions, but I cannot guarantee that the answers will always be what you want to hear.'

'If I find you answer false, or give us misinformation, you will suffer for it in ways you cannot even start to imagine,' the seigneur said threateningly, thrusting his face close to Robert's. 'So think on it, and be wise. Believe me, you must accept the word of the Duc de Beauvais.'

'Come! Time is pressing.' De Beauvais grasped Robert's good arm and pushed him outside.

Robert was not surprised that the man everyone addressed as 'seigneur' was a duke. That fitted in with the royal quarter on his coat of arms and it showed what an important and well-organised raid this was: it was not just a brief excursion of a group of privateers, but probably part of an extensive invasion.

Smoke was billowing down the street and engulfed them as they walked towards the main square. Soldiers were running everywhere, some carrying sacks of plunder towards the shore and the waiting ships, others prancing about, torches or bottles in their hands. The buildings near St John's Church were well alight, flames leaping high into the sky, sending showers of sparks shooting up. Some burning fragments were carried by the wind across the Solent, but others drifted back down and settled on the ground, to glow awhile before dying. Some were falling on the thatch of other buildings, and even the church itself, starting

Evening

them smouldering. The old reeds, dried by the summer sun, would soon burst into flames that would lick upwards and burn through until the whole roof fell in with a shower of sparks that would further spread the fire. It would not be long before the whole town was in flames.

A brilliant flash of lightning illuminated the scene, sending everything into stark relief for an instant. This was followed almost immediately by an earsplitting crack of thunder that then rolled and echoed on for ages, it seemed. The storm was very close now, almost overhead.

The duke drew his sword and started laying about him with its flat side. He shouted for his knights to order the men to leave the burning and looting, and to form into marching order. They, copying their leader, also set about them and forced the men to come to their senses and form their platoons. A bugle call blasted out, only to be drowned by another clap of thunder, but the hurrying men stopped, turned and came towards the group in the square. Discipline was being restored. Upwards of 500 men finally assembled.

Robert stood behind de Beauvais and his knights while they conferred. The duke ordered that a garrison should be left to guard Yarmouth and protect their avenue of retreat to the ships, should it be necessary. The rest were to march to Francheville, and Robert thought they would then undertake a camisarde, a night attack. Under cover of the storm they would be able to gain complete surprise, unless a warning had reached them from Yarmouth. Robert was jubilant because he was sure that they would find the town abandoned, just like Yarmouth had been. Little did he know that the French were already in possession of the other town too.

'You will come with me, and make no tricks,' de Beauvais said to Robert. Then he turned to his squire. 'You! Look to this English knight. He has given his word not to attempt to escape, but if he does, kill him. He may be valuable, but he cannot be allowed to jeopardise our mission.'

De Beauvais mounted a fine stallion that had been brought up and turned to the massed troops, swept his arm towards the east and shouted '*En avance!*' The troops cheered and platoon by

21 August 1377

platoon marched out of the square and eastwards on to the high road, led by the mounted knights and squires. There was a blinding flash of lightning that sizzled as it rent the air, followed immediately by an ear-splitting crack of thunder. The storm was directly overhead. A few large drops of rain spotted into the dust and then, with a loud hiss, the heavens opened and torrents of rain mixed with hail pelted down. The men put their shields over their heads in protection, but Robert remained exposed and within seconds was wet to the skin, his hair plastered over his face and the remnants of his shirt sticking to him. The rain was cold after the heat of the day but was refreshing, nonetheless, despite the sting of the hail stones. Robert joined the marching column, on foot beside the mounted squire. By the time they reached the eastern gate to the town, and passed through the ditches and dykes, and the fortified palisade of sharpened tree trunks, the road was rapidly being churned to slippery and clinging mud. The moon had disappeared behind the clouds, but the leaders could see their way through the open fields and into the woods by the frequent lightning flashes.

21 August 1377

Night

The column of French troops marched for an hour or more at a good steady pace along the well-marked track towards Schaldefleet. The soldiers were fearful of a possible ambush, and were quiet, except for the thudding of their footsteps and the occasional jingle of weapons. Eventually the rain had stopped as the storm moved northwards across the Solent, and the sky was bright with stars, and the big disc of the full moon. The moonlight dappled through the trees and the rain dripped on the marchers as a light breeze stirred the branches. Despite the humidity, the warm night air and their exertions were drying their clothes, but their feet were still wet and muddy.

De Beauvais was comfortable and dry on his stallion, protected as he had been by a thick cape. He set a fast pace, urging the troops to keep up, clearly eager to maintain the element of surprise. Robert in particular was tired; his stride had become uneven and he continually stumbled. His arm, despite the sling, was throbbing and felt swollen and inflamed from his shoulder to his fingertips. He occasionally flexed his fingers to try to ease the stiffening. He gritted his teeth and carried on, determined to show his captors the strength that an Islander would have.

A vanguard had been sent forward to scout the way and make sure it was clear. As they came out of the trees and onto the fields surrounding the village of Schaldefleet they stopped and saw the glow of fire way off in front and towards their left. In the village, dogs were already barking at the intruders and the unusual skylight. A report was passed back to de Beauvais and they awaited orders as to whether an attack would be mounted.

On receiving the message de Beauvais stopped the column and trotted back to where Robert stood. He wheeled his horse

21 August 1377

beside Robert and demanded, 'Tell me, Affeton, what is this town? How large is it?'

'It is only a small and poor village, sire. With the warning the dogs have made, I expect that the inhabitants will have fled. It will not be worth your while bothering to spend time here.'

'And could that fire be at Francheville?'

'Yes, sire. I think it most probably is,' replied Robert, thoroughly dispirited.

'Excellent. How do we get there quickly? It is possible that the other battalion might need our support immediately.'

'The only way is through the village there.' Robert pointed to the church tower shining in the moonlight in front of them, 'Past the church and across the bridge, then to the left at the top of the hill. That will lead us to the causeway.'

'Ah! This causeway, is it likely to be defended?' de Beauvais asked.

'I doubt that it will be defended, but the bridge in the middle might be raised. That would mean swimming across, or about an hour-long march around the marshes.'

De Beauvais called a messenger to ride out to the scouting party with orders to progress through the village, and tell them to beware an ambush or resistance at the causeway. Robert, however, was convinced that the people of the Francheville had long left, and that any opposition would have been brief.

That is how it transpired. When they approached the causeway half an hour later, it was to discover that the bridge had been dismantled by townspeople as they fled. The Frenchmen on the other side hailed their comrades with news that the town was theirs. Behind them the town was now well on fire, and further troops could be seen rushing around the buildings, looting and pillaging.

De Beauvais gave orders for the planks of the bridge to be hauled out of the mud and laid across the gap in the causeway so that the men could cross. Once this was done they crossed one by one on foot with trepidation, not relishing overbalancing into the black water beneath. De Beauvais and the knights had to leave their mounts behind with a detail of a dozen men ordered to stay and guard the causeway in case of a counter-attack.

Night

Robert was taken up to the village and locked in a shed while de Beauvais sought the leader of the other battalion. Robert was too tired to care about examining his temporary prison, but lay down on the bare earth floor and immediately fell into a deep sleep. He was oblivious to the noise, shouts and screams coming from outside.

The next he knew was that somebody was violently shaking his good right shoulder, and it was with extreme difficulty that he fought his way out of the fog of sleep and awoke. He had been summoned to a council of war that de Beauvais was holding with his lieutenants in the building next door. Robert found that the short sleep had refreshed him somewhat, but he had stiffened up considerably. It felt as if he was carrying an immense weight on his left shoulder and he walked with a marked list to one side.

He was ushered into the room lit by a multitude of torches. He blinked at the unaccustomed bright light. The Duke was surrounded by at least a dozen knights. Surely these must be the elite of the attacking force, he thought.

De Beauvais was seated before a table on which stood pitchers of wine taken from one of the better houses in the town. Robert wondered whether some of it was the same wine he had drunk only a month ago in his cousin's house after the tournament at the fair. That now seemed to be a different world. One of the knights was refilling de Beauvais' mazer. They were obviously discussing tactics for the morrow. As he entered, the talk stopped; some of the knights looked at him with curiosity and others with contempt or antagonism. But for the protection of de Beauvais it was quite likely that Robert would have been dispatched or called out for single combat, despite the fact that the code of chivalry demanded that knights were well treated and either freed or ransomed.

To de Beauvais' right a dark and rather pensive knight was seated. He had a long thin face and his black eyes were deep-sunk in their sockets. He looked at Robert with a detached interest as he sucked at his thin lips. His elbows rested on the table and his hands were steepled in front of him. Robert was surprised to see that some of the other knights were also dark-skinned, with black eyes and hair. They were distinctly different from the more

21 August 1377

familiar French, many of whom were difficult to separate from the English in looks. He was to learn that these were Castilians, rather uncomfortable political allies of the French. There was considerable friction and rivalry between the two forces, who had different languages and cultures, despite their common objectives against the English.

'As you see, we have taken the town and your people are either dead or they fled. The resistance was puny,' de Beauvais said with satisfaction.

'Come here, sir knight, and draw me a map of this island with the locations of the main towns.' De Beauvais gestured to Robert to approach the table, smoothed down a piece of parchment and pushed across a quill pen and a small pot of ink.

Robert licked his lips. He was very thirsty but he would not deign to ask a favour from his captor. He drew himself up, squaring his shoulders, and looked round the expectant group.

De Beauvais clicked his fingers and indicated that Robert should be given a mazer and some wine mixed with water. One of the knights filled it, and Robert thankfully took a mouthful. He picked up the pen, and dipping it frequently into the ink drew a rough outline of the Island. It was diamond-shaped, but with five indentations on the northern side, on each of which was a town. As he went he gave a brief explanation in French. At the westernmost he indicated Yarmouth, and on the next drew in Francheville, explaining that's where they were at that moment. The third stretched southwards from the northern tip of the Island, penetrating almost to the middle, almost splitting the Island into two equal halves. At the end of that estuary Nieuport was situated. The next to the east had Wootton, and finally the easternmost led to Brading. He indicated the chain of chalk downs that ran from west to east, and the large area of downs near to the southern tip.

'Good. Now, where is the castle you call Caresbrooke?' de Beauvais demanded.

Robert indicated a spot just to the west of Nieuport.

De Beauvais looked hard at the map, then at Robert, and then he held out his hand to the knight to his immediate left, who was apparently one of his squires. This knight put into it another parchment fastened with a coloured tape. De Beauvais unrolled it and put it on the table beside the first. It, too, was a map of the Island. The duke bent over, comparing them, while Robert breathed a sigh of relief. Obviously he had just been tested for his honesty. It was a good thing that he hadn't tried to mislead them. He guessed that the second map had been drawn by traders, or from the descriptions of wandering minstrels or friars. De Beauvais was obviously satisfied by his comparison.

'What is this other castle shown on this map?' he asked. Robert looked at the point indicated on the French map, and puzzled for a moment. Then the answer came to him.

'That is no castle, sire. That is the abbey of St Mary of Quarr. It is of Cistercian foundation, and is associated with the abbey of Lire in Normandy. Part of it is fortified, that may be why it has been mistaken for a castle.'

De Beauvais sucked his teeth, saying, 'I think that we would be best to leave that untouched, otherwise we may bring down the wrath of God and the Pope on us.' He continued, 'Now to the castle proper. How is it disposed?'

Robert described the castle site, its fortifications and defences; nothing that an observer wouldn't be able to see for himself. He then explained how the militia was formed, how they were trained, and how good their reserves of food and armaments were. Here he exaggerated, making the castle sound impregnable, and the defenders more numerous. He emphasised the number of bowmen in particular.

The French were understandably wary of the English long-bowmen. They had experienced the dreaded *grey goose wing* at Poitiers and at Crecy. The arrows were fletched with goose feathers, and the hail of arrows that the archers could release had been impenetrable for the French cavalry, even with their good Milanese armour. The French crossbowmen had been completely overwhelmed by the speed and sheer magnitude of fire, as well as the distance that the longbow could shoot. Consequently Robert made much of the archers that were in the castle garrison, as well as those likely to be hastening there for shelter and to fulfil their sworn or indentured duty.

The assembled knights had been jubilant that they had been able to occupy two of the Island towns so easily, but they were

21 August 1377

dismayed they had not been able to catch the English completely unawares, and that apparently so many remained to fight from a position of strength. Nevertheless, they knew that they had the upper hand, and they fell to discussing the next day's actions. It became apparent to Robert that this was not the total of the French force. They had also dispatched a group of fully armed ships to sail and to row up the Medine to Nieuport, and a land attack was planned at the same time as they were due to arrive, so making the defenders fight on all sides at once. The morning was the planned time for the assault.

Robert was also appalled to hear that another fleet was attacking the east part of the Island and were likely to attack Brading and Nunwell. Also raids were being carried out further along the coast at Winchelsea and Rye.

'If what we are told of the castle defences is true, then we will need to make sure we protect our flank when we approach Nieuport,' said de Beauvais looking searchingly at Robert, as if to ascertain whether he was telling the truth.

'If we approach the town from the west there will be less than a league between us and the castle. To go round to the south would need a good day's march, and we do not have that time. Half of our force, one battalion, will surround the castle, and make as if they are simply the vanguard and more troops are coming behind. Make sure they do not venture out to outflank us when we attack the town. The English will not have information on the disposition of our troops; they have been too busy fleeing and trying to reorganise.

'The other half will march straight to Nieuport and attack as soon as they can, whether the ships are there or not. We must not give the town time to muster their defences.'

He then directed his various knights as to where they would be in the attacking force. He would lead the battalion aiming for the town. His right-hand man, the Comte de Mortagne, was to lead his Castilians to the castle.

Robert quickly reappraised the count, now his role was clear. De Mortagne was tall and though slender was probably sinewy and strong. His thin face was solemn and withdrawn and his black eyes glittered, revealing little of his thoughts. Robert found

Night

his steady gaze rather intimidating. De Mortagne moved his arms and shifted his position and in so doing showed that he had a large red cross on his surcoat.

Such a cross had been the emblem of the Knights Templar. This select band of knights had been holy warriors, sworn to punish opponents of Christianity and uphold Christian virtues. They had fought the Saracens in the Holy Land during the Crusades and were reputed to be zealous, single-minded and unemotional, but they had been disbanded by Pope Clement in 1314. Their dedication and unity, together with the wealth of their order had made other parts of the Church jealous, and they had accused the Templars of corruption and ungodly practices. The Templars had been tested by the Inquisition, tortured and mutilated until they confessed of any sin that they were accused of. They had been imprisoned, had died of their wounds or been burned. It had become obvious from the way that the order's riches were taken and used that the accusations had been falsely laid through greed and jealousy, but the order was broken. Nevertheless, despite the years that had gone by, the principles by which the Templars were established were still favoured by some. Perhaps this count was one of these followers.

'And,' de Beauvais ordered, 'de Mortagne, you will take this knight, de Affeton, with you. Show him at the castle and say that we have him as hostage. Say he will not be harmed as long as we are not resisted. Tell them that we are prepared to accept ransom terms for him. Then report to me tomorrow evening. Now, we are all tired. We will need to march again before prime, and we need an hour or so to sleep. *Bonne nuit.*'

With that Robert was taken back to his shed and shut in, with a guard outside. His bed was the bare earth.

★

Rachel had spent the evening at Kingston talking to her mother, alternately tearful and angry. When Rachel had told her father that she had been meeting Robert and that he would be coming to visit Kingston in two days' time, and the purpose of the visit, he had become very angry. He had made it plain that it was a father's

21 August 1377

duty to find a husband of wealth and standing for a daughter and in his view, there were few on the Island who were fitted for Rachel. All of the single men were too old and weak to give him the grandson and heir that he badly wanted, and the younger ones too feather-brained, or with too limited prospects for him to tolerate.

Rachel argued that he was looking for someone who was equal to him, not someone who was equal to her. Her feelings and desires appeared to count for nothing with him. She insisted she loved Robert and would marry no one else. The exchange developed into a heated argument, and her father had left for Nieuport – where he had to attend court sessions the following day – in a thoroughly bad temper.

The one consolation for Rachel was that he had not refused to receive Robert when he was to come. Rachel's mother, Isabel, tried to console her by saying that her father had always been prone to fits of temper that he later regretted, as well she knew. She thought it was more than likely that during his absence he would think about the arguments, come to appreciate the depth and strength of Rachel's feelings, and change his mind. Perhaps he would see the advantages of a union with one of the oldest and most respected families on the Island.

Eventually they had both gone to bed, emotionally exhausted. During the afternoon no one had seen the thin warning column of smoke ascending in the mist from the beacon on Hetdone.

Rachel was awakened in the middle of the night by someone hammering on the thick oak door of the manor. The patrol sent out from the castle had made good time along the road to Shorwell where two men had gone to Brixton, and the others were going on to Chale and Whitwell after calling at Kingston. On the way they were rousing the inhabitants of as many cottages and farmsteads as they could, before rushing on. They were eager to return to the castle before dawn.

Rachel hurriedly put on a shift and reached the bottom of the stairs just as the bleary-eyed steward, Michael Apse, was unbolting the door. Before it was fully open the soldier blurted out the news, urging them to make haste to Caresbrooke. Then he turned and galloped away to catch up with his compatriots.

Night

Because her father was in Nieuport Rachel immediately took charge, knowing that her mother would dither and not be able to decide what to do. It seemed rather odd to be fleeing towards the attackers, but Rachel was sure it would be the right thing to do. And Robert, she thought, was more than likely to be at Caresbrooke and they could be together again.

'Light the house, and wake everyone,' she told Michael. 'Tell the servants to saddle up the horses. We will only be able to take what we can carry. Prepare to leave for Caresbrooke immediately, then collect the money box and the silverware. Hide all the other valuables. I will go to my mother's room to help bring her jewellery and other things downstairs.'

She rushed back upstairs into her mother's room. Isabel was sitting up in bed, dazed and sleepy. 'What is going on, Rachel? What is all the commotion?' she asked with concern.

'Mother, the French are invading. They have attacked Yarmouth already. Sir Hugh insists that everyone must go to the castle for protection until it is safe.'

'Oh dear, oh dear! Your father is away. What shall we do?' She dithered, just as Rachel thought she would.

'Hurry up and get dressed. Put on something suitable for riding, for we must go immediately. We can only take the valuables and a few clothes. If we stay too long we may not be able to get there.'

Just then the maid Sarah came into the room sniffing back her tears. She had heard the news.

Rachel took her by the shoulders. 'Pull yourself together, Sarah, and help my mother dress, then go and fetch your own things, and get ready to come with us to the castle.' Not that the poor girl had very much of her own possessions, coming from a poor cottar family. To her, a trip to the market was usually as much excitement as she would get in a year.

Rachel left her mother and the maid looking through the clothes, ran into her own room and opened the chest by her bed. From it she pulled a linen dress and her riding attire, thick hose and a jerkin. Throwing off her shift she dressed for the ride, and folded the dress, a cote-hardi, and an acton, a quilted jacket, into a bag that could be thrown over the saddle. She went back to her

21 August 1377

mother's room to find her standing wondering which clothes to put on.

'Mother,' she said impatiently, 'for heaven's sake put this on and pack these things to take with us.' She quickly sorted through the pile of clothes her mother had pulled out onto the bed and selected some suitable for the journey and some practical clothes for wearing at the castle. Sarah hastily started packing the clothes, and then left to collect her own. As an afterthought Rachel put in a selection of her ointments and medicines in case they might be needed.

'Here, put these on. Hurry up! I will go and make sure the servants are ready.' She collected her mother's jewels into a bag, ran down the stairs, through the hall and out into the moonlight.

The groom had assembled a motley collection of horses, hobbies, her mother's jennet and sufficient hackneys for all the eight servants, and some over as pack animals for the baggage. The other two servants were with their lord in Nieuport – their belongings would have to stay where they were. There was just not enough time to sort them out.

Apse appeared from the hall, staggering under the weight of two heavy boxes containing the family plate, money and valuables. Together with the groom he strapped them across the back of one of the horses.

'Good!' Rachel said approvingly. 'Now fetch the bag from my mother's room, while I have a last look to make sure we haven't forgotten anything.' Then she ordered two of the servants to fetch some food and drink, and one to help her put the lights out.

Carrying a candle she went from room to room, casting her eye over the familiar objects, wondering whether she would ever see them again. She heard her mother come downstairs, and go outside. She pulled a sword and buckler off the wall where they were customarily hung, thinking that they might be useful, and went outside herself. She blew out the candle, threw it on one side and shut the door. There was little point in attempting to lock it: the local peasants wouldn't dare to steal and the French, if they reached this far, wouldn't be stopped by a mere lock.

Night

'Are we all here, Steward?' she asked.

'Aye, miss,' he replied, helping Lady Isabel into the saddle. 'I reckon it should take us about one hour and a half to the castle – it's about four miles as the crow flies.'

With the steward leading, the company cantered in the moonlight down the track to the main road. On Rachel's insistence they didn't turn along the road towards Shorwell, but pressed on at a trot across towards the open downs above Chillerton. This meant that they would approach Caresbrooke directly from the south, keeping off the main roads. The going would be quicker in the bright moonlight and it would keep them further from any possibility of encountering French patrols – the French would be much more likely to keep to the main roads.

As they climbed higher on the downs they could see a thunderstorm away to the north-west, passing across the Solent to the mainland. The flashes of lightning were still bright, but the thunder was faint. The storm had passed west of them, rain had not fallen where they were, the riding was dry and they should make good time. The glow from the burning towns was plainly visible, reflected on the underside of the storm clouds, and this spurred them on. Above them the sky was a deep dark purple, studded with bright stars, with the moon above and behind them.

Rachel gazed into the heavens and wondered where Robert was. An aching need for him welled up inside her. She said a little prayer, and a Hail Mary, for his safety and crossed herself. 'Please God, keep him safe for me. I love him,' she whispered to herself.

Her mother, riding beside her, seemed to sense her feelings; she leant across and squeezed her hand. At times Lady Isabel was intuitive and sensitive to people's feelings, despite her vagueness.

After cresting the down they met a solitary shepherd who knew nothing of the alarms. They persuaded him to follow them to Caresbrooke. Then they rode down the wooded valley past Gatcombe and along the narrow winding lanes through the night-time moonlit shadows. They met no one, all the cottages being deserted. Their imaginations played tricks with every noise; every shadow became a French invader. They were sure their hoof beats could be heard for miles, as they sounded deafening to their own ears. Birds disturbed from their roosts fluttered noisily away,

21 August 1377

making the horses and the riders start, and their hands clutched nervously at sword hilts. A vixen's eerie wail made them shiver with fright and a ghostly white barn owl flew soundlessly across the path, startling them. They were happy to only have a further two miles or so to go to safety.

Half an hour later they crested the hill to the south of the castle. There it stood, slightly below them, gaunt, solid and grey in the moonlight, starkly silhouetted on the other side of the shallow valley. They could see the banner on the top of the keep was hanging limply, and around the gates was a bustle of activity, lit by numerous torches. The campfires and torches within the castle radiated a glow into the night sky, against which sentries moved, patrolling the curtain walls.

The party was thankful to have arrived safely, feeling tired now the tension eased. They joined the stream of peasants heading for the gates and, as they approached, a sentry demanded to know who they were and from whence they came.

Michael Apse called out, 'Lady Isabel and Rachel de Kingston, and servants.'

This caused a stir inside and the sergeant of the guard came to meet them at the gate as they entered. 'My lady, is Lord John not with you?' he asked.

Lady Isabel looked worried at this. 'He is not. He was due at court in Nieuport today. He travelled there last evening, and is not due to return home until tomorrow morning. Has he not come here yet?'

'We have had few come from Nieuport, my lady, and they say that the burgesses are going to defend the town. Perhaps he is staying to assist them.'

'Just the sort of foolhardy enterprise he would get involved in,' said Lady Isabel tremulously.

The sentry waved them to enter, saying, 'Sir Hugh would wish you to join him in his quarters, which are over there. The servants will be housed in the camp behind the chapel.'

As she was riding past the sergeant, Rachel leant over and asked, 'Is there any news of Robert de Affeton. Has he come in yet?'

'My lady, he has not,' the sergeant replied. 'It has been reported by his bailiff, and a yeoman from Freshwater, that he was shot by a French crossbow while rescuing a boy at Yarmouth. The boy himself is with them and has confirmed it. We fear that he is either dead or taken prisoner. But servants have brought his father, Sir Roger, in. He is very ill and hardly survived the journey.'

Rachel gasped, her head drooped and tears started rolling down her cheeks. Her mother immediately took her hand to console her. They crossed the courtyard and dismounted. Rachel wiped away the tears and clenched her fists with determination, as if willing Robert to be alive.

'I know he is not dead. I feel it. He must be alive, for I feel him here, in my heart.'

Lady Isabel hugged Rachel, saying, 'I hope you are right, my daughter. You *are* right, I am sure, for you can sense these things.'

Rachel's chin went up, her eyes glistened and a new strength appeared in her voice. 'I will go and find Sir Roger and see what I can do to ease his sickness. That is what Robert would want me to do.' Then to the steward, 'Michael, you and Sarah must look to my mother and make sure she is comfortable, and store our possessions away safely. Also, search out the boy from Yarmouth, for I want to question him. Bring him to me. I will return shortly.'

With that she set off, determined to find out where Sir Roger was lying abed, and to help him if she could.

★

At the castle a continual stream of people – peasants, yeomen, cotters and their families – had arrived throughout the early part of the night. Sir Hugh wanted to keep the great gates open for refugees as long as possible. He ordered a routine to be set up for operating the treadmill to raise water. Normally this task was a punishment, but now the demand would be too great for that to be enough. He had posted forward pickets on the main tracks to the castle to warn of any approaching French warriors so that the gates could be closed in time before an attack. Then he had slept fitfully for a couple of hours before rising to check on the information coming from the patrols and from the newcomers.

21 August 1377

The eastern sky was beginning to lighten, heralding the early summer dawn.

Some of the lords had also arrived, together with their families and retinues, and the castle was becoming rather full with makeshift shelters and tents. The horses and other livestock were enclosed in an area that had been partitioned off near the stables, but some of them had escaped into the castle kitchen garden. Chickens and pigs were happily eating the strawberries and the horses were munching the unripe apples off the trees. Some of the boys were trying to round them up and drive them out, and catch the hens, but with little success. The noise was considerable, but tiredness and the anticlimax from the worry and the excitement of the preceding day were at last beginning to make everyone seek their beds and sleep.

Sir Hugh asked who had reached the castle while he was asleep, and was told that the group from Affeton had just arrived, including his old friend Sir Roger. William and Alice had succeeded in getting Sir Roger into a cart and, together with the other estate workers, had travelled slowly along the track over the downs. The stress of the journey, the bumping and jolting, had weakened Sir Roger considerably and he failed to recognise Sir Hugh when he leant over and spoke to him. Sir Hugh insisted that he should be taken to his own apartments, and he was carefully put to bed with a warming pan to stop him shivering, despite the warmth of the night.

At this stage Peter de Heyno and Rebecca arrived, with their retainers. Rebecca, now in the late stages of her pregnancy, had been laid in a cart for the journey and at every bump Peter was convinced she was going to go into labour. However, despite her condition she immediately took over control of her father's care, ordering medicines and more warm blankets to supplement the warming pan. He felt chilled even though the weather was hot, and she was convinced that he would develop a fever, especially if others were left to look to him.

Shortly after, the message that Robert had been hit by a crossbow bolt and either been taken or killed had been relayed by the bailiff, Thomas and Harold when they arrived. Rebecca was desolated to hear this, for she loved her brother dearly, and questioned the three of them closely to convince herself that he was still alive. Peter had tried in vain to console her and stop her tears. She insisted that no one spoke of it in the chamber, in case her father could still hear, even though he appeared to have fallen into a coma.

She sat by her father's bed looking at him lying motionless. He seemed such a small, weak and fragile being, when her childhood memories were of him big, strong, handsome and dependable. Now his breathing was shallow and uneven and his face was almost transparent, waxy and colourless. His lips were just thin blue lines. She thought that he was unlikely to survive the night, and might not ever see his first grandson – or would it be granddaughter? – so soon to be born. The baby moved inside her as if sensing her thoughts.

She leant over the bed and took her father's hand. It was cold and limp, the blue veins showing through; simply bones covered with skin. All his flesh seemed to have melted away, just like his life.

A soft knock came at the door, so soft that Rebecca almost missed it in the noise that penetrated in from outside the window. It came again, a little louder this time. Rebecca placed her father's hand back under the sheet and went across to the door and opened it.

Rachel and Rebecca stood and looked at each other for a brief second. The mutual recognition was immediate. Of course, Robert had told Rachel of Rebecca during their meetings, when their minds had not been otherwise occupied. She could see the likeness of Robert in Rebecca's eyes and mouth. Rebecca knew about Rachel from what Peter had told her of her ministrations to him at the tourney and guessed this was her brother's lover.

They simultaneously clasped each other in a long embrace and, when they realised both knew of Robert's fate, they both started to cry afresh, Rachel crying for Rebecca's brother, and Rebecca crying for Rachel's lover.

They crossed to the bed and, still holding hands they knelt beside it and prayed, both for the old man before them and for their beloved Robert. After a while their grief subsided and they talked in whispers about their hopes and fears.

21 August 1377

The door softly opened and Peter came in. He looked at the two women beside the bed and smiled at his wife, and the girl beside her whom he hoped would become his sister-in-law.

'How are you, my dear?' he said, putting an arm round Rebecca and kissing the top of her head. 'Don't you think you should lie down and rest? You have had a long journey. I don't want you to become overtired.'

Then, turning to Rachel, he kissed her on the cheek, gave her a hug and added quietly, 'You have no need to worry. Robert is a survivor, it will take more than one bolt from a crossbow to despatch him. He is as hard as nails.'

'I know,' Rachel replied. 'I am sure he is alive.' She clenched her fists as if to help convince herself. 'I know it. He is alive. He must live.' Her lip trembled and tears welled into her eyes again.

Peter knew what the best remedy would be. 'You need something to eat and drink. You are both exhausted. I'll go and see what I can find. Just rest here until I come back.'

When he came back ten minutes later with some bread and cheese, cold meat, sweetmeats and a pitcher of wine mixed with water, he found them on cushions on the floor leaning against the bed and asleep, just like Sir Roger. He put down the food, so that they could eat when they woke, and crept out to do his duty in helping to organise the defence of the castle.

22 August 1377

Morning

The sun was just peeping over the horizon and the dawn chorus welcomed another fine and warm summer's day. The sky was clear and the dew was already evaporating from the grass.

Within the castle it was fairly quiet as the exhausted refugees slept beyond their normal waking hour. A trickle of people still came through the gates as small family groups or as individuals, some of them shepherded by the returning scouting platoons. Few were expected once it was daylight, because of the risk of meeting the invaders en route. The country folk would feel safer in their familiar woods and valleys where the attackers were unlikely to penetrate. Certainly, if they did, their local knowledge would help them avoid capture and they might eventually move south, away from the invaders to find comfort with relatives.

Michael Apse had found the boy Harold, and led him to Rachel, as he had been instructed. Harold was tearful because he had not found his father, his mother having died some years before. It was thought by others from Yarmouth that he had returned to the town to find his boy, and had been caught by the French. Nevertheless, Harold told Rachel all he could of Robert's bravery, looking dolefully into the eyes of the beautiful lady.

Sir Hugh called the lords to a council of war, in order to discuss the situation, anticipate the possible actions of the French and try to establish a strategy for defence. Eight lords were there, including Peter, Adam de Cumpton, and Theobald de Gorges. Nothing further had been heard of the whereabouts of de Kingston, and it was assumed that he was still in Nieuport. All were disappointed to hear the report that Robert had either been taken or killed at Yarmouth – the first knightly casualty they knew of.

Reports had come back from the patrols sent out to spy on the French, one having only narrowly avoided being taken themselves. It was only their knowledge of the tracks in the woods and the best crossing of the streams that had allowed them to escape from the hail of bolts and the pursuing horsemen.

At Yarmouth there must have been many other casualties as well as Robert, but no one knew how many. The refugees had reported other men going back into the town, but nothing was known of their fate. At Francheville the situation was much graver: upwards of a hundred men, women and children must have been killed or captured. The general assumption was that prisoners would not be taken, as they were a liability for troops on the move, unless they had obvious hostage and ransom value.

When the reports were pieced together the lords were astounded at the estimates of the numbers of French in the invasion. Two battalions with upwards of 500 men in each had separately attacked Yarmouth and Francheville and were now marching towards the castle and Nieuport. There was a lengthy discussion as to the alternatives of defence or attack. Should they rely on the strength of the castle, and sit out what could be a lengthy siege, or should they venture forth to meet the attackers head-on?

An accounting of the militia available within the castle at that moment totalled about 550 men; only about half had mounts. Many of those raised from the Island had not yet reached the castle, or were not likely to. It appeared that they were outnumbered by the attackers, and though the English had won at Poitiers and Crecy while at a similar numerical disadvantage, they had been much better prepared and could choose their own ground. The decision had to be to remain in the castle and await developments. At least from the castle they would be able to harry the invaders with occasional armed sorties. Word of the invasion must reach the mainland before long, though no message had been sent, but to raise a relief force, and for it to reach the Island could take several weeks. Nevertheless, it was unlikely that the castle could be taken before assistance came from the mainland.

Sir Hugh's immediate worry was the situation at Nieuport. Few of the inhabitants had yet appeared at the castle, and those who had said that the burgesses were aiming to defend the town, and were trying to stop people leaving. They thought that the

French would not be rash enough to try to attack such a large town. From the battlements of the castle keep the town could be seen. It appeared to be calm; the western gate, at least, was still open. But messengers sent down earlier in the night to warn the townsfolk came back discouraged. They reported the burgesses and most of the townsfolk were full of confidence, saying they would be able to beat off the French.

The town was bounded to the north by the Lukely Brook, and to the east by the Medine River. Both normally provided good wharfage for shipping as far upstream as the water mills, and made good natural defences in time of war. But the other two sides of the town, the west and south, were not quite so secure. Ditches and wooden ramparts had been made in days past and were not in particularly good repair. There was a strong gate on the western end of the town, on the road to Caresbrooke, where the walls made an abrupt turn and ran down to the Lukely Brook. There was a further gate to the south and one to the east, which led to a bridge over the Medine. The town was defensible, but not against a strong force, as the perimeter was long and would require many defenders against a concerted attack.

In Sir Hugh's view there were likely to be too many attackers; the town was underestimating the number of the enemy and overestimating the defenders' capabilities. Sir Hugh sent urgent orders for the town to be evacuated and for the people to retreat to the castle. There was a pause while these were dispatched.

At that point a message arrived from one of the outlying pickets that a large French force was approaching through the forest north of the village. This was almost immediately confirmed by the lookouts on the keep. All of the assembled lords followed Sir Hugh to the top of the keep to see for themselves. In the distance there was still early morning mist rising from the forest, but they could clearly see a large mass of troops. Sun glinted off their weapons, half hidden in the cloud of dust rising from the marching feet.

It became obvious to the watchers that the column of attackers was dividing into two, one heading for Caresbrooke and the other continuing on towards Nieuport. Sir Hugh immediately ordered the drawbridge to be raised and the portcullis gates lowered. The

22 August 1377

postern gate was to be left until the last moment so that any further refugees and the scouts could still be let in. On the route they were taking, the battalion heading for the castle would pass into some dead ground behind the hill on which the village of Caresbrooke itself was located. Where would the French reappear? They were trapped in the castle, and the townsfolk of Nieuport would not have time to evacuate now. The church bells started tolling a mournful warning. Their fate was sealed.

★

Robert slept a sleep of pure exhaustion, without dreams, until he was roused before sunrise. During the night the French scouting parties returned from plundering the outlying farms and houses with horses of various shapes, sizes and colours, and a number of ox carts. So, when the march towards Nieuport resumed, many of the sergeant men-at-arms and archers would also be mounted, even though most would have to ride without saddles – they were accustomed to that.

One of the patrols had seen an armed rider they took to be a scout sent out to determine the French dispositions but they had been unable to catch him before he rode away eastwards. Robert took great heart in this, for it meant that the messages had reached the castle and preparations were being made for defence.

Each of the French soldiers had taken a quick bite of bread and dried meat or fish, and a drink of water, or some of the plundered ale, as soon as they awoke. They didn't know when they would next be able to fill their bellies, so they made sure they packed some more food for later in pouches hung on their belts. Some of the horses were also laden with panniers of food and drink in case the troops were unable to plunder enough in the farms and cottages as they marched. Robert had not been able to eat, as he still felt sick and dizzy, but he drank a long draught of ale mixed with water to quench his raging thirst.

The column of marchers formed up and set out. De Beauvais and the main group of knights rode in the vanguard, and a further group rode behind to chivvy along stragglers and to be able to quickly come to the assistance of any part of the column should it

Morning

be attacked. In all, Robert estimated that there were more than 300 marching, as well as 200 mounted – a formidable fighting force. A further hundred had been left at garrisons in Francheville and Yarmouth.

The marching soldiers were armed with crossbows, but they couldn't carry them cocked and ready to fire, otherwise the bowstrings would stretch. The mounted knights had lances at rest, held vertically with their ends cupped by their stirrups. Their swords were loose in their scabbards. They were all tense and nervous, because today was likely to be a much more severe test than the surprise attacks of yesterday – a test that some of them might not survive.

After the overnight rain it felt damply cold, and a layer of thin mist hung over the marshes behind the town. Trees stuck above it like ships on a ghostly sea, and dead branches appeared like the hands of drowning men cut off at the wrist. The sun reflected blindingly from the mist, but it would not be long before it burnt off as the sun gained warmth. The dawn chorus was loud and harmonious, as if the birds were singing in delight that they had survived the thunderstorm.

Robert was feverish. His face felt burning hot, his eyes were smarting, his head was heavy and all his muscles ached. He kept involuntarily wiping his hand across his forehead, as if to ease his headache. He would dearly like to sit or lie down and eyed the riders with envy.

De Beauvais had assigned a young squire to act as guard to the captive he thought so valuable and he rode alongside Robert on a small, thin pony. The youth must have been about seventeen, though well grown, upright and strong. He was dark of face and eye beneath his helmet, and carried a sword and shield. He reminded Robert of how he must have been at that age when he was a squire fulfilling his duty in Gascony. The lad was voluble; he chattered away to Robert about his home and family, who appeared to be reasonably wealthy, about the glorious adventure that he was on and how he eventually hoped to become a knight himself. Robert forced himself to listen, though it was only with half an ear, hoping to find out useful information. He made enough conversation in reply to be courteous, but much of his

22 August 1377

energy was concentrated on simply putting one foot before the other. After they had gone a few miles all Robert wanted to do was to lie down. If he had, he knew he would have immediately gone to sleep.

They were travelling along the main road to Nieuport, which passed through the edge of the vast Avington Forest. The track was wide enough for about three soldiers to march abreast. Riders could only go in pairs, and carts singly. In places where the track dipped the ruts were muddy and wet and two of the marching lines of troops had to splash through the water. On the mainland, roads between market towns were cleared for a bowshot distance on either side to deter ambush and thieving. But here trees overhung the track and the surrounding undergrowth often was thick on either side. This made the men nervous and their senses were alert and straining. But there was the consolation that the trees at least afforded them shade from the rising sun.

The forest was quiet and eerie with only occasional birdsong to break the ominous silence. There was a heady smell of wild garlic, which reminded them of their own forests. This occasionally mingled with the sweetness of the misty flowers of the cream-coloured meadowsweet that grew in the sunny patches. Echoing through the trees came a distant alarm cackle of a blackbird. Hands immediately tensed in fear in case it was a signal for attack.

Suddenly there was a commotion ahead and several shouts and screams. Half a dozen arrows had come out of the forest and struck down some of the marchers. Several lay screaming on the ground with arrows sticking out of their bodies; one or two lay absolutely still. Immediately the column stopped and the men rushed for cover into the trees. The archers immediately started winding their crossbows and slid bolts into their bows. Though they fired them in the direction the ambushing arrows had come from, the attackers had already melted into the quiet forest. Others had drawn their swords ready for an attack, but none came.

In response to shouted orders, groups of swordsmen from further along the column disappeared into the trees to try to encircle the ambushers, and mounted knights came galloping up

Morning

from the rear to forestall attack. The thick trees and undergrowth hampered the riders. As they couldn't move as quickly as the infantry, the knights dismounted and with drawn swords peered into the surrounding trees.

Robert guessed that he might get a few minutes' respite, and took the opportunity to sit down and have a rest, with his back against a tree. His guard dismounted and stood over him with sword drawn to ensure that he didn't sneak away while attention was concentrated elsewhere. From deeper in the woods came the taunting laugh of a yaffle, followed by its drumming on a hollow tree. Could it be another signal?

After a few minutes the archers returned, having seen no one. Two marchers had been killed and others were badly wounded; the impact in terms of morale was much greater. The invaders had been reminded that danger was everywhere, and this was definitely foreign territory. Unfortunately, such a surprise would be difficult again.

The bodies were heaved on to horses for burial later and the wounded were placed on litters made from stakes cut from the undergrowth, tied together with linen strips, and covered with grass. These litters were carried by pairs of men, and the column reformed.

Robert scrambled to his feet and stood, dizzy and swaying. He felt worse now than before he had rested, but he was forced to move off with the column. He had to concentrate hard to put one foot before the other, and sweat soon coursed down his chest. Left, right, left, right, until the rhythm became all he could think of.

Occasionally a marcher would stop by the side of the track, lay down his arms and relieve himself, to the ribald comments of his comrades. No one waited; he would have to rejoin the column further back or come trotting up later with his equipment thumping against his back.

In the middle of the forest was a pungent smell of wood smoke and the trees thinned out as the track entered a clearing. In the centre was a turf-covered mound. Blue smoke wreathed out between the turfs, rising slowly through the sunbeams to diffuse in overhanging branches. Beside the mound were a heap of charcoal and a stack of billets and staves of wood. It was clear that the fire had been tended recently and the charcoal burners were probably close at hand – they may even have been the illusive bowmen. To one side of the clearing was a crude lean-to shelter with a roughly thatched roof, where the charcoal burners lived while the burning lasted.

Two of the marchers crossed to the fire and with some of the staves attacked the mound, prising off the turves. The sudden inrush of air caused flames to break out and grey smoke and sparks billowed upwards. One of men took a burning staff and went across and set light to the shelter. A rather spiteful and pointless retribution for the attack, thought Robert.

A thudding of hooves heralded the appearance of de Mortagne, who came galloping up from the rear to see what was holding up the column. When he saw the crowd of men watching the flames devour the little hut, the contempt that knights customarily had for the infantry came out in scathing comments.

'Resume marching, you lazy laggards,' he said with a lip curling in scorn. 'If there are any more delays, I will personally tie you all to trees and let the cursed English archers have target practise with you.'

Turning to Robert he added 'We have clearly lost the surprise that we might have had. The whole countryside has fled to your Caresbrooke Castle. However, we will see whether the rest of the fleet has reached your Nieuport yet.'

The significance of this statement didn't fully register with Robert until later. Then de Mortagne turned to the squire. 'Look after our hostage, Charles,' he said with a sinister glance at Robert. 'We will have use for him later.'

The ranks reformed and the men started off again, muttering, aggrieved at being denied their bit of fun. Robert judged that there was only about a mile before the troops would need to separate, with one battalion heading for the castle, and the other for the town.

After less than half that distance the trees thinned and the track widened. They had come to the common grazing land on the edge of the farms and small hamlets surrounding Nieuport. Caresbrooke was about two miles off to the right. The column of marchers was now exposed to the full heat of the sun. It was baking hot in the early morning, and the sun was glaring directly into their faces. Those with helmets had the advantage of some protection for their eyes, but sweat matted their hair and ran down their faces, for they were heavily laden with food and drink, as well as their weapons.

Robert had only his tousled hair to keep the sun off. His eyes hurt and his head throbbed. He ran his dry tongue around his parched lips, but got no respite from it. He stumbled. The squire, Charles, saw his discomfort and offered Robert his leather bottle of water. Robert gratefully took it and swilled a mouthful around before swallowing it and taking another. This settled his nauseous stomach and he felt somewhat better.

Charles dismounted, and told Robert to mount and ride for a while. However, he kept a firm hand on the horse's bridle. Robert felt grateful to the chivalrous squire, for the respite from walking was very welcome. After a little while Robert felt more able to take in what was going on around him.

In front of them was flat, open farmland, peppered with occasional copses and groves of trees. A few cottages stood on the western side of the trees, facing towards the sun, using their protection from northerly winds. The scene was one of fertile tranquillity.

To the south the land undulated and rose slightly towards the steeper slopes of the downs. Immediately to their right the downs were high, but the top of the keep of the castle was visible, with more hills in the distance behind. The downs gradually descended to the east to the gap in the ridge, through which roads converged to reach the southern half of the Island. In this gap Nieuport was located at the head of the tidal River Medine. It was the obvious location for the main market town, being in the centre of the Island, and accessible to the sea as well. Robert knew that somewhere to the left lay hidden the valley in which the Medine estuary ran the six or so miles from the Solent up to Nieuport.

Robert realised that the only unusual feature about the landscape that day was the lack of people in sight: no one tilling the fields, no one tending the animals. Some cows were straining

22 August 1377

at the ends of their tethers, lowing demandingly for want of being milked. A flock of geese came running towards them with wings outstretched, honking and hissing loudly. Some of the men broke ranks and, using their swords, quickly either decapitated them, or broke their necks. They would be a welcome addition to the next meal. The birds were slung from the packhorses with their blood draining out and dripping onto the ground on either side of the track. The horses, smelling the warm blood, pranced, wild-eyed and nervous. The men leading them either hit them with their sticks to keep them from plunging off across the fields or soothed them with calming words.

A squire from the vanguard of the column appeared with instructions for the Castilian battalion under de Mortagne to break off for the castle. De Beauvais would lead his battalion straight on along the well-trodden track towards Nieuport. De Mortagne pointed to the right and started trotting off towards Caresbrooke across the fields. As the battalions parted there was much ribaldry, laughter and friendly insults as the compatriots argued which would have the most honourable conflicts and the largest spoils.

The marching infantry found the going much harder over the fields of peas and beans, ripening wheat and rye. The long stalks kept tripping them up and biting flies rose in clouds around them. They sneezed and coughed and became hot and irritable as they tried ineffectually to brush the insects away. Occasionally one or another would stop and take a drink from the leather bottles slung from their baldrics. Those who were mounted fared little better.

They began to pick their way around the worst-looking patches, endeavouring to find easier going, with the result that the marching column broke up into little groups advancing over a broad front. The knot of mounted knights surrounding de Mortagne got further and further ahead and detached from the marchers. Eventually they found a good track leading them in the right direction, and waited while everyone gradually converged again.

Robert found his mind wandering. He looked at the trees under the downs and thought they were dancing and waving to him, but it was just the heat haze. The archer marching next to him appeared familiar and Robert looked at him more closely. Could it be his old friend from the days in Gascony? Robert didn't realise that he was getting light-headed and feverish; the combination of the wound and the heat were having their effect. He had ceased to feel any sensation in his left arm, and though he thought he was sitting upright on the horse, he was actually swaying from side to side and was gradually slumping further and further forward.

Marching was hot, thirsty work. Robert's squire companion emptied his water bottle down his throat and took another from the saddlebag. After a swig himself, he passed it to Robert who, once he realised what was happening, took a grateful drink, then rubbed some over his face and neck. The talkative young man had lapsed into silence as he plodded along at the horse's head but the water had revived Robert and he felt somewhat better again.

They eventually reached the long stretch of woodland at the base of the downs and turned left to follow the track to the village of Caresbrooke. Beneath the beech trees it was cool and refreshing and smelt of garlic and damp earth. Immediately spirits began to rise.

Because they were nearing the castle and there was a greater possibility of serious opposition, de Mortagne called a halt so that the men could refresh themselves and reform into their platoons. The hot and weary men took off their kettle hats to let the air get to their heads and sat or lay on the ground to relax their aching backs. Those in the saddle dismounted, stretched and eased their sore backsides. Belt pouches were opened and bread, cheese and meat appeared, to be quickly wolfed down, followed by a long satisfying drink. Some then took off their boots and let the air refresh their feet as they massaged them. Many found a convenient tree trunk against which to urinate.

Robert sat with his back against a large mossy trunk and eased his left arm within its makeshift sling. It was starting to hurt again and, peering under his torn and bloody shirt, he could see that the wound was inflamed and oozing red watery fluid. It didn't look very good, despite the cauterising, and needed some soothing ointment to cleanse it. He leant his head back against the trunk and closed his eyes. A vision of Rachel came into his mind; he felt

22 August 1377

she was trying to communicate, telling him that she loved him and that she knew he was alive. He felt new energy flowing into his veins and hope for the future lightened his mind.

All too soon the call came to form up to march on and, stiffly, they all clambered to their feet and collected their arms. Robert had felt better sitting down. Standing up again, he felt sick and dizzy but he forced himself to try to appear normal and bear himself like a knight. The column moved off cautiously through the woods, alert and ready for possible ambush. The woods were cool and quiet. Even the birds did not sing, as if they were afraid of the intruders. The only sounds were the occasional chink of metal as weapons jingled, and the soft footfalls in the decaying leaves of the peaty earth.

Some minutes later they emerged from the woods above Caresbrooke, not far from where Robert had stopped some weeks before to look down on the village. It was quiet and deserted, only the thin wisps of smoke rising from the roofs of some of the houses where fires had not been properly damped down. On the other side of the wooded valley the top of the castle keep peeped over the trees, with several colourful banners fluttering in the breeze above the figures of the defenders. Some of the braver knights, eager for glory, broke away and cantered down the steep hill with their swords drawn or lances presented, oblivious to the possible threat of hidden English archers. But the only things to appear were several dogs, which immediately started barking and snapping at the heels of the horses. There was a sudden yelp as one was hit by a swinging sword and it went howling away, trailing blood from a long cut in its side.

The knights drew to a halt at the crossroads at the top of the main street. The squires dismounted, and with the vanguard of the marchers, who had run down behind the knights, started entering the houses, searching for valuables and anything else attractive. De Mortagne had given instructions not to fire the village yet – it was directly under the eyes of the castle, they could use it in bargaining later on. Sounds came of breaking wood and pottery as the contents of houses were turned upside down, cupboards ransacked and chests forced open. The men emerged clutching trinkets, cups, mazers and anything else that took their fancy, much of which would be discarded as soon as something else took their eye.

Down the street the column went, gradually becoming a rampaging mob. Discipline was on the verge of breaking down when an argument started over some of the spoils but a shouted instruction soon restored order. De Mortagne and the other knights sat on their horses and watched, partly in case of surprise attack, and partly because they knew that they would be offered, or could purloin, any really valuable finds.

They progressed down the hill as far as the church, only to be met at the churchyard gate by the prior and two monks, for the church was part of a small Benedictine priory. Though small, the church of St Mary was the grandest on the Island, and the many chapels and granges it had elsewhere made it relatively wealthy. The temptation to rob the church would be hard to resist, though undoubtedly the best valuables and plate had already been hidden.

The prior, with head held high and white beard stubbornly thrust out, held up a cross to try to prevent the Castilians from robbing the church. He and the monks were singing Latin chants, and since most of the Castilians were religious men they were fearful of enraging the powerful Church and went down on bended knee and crossed themselves. The power of the Church was such that robbing of a religious building, which would be seen as a sacrilegious act, could result in excommunication, even in Castile. The men passed on to other houses, although some sneaked round the back of the church to see what they could find in the byres and granaries outside the sacred ground.

De Mortagne called the men to reform their marching ranks, and he pointed to a narrow alleyway to the right, which led down the hill between the houses to a ford across the brook. On the stones beside the water lay wet clothes, washing abandoned in the women's rush to find sanctuary either in the woods, the castle, or in the church. The clothing was speared, and with peals of coarse laughter held aloft on the end of lances and pikes.

The archers splashed through the water of the ford; some, reluctant to wet their feet, picked their way over the nearby stepping stones. Once across the stream the path led through the trees and up towards the castle. All laughter and conversation

22 August 1377

ceased as a nervous expectation descended on the invaders. Everyone unconsciously adjusted their weapons and cast glances to either side, trying to keep their breathing regular and quiet so that they could hear more clearly.

As soon as the grey walls could be seen, the column stopped in the trees and de Mortagne went slowly forward to look more carefully at the castle. The ground around was kept clear of trees and undergrowth for a distance of several hundred yards, at least a long bowshot. This meant that any attackers would have to cross open ground and be exposed to arrows from the high battlements for a long time before they could return fire.

Following a signal from de Mortagne the marchers kept in the trees and moved westwards round the walls until they were opposite the gatehouse. The drawbridge was raised and secure, and many guards could be seen on the battlements watching them, the sunlight glinting off their helmets as they stood in the embrasures.

Taking a couple of knights with him, de Mortagne started on a circuit of the castle, keeping close to the trees. They could be seen by the defenders, who were lining the battlements, but were out of range; the few arrows that were loosed fell short.

While their leader was gone some of the men sat on the ground and rested while others stood guard. All were apprehensive. Their foes were in sight and they anticipated the forthcoming battles with a mixture of jubilation and dread. Robert moved slowly to the edge of the trees, straining to see whether he could recognise any friends on the battlements, and praying that Rachel was safely inside. In his tiredness and pain he could not recognise anyone. Charles, had followed closely and warily, ready to use his sword should Robert decide to make a break for the castle.

After about half an hour De Mortagne returned from the opposite direction, having made a complete circuit of the castle. He looked rather sombre and he came straight across to Robert, glowering, and demanded, 'What lies at the foot of the walls? Because of the curve of the ground I cannot see.'

Robert explained that there was a deep moat all the way round the castle. Though it was not full of water, it was steep-sided and full of sharpened stakes and thick thorn bushes. It would be difficult to penetrate, and all the while the invaders would be exposed to arrows from archers above as well as boulders and boiling oil. Robert would have liked to have seen the invaders try to storm the walls and be defeated in attacking the impenetrable castle, but thought it would be better to try to get them to retreat rather than to inflict great loss of life on both sides.

'Very well,' said de Mortagne. Obviously the description was no more than he expected. 'I want to talk with the captain of the castle, and will need to get close enough to be heard. As this will be within bowshot, you will carry a white flag and walk in front of me. They will recognise you and this should reassure them that we do not intend any trickery. But be wise and remember that you are under oath, and there will be several crossbows aimed on you by our best marksmen. Make any mistakes and you are a dead man! You will translate for me if they do not understand my language.'

So saying, he told one of his squires to tie a white banner to the end of his lance. This was then thrust into Robert's hands, and he held it aloft, as high as he could with his bad shoulder. Prompted by de Mortagne, who quickly donned his helmet, he started walking towards the castle. He was feeling very weak and sick, and his head was throbbing. He stumbled over the uneven sward. Behind him he could hear the French commander's horse prancing. A quick glance round showed a line of archers at the edge of the trees, several with crossbows set and trained on him.

When he thought they were within hearing de Mortagne prompted Robert to speak. He summoned his strength and shouted. 'Hold your fire. This is Robert de Affeton. I am a hostage, and the French commander wants to negotiate with the captain. Please summon Sir Hugh. Hold your fire!'

He could hear this instruction being echoed inside the castle. More heads appeared at the battlements, to watch and to hear the exchanges. A voice came strongly back from the battlements, a voice that Robert recognised as that of Sir Hugh.

'Robert, this is Sir Hugh speaking. I see you are injured. Not badly, I hope! Tell the commander that we are secure with enough food and arms to withstand whatever siege he wants to inflict on us. What does he want to say?'

22 August 1377

Robert repeated this in French to de Mortagne, who replied, 'Tell the captain that we come not to make war on women and children, but to revenge the many who have died because of the wrongful English claims to French lands, and the unjust wars against France. We will only harm those who resist us. We have spared Caresbrooke the fire, and we will do the same with Nieuport if the castle is surrendered. The people will be allowed to go unmolested provided they do not resist.' He obviously did not expect the castle to fall so easily but had to go through the expected routine of the code of chivalry.

Robert shouted this to the castle. There was silence that appeared to stretch for minutes and he felt himself holding his breath for the answer. Sir Hugh was obviously consulting with others of the defence committee who might be with him. Standing in the hot sun and holding the lance aloft, Robert began to feel dizzy and light-headed. His heart was frantically beating, and the blood was pounding in his ears. He could feel his knees beginning to tremble, so he grounded the butt of the lance to take the strain off his arms, which felt like they were made of lead.

The answer came back. 'We will not surrender. The French had better return to their ships quickly and leave, for there will be reinforcements coming from the mainland within hours.'

When de Mortagne heard the translation he obviously thought it was a bluff. He snorted, and muttered under his breath about reinforcements being like a mirage to a thirsty man. He then said out loud, 'Be it as you will. You will regret your resistance. However, we will accept ransom for the young knight here for the sum of 200 marks.'

Again there was silence. Robert felt sick and he found his eyes would not focus properly. He blinked hard to try to clear his vision, but found that he could not keep the lance upright any longer despite his best efforts, the tip started drooping and the pounding in his ears became a rushing. All he could see was a pulsating red film and he collapsed to his knees. The lance slipped from his grasp as he slumped to the ground. He could not hear the answer that came from the battlements or the cry that came from Rachel.

De Mortagne looked at the slumped body with a sneer on his face but signalled for men-at-arms to come and carry Robert back out of range. One picked up the lance and handed it to the commander, and he followed them at a trot back to the cover of the trees.

★

To the watchers on the battlements it was not clear how big the force was that they could see approaching in the trees. From the keep the lookouts had been able to see the invaders pass through Caresbrooke and start across the stream towards the castle. Then all went quiet for almost half an hour, and people drifted away. When the French reappeared the shouts sent everyone back to the battlements and windows, and they watched in awestruck silence.

The group of knights led by the knight with the red cross on his surcoat made the circuit of the castle well out of bowshot, stopping every so often to appraise the state of the walls and the defences. At each stage the defending bowmen drew their bows just in case they could reach the foe, but it was too far, even though the height of the walls gave them added range.

Rachel was woken by the noise, and immediately ran to the window. She could see only the courtyard, not outside the walls, but the people were running with obvious urgency. The reason was obvious. Holding her finger to her lips, she woke Rebecca, who was still sitting on the floor asleep, leaning on the end of her father's bed. As he appeared to be calm and comfortable, they both tiptoed out of the room and hurried up to the battlements.

When the white flag was carried out across the grass it was not immediately apparent, except to Rachel, who the bearer was until he announced himself. Robert was bloodstained and dirty, his clothing torn and his body drooping. He was followed by the tall French knight, mounted on a prancing white palfrey bedecked with an ornate caparison. The knight had gleaming armour, and was wearing a modern style basinet that had a chain-mail eventail guarding the neck and shoulders. It would have been stifling inside, but the knight must have donned it especially to impress the defenders. The short white surcoat covering the body armour

22 August 1377

was emblazoned with a red-cross emblem similar to that of a Templar. Perhaps he was a warrior knight who believed in the same principles and had eschewed the vanities of the world to spread the word of Christendom and fight the infidel. Why he should be part of the French force caused puzzled comment and astonishment amongst the onlookers – was he a mercenary?

Rachel recognised Robert immediately he appeared and her heart leapt. She gasped and her hand went up to cover her mouth to prevent further cries. Tears flooded her eyes, but she wiped them away abruptly as she leant forward to get a better view of her lover. 'I knew he was alive,' she cried, 'but he's been wounded. Look at the bloodstains on his shirt.'

Rebecca took her hand. She, too, was agonising over her brother's apparent condition. Peter came hurrying around the parapet and put his consoling arms around them.

'Don't worry, my dears,' he said, 'he is too valuable for them to harm him any more. They will want to ransom him, I'll warrant.'

And he was proved right when the knight shouted his demand. But then Robert collapsed on the ground, and Rachel cried out his name in agony. She burst into tears again and could scarcely keep still, so deep was her agony of mental torture. Her hands twisted together, her shoulders hunched and her body appeared to shrink with the inner turmoil. A lesser woman might have fainted but she regained her composure as Robert was carried towards the trees.

Once the French had reached the safety of the trees a number of warning bolts from the invaders' crossbows rattled against the walls, or soared over into the courtyard – everyone involuntarily ducked. A scream came from a woman below who received a bolt in her thigh, but the children fought to collect the others. Rebecca started towards the steps to go and attend to the injured woman, but stopped when it was clear that there were many other people there looking after her.

'Peter,' Rachel asked pleadingly, 'can we raise the 200 marks they are asking? I have but ten in my purse, but Robert's father may have some, and perhaps we could raise the rest amongst the other lords.'

'Indeed we might, Rachel,' he answered, 'but it will take some time to get that sum together. It is a lot of money, and many will have buried their valuables rather than risk carrying them on the road. I am sure that they will be coming back to parley again, and there will be plenty of time yet.'

Sir Hugh came round the battlements just as Peter was talking, and agreed that there would be many other opportunities to respond to the ransom demand. 'It is quite possible they may reduce the asking price as they get other booty to satisfy their greed. I would be happy to contribute to the ransom but if we respond too readily they may increase their demands with other hostages they may capture. I think we must be cautious to start with, until we can see how the situation develops. I am sure he will be safe with them for the time being. They will not harm him.'

Rachel wanted to argue strongly the way her heart led her, but her head told her the rightness of Sir Hugh's reasoning. With patience, she knew all would work out eventually.

Looking from the battlements they could see that the attacking force had decreased in number. Though some of the French force remained in the trees, it was unclear whether the rest were just out of sight further away in the trees, or whether they had gone to join the other battalion attacking Nieuport.

Some of the lords who had gathered round Sir Hugh said that now was the time for a foray to catch the invaders when they were least expecting it. But Sir Hugh thought that it would be better to wait until they were well prepared in order to win such a battle. Because of the disarray within the castle it would be rash to embark on a sortie yet, especially as they didn't know precisely where the enemy was.

Though the men had trained into efficient fighting units over the last few months, only a fraction of the able-bodied men with fighting ability had managed to reach the castle. The men would have to be regrouped, arms would have to be issued and tested and new disciplines of combat understood. Fighting organised battles on open ground was a different matter from skirmishing from a strong castle into areas where, though the ground was familiar, the strength and disposition of the enemy was unknown.

22 August 1377

Time was needed to reorganise, and to weigh up the strengths and seek out the weaknesses of the enemy. These considerations had been fully discussed and agreed at the meeting of the defence council earlier that morning, and the principles remained correct now that events had come to a head.

Sir Hugh also resolved that in future the battlements would be out of bounds to all but the armed defenders and that women, children and non-combatants would have to remain below, or look from the narrow windows where they were safer from enemy arrows.

Once it was obvious that the immediate activity and excitement was over, the onlookers on the battlements began to drift away down the steps to the courtyard below. It was littered with the belongings of the refugees and with weapons ready for distribution to the men. After a further brief discussion between Sir Hugh, Peter and three of the other lords, they busied themselves in issuing orders to organise the chaos and get some space cleared for training.

The two ladies returned to the chamber in which Rebecca's father lay. As they climbed the steps up to the room Rebecca gasped, stopped and pressed her hand beneath her belly. Strain showed in her eyes and in the tension around her mouth. She gasped again and bit her lip.

'I think that my time is near. The birth pains have started.'

Rachel, who was leading the way, turned with concern, took her hand and helped her into the chamber where Sir Roger lay sleeping.

'Sit down on that chair,' she said. 'I will go and get the midwife and tell Peter. Will you be all right while I do?'

Rebecca, with white face and pursed lips, nodded, and Rachel ran from the room.

High above them on the parapet of the keep the lookout shouted that he could see fighting around the western gate to Nieuport, and the masts of French ships coming up the Medine.

NIEUPORT

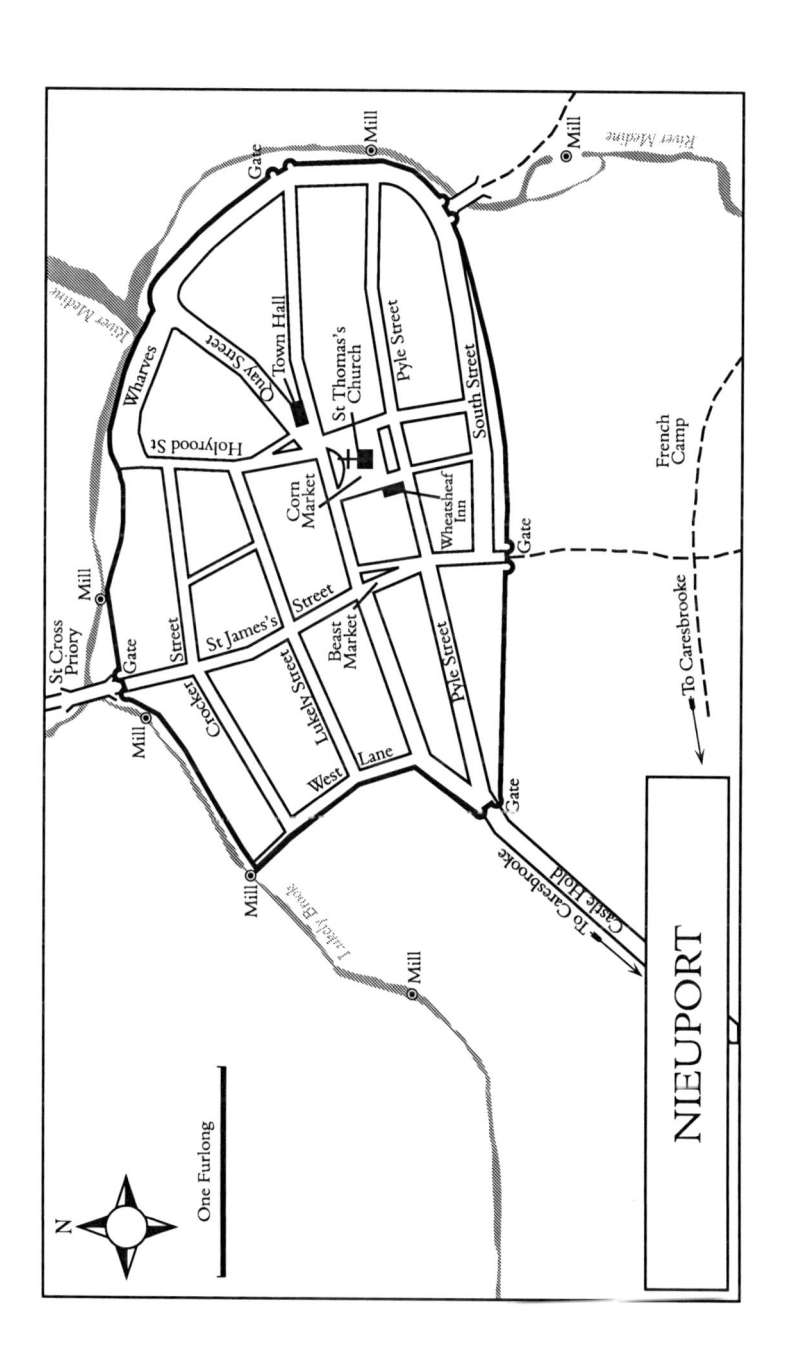

22 August 1377

Morning (Nieuport)

John de Kingston was in a bad temper when he awoke, despite having slept well. He had one of his customary headaches, and was feeling rather dopey. It was not unexpected as the migraines always seemed to come after some emotional upset; it would probably pass after an hour or two.

He had ridden to Nieuport late the previous afternoon in a black mood following the argument with Rachel. The ride had been a silent one, the two servants accompanying him casting wary glances, careful not to incur an outburst of his wrath. Normally such a ride through the lanes and byways of the island would have lightened his mood and lifted his spirit. But he pondered on his daughter's stated love for this lad de Affeton, whom he would have to welcome to his house in a couple of days. In his eyes the young man was but a country landlord, with little wealth or social standing, even though the Affeton estates were extensive around Freshwater and Yarmouth. He loved his daughter dearly, and one part of him wanted her to be happy above all else, but the other side of him kept insisting that she was worth better.

Did he really want to have his estates tied to parochial Islanders as part of Rachel's dowry? Eventually everything would pass to her husband when he died. Would de Affeton be worthy of this inheritance? Would a grandson grow up to be Kingston or Affeton?

He realised he knew little of de Affeton. The fair the previous month had been the only time he had really taken any notice of the man as anything other than a youthful acquaintance who was on the fringes of his consciousness, someone who did not weigh much in his affairs. There was nothing that Robert had done to gain his respect or make him think that Robert was equal to the task of siring and raising his grandson in a manner befitting the Kingston ancestry.

He would have to decide how he was going to receive Robert. He would have to get used to the idea of calling him Robert! Was he going to agree to a betrothal or refuse to countenance the idea – and risk Rachel's turning against him and running away and marrying the man anyway?

He could not decide. He would have to mull it over and try to make his mind up. Perhaps friends in Nieuport could help shed light on the tricky subject and help him with useful information that might clarify some of his worries.

That evening he had dined with a burgess of the town, who knew all there was to know about everyone and everything on the Island. They had eaten very well and had continued drinking good Gascony wine until after dark. De Kingston had discreetly found out more about the Affeton family without disclosing the reasons for his interest. What he heard inclined him a bit more favourably towards the suitor: the family had very good connections on the mainland through Robert's mother, and his father had been valiant in the French wars, being dubbed a knight on the battlefield. Apparently Robert had shown the same honour in his service as squire to the Duke of York, had been wounded while saving the life of a friend and was looked upon with considerable favour by that lord.

De Kingston had been aware that Robert had served abroad, but these details explained why Robert had surprised him by being such a good marksman and so proficient at the joust. Perhaps his daughter's choice had not been so bad after all! Uncharacteristically, he wavered between one decision and the other. Normally he was prone to making a quick decision and being prepared to live with the consequences.

It was during their drinking and conversing that messengers had arrived. The first came from the castle at Caresbrooke, sent by the captain Sir Hugh, saying that there were reports of French invading Yarmouth, and advising the people of Nieuport to take refuge in the castle until the situation became clearer. The Elder Bailiff immediately called the burgesses together, to discuss what

22 August 1377

should be done. De Kingston had been included in the meeting out of courtesy, because he was one of the King's magistrates.

The burgesses were divided. Some thought that the reports must be exaggerated and tinged with panic. There was a history of rivalry and disagreement between the town and the castle. The town resented having to pay taxes for support of the castle and the infringement of what they saw as their liberty to trade and to make money. This was exacerbated by the town's people having to erect and maintain defences at their own expense, with little support from the castle.

The dissenters argued it was not worth the trouble to round up all the people and trek up to the castle, only to have to return the following day when it became obvious that the reports were unfounded or exaggerated. What was the point, if they had adequate defences, in abandoning them and running away at the first sign of trouble? Surely with a town the size of Nieuport the French would be loath to attack. It was well defended, after all! Anyway, if everyone retreated to the castle it would leave all the houses and businesses open to looting by the French invaders.

A minority took the opposite view: they had better go, just in case. What was the use of worldly wealth if one lost one's life, or had one's family injured? The memory of the last French incursion was still fresh in their minds.

The arguments went round and round for a long time, with first one faction gaining support, and then another. Words such as 'cowardly', 'complacent', 'pessimistic' and 'optimistic' were used; the atmosphere became heated.

De Kingston, too, was torn. He felt that he should go to his family but, on the other hand, he knew that they were far from any immediate danger in the south of the island, and he had his duty to perform in the court the following day. It would not give a very good impression if the King's Justice were to turn tail and run at the smallest sign.

He was due to hear evidence at a murder case: where a merchant from Brading was accused of killing a sailor from one of the trading vessels who, it was alleged, had attacked him after he had caught the sailor watering down the wine in the barrels. However, some said that it was the sailor who had caught the merchant diluting the wine. Since the King took a duty on the wine imports, and claimed two casks in every load as prisage, a watered-down barrel represented a considerable gain for both the sailor and the merchant, and a loss of tax. The trial had already been delayed too long, with the merchant languishing in the town gaol, and his friends agitating for action.

Just when the argument between the burgesses seemed to be converging on caution, the second messenger arrived. He came from the Brading area in the East Medine with reports of French landing at St Helen's and attacking Nunwell and Brading. Immediately the supporters of doing nothing saw this as evidence of confusion on behalf of Sir Hugh, and they voted that the town gates should be locked until daybreak, and that the town militia should be alerted and guards posted. Come the morning, the situation should become clearer.

This motion was passed by the majority of burgesses and the meeting broke up, with some going to their beds and others setting out to tell the captain of the militia to see the gates were locked. A few were determined to set out for the castle, incurring the scorn of their fellows, but in the end they were turned back at the closed gates by the guards. No one thought it worthwhile to send a message to the castle passing on the town's decision.

There had been a small crowd outside the town hall, waiting to hear what they should do, and they were visibly relieved when they were told to go to their beds. De Kingston also decided that he might as well go to bed, but not before he had walked to the gates and seen the guards being posted. He sent a message to his servants saying that he would meet them in the late afternoon of the morrow, as previously arranged. They had a number of purchases to make on his behalf in the markets and from the merchants, which would keep them busy enough. Then, leaving instructions that he should be called if any further news arrived, he too retired.

As usual he had stayed the night in the Wheatsheaf tavern, while his men lodged in a boarding house down by the quay. This tavern, one of the two best in the town, overlooked the corn market, on the opposite side to the church of St Thomas. Elsewhere in the town were the butter and beast markets, so it

22 August 1377

was difficult to find anywhere less noisy. Because the markets would normally be a bustle of activity early in the morning, he had learned to his cost on his first visit that he would be disturbed early if he had insisted on the best room, which was at the front of the building: the clamour began long before daybreak as the carts arrived laden with produce, were unloaded, and trading started. Consequently, the room he had now was at the back, quiet and comfortable.

He was awoken by a knock on the door and, following his growl, a maid came timidly into the room carrying a pitcher of water and a bowl. De Kingston was by now a regular visitor, as he sat in court regularly, and the landlord and his servants had become used to his foibles and had set up a routine that satisfied him. The maid placed the water carefully on a table and, with a small curtsey, went out. A few moments later she was back with a platter of cheese, meat and bread, and a pitcher of ale.

De Kingston threw off the covers, went to the window and opened the shutters wide, scratching with annoyance at a fleabite under his left armpit. He surveyed the scene as he chewed on some of the food. The room looked out over a jumble of roofs, in various states of repair, nearly all of them thatched. Some looked as if they wouldn't keep out even the lightest shower of rain, whereas others were freshly thatched or repaired. One or two houses even had chimneys, which were a comparatively new innovation. Between the houses were many trees, orchards and gardens, forming extensions of the countryside into the town. Somewhere a cow lowed, asking to be milked, and there were cockerels crowing from several of the yards. It was a pleasing view, mixing the rural with the urban, normally quiet, peaceful and full of birdsong.

Nieuport was the main town of the Island, and had a population of upward of a thousand people, but very few were rich. Most made a living tilling the fields around the town, trading with the villages, and selling their skills as artisans across the Island – thatchers were in great demand, judging by the state of the roofs. The merchants who brought goods in from the mainland and sent back wool, woven cloth and local produce were the ones who were rich, rich enough to employ servants, grooms and maids. But even they did not have the same status as the lords of the manors, whose time could be spent hunting, knowing that their villeins would be doing the work for them, and supporting them with their dues of produce and labour. Nevertheless some of the lords had duties of their own.

De Kingston was aware that times were changing and that he would have to change too, but it was too easy to carry on in the ways he had been brought up with. Today his conscience was pricking him. Perhaps he should have gone to his home last night after all, and escorted his wife and beloved daughter to safety. He thought about Rachel, the daughter that came instead of the son that he had so dearly wanted. She was headstrong, he knew, and smiled as he thought of the arguments they had had. It hurt him to think she was so like him, but also gave him great satisfaction to see his own characteristics being passed on through the generations, just as he had inherited them from his own father and mother. Since she knew her own mind, and was as determined as he was, perhaps it would be better having Robert as a son-in-law than some of the other suitors he had tried to get Rachel to agree to marry. Some had been as old as he was, others too soft, with no spine. He regretted his choices, and was secretly pleased that Rachel had refused them. Perhaps he should receive and welcome Robert, and judge him more seriously later.

He pulled himself out of his reverie and gave himself the luxury of a comprehensive wash. Feeling better, and with the intensity of the headache diminishing, he dressed, strapped on his sword, went downstairs and out into the market to try to find out what news had come in, and whether anything had transpired in the night. Despite the rumours of invasion, there was a crowd of yeomen and franklins come to the market with corn for sale, so the town gates must have opened at daybreak.

Since it was August, only the winter-sown wheat and rye had been harvested; the Lenten seed would be harvested later in the month and in September. Sacks were being unloaded from carts, the men straining to lift them. Some carts also had fresh hay, smelling sweet and fragrant. The large bushel bags of the corn were stacked in piles, one with its top open so that the buyers could feel the grain, crack it beneath their fingernails, feel the

22 August 1377

moisture of it, and smell that it was fresh and without mildew. The vendors would also be selling for their local cottars, and taking a portion of the grain in payment for their trouble. The cottars would have kept enough for themselves for the winter, and for seed for the next harvest; in good years there would be enough left over to sell. In bad years they would have to eat their seed corn and then borrow money to buy the seed for the next sowing. But this looked like a good year.

The grain was fat and golden, the smell of it filled the air with its dry sweetness, and the dust danced in the early morning sunbeams. The prices were always low if there was a good harvest and the farmers would grumble, but they took a measure of satisfaction in the grumbles; at least there would be enough to last the winter and for seed, so hunger would not be a problem for the next year.

Pigeons and sparrows were trying to steal a breakfast from the spilt grain but fluttered away between people's legs whenever they got too close. Several dirty, barefooted little boys also scrabbled on their knees collecting the grain and putting it in their pockets to take home to their mothers for the family meal.

There weren't as many people present as on a normal day. Some of the people had heard of the possibility of invasion and hadn't come; others had come despite the news. Though there was an air of uncertainty, the fact that all seemed normal acted as reassurance, and it looked very much like business as usual. Nevertheless, there was a certain tension, as if everyone was mentally looking over their shoulders, especially those who had not heard of the reported attacks before they reached the town. They demanded new information from all they met. Speculation was rife as to whether there was actually an invasion or not. Small knots of people formed, shared opinions and then split up, only to reform elsewhere.

Nevertheless, millers and merchants walked round the market plunging their hands deep in the bags to ensure that the best had not just been placed at the top, and haggling over prices. Each merchant had an assistant or two to mark the purchases and settle the accounting.

There were six mills around Nieuport, four on the Lukely Brook, which formed the northern side of the town. One of these was owned by St Cross Priory. The other two were on the

Morning (Nieuport)

Medine to the east. The millers were always prominent as purchasers of the best grain, most of them being well dressed and portly, full of their own importance.

One or two of them noticed de Kingston standing in the tavern doorway and acknowledged him, doffing their hats and muttering words of greeting. One, a burgess who had taken part in the arguments of the night before, came across to tell him there had been no further news from either east or west of the veracity of the various reports, and he thought that it was all scaremongering. He was sure they had come to the correct conclusion, but nevertheless, as a precaution, the armoury was being opened and all the able-bodied men would be issued with swords and bows and arrows.

De Kingston thanked him and was relieved. He was sure that if the reports were correct they would have heard more before now. However, there was still a nagging doubt in the back of his mind that Sir Hugh was unlikely to make a mistake over such an important issue. Perhaps he had considered that being prepared was the wisest course of action under the circumstances.

He moved along the wall of the tavern to avoid the press of people in the market and went into the barber's shop round the corner in the High Street. Despite the fact that it was full, he was shaved immediately, someone else giving up a place for him. Giving the barber a penny, he returned to the tavern to finish his breakfast and fetch his court papers. After that he felt in better humour, ready for anything the day could offer.

He crossed the market square and went down a narrow alley behind the church. This brought him out into the main street almost opposite the town hall. In front of it was a dense throng of men and young lads grouped round the steps leading down to the armoury, which was in the cellar below the hall. They had formed into two lines. Each man in one line was being issued with a bow, from the long chests in which they were stored. They then took a sheaf of arrows wrapped in canvas from the barrels, and inspected the flights to make sure they were still well attached and not damaged. The second line was for the issue of swords.

The Elder Bailiff and his deputies were arranging shifts of men for sentry duty at the gates and on the ramparts surrounding

22 August 1377

the town. In all there must have been about 200 men who could be called on to defend the town, though some were rather old and weak, and some very young. At least half that number again were attending the markets. Together they would make a formidable force, and all were reasonably well trained although untested in real conflict.

De Kingston went up the steps into the town hall and found the clerk who would be administering the court proceedings. The plaintiff had been brought from the cells, but many of the witnesses had yet to arrive, even though the time for the trial was approaching. He suggested that the start of the proceedings should be delayed for an hour and decided in that time to go to the western gates to judge for himself the state of readiness of the guard.

Just at that moment the big bass bell in St Thomas's Church started slowly tolling – the general alarm call!

His heart gave a lurch, and he cursed under his breath as he started running up the High Street, his sword banging against his thigh. People were standing frozen and open-mouthed looking at the church tower. Though they knew well enough the significance of the bell, they were too shocked for it to register and spur them into movement. Some of the women shrieked and burst into tears, calling for their children.

'The Noddies must be attacking. Get your weapons. Man the ramparts,' de Kingston bellowed. He urged some of the men into movement as he pushed past them, others he had to strike to get them moving. As they came out of their daze they started running too, and the movement spread until everyone was hurrying, some to their homes to find their families and children, some towards the armoury and some to the town walls.

In the middle of the beast market, a heaving mass of bellowing oxen and cattle were penned. The animals had been upset by the bells, and they were bucking and rearing, smashing down the hurdles keeping them in. Some of the men were trying to quieten them down and reinforce the fences, as it would be no help at all to have rampaging cattle roaming the streets while the defence was being organised.

De Kingston ran on up the High Street towards the western gate, his heart still pounding. He could see that the gates were

Morning (Nieuport)

shut and there was a crowd of militia clambering onto the ramparts on either side.

The gate was sited on a right-angled bend in the defences; it was an obvious point for attack, as the defenders would have to cover a wide angle of fire. To the right, the ramparts ran down the gentle slope to the Lukely Brook, where they again turned at a water mill and ran eastwards beside the brook, which formed a good natural line of defence, towards the town wharves. To the left of the gate the ramparts ran around the southern side of the town towards the Medine.

He climbed up the inner side of the bank and up the steps on to the walkway that ran around inside the wooden palisade. The palisade was pierced at intervals with embrasures so a watch could be kept with a certain amount of protection, and through which archers could shoot without being totally exposed.

He pulled an archer away from an embrasure so that he could see what was happening outside. There was a fall of about ten feet down to the sloping earth rampart, and a surrounding moat about six feet deep that was full of scrub, brambles and thorn bushes. Beyond that, fields stretched away to the woods and in the distance, peeping over the trees, the keep of the castle could be seen.

About 200 yards away a column of French men-at-arms was spreading out parallel to the walls, just out of bowshot. The knights' horses were being led to the rear and shield walls were being constructed for the protection of the archers. Undoubtedly other men were busy cutting branches in the woods to build more substantial protective barriers. A number of wooden ladders were being brought forward. Attack was imminent.

The church bell had stopped its mournful warning, and there was an unnatural silence, with only the distant cries of the invaders, and the scramble of townsfolk on to the ramparts to be heard.

One of the burgesses organising the defenders had marshalled a number of archers into a reasonably sized group and had ordered them to spread out along the palisade and to start shooting at any who came in range. However, the French were wary, and judged well the range of the English longbows. The arrows generally fell short, much to the defender's dismay.

22 August 1377

There was a sudden swish and a scream, a cry of mortal agony. One of the archers collapsed to the ground, a crossbow bolt sticking out of his hard leather head cap. He slumped to the ground but was dead before he got there. His neighbour crossed himself as he knelt to cradle his fellow in his arms. When he realised the man was dead he pulled him out of the way and took his place. Another bolt thudded into the wooden palisade beside de Kingston.

'Get down,' he shouted. 'Take cover!'

Many of the archers had not experienced crossbow fire before, or had forgotten that crossbows could shoot farther than their longbows, though at a much slower rate. Longbows were most effective when used en masse in the open against moving troops. In siege conditions crossbows could be deadly picking off individuals.

Peeping through an embrasure, de Kingston could see a lone horseman riding round the town from the south across the fields through the crops. He headed towards the group of knights that, de Kingston guessed, contained the leader. There was much gesticulating and earnest discussion, and the horseman rode back the way he had come. The knights then dispersed towards their respective platoons.

De Kingston realised that there must be another group of the enemy elsewhere, but inside the town they had heard nothing from other sectors of the defences as to whether they were confronted by attackers. Since no communication system had been set up within the town, the defences would be uncoordinated and there would be major problems if attacks came from several places at once. It was essential that messengers relayed information so that reinforcements could be sent to parts of the ramparts under pressure.

De Kingston turned to the burgess commanding the gate, saying, 'I think there might be more French troops to the south and east of the town. We need information from further along. You, lad!' he shouted at a youth hovering frightened in the background. 'We must find out what is happening on the other quarters of the town. Go and see! Tell them that we have a force of about 200 French forming up to attack. Bring us back information on what the situation is elsewhere.'

Morning (Nieuport)

The youth ran off, relieved to have something positive to do, especially something that took him away from the immediate danger.

There followed a period of quiet while little seemed to happen. The French had formed into an attack pattern with groups of archers spaced some dozen or so yards apart, and supported by a knight or two and some men-at-arms with swords and shields. In the trees behind, the horses were being tethered by the younger squires. The archers were well accoutred, some groups dressed in brown jupons and some others in black, green or red. Most likely these were platoons or divisions owing allegiance to one or other of the knights and coming from the same town or region. Their crossbows were strung and drawn, with bolts in place ready for firing. They were not talking to each other, but were looking fixedly ahead as if keyed up and concentrating on some distant mental target. They were obviously waiting for the signal to begin the attack. And the defenders were still not adequately organised.

The messenger came running back and pushed his way up to where de Kingston and the burgess were standing at the ramparts. He was gasping for breath and sweat was running down his face and staining his shirt.

'Sire,' he puffed, 'there are French troops crossing the ford to the east of the town and French ships are coming up the Medine. There must be a thousand or more, counting those here. The Elder Bailiff says that we should consider parleying for terms; we cannot hold out against so many. He is going to show a white flag of truce.'

However, before anything could be done, a trumpet blast sounded from the other side of the town, and it was echoed by another, and another from the troops before them. De Kingston drew his sword as a shout of triumph came from the French. This must be the signal they had been waiting for.

Each group of archers started moving progressively forward. The front rank moved several paces behind the cover of their shields. They stopped, raised their crossbows, took aim on a target, either someone on the ramparts, or a longer higher shot over the palisade into the streets, with the chance of hitting

22 August 1377

someone beyond. When they had fired, the second rank moved through the first and they themselves fired, while the first rank reloaded. Then the third rank moved through to fire, by which time the first could shoot again. All the while there was a protecting screen of moving shields.

Those who could watch the flight of the arrows ducked as the bolts thudded into the wooden stockade, or went over into the streets and buildings behind. Cries of agony showed that many of them hit their mark.

'Right men!' shouted de Kingston. 'Steady! They will be in range of your longbows shortly. You can shoot faster than they can, but we have only a few arrows. Pick your targets well, and don't waste arrows. We must stop them before they can rush us. When they are in range, shoot as you will.'

A chorus of cheers rose from the defenders, which was more to help boost their flagging confidence, in the face of such well-trained men and such a disciplined attack, than any feeling of impending victory. They dried their sweaty palms on their clothing, so as to hold the bows more firmly, and several turned to their neighbours and wished them God's grace.

The defenders' arrows began to soar towards the attackers, but there were pitifully few of them; it was obvious that the defenders were outnumbered. Along their sector of the ramparts, which was about a hundred yards long, there were only about twenty archers, and half a dozen men-at-arms with swords – scarcely one soldier every twelve feet. Each archer had a sheaf of four dozen arrows, enough to last at most five minutes of shooting at maximum speed. They had to conserve their stocks and shoot sparingly when they were sure of a hit. They could not call on reinforcements either, because they could hear the shouts and screams from the other quarters of the town as they, too, were assailed simultaneously.

A grunt came from the man to de Kingston's right, and he slid to the ground with a bolt protruding from his chest. De Kingston dropped his sword, grabbed the bow and, nocking an arrow into the string, drew and aimed at one of the advancing crossbowmen. He missed and cursed roundly. He quickly drew the bow again, and had the satisfaction of seeing his target fall and remain squirming on the ground as the phalanx of the French bowmen marched on, stepping over and around him. Very few of the defenders' arrows were finding their mark, judging by the small number of the attackers being left behind lying on the ground or limping back to safety.

The advancing foe were now within a hundred paces or so of the ramparts and with another trumpet call they all started running, their kettle helmets bobbing up and down over their eyes and their shields held high. One rank stopped to act as marksmen to keep the defenders' heads down, and allow the others to get across the moat to the foot of the ramparts. Ladders appeared at the back of the attacking force and these were rapidly brought to the fore to be put against the ramparts. The defenders were now very exposed, because to fire on the French below them in the moat or on the ramparts meant leaning out of the embrasures in full view of the marksmen. Several who tried were quickly left draped over the wooden walls with arrows through them. Few of the attackers were injured by the defenders' efforts.

Within no time at all the ladders were in place and the French were clambering up, swords in hand, knights and men-at-arms leading. The marksmen below could not fire now, because of the risk of hitting their own men. They dropped their crossbows, took the swords out of the belts and ran in to start to ascend the ladders too. One of the ladders was pushed away with a long pike in time to tip off the attackers before they reached the top. Elsewhere, the defenders hacked at the first man up the ladder, but the knights were well armoured with heavy helmets and chain mail, and little impression could be made on them. The attackers clambered through the embrasures and were soon in hand-to-hand combat with defenders on the walkway.

De Kingston had thrown down his bow and, with his sword in one hand and a small shield in the other, met one of the first knights to clamber up the ladder nearest to him. A hefty swipe knocked the knight off balance, but he recovered before de Kingston could get in close enough to strike again. The knight was tall and powerful, with a harness of shiny Italian plate and a bascinet surmounted by an eagle's wing covering his head – obviously one of the leaders, de Kingston thought. This

22 August 1377

contrasted with de Kingston's attire. He had no helmet, so that the white streak in his hair showed distinctively, and he only had a rather ornate cloth cote, and breeches. Nevertheless, he was a commanding figure, obviously one of the local lords or dignitaries.

The knight and de Kingston cut and parried, thrust and side-stepped, and circled round each other, oblivious of what was going on around them, and of the other attackers swarming over the palisade. Their swords clashed and sparks flew. The other combats gradually ceased as the defenders one by one conceded defeat, were killed or wounded. Extra space was created as the other fighters moved aside and watched their leaders clashing.

De Kingston managed to get through his opponent's defence and struck him heavily on his helmet. The knight drew back for a second, but then counter-attacked vigorously. De Kingston was the older of the two and rapidly realised that his opponent was at least his equal in experience, and had the advantage of being somewhat younger. However, he didn't have the weight of armour to carry, and wile could take the place of youthful strength. He started to draw the man forward, trying to get him off balance. A thrust and a step back, which the knight followed with a counter-thrust meant the knight had his weight on his right foot. A quick step to the left forced the knight to step around to the right, a movement that is not easy with the encumbrance of armour. He was marginally off balance, and with a quick movement de Kingston caught him with a cut across his back. Because of the armour the knight was not blooded, but the blow hurt him, and he grunted, more with surprise than pain.

De Kingston immediately attacked with his sword swinging, each swing being accompanied by a sharp exhalation of breath. The knight gave ground, and warily parried. They circled and the knight then attacked with his sword swinging. This time it was de Kingston's turn to retreat, and he took a blow on his shield denting it badly. Both started to tire and slow down.

De Kingston was not aware what was happening around him until his opponent suddenly drew back, lowered his sword and reached up and took off his helmet. Looking around him de Kingston realised that the defenders had lost. There were many bodies lying contorted, and injured, nursing wounds often pouring with blood, with their victors standing over them. He was surrounded by French swords all pointed at him. There was no way in which he would be allowed to win. There was no alternative but for him to either surrender or be killed outright. He lowered his sword until its tip was on the ground and he bowed proudly in defeat.

'Well fought, sir knight,' de Kingston exclaimed, searching for the French words that he used to know so well, but which were now rather rusty. 'It appears that I have to concede that victory is yours. Whom do I have the honour of crossing swords with?'

The haughty manner and the pointed beard showed the distinction of the victor. However, his cheeks were red with exertion, and he was breathing heavily. A satisfied smile lifted the corners of his mouth, but his eyes stayed cold and sharp.

'I think that you must consider yourself my prisoner, monsieur, though you have acquitted yourself with honour. Give me your sword and your word not to interfere, and you will not be harmed.' He sheathed his sword and took off one of his gauntlets. 'I am the Duc de Beauvais. And your name?'

'My name is John de Kingston,' he replied, understanding the gist of what was said. 'You have taken the main town on the Island, but it is poor, and of little wealth. You will find it more difficult to take the castle at Caresbrooke.' He pointed to the castle keep in the distance; he couldn't help boasting a little to take some of the satisfaction away from the victors.

Just then another French knight came up and made it obvious that the town had fallen and that the French were in complete control. De Beauvais smiled with satisfaction, while some of the French archers raised a cheer.

'We have plans for the castle that we will carry out in due course. Meanwhile you are likely to be a valuable hostage, and I can see you should command a goodly ransom. You are my prisoner and I put you under oath of chivalry not to try to escape or harm my men. Now lead me to the mayor and the chief citizens of the town. I wish to make a proposition to them.'

De Kingston did not understand all that was said, but guessed correctly what the meaning was.

22 August 1377

De Beauvais gave orders to his entourage of knights who were gradually assembling. Men were detailed to stay on guard, in case of a counter-attack or foray from the castle. Others had specific instructions for disarming the militia and impounding all the townspeople's weapons. Gesturing imperiously, he gave instructions that the dead should be prepared for burial, and the wounded given assistance. This was taken to mean both the invaders and the defenders, but the surviving Islanders were already seeing to their friends and compatriots.

De Beauvais descended to the street, where some of his men were opening the gates to let in the rest of the French troops. He turned and, beckoning de Kingston to follow him, strode down the street towards the beast market. Behind them followed a column of the enemy who peered around at the unfamiliar English streets and houses, and menaced everyone they saw, driving them down the road, sending children running, and making the womenfolk cover their faces in fear.

When they reached the market it was obvious that the fighting had continued right into the heart of the town. Several bodies lay in pools of blood, which gave off a distinctive sickly smell. The occasional Frenchman was being covered with cloth while the Islanders' bodies were being dragged into a pile at the side of the market square. Groups of dejected townspeople were being herded by armed Frenchmen who were pushing them with their shields, or the flat of their swords, and swearing and cursing at them. Some of the women were crying, with their children clutching their hands or hiding behind their skirts. Others were helping those wounded in the fighting, and binding up their wounds. The remnants of the fighting men wearily, but proudly, marched along, now disarmed and closely watched by the wary crossbowmen.

De Beauvais stepped on to one of the mounting blocks that were placed round the square for the convenience of horsemen. He surveyed the congregation of townsfolk with a look of disdain, not seeing very much of fashion or wealth in their dress and accoutrements. They were simply peasants of the enemy, people who could be stamped on and cast aside because of the needs of war.

He waited for some minutes, flicking imaginary dirt off his armour, and conversing quietly with his knights. De Kingston stood to one side between two men-at-arms who intimidated him with unsheathed swords. Many of the people looked at him, recognised him as a captive and whispered to each other.

Then there was a flurry of activity in a side street and the Elder Bailiff and some of the burgesses were ushered out, surrounded by armed guards. They were pushed before De Beauvais and forced to their knees. They looked a sorry sight, with all of their dignity gone. The Elder Bailiff had a fashionable hat, which was composed of the end of a long coiled liripipe, which would normally have hung down his back like a long tubular stocking. This was now askew over one eye and partly uncoiled, looking more like a pile of old washing. He also had a hole in the knee of his hose and dirt all down the front of his brown velvet jacket. He was not an impressive sight, though he tried to keep as much dignity as he could.

The other burgesses also formed a pitiful group, with dishevelled clothing, dirty and torn. Some of them had obviously put up resistance, or been involved in the fighting, and had been manhandled with a certain amount of brutality as a consequence. One had blood running down his face, and a rapidly closing eye, puffed and swollen, and turning purple. Another was holding an arm that may well have been broken. After kneeling for a few minutes, some of the weaker ones collapsed and ended sitting in the muck of the market square.

De Beauvais' voice rang out clearly above the general murmuring and shuffling. As he spoke in French not many understood what he said, though the meaning was fairly obvious.

'We have no fight with women and children, only with those who resist us. We have taken this town; you have resisted and we have dead and wounded to revenge. What ransom will you give us? Unless you pay we will take further retribution. We will burn your town to the ground, and hang your menfolk! Bring out your money, your jewellery, and your valuables, and let me see whether there is enough payment to satisfy my men. First of all you,' said he, pointing at the Elder Bailiff, 'what have you to give us?'

22 August 1377

The mayor cringed, and muttered something about the town plate being but poor, and not even of silver, and anyway the key being in the hands of someone who he knew had been killed. The Duke laughed at him, recognising the attempted excuses, without understanding the English the man gabbled. He drew his sword and with a wave swept the hat off the man's head. A second swipe sliced the front of his jacket wide open, and left a cut from which blood welled up and ran down his fat belly. The Elder Bailiff turned grey and fell flat on his face, sobbing and crying for mercy in the name of Our Lady.

'Enough of these excuses! You will take us to where these pieces are kept, or my sword will cut deeper and more often.' Then to everyone else he shouted, 'Go to your houses and bring out the ransom, otherwise the town will be put to the torch. Anyone who shows a weapon or harms my men will be killed.'

The Elder Bailiff and burgesses were hauled to their feet and prodded to lead the way to the town hall where they had to open the chest in which the town silver was kept. The Duke ran his hands through the contents and held up one or two of the pieces to the light. He grimaced at their poor quality and their light weight. Nevertheless, the chest was hauled out and loaded into a nearby cart, ready to be taken down to the wharf and loaded onto a French ship.

The Duke was not satisfied with this ransom and sent each of the burgesses back to their homes to add their own valuables to the collection. Armed guards ensured they did not hide any valuables instead of bringing them back to the communal sacrifice.

The Duke then gave instructions to his knights and squires to start a separate search of all the properties to confiscate goods and chattels, and to organise collection of food and drink for the men. De Kingston watched these deliberations with sinking heart, thinking of the possibility of his manor being ransacked and his family being treated in the same way. He could do nothing, nor go anywhere.

De Beauvais went into the council chamber followed by the rest of his knights. He sat in the Elder Bailiff's seat at the head of the table, and put his feet upon it. Taking a drink from a cup that was put before him, he started a council of war. After some discussion, the Duke decided to make camp for his men on the open common land to the south of the town, rather than billet them in the town. There were too many townsfolk and there was too great a risk of a night-time attack against the invaders while dispersed and asleep if they were billeted separately in the town. To minimise risk, the town gates could be shut and barred, and guards could ensure that all the townsfolk remained inside. Then, in the camp, they would be much safer, especially if all the hidden weapons could be found and confiscated. A curfew would ensure the townsfolk stayed in their houses, and this would be enforced by regular patrols. Other patrols were sent out to scout the surrounding countryside, to round up horses to improve the invading troop's mobility, to find more ox carts for carrying booty to the ships, and further supplies of food, drink and arms, and, of course, to loot and pillage.

22 August 1377

Afternoon/Evening

Eventually de Kingston was taken out to the site of the camp. The spot they had chosen was only half a mile to the south of the town and situated on a slight hill of common land. It was only about fifty feet higher than the town, but as the land was clear of hedges and trees there was a complete view of the town, the river and the land away to the north. The common land continued south of the camp over fields and small coppices, so the campsite would be difficult to take by surprise, provided it was adequately guarded.

From the town some columns of smoke were beginning to rise, despite de Beauvais having ordered no wholesale burning. Beyond, de Kingston could see the masts of at least twenty ships moored in the Medine River. He was sure that not all of them were French and some of them must be English trading ships captured while at anchor or unloading at the quays. Undoubtedly they would be commandeered to help carry back to France the goods and valuables that were worth taking. Nevertheless, upward of a dozen of the ships must have been French. When added to those remaining at Yarmouth and Francheville it made a very large force. He wondered how many more there must have been at Brading or St Helen's, since additional invaders had obviously come from the east in the concerted raid. It was no wonder that the town had fallen so quickly when being attacked from two directions by land, as well as from the water. This was much more than the defenders could be expected to withstand, despite their valour.

Defences were quickly being constructed around the camp. Many of the soldiers were weaving a palisade out of brushwood, fastened with sharpened stakes set only a foot or so apart, and set at an angle pointing outwards so as to impale any prospective attackers. Even though it was only about four feet high, it would be very effective against both foot soldiers and cavalry, despite its simplicity. Entrances were being made on each of the four sides. These comprised an eight-feet-wide gap in the palisade, but each one was protected by a further stretch of palisade in front and overlapping it on either side. Though obvious weak points, they would be easy enough to guard and defend. The main problem would be having to zigzag through the tight bends in a cart, especially an oxcart, as these creatures were only used to going in straight lines.

Inside the defences, rows of simple lean-to shelters separated by wide avenues were being built, each large enough for two men, and their equipment. Two forked sticks about four feet long were thrust into the ground about six feet apart, and a long straight hazel, or ash branch between them formed the ridge. Then other branches rested against the ridge and these were covered with leaves and long grass. The majority of them were set out with the open side facing north, giving them cool shelter from the sun during the day, and some protection from the prevailing wind. Groups of six or ten of these shelters were located around a central fire so that communal cooking could be done, relieving those on guard duty from other tasks. Each man would have to take his turn at standing guard and at other duties, such as cooking, fetching water and supplies, and sleeping, as well as soldiering.

De Kingston was guarded by a man-at-arms who walked warily with his hand always on the hilt of his sword and one eye on his charge. He was one of de Beauvais' squires, but was morose and disinclined to talk. He probably felt that the duty he had been given was too far from the glory and excitement, and was really a punishment of some sort.

Because no command otherwise had been given, de Kingston felt free to walk about at will within the compound. He set out to make a complete circuit of the camp, the guard trailing after him. He found his knowledge of French gradually returning the more he heard the language spoken, and he listened surreptitiously to the conversations, for it was always surprising how much information could be gleaned from the ordinary men. Some of the crossbowmen were mercenaries from Genoa. It was obvious that Charles V had a very definite interest in the expedition. De Kingston was amazed to hear that there were similar raids in progress at the same time elsewhere on the south coast of England – he heard Rye and Hastings mentioned. So this wasn't just a skirmish, but a well-planned and thoroughly organised series of concerted raids aimed at harassing the English. Could it be that there was a subtle agenda and the French were intending to remain in occupation of the Island for a long time? It was a plausible theory, since the Island would be difficult to recover from the mainland, given a well-organised and alert defending force. De Kingston resolved to try and find out more from some of the knights: where they came from, to whom their allegiance was due, and what they had been told of the purpose of the attack before they embarked on it. Particularly he wanted to know how long they expected to be away from home.

His circuit eventually led to a slight hillock in the centre of the compound, on the crest of which a tent had been raised for the Duke's use, conveniently placed beneath the shade of a solitary old oak tree. Furniture plundered from the town had been placed within the tent, and benches and chairs were being set round the fire as a meeting place for the commanders. Some had rich tapestries and cloths thrown over them. Sitting in one of the chairs, his legs splayed out in front of him, was a knight drinking thirstily from a large goblet. He looked well travelled, dusty and drawn, with lines of strain and tiredness around his eyes and a frown creasing his forehead. De Kingston was to find out later that this was the leader of the Castilian battalion, the Comte de Mortagne, recently arrived from his foray at the castle.

The swarthy knight looked up appraisingly at the English captive, and interest lit up his dark eyes. He rubbed his jaw and scratched in the stubble beard. He spoke in French, obviously expecting to be understood.

'Ah! You must be the other Englishman I've heard about. You will find a young man that you may know over in that tent,' he said, gesturing with the goblet and spilling some of the wine in the process. 'He is wounded and delirious, and may die before tomorrow comes. You had better see him in case there is anything you can do for him or his kin. I have asked for a priest to attend him so that he may die properly shriven.'

With a gesture of acknowledgement de Kingston turned and hurried to the indicated tent. When he reached the tent he was very surprised to find there the one who was his daughter's lover. Considering the position that they were all in now, it seemed trivial to worry about anything except helping Robert to survive. Rachel's happiness could be so easily destroyed if the young man were to die and he couldn't risk the accusation that some blame might attach to him.

He looked down at Robert, who lay on a rough bed of grass and straw. His clothes were saturated with sweat, and yet he was shivering. His left shoulder was exposed where the shirt was torn, and fresh blood glistened amongst the darker dried blood and burned flesh of the cauterised wound. He writhed and muttered, but the words were unintelligible against the grinding of his teeth. His eyes were wide open, but rolled around staring, appearing to take in nothing that they saw.

De Kingston wished his sister were there to administer her potions and remedies. He was sure that she would know what to do to break the fever. He knew also that Rachel had acquired some of her expertise and talents. He wracked his brain, but couldn't remember anything of what he had seen her do that he could use. Perhaps feverfew... but where he could get some and how much to administer he didn't know.

By dint of signs and gestures he succeeded in making the guard understand that he needed some water and a cloth. When it came he started to cool Robert's brow and squeeze water into his mouth through his parched and cracked lips to replace the water he had lost as sweat. He appreciated that Robert had probably not had enough to drink since his wounding and through the heat of the day.

De Kingston sat many hours with Robert, cooling his brow and wetting his lips. Robert became delirious and raved about Rachel, his father and a boy called Harold. It was difficult to pick out the reality from imaginary events, as the sequence was so garbled, but, after a while, he was able to piece together much of the story of Robert's rescue of Harold at Yarmouth, the

22 August 1377

wounding, the capture and the long march to the castle. Questioning of the guard clarified Robert's role in Harold's escape from Yarmouth. He also came to realise the depth of Robert's feelings for Rachel, and could see now why she was in love with him. Though he would have been loath to admit it, de Kingston now began to respect Robert as an honourable, courageous and worthy man.

De Kingston's eyelids drooped occasionally as exhaustion overcame him. He fought against it, but his eyes simply would not stay open, and he slept, only to be awoken occasionally by Robert's moans. At one time, just as night was falling, the flap of the tent was thrown open and the Duke de Beauvais entered. He enquired after Robert's health and leant over him, peering intently. Without his armour the Duke was a much less physically imposing figure, but his eyes burned with a remarkable, almost hypnotic intensity, and his haughty manner distinguished him as an unusual leader. De Kingston felt instinctively that this man loved the ideal of chivalry above all else, and could be trusted to honour his word, protect ladies and welcome death when it came. This feeling instilled a deference in him that he felt for few people. Nevertheless, de Kingston was sure that de Beauvais was capable of considerable cruelty to those outside of his interpretation of the code of chivalry. Obviously a man to be very wary of, he concluded. He was unsure whether the Duke's interest in Robert was through chivalrous feelings or simply because of his worth as a hostage.

De Beauvais seemed to be happy to linger in conversation with his new hostage, and asked him many questions about the Island, its defences, and about de Kingston himself. He did not appear upset when de Kingston refused to answer questions he felt would be too revealing, though his eyes glittered and his lips twitched. To de Kingston's surprise, it transpired that de Beauvais had met Robert during the capture of Yarmouth, and the Duke considered that Robert had been instrumental in getting early warning of the raid to Caresbrooke and foiling the French attempts at surprise. However, he seemed to bear no ill will for all that – it was just the fortunes of war as far as he was concerned, and he respected an enemy that did what he would have done in the same circumstances. He appeared to approve of Robert's chivalrous act in saving the boy.

It was also clear that de Beauvais and de Mortagne had ridden up to the castle in the evening twilight and taken a look at the state of the defences. De Kingston got the distinct feeling that they were impressed and even awed by the scale of the fortress, its tall walls and impregnable appearance. The chances of success of a full frontal attack were small and he thought they would have to consider a more subtle approach. It would have to be starvation or intimidation. Nevertheless, to his surprise, de Beauvais was not discouraged at all, and hinted that they had something planned which would turn out to be a major surprise. The worrying thing was that de Beauvais thought that a siege could all be over in a few days. De Kingston pondered on this, and determined to solve the mystery.

Shortly after de Beauvais had left, the squire appeared with food and drink for de Kingston, obviously sent by the Duke. After that de Kingston could keep his eyes open no longer and, despite the moaning and continual movements coming from Robert, he slept.

Some time in the middle of the night he awoke, wanting to relieve himself. He stumbled outside, still half-asleep, and when he returned he found that Robert was sleeping peacefully too. His forehead was cool and the fever had obviously broken – recovery was now guaranteed, though Robert would be weak. De Kingston was surprised at his own relief and satisfaction, and thought that he really quite liked the lad.

23 August 1377

Morning

In the afternoon of that first day, and over the first night some semblance of order was established in the castle, with a planned pattern of activity; soldiers came on and off watch, sword and archery practice sessions were set up and meals were cooked and eaten.

Everyone now had a small area to call home, and most had found relations, or friends and neighbours, to set up their temporary shelters next to and share griefs and worries with. The castle surroundings and its routines became familiar, and after the refugees' initial intense fright and anguish, in the security of their surroundings, they became more optimistic about the future. Though they all had worries for missing relatives, they gained strength from each other's presence.

The display of might by the invaders and the exhibition of Robert de Affeton as a hostage had brought home to them all that they were lucky to be safe and sound, even though such respite might only be temporary, although their worries about the others left outside deepened. Speculation about the fate of the rest of the Island was intense, especially when they had heard the sound of the church bells tolling in Nieuport. The fighting around the west gate was visible from the keep, and it was obvious that the defence was quickly overcome. Since then regular comings and goings of the French soldiers through the gate could be seen. The news that the town had fallen quickly spread throughout the castle and cast a cloud of gloom over everyone.

In the twilight of that first evening two mounted and armoured knights were seen circuiting the castle in the shelter of the trees, stopping every so often to point at the castle and to bend their heads in discussion. One was the knight who had appeared with Robert de Affeton during the morning, the dark-skinned one with the red cross on his jupon. The other appeared older, and even more richly apparelled, and to him the other knight deferred. The defenders surmised correctly that this older knight must be the overall commander of the French. The two must have been reconnoitring and planning their attack, looking for the weak points in the battlements and considering whether an attack was possible. Eventually they turned and disappeared.

For the first full night, worries that they may return with troops for an onslaught made the sentries nervous of every sound. They stared out into the moonlight until their eyes ached, and they paced around the walls, following the orders they had been given not to become stationary targets for snipers. An owl's hoot or a fox's scream would have them starting and grasping their weapons; by dawn, however, the tension ebbed somewhat, since the relief guards had had a good night's sleep and a meal to comfort them.

Sir Hugh made a round of the sentries as soon as light started in the eastern sky, asking what they had seen or heard, then asking after their families, speaking calming and comforting words. In the courtyard below the refugees began to waken. Children clamoured, and babies wailed, in hunger. Movement around the fires heralded the preparation of the first meal of the day, breaking the fast of the night, and women carried beakers and pitchers to the well for water. To a casual observer it all seemed fairly calm and relaxed, but an exaggerated politeness and concern between neighbours showed the underlying tension.

Suddenly two well-aimed bolts came zipping out of the trees. One hit a guard on the battlements, killing him outright. The other ricocheted off the battlements into the courtyard below, where some fought for possession of it. Thereafter the sentries were much more vigilant. The enemy were out there in the woods, even though they could not be seen.

The dawn light filtered through the narrow, glassless window into the room that Rachel and Rebecca were sharing with Rebecca's ailing father. They stirred. Rachel's contractions had stopped and, though feeling tired and uncomfortable, she had not felt them again.

Yawning and stretching, Rachel combed her fingers through her fine, straw-coloured hair. She looked across at the young

23 August 1377

woman who was now her best friend lying on rugs beside her, hands folded across her swollen belly. During the last day and night they had grown to love each other as sisters of the womb. Their minds seemed to be in such accord that they often started, together, to say precisely the same thing, the same thoughts being triggered in both of them by an action or a word, or sometimes nothing at all in particular.

Rebecca opened her eyes, saw her friend watching her and smiled before turning towards her father. He was pale and still, his cheeks sunken and drawn, and his skin grey and waxy. For a moment Rachel thought that he had ceased breathing altogether, but his breaths were shallow and slow, often with time between them that seemed to stretch into eternity. With a sinking heart she recognised that he was slowly slipping away and Robert did not know, could not be here to share her grief and comfort his father. She was now very glad that the priest had been prevailed upon the previous night to shrive him, give him the last rites, and that he now had the peace of God enveloping him.

'I will go and get some food and water,' Rachel said, seeing Rebecca's concern and realising she must want to be alone with her father. Also she needed to see her own mother was comfortable and adequately looked after by the servants.

Rebecca gratefully nodded as Rachel quietly slipped out and closed the door gently behind her. Taking her father's cold hand in both of hers, Rebecca sat thinking of the sunny, happy days of her childhood with her strong and reliable father, and her long-dead mother, calm and beautiful. Soft tears fell down her cheeks and wet their clasped hands. She felt his hand stir in hers and his eyes opened. Seeing her there, and obviously recognising her, he winked one eye, and though his face did not change, she knew he was smiling encouragingly at her. Her heart lifted and she did not feel sad any longer; she knew that he had triumphed over life and over death. He wanted her to rejoice for his life and carry his memory with her and pass it on to his grandchild, soon to be born. He could not speak, but his words were obvious. His eyes closed and he gave a gentle sigh.

Five minutes later, when she was gently smoothing his forehead and thinking about their past lives at Affeton, she realised that it had been some while since she had heard him take a breath. He had died without a sound, without her knowing. It was then her grief burst forth; she clasped his still form to her and the tears flowed anew. But though she was crying, the tears were tears of relief rather than sorrow; relief that his suffering was ended and he could now rest in peace, together with her beloved mother. She gently covered his eyes, her throat aching with the tears, and she crossed herself and quietly said a Hail Mary.

The door opened and Rachel came in, together with Peter. They saw the look on her face, and the tears, and knew that they were too late. Rachel flew to console her friend, and Peter stood beside them as they quietly paid homage to the old man, each praying for his soul in their separate ways.

After a minute, Rebecca turned to Peter and put her arms round him. They stood there taking strength from each other, and the baby moved between them.

'Peter,' Rebecca whispered, 'I know the baby will be a boy and will be the image of his grandfather. I know that my father would like him to be called Roger, after him. He must be called Roger. Please agree.'

'Yes, my love,' he replied with a quiet smile. 'Roger shall be his name, and I am sure he will bear it with the same honour as his grandfather did. Now,' he added with more urgency, 'as your brother is not here to make the arrangements, will you please excuse me so that I can inform Sir Hugh, and ensure that your father is laid out and properly prepared for a funeral. Then Robert will know that we have done all that's necessary and have not dishonoured his father.'

Peter took the old man's hand, and stood for a few seconds with his lips moving as he said a quiet prayer. He then bent his knee and bowed low before his father-in-law, just as he had done when he had asked for Rachel's hand in marriage. Rebecca kissed him before he went out.

It was then only a few minutes before many other people came: the priest again, two old women to wash and bind the body, and Sir Roger's servants, Alice, William and Timothy. Following them came the boy Harold, who had become an ever-present shadow behind Timothy, traumatised as he was through

23 August 1377

not knowing where his father was, and the shock of seeing his rescuer a captive. He held on to the bailiff as the only rock available.

Sir Hugh also came, despite his other worries and duties, and consoled Rebecca with kind words of sympathy. He insisted that the body should be placed to lie in state for a few days in the castle chapel, in the hope that the interment could eventually be directly in the church at Freshwater. If not, the coffin would be placed in the chapel vaults until the present warfare was over.

★

Before the break of day, when the French camp was stirring, and the guards were changing, de Kingston was woken by the sharp boot of the squire who had guarded him the previous day. He brought more food and some ale that he put down on the ground. He looked closely at Robert and grunted with satisfaction at seeing that he was somewhat recovered.

'The Duc orders that you go with him to the castle,' he said in French to de Kingston, accompanied by signs and gestures. 'But he can stay here.' He pointed at Robert. 'We will leave in a few minutes.'

Robert had woken at these words, feeling weak and tired, but remarkably clear-headed. He struggled to raise his head. 'Where am I?' he asked. He saw the French squire and immediately realised the position he was in, even though he didn't know where he was. Then his gaze settled on de Kingston, and he said with surprise, 'Ah! My lord de Kingston! So you are prisoner too. Is your family also prisoner? Where are we?'

'Take it easy, lad. Do not strain yourself. We are both prisoners – hostages – at the French camp outside Nieuport. Eat some of this, and have a drink.'

The guard repeated his instructions, and was relieved to see that Robert understood, even if de Kingston didn't. Thankfully he then left.

De Kingston offered Robert some of the bread and ale mixed with water left from the previous night, and helped him to sit up, propping some clothing behind him. While they ate he recounted the unsuccessful defence of Nieuport, and finished by expressing his worries about his wife and daughter, wondering whether they were still at Kingston Manor, or safe in Caresbrooke Castle. He thought it wise to say nothing about what he now knew of Rachel and Robert. He decided to wait and see how things developed.

In return, Robert told about his escapades in Yarmouth, of the trek to Francheville and to the castle, confirming what de Kingston had already surmised. Of the latter part Robert obviously had only vague memories. Since he had been due to visit Kingston anyway, he had no way of avoiding comment about his concern for Rachel, and with trepidation confessed that he and Rachel were in love and wanted to marry. Robert thought that de Kingston didn't seem to be particularly dismayed or upset about it, only nodding slightly and making non-committal noises about reviewing the situation after the French were beaten. Despite his poor condition, Robert was surprised and thought that sounded much more hopeful than he had ever thought possible. As a consequence, he felt even better.

Further conversation was interrupted by shouting outside the tent. The squire and two guards burst in, and gestured for de Kingston to go with them. Robert tried to get up too, but was firmly pushed back down by one of the soldiers with instructions to stay where he was.

De Kingston put out his hand to Robert and said, 'Don't worry! I think de Beauvais wants to exhibit me at the castle as a hostage for ransom, just as you were yesterday. You'll be looked after well here, I'm sure, for you are too useful to them to be dispensed with yet. I will be back later. I hope that I can at least get some news about what has happened to the rest of the Island.'

With that he shook Robert's hand and, with an encouraging smile, turned and joined his captors as they departed.

★

The lookout on the keep saw them first just after dawn, and even heard them coming before that: a large band of soldiers was approaching through the trees, up the track from the direction of Nieuport. He called to the captain of the guard, who had the

23 August 1377

trumpeter sound the alarm. All the able-bodied men grabbed their arms and ran to the battlements, even those who had just begun sleeping after their night-time shift of sentry duty. The older children did as they had been instructed and stood at the bottom of the steps so that they could fetch new supplies of arrows when they were needed, or do any other fetching and carrying from the armoury or the larders. All except a few fires were put out in case they were a hazard, and buckets and pitchers of water were filled to douse any fire arrows that might come over the battlements.

Some minutes later the first of the French could be seen by those on the battlements. They were led by an imposing fully armoured knight wearing a bascinet surmounted by an eagle's wing, and riding a white charger with full caparison. He was the knight who had led the covert survey of the castle the previous evening. Beside him was the knight, who had accompanied him and had parleyed with them the previous morning, as well as half a dozen or so other lesser knights. Behind were more lightly armed squires on smaller hobbies and palfreys, many of them taken from plundered farms and stables. Behind them again was a long column of archers armed with their crossbows, swords and shields. There were many more than had been present the previous day, and Sir Hugh could see from their colours and accoutrements that several different divisions were represented.

The marching column was silent. All that could be heard was the steady thump of the marching feet, the jingle of armaments and the occasional snort of a horse. Clouds of dust rose from them as they marched, making some of those at the back of the column cough and splutter. They cast glances at the castle, mentally assessing their chances of eventually capturing it, but their eyes were generally on the person in front, as they had been ordered.

The defenders on the battlements were also silent, each person counting how many attackers there were and estimating how many more might be left elsewhere. They were dismayed to see they were easily outnumbered, even without those likely to have been left to secure Nieuport, Yarmouth and Francheville.

Sir Hugh and the other lords walked round the battlements keeping pace with the besiegers, having ordered the archers to hold their fire until he gave the order. Though they expected the column to stop at the gatehouse, the French went on past. To the puzzlement of those inside, they continued marching and went completely round the castle, and then went round a second circuit, all the time taking care to stay out of bowshot. Within the castle the progress of the column was followed first with curiosity and then with increasing apprehension. The silence of the marching men and their strength and discipline, became overwhelming, the hearts of the watchers steadily sinking into their boots. Suddenly, the silence was broken by a defender's comment.

'Anyone would think that we were the city of Jericho, and this was Soloman's invading army. But marching round won't break our walls down – they've forgotten their trumpets!'

This was met with hoots of laughter, and Sir Hugh breathed a silent prayer of thanks for the indomitable spirit of the unknown man.

At the end of the second circuit the leader held up his hand and the knights stopped in front of the barbican and dismounted. The rest of the column came to a halt on either side of the knights, still half-encircling the castle. One of the squires produced a white flag and it was attached to the end of a lance, and several of the knights stepped forward with the flag held high. They obviously wished to begin confrontation and possible parleying. A rather dishevelled man, broad and upright, with a white streak in his dark hair was brought forward to join the group.

'Good Lord,' said Peter de Heyno with surprise. He had joined the group on the battlements halfway through the final circuit. 'Isn't that John de Kingston there with them? They must have taken him prisoner in Nieuport.'

The knight with the eagle's wing stepped forward of the rest, together with de Kingston. After a few words between them the knight shouted to them in French.

'I am the Duc de Beauvais, representative of the King of France. We have taken your town of Nieuport, as well as Yarmouth, Francheville, Brading and La Rye. All of your people are our prisoners.'

To start with it wasn't clear what he was saying; few understood his language and dialect, but soon a ripple of whispers and gasps spread round the walls as the meaning was understood. It

23 August 1377

was the first indication that parts of the Island other than the West Wight had been overrun.

De Beauvais continued. 'Our fleet is in your River Medine and we have the Island completely in our hands. We can desolate it, or we can leave it alone. That is entirely up to you. We also have another hostage here – Lord de Kingston.' At this point de Kingston was pushed unceremoniously forward. 'We call for ransom for him. Otherwise he will be put to the sword, together with the hostage of yesterday, and all the burgesses of Nieuport and the peasants.'

'Robert must still be alive,' said Sir Hugh with some relief. 'Thank God for that! But de Kingston taken as well…' He shook his head in despair.

'We wish to negotiate with you,' continued de Beauvais. 'We will ransom our captives and the towns, villages and farms so far undamaged. Five thousand marks is our price. I will give you until this evening to agree. Do not think that there is any point in resisting. You can see from the army here that you have no chance,' he waved his arms to right and left. 'These are only a fraction of my army. If you think that your castle is secure, you must think again, for we have the means of defeating your thick walls.'

So saying, he turned on his heels and led the way back to the ranks of his men. A few commands were shouted and the column wheeled and started back down the track towards the town, leaving a token force to watch the castle. The hundred or so soldiers were quite adequate to prevent the desperate besieged making sorties to harass the invaders, and to stop any local people from sneaking in with fresh provisions or reinforcements. A number of men called engineers were left at the castle with axes and other tools.

Not all of the Duke's words were clear to the defenders as most of them didn't understand French at all, and those who did only had a smattering, but it was obvious that they had to make a choice between paying money or risking heavy retribution. Quite what his final comment about defeating their walls implied raised a great deal of speculation.

Morning

★

When the marching column returned to the encampment, additional platoons of French men-at-arms were detailed to scour the Island for victuals, horses and any valuables they could find. Their instructions were not to burn and despoil, but merely to plunder, otherwise their ransom demands would be valueless. Additionally, a number of carpenters and specially trained skilful and experienced engineers were dispatched to procure timbers, ropes and heavy stones to be taken to the castle.

De Kingston returned to where he had left Robert to find him stiffly, and with some difficulty, hobbling round the tent trying to loosen his tight muscles. He was looking somewhat recovered, had some colour back in his cheeks and was ravenous. They asked one of the guards to fetch some victuals and drink and, when it came, sat down and discussed the events of the morning.

Their main concern was to try to work out whether there was any way they could cease being anything other than helpless onlookers and help to turn the tide of fortune in the Islander's favour. The rest of the day they spent kicking their heels around the camp, as they were not allowed to go further, but Robert was able to talk to more of the French troops. In particular, they were both interested in finding out more about the task that the engineers were engaged upon.

★

Rachel was overjoyed to see her father and hear that Robert was alive and likely to be well, even though they were both hostages. Rebecca too was happy at the news and it relieved, to some extent at least, her sorrow at her father's death. But she was desolated that there was no way in which she could tell Robert the bad news. Now that her father's body was being attended to, she and those around her had time to consider their own plight and take more notice of their surroundings and of the other refugees in the castle.

Rachel went to console her mother, who had not seen the enemy parade round the castle. She had obviously been very

23 August 1377

worried as to the fate of her husband in Nieuport, and was extremely relieved to hear that though he was in the hands of the enemy, he appeared to be reasonably unharmed and well treated. Together they talked about the possibility of raising some ransom money to get him released. But most of their valuables were hidden back at Kingston Manor, and there was no way they could get at them without putting themselves or their property at risk. They would not be able to raise all of the money anyway, and they were unsure as to whether Sir Hugh would be able to provide any of the rest.

It seemed only a few moments though before one of the de Heyno servants came to ask Rachel if she would return to the other chamber, because Rebecca's birth pains had begun again and she was asking for her.

When she reached the chamber so recently vacated and cleaned, she saw Rebecca lying on the bed with a hand clasped to her large belly. Beads of sweat stood out on her forehead, her eyes were closed and screwed up as a new pain started. A slight moan escaped her tightly pursed lips. Peter was already there looking concerned, holding her other hand. Her fingers turned white as she squeezed his hand hard to help her bear the pain. He looked round at Rachel as she came in, with a pleading look on his face. The strain shone quite clearly in his eyes. He was obviously at a loss for what he could do to help.

'It seems her pains started just after her father died, though she didn't mention them at the time. I think that the grief may well have started things off; the baby should not be due for a couple of weeks yet,' Peter told her.

Rachel nodded and moved to the other side of the bed. The servant was hovering just inside the doorway, not knowing whether he should go or stay.

'Go and get old Mrs Baker,' Rachel said to him. 'She's a good midwife and has attended many births. She hasn't lost a baby or a mother yet, so I am told. When you have done that fetch some clean cloth and boiled water. I think that the baby may not be long.' He scuttled off with relief to get away.

Then, turning to Peter, she said, 'I am sure you will not want to stay for the birth. If you do, you must stay out of the way and

Morning

not faint. It might be as painful for you as it will be for her,' she added with a smile.

Peter looked questioningly down at Rebecca who was lying back regaining her strength as the pain diminished.

'Peter,' she whispered, 'you have important things to do elsewhere. I will be all right here with Rachel, and you cannot help. Please go, my love.'

Relieved that he was to be spared the ordeal of seeing his beloved wife suffer, Peter bent down and kissed her. She half sat up, put her arms round his neck and kissed him back, but then dropped back with a sharp intake of breath as the next pain started.

Rachel ushered him out of the room, assuring him that he would be told as soon as there was any definite news. He left the chamber with a long face and a worried backward glance at his wife, who was now oblivious to him.

The midwife came in as Peter left. She was a wrinkled and bent old woman, with one solitary tooth in her lower jaw and thin grey hair hanging low over her narrow shoulders. Not a sight that inspired confidence, but one look into her eyes dispelled any concern Rachel might have had. The eyes were bright, sparkling and filled with joy of life and with humour. Rebecca obviously could not be in better hands. The old woman rolled up her sleeves, revealing strong forearms and capable hands. She started to strip off Rebecca's clothes, revealing her distended belly veined with blue.

A hasty knock on the door heralded the return of the servant carrying a large pan of steaming water, which he placed on the floor. He was followed by another man laden with a number of not-too-clean cloths. They departed quickly.

'If you are going to help me, my dear, you had better put a cloth around yourself, otherwise you could spoil your fine clothes.' The old woman's voice was firm and strong. She was used to having her every order obeyed when she was in the birth chamber. At that moment Rebecca's waters broke and a flood of the protective fluid spurted from between her legs.

About three hours later a small wrinkled and red boy was delivered into the woman's hands. She held the baby up by his feet and slapped him on the back until he cried with his first

23 August 1377

breath. She then cut and knotted the umbilical cord. Rachel watched with joy in her heart and a wide smile on her face at the start of a new life, but she then helped wipe and wash the little child, and clear up the blood-stained cloths and the afterbirth. The exhausted Rebecca lay back, relieved that the baby was fit and healthy. She looked at her baby with supreme love, her face shining, when, neatly wrapped, he was put in her arms.

Peter rushed in to find his beloved wife sitting up in the bed holding the baby close. Her hair had been combed and she had had a drink of water and had washed her face. She looked rosy and glowed with happiness. He was overjoyed to find them both so content, and that the birth had been so quick and easy. He was so happy that he kissed the old midwife; she was startled but immensely pleased at his joy. He then kissed Rachel, before kneeling beside the bed and taking both Rebecca and Roger in his arms.

The baby had his eyes closed, as if recovering from a long and tiring journey, but he had a respectable amount of light brown silky hair framing an already determined-looking face, with a little button nose in the centre. His fists were tightly clenched in front of him, as if ready for another tussle.

Rebecca smiled up at Peter and said, 'I feel there is a portent in the way our son was born just as my father died. Their souls must have passed at the gates of heaven. I am sure it's right that we have been destined to call him Roger, after his grandfather.'

Peter looking proud and happy, could do nothing but agree wholeheartedly.

★

In the constable's solar Sir Hugh and the other lords were in deep discussion over the ransom demand.

'Surely it is simply not possible to find that much ransom money, or even its equivalent in valuables, jewels or fine cloths? How much is there in the castle exchequer, Sir Hugh?'

A mark was the equivalent of about ten days' wages of a skilful archer, or about two days' of a man-at-arms. Five thousand marks was therefore enough to pay a small army for at least a summer's warfare. Reckoned another way, it was almost one mark for each man, woman and child on the Island. In those terms it didn't sound so bad, but most of them would not see a one-mark coin in a month of Sundays. Most families would think themselves lucky to have a few pence saved up, or perhaps a shilling, and a mark was six shillings and eight pence. How could such a small island find so much?

'There should be about 800 marks in the castle chest,' replied Sir Hugh frowning, 'together with some gold rings and silver goblets. I suppose, in all, the castle has about 1,000 marks.' There was a general agreement, as this was the amount that would have been expected.

'I am sure the rest of us can only produce much less than that amount immediately. Given time and the opportunity to go to our homes for the savings that we've hidden, together we might be able to double what the castle has,' said John Urrey.

'They won't be expecting us to agree to their first demand. They will be prepared to bargain, surely,' said Adam de Cumpton. 'We have no proof that the whole island has been taken. Anyway, what means have they for taking the castle? It is strong and sound.'

'The only way in which we could raise such a sum, or even near the amount, would be to ask the Abbot of Quarr Abbey to put in some of the wealth they must have,' suggested Theobald de Gorges. 'The abbot and the monks have not come here for protection because they have sanctuary enough of their own. I doubt very much that the French will have attacked the abbey yet, and it is unlikely they will anyway since it has been fortified well and has holy protection. There will only be the monks and their estate villeins – not very many defenders. I expect they will rely on the power of the cross rather than the power of the sword to avoid giving any of their wealth to the invaders.

'Nevertheless, the abbot has been zealous in helping to regulate the defences of the Island, and might help,' he continued thoughtfully. 'I was involved in supervising the construction of the walls and battlements of the abbey and have worked extensively with the abbot. Naturally he was keen on protecting both the island and his abbey.'

23 August 1377

'That's a very interesting suggestion, Theobald,' replied Sir Hugh. 'But there is the problem of how we get a message to him. Perhaps we could get someone to slip through the French forces to the abbey. Under the circumstances, the French commander might grant us safe passage if it meant him getting his ransom quickly.

'I think we should wait a while, see how persistent the French are, and how much they may be prepared to accept. We really need to know what they have up their sleeves. They could be bluffing, and they may be willing to bargain if we hang on and if they know how poor we really are. At the moment I cannot see that we can do much more.'

Murmurs of agreement came from around the table, and the meeting broke up.

During the morning and throughout the rest of the afternoon the French soldiers and a new group of unarmed men were very busy outside the castle. In the woods the sound of chopping resounded, with the occasional crash of falling trees and shouts of the men. Teams of oxen appeared, together with motley collections of a large variety of horses. These were driven by soldiers with whips, and dragged the tree trunks to the highest point of the hill outside the walls, about 200 paces south of the gatehouse. At that point two enormous pits were being dug and a large area of ground cleared and flattened.

Within the castle there was great speculation as to what was being done, and a perpetual line of watchers on the battlements marvelled and commented on every movement. No one knew what it might mean, but there were many prepared to guess.

The French marching column returned in the evening, and this time they had both de Kingston and Robert with them. The performance was a repeat of that of the morning: the column formed a procession round the castle, doing two circuits as before. However, this time the men were singing lustily both French and Castilian marching songs. Their steps were precise and regular, beating a steady rhythm. Everyone within the castle was impressed by their discipline and confidence.

After the second circuit de Beauvais and his group of knights again stopped in front of the gatehouse barbican, out of range of the long bows. De Kingston and Robert were plainly visible standing among the mounted squires.

At a signal the singing stopped abruptly. The knights didn't speak and their mounts scarcely fidgeted. The column of men-at-arms and archers stood still and gazed at the castle. Nothing was said. No parleying was attempted. The defenders were expecting to have to argue, explain, and attempt to gain a compromise; they found the silence oppressive and very intimidating – everyone was afraid to be the first to break the silence, and it set them wondering whether the French were going to bother to negotiate before attacking. They found their hands holding their weapons sweating with apprehension.

The French stood still for at least ten minutes. Then, at a signal, they turned away without showing the white flag and disappeared into the trees down the track towards the town.

The watchers from the battlements included Rachel, who was overjoyed to be able to see both her father and her lover alive, if not safe. To her eyes Robert looked weak and ill, even though he was holding himself erect, and trying to walk steadily. She dearly wanted to call out to him, to tell him that he was now uncle to a splendid little nephew. But the silence stopped her, the silence that no one felt that they could break. It was almost as if a spell had been cast over the scene.

The opportunity passed as the attackers moved away, and a buzz of relieved conversation and comment broke out once the French were out of sight. Rachel felt a great weight on her spirit. She yearned to hold Robert, run her fingers through his hair, feel his strong hands in hers and to be able to comfort him in his grief.

On the way back to the town, Robert and de Kingston were behind the main group of the French commanders, but they could hear a heated discussion going on between de Beauvais and de Mortagne. There was obviously a conflict of attitude between them: De Mortagne was arguing for a more ruthless approach than de Beauvais, who was inclined to take a subtler, less brutal approach. The comte wanted some of the leading citizens of Nieuport, particularly the burgesses, to be brought to the castle and one by one hung where the defenders could see, until they gave in to the ransom demands.

23 August 1377

He was taking an attitude that would have been typical of the Knights Templar, which was rooted in their origins during the days of the Crusades. If he had been one of them, he would have sworn to uphold Christianity by the sword against all unbelievers, and his conduct would have been entirely focused on obeying those principles. His definition of unbelievers probably encompassed all who disagreed specifically with him. His code of ethics seemed to be governed by the military aspects of life, and as far as he was concerned the peasants were entirely disposable; they were equivalent of animals, and were there entirely for him to display his fighting prowess.

However, de Beauvais was a man whose principles of chivalry were much more courtly and gracious. The French aristocracy had led the whole of Europe in developing chivalry as an ideal of treating others as one would like to be treated oneself, for the knightly class at least. In particular courtly love and respect for ladies was considered to be a manly characteristic, in contrast to the older view of women as chattels to be treated as the way of securing sons and succession of the family line.

This new attitude was slowly gaining ground in England, and though de Kingston had heard about it, he had never really experienced it. Robert, on the other hand, had met such attitudes before, during his time in Gascony. There he had argued the pros and cons through by himself and with the other squires, and they had come to the conclusion that the older ways would inevitably have to change. He would be happy to have a relationship with the serfs based on mutual respect and knowledge of the responsibility of each to the other, rather than one based on fear. In this respect de Kingston was of an older generation and a different persuasion.

De Beauvais was countering de Mortagne's arguments, saying that such a hasty approach would gain them little in the short run, and might lose them a lot in the long. More time and the threat of the siege weapon that was being constructed was likely to instil morbid fear in the defenders, sufficient to make them produce their valuables from their secret hiding places that otherwise might remain hidden. The extra time would be valuable in allowing the French to search out and capture those who had so far eluded them and who had not found safety in the castle and give them time to loot the surrounding manors and hamlets. They could rely on the trebuchet to break the walls, and probably also the spirit of the defenders, within a couple of days.

De Mortagne also argued for sacking the abbey at Quarr, which was likely to be rich with altar gold, silver and jewels, and which so far they had spared. De Beauvais did not agree with this as the abbey was Cistercian; his sister was in a Cistercian nunnery, and he was determined that their argument should not be with God, but with the English who had so long attacked and despoiled France. He didn't want to have the killing of holy men or sacrilege on his conscience. De Beauvais found it difficult to understand how de Mortagne could wish to do so when he had sworn oaths on the cross to protect Christianity.

De Mortagne didn't press the arguments too far, but it was obvious that they would return to it again and, should there be any setbacks to the strategy de Beauvais was adamant to follow, his case would be made more strongly. The difference of attitude between the two leaders was something they would have to resolve before their return to France, as they might have to justify their actions before a critical king. Neither of them would want to appear to have been supporting a policy that failed.

Back in the French encampment a puzzled de Kingston said, 'Do you know anything about this machine the Duke mentioned, Robert, this trebuchet?'

Robert had experienced the construction and firing of one in France during the siege on an isolated but very strong castle. He explained to de Kingston how it worked.

'It is rather like a gigantic sling, or catapult,' he said. 'Two large tree trunks can either be fixed upright in the ground, or supported on a framework moving on wheels. Across the top of the two uprights is an axle carrying a throwing arm that may be up to thirty feet long. On one end of the arm is a sling that carries a stone weighing two or three hundredweight. On the other end is a counterweight, which is most likely to be a basket filled with rocks or earth, and weighing several tons. A capstan wheel is used to pull down the sling against the weight. It takes about forty men to pull it down, and when it's released the stone flies through the

23 August 1377

air and can do tremendous damage to the battlements. It doesn't take many shots to breach the walls of a castle. Sometimes they attach flaming brands to the shot and fire it over the walls to set light to the buildings inside. I tell you, it is very frightening!' The hair on the back of his neck prickled at the memory.

De Kingston looked both impressed and worried, sucking a fingernail. 'How long does it take to build such a machine? And how many shots can it fire? It must only be able to fire a few shots a day.'

Robert thought a moment. 'I believe experienced engineers can build one in about three days, and I have heard of such a machine firing a hundred shots a day, providing that enough good large rocks are available.'

'But surely bowmen can stop it by firing at the operators from the battlements, or is the range too far?'

'Generally the trebuchet is set up out of arrow range – at least 250 yards,' Robert countered. 'If they get it constructed, I don't think the castle will have much chance of holding out for long once it starts firing.'

Both fell silent as the implications of what he had said sank in.

Robert yawned and stretched. 'I could do with some sleep. Perhaps we'll have some ideas as to how we could stop their plans in the morning.'

He lay back and was soon snoring, while de Kingston sat, his head resting on his hand, and pondered.

THE AMBUSH OUTSIDE NIEUPORT

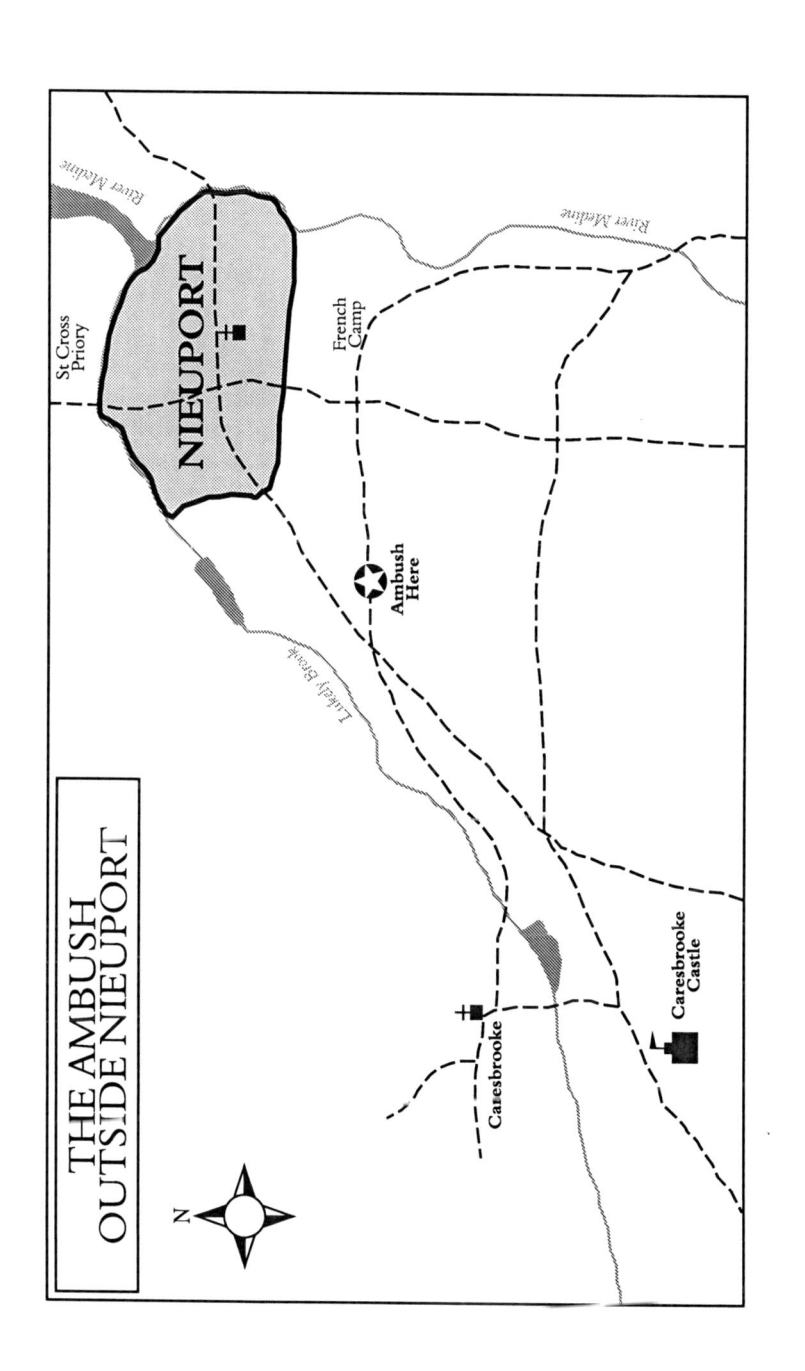

24 August 1377

Morning

The previous night Robert had managed to purloin a bucket of water from one of the nearby archers. He had used it to wash himself as well as he could, using a scrap of cloth as a flannel, much to the amusement of the Frenchmen, who obviously didn't do very much washing. After this, he washed his shirt and hung it on the shelter overnight to dry.

In the morning he woke feeling much refreshed. He stood outside the shelter feeling the dew on his feet, and took a few deep breaths of clean morning air. The sky was blue but with the feathery high white clouds that he had always thought of as angels' wings. Did these precede a change in the weather? he wondered – they often did. After some stretching he found much of his stiffness had eased, and inspection of the wound in his shoulder showed new pink skin sealing it over. It was still tender, but providing he didn't stretch too far, he didn't think it would open up again. He washed it again carefully and then put on the shirt that he had washed. It was cleaner, no longer stained with blood, mud and sweat, but still tattered and torn.

It was obvious that he and de Kingston were to accompany the early-morning sortie to the castle. They walked together and were deep in discussion as they ascended the leafy lanes to the castle. Some careful listening and watching revealed that the group of men, who called themselves engineers, had gone to the castle the previous day to start construction of the trebuchet.

When the column arrived Robert could see that work on the machine was advancing quickly. A flat area had been cleared on the crest of the hill, with an unobstructed line of fire to the wall to the south of the gatehouse where the battlements appeared to be relatively weak and in need of repair. The first upright was being slid into a hole and levered vertically into place. The hole for the second upright had been dug, and a massive tree trunk was being shaped into a smooth cylinder, presumably for the axle. At least fifty men were working on it, and there was a continual procession of others driving teams of horses and oxen to bring in the trees and rocks needed. The busy engineers were covered in sweat and dust, despite the early hour, and took the opportunity to rest and raise a cheer when the column of marching troops arrived.

After what seemed now like the obligatory two circuits of the castle, the column stopped. De Beauvais then stepped forward under the white flag to parley once more. Sir Hugh was on the battlements waiting.

'*Bien, Monsieur le Capitaine du château!*' shouted de Beauvais, and continued in French, 'You heard yesterday our terms for ransom of your countryside, your towns, your houses and your people. We will release them for fair payment. We seek fair retribution for the harm you have done to us in our lands. What is your reply?'

Sir Hugh waited a full half-minute before he replied, during which de Beauvais' horse became fractious and started prancing around, much to his chagrin.

'My Lord,' he shouted, 'we have understood that you want us to pay ransom of 5,000 marks. We would like to avoid unnecessary conflict, injury and death, for it would affect both yourselves and us. However, now you have had time to assess the Island's wealth and resources, you will have seen that we are not rich. The Island pays rent to our lord, the Duke of York, of only a few hundred marks a year, and there are years when we are hard-pressed to find even that and we have to plead for remission of the rents.' He neglected to say that the remission was because of the difficulty of retaining people living on the Island because of the threat of invasion.

'Many of our people have left the Island for the mainland because of the threat of invasion from your country, and there have been other invasions within our lifetime that have killed our people and animals, violated our women, and taken our possessions. We do not have 5,000 marks to pay the ransom. We would have to get assistance to pay from the mainland, and that

24 August 1377

will take a long time.' Sir Hugh was aware that the French might be concerned about staying on the Island too long, and being trapped by reinforcements sent from Southampton, especially since the burning towns would have acted as excellent warning beacons.

De Beauvais turned sideways and asked Robert to clarify some parts of Sir Hugh's speech that he did not understand. Then he shouted a reply. 'Your answer is no more than I would expect, and I do not believe that you have not money, jewellery, plate or valuables to that value within your castle, and with the knights and yeomen you are succouring. I think that you need some persuasion to think again. We have the town of Nieuport at our mercy, and we will start to exact our ransom from them, in blood if necessary. Their blood will be on your head, and your conscience.'

He waved his arm towards the tree trunks rising into the air. 'You will see that we are preparing to bombard the castle with the trebuchet. You will not like it. Many of your people will be frightened and many killed. Your castle will eventually succumb. Just consider what little you gain by delay. We will return, and I expect a more positive response.'

No answer was forthcoming from the battlements, nor was one expected. The French withdrew.

On the way down the road from the castle, Robert and de Kingston could see de Beauvais and de Mortagne in deep discussion, though this time they were too far behind to hear what was said.

About halfway to the town the road came to a junction where it was joined by the road coming straight down from Caresbrooke village and heading on to the western gate of the town, the one that de Kingston had helped to defend. At that junction a narrower road forked off to the right and round the southern side of the town. It cut between high banks, with oak, sycamore and elm trees hanging low overhead and thick bramble undergrowth on either side. This road led directly to where the French encampment was.

At the junction the force divided. De Mortagne took a group of knights and squires, together with a platoon of archers, straight

Morning

on down the road to the town, while the rest of the column went up the side road towards the camp. The two Islanders had to go towards the camp. Robert kept his eyes open to all that was going on, just in case it might turn out to be useful information later. He noticed that the French column stayed as a compact marching mass of men, just as they had the previous evening, as well as on the way to the castle that morning. There were no scouts or outriders. The French obviously thought that the Islanders were defeated, and there was no risk of any attack, all the able-bodied soldiers either being safely cooped up in the castle, or being hunted across the Island by the French patrols.

When they reached the camp the two prisoners were shepherded back to their shelter where they had something more to eat, but where they could watch the comings and goings. As they watched, Robert and de Kingston started discussing various ideas that they had had.

There was a lot of activity around the camp, with men coming and going all the time. Now they were familiar with the camp routine, the surroundings and the whole pattern of their existence was losing its strangeness.

It was now two days since the French had attacked Nieuport, and three days since Yarmouth and Francheville had been sacked. Patrols had been sent out to explore the Island, particularly the south, to raid the outlying farms and villages, to find supplies of food, and to bring in anything of value they could find. Those patrols were returning from their forays, sometimes with pack animals laden with the contents of the barns and storerooms. Occasionally stolen carts would be used to carry barrels of ale or wine, and other booty. All of the valuables were separated, noted down on a list by a quartermaster, who was one of the Duke's stewards, put into a tent and guarded. The rest was put into an enclosure for later distribution. Obviously the intention was to share out the loot when they returned to France. De Beauvais and the King would take the major share, with smaller shares going to the lesser knights and even smaller ones to the common archers. Specific instructions had been given to the troops about leaving churches and holy places alone, but who was to prevent it when the men found something they fancied and were half-drunk on

24 August 1377

stolen ale? Many houses and homesteads were put to the torch in drunken glee.

A small but growing graveyard had been dug, because some patrols were returning with dead and wounded. They were meeting with opposition from the yeomen and peasants who had failed to reach the safety of the castle. The locals knew the paths and tracks through the woods and heaths, the places to hide and see without being seen, and they would fire a hasty but well-aimed arrow and then disappear into the trees. Particularly at night they were able to sneak up behind a guard and slide a knife beneath his ribs. In the end the French were always nervously looking over their shoulders and could see enemies in every bush and over every hillock. Their retaliation was to kill anyone they could catch. Many a serf was later found pinned to a tree by crossbow bolts, having been used for target practice. Any women caught were stripped naked and raped, often being used by the whole patrol in turn; they were then left in shame to fend for themselves. Nine months later quite a number of French bastards were to be born, to be called de Norman, or Black, because of their swarthy skin.

Robert and de Kingston heard the boasts and bragging of the men over their conquests, but it became clear that the patrols were not venturing too far from the protection of the main force. It seemed to them highly likely that many manors and farms tucked away in the isolated areas might survive intact. De Kingston had hopes that his secluded manor far to the south might remain unmolested, but Robert wasn't that confident that Affeton Manor would be: it was too close to the place of the first landing.

From overheard conversations amongst the men-at-arms, Robert understood that they expected to remain on the Island only a few more days. Orders had been given that the valuables should be taken on board the ships moored in the river, and carts and horses were starting to take away the contents of the store tents.

At about noon a squire came from de Beauvais ordering them to accompany him on a trip into Nieuport, as there was something there he wanted them to see. Both reluctantly rose to their feet, perturbed at the prospect of a new experience, but it wasn't to be quite what they expected.

In the centre of the camp a large contingent of troops had assembled. De Beauvais was riding with a number of squires and men-at-arms at the van. He gestured that the two hostages should join in directly behind his group, but said nothing about the purpose of the trip. Robert was surprised that de Mortagne was nowhere to be seen.

They marched down the well-beaten track towards the town. The sun was peeping between the clouds, and there was a strong breeze that sent them scurrying quickly overhead. It was the sort of day that normally would have given a lift to the heart and sent the senses singing. But this day was to be far from normal.

When they entered the town it looked much as it usually did. Piles of litter cluttered the streets, but none of the houses or shops appeared to have been destroyed, and few showed any sort of damage at all, apart from the occasional broken window shutter, or missing door. However, as they walked past they could see signs that they had been plundered of their best goods, and discarded items lay within the gardens.

The people were subdued and unsmiling. They scarcely looked up as the troops rode by. Fear was apparent in their eyes. Many of them had bruises or cuts about their faces, and they looked drawn, hungry and tired. They spat at the feet of the marchers and the few women hastily retreated. Those seeing and recognising the hostages showed little emotion. The soldiers had taken the best food, leaving little for the townsfolk, and at night the drunken soldiers enjoyed playing games. They would catch the old men, tie blindfolds over their eyes and taunt them with swordpoints and drive them until they fell into the drains and sewers or the river. The most comely women were abducted and forced to entertain the soldiers in their own marriage beds, though they hoped that in doing so they might lessen the demands on their families and get some favour in return. The younger girls were abducted and taken back to the French camp. The able-bodied men were being used as serfs to load and carry and attend to the soldiers' slightest whims, that is

24 August 1377

those who had not been locked up as potential troublemakers. Many others who had resisted had been killed.

A line of soldiers ushered the townsfolk along the street, driving them like cattle towards the main square. Robert and de Kingston began to worry that they were about to witness some real unpleasantness. They reached the large open square of the beast market and were horrified to see a set of three gallows had been constructed in the middle.

'So that's what de Mortagne has been doing all morning,' breathed Robert as his eyes met those of de Kingston. He grimaced, knowing that the rest of the day would be unpleasant.

A number of the soldiers, who were probably carpenters in peacetime, were still hammering at the supports for the uprights, and a large wagon was standing nearby with a dejected horse between the shafts. The soldiers formed a ring around the gallows, facing outwards, keeping the local people away. De Beauvais together with his squires, stood inside the ring facing the ominous structure. Robert and de Kingston had to join them.

There was a commotion on the other side of the square, which eventually resolved itself into another group led by de Mortagne appearing from the direction of the town hall. In the centre of the group were all of the burgesses, staggering along with bound hands and linked together with loops of rope around their necks. Their shoulders were slumped, their feet dragged and some were crying, for they began to realise what was going to happen to them.

The cart was backed up under the gallows, and two of the soldiers clambered onto it to sling ropes over the bars. Three of the burgesses were picked out by de Mortagne and thrown up on to the cart. With their hands tied they couldn't stand and lay struggling on the straw. On de Mortagne's instruction the nooses were placed over their heads and they were hauled by the throat to their feet, coughing and spluttering. A priest moved forward and gave them a blessing and told them they should confess their sins before they met their maker. Now that the time had come, and there was no possibility of reprieve, two of them regained their dignity and stood resolute, staring at their tormentors. The third had a terrible possessed look on his face with staring eyes, a working mouth and a rigid body. He cursed de Beauvais and prophesied that he would be killed before he left the Island.

De Beauvais blanched at the curse, but turned to face the crowd. He raised his voice and shouted, 'Your comrades and leaders are in the safety of the castle at Caresbrooke and will not pay ransom for the people of Nieuport. Even in times of war we are willing to be generous, but they will not help us to save you unnecessary suffering. Consequently, it is necessary to make them realise that we are serious in our demands. We are not here for pleasure, or for the good of our health. May God rest your souls.' Since he was talking in French, most of what he said went without being understood by the general populace.

So saying, he gave the signal for the cart to be driven forward. It lurched and the three victims fell, the nooses tight around their necks. They struggled and coughed, and tried to regain their feet but the cart continued to move. One by one they fell off the back to jerk upright on the end of the rope. The crowd shouted and cursed, and one or two struggled against the mass of Frenchmen to break through and release their friends and relations. The soldiers enjoyed pushing them back with blows from their bucklers or swords. The hanging bodies swung, banging into each other as they writhed and kicked. Red, then blue in the face, with their eyes starting from the sockets they slowly strangled. Eventually they hung rigid and quivering, with purple tongues protruding and wet patches staining their hose. It took a good five minutes before they were completely dead.

At a sign from the Duke the bodies were let down and thrown to one side and the ropes made ready for the next victims.

Those whose turn was still to come stared transfixed. They could not tear their eyes away, seeing their friends as they themselves would soon be. One or two collapsed on the ground, fainting. Robert felt the bile rising into his mouth; he turned away and was violently sick. De Kingston tried to remonstrate with de Beauvais, but was silenced with a back-handed blow across the mouth.

The same performance was repeated twice more until there was a pile of nine burgesses beside the gallows platform. The watching townspeople had fallen silent. They could do nothing

24 August 1377

but watch and pray. If they tried to do anything they would risk starting more brutality and even finding themselves dangling at the end of the rope.

Robert and de Kingston, pale and shaken, swore to themselves that their friends and fellow Islanders would be revenged by some means or other. Nevertheless, Robert thought that de Beauvais himself looked rather pale and he kept raising a scented glove to his nostrils. His lips were firmly pressed together and a little muscle continually twitched on his jaw.

'Take them away and bury them,' ordered de Mortagne, and the families and friends looked at each other before they pulled the dead men out of the pile. By mutual consent they were all carried towards the church in the corn market, where they could be laid out and honoured as martyrs.

The other townsfolk stood around whispering to each other, casting hateful glances at their tormentors.

On the way back to the camp, both Robert and de Kingston were occupied with their own thoughts, until the Duke turned, paused and waited until they caught up with him.

'Have either of you seen a trebuchet, or been in a siege where one was used?' he demanded eyeing them closely.

Robert was unsure whether to admit that he had – not knowing what might be the outcome. If he did then he might be forced to take a part in its construction, or in using it against his own people. His hesitation and the look of indecision on his face was immediately pounced on by de Beauvais.

'*Eh bien!*' he said with satisfaction. 'I think that you must have seen one while you were at war in France.' Robert had to nod his head. 'You know then,' the Duke continued, 'how easy it is to demolish the castle walls and frighten the defenders into surrender. In two more days we will be in possession of your castle and its contents.' He wheeled his mount around and cantered off toward the encampment.

Before they reached the camp they became aware that the wind had risen further, and some of the gusts were of gale force, tearing leaves off the trees and whirling rubbish across the ground. The clouds were thick and a sombre grey, rushing past close overhead. Rain could not be far away.

24 August 1377

Evening

On the way back to the camp after the executions they heard de Beauvais expressing concern about the likelihood of the bad weather and adverse winds delaying the return to France. Normally expeditions such as this one only lasted during the fine summer months and, after all, it was almost the end of August. Hostilities were generally abandoned with the advent of autumn; food became difficult to find, the tracks became too muddy to travel, and the wet and cold made the troops fractious. Robert thought that this sense of urgency may have been the critical thing that provoked de Beauvais into the hangings they had witnessed in the town. Perhaps his main intention was to try and resolve the impasse quickly in order to hasten the French withdrawal.

Back at the camp the mood had changed. The French and Castilian soldiers went listlessly about their tasks, without enthusiasm or any of their customary ribaldry. Robert and de Kingston, also dispirited, sat in their tent watching them. They talked and plotted with added urgency, trying to think of any ways to hasten the French defeat or departure. The afternoon continued very windy with occasional showers of heavy rain.

After a brief meal the column formed again for the regular evening march to the castle. The wind was still blustery and the sky was filled with scurrying clouds, but the sun occasionally broke through.

The march was quiet and rather contemplative: the marchers complaining about their wet clothes and muddy feet. When the column drew up before the castle gates after their two circuits of the walls, the battlements were lined with defenders, who were squinting into the bright evening sun. From outside the castle each defender was clearly outlined, and Robert was even able to recognise some of them.

24 August 1377

I wonder whether Rachel is there watching, he thought. But he couldn't see her. She could see him, however, as she was peering through one of the arrow slits in the gatehouse. She was overjoyed that he looked so much recovered and clapped her hands in relief, with her heart thumping madly.

The squire with the white flag of truce stopped on the sward in front of the gates. De Beauvais reined forward, took off his basinet with its fine black wing, so that his hair blew free in the wind, and shouted, 'Because you are unwilling to pay the ransom we demand, I have taken retribution on the burgesses of Nieuport. They have all been hanged. If you continue to resist I will carry out more executions.'

Curses were shouted in return when what he was saying was translated. Fists were shaken and tears of anger and frustration coursed down many cheeks. Though some sort of retaliation or escalation of pressure had been expected, they had not expected anything as drastic. The defenders began to realise how few options there were left for them.

The Duke continued, 'The day after tomorrow the trebuchet will be ready, and I will demolish your castle.' He waved his arm towards the clearing out of range from the castle where the frame was rising. 'You may not know the terror of the machine, the rain of stones and fireballs it can bring.' He gestured towards Robert. 'Your compatriot here does. He has experienced the true power of the awful machine. In case you do not believe me, I will release him. He will vouch for the truth of what I say, and he will tell you that we will be magnanimous when you surrender. His release is a gesture of good faith, to show that we are merciful and honourable knights. We will return tomorrow for your answer, and it had better be a positive one; we will give no quarter if we have to storm the ruins after the bombardment.'

He prodded Robert with his sword, and pushed him towards the gatehouse. 'You will tell your people to surrender. If they do, we will harm none of them. If they do not, everyone will be killed when the castle falls. Be sure you do not fail me, or your colleague here will be the first to feel the results of my anger.'

Robert looked round at de Kingston, and made to try to persuade him to take his place but de Kingston shook his head

Evening

and encouraged him with a smile. 'You must go. You have youth and vigour on your side. I am sure that you will tell Sir Hugh what needs to be done.'

They had already discussed whether an armed sortie from the castle would have any chance of destroying or disabling the trebuchet. The aggression in de Kingston had come to the fore when he said that it was better to go down fighting with honour than to sit in the castle while it was destroyed around them. In either case their island and their homes would be ravaged. He had become passionate in advocating that the castle should take matters into their own hands. He didn't believe that there was any future in trusting the French.

Robert understood what he was suggesting, gave a nod and, grim-faced, held out his hand for de Kingston to grasp. De Kingston did more than that: he put his arms round Robert and pounded him warmly on the back. 'God be with you, my boy!' he said.

Robert, with surprise, blurted, 'And with you, sire!' in return.

He turned and walked towards the gatehouse, with his head held high and a spring in his step. As the drawbridge was still raised, he could only stand on the edge of the moat, and wait. It was obvious that the order to lower it would not be given while the French were there, just in case the move was a ploy for them to storm the castle. So he turned and stood and watched while de Beauvais wheeled his horse and signalled that the French contingent should withdraw into the trees and march back along the track towards Nieuport. There was silence from within the castle as they too stood and watched, cursing under their breath, but wondering what was happening.

A full five minutes passed and all of the French were out of sight before Robert heard a shouted order and sounds of movement from within. The drawbridge creaked and groaned as it gradually descended to the horizontal, clunking into the grooves close to where Robert stood. The portcullis was only half-raised, and the massive nail-studded oak doors behind it opened slightly, and half a dozen men squeezed through. The battlements were lined with archers, to provide covering fire in case the French made a last-minute attempt to gain entry.

24 August 1377

The militia men ran over to Robert and hastily shepherded him through the gates and into the courtyard. Immediately there was a satisfying thud as the gates were slammed shut behind them and the portcullis clanged into place. With clanks and squeals the drawbridge was raised and Robert was safe amongst his own again.

Once through the gate he was welcomed by a crush of people all clamouring to greet and congratulate him on his release and question him about his capture. The battlements around the courtyard were lined with defenders who cheered and clapped as if he were a victorious hero. Rachel stood in the doorway of Sir Hugh's residence, flushed and radiant in her joy at seeing him free again. Because of the crowd they were unable to reach each other, but exchanged longing looks. Robert shrugged his shoulders in resignation. Then Sir Hugh strode forward, closely followed by Peter. The crowd parted before them, and Rachel managed to get in close behind before the crowd closed again. Harold wriggled through between the legs of the guards who were trying to restrain him and kept up with the welcoming group. Robert took Rachel's hand, but a brief touch was all they managed before Sir Hugh congratulated him and told him the news of his father's death.

Robert reeled with the shock; he felt as if he had been hit with a hammer blow. Sir Hugh realised that now was not the best time, nor the best place, to find out why Robert had been released and what he could reveal about the French plans. That would have to wait until later; an hour or so would make little difference.

It was some minutes before Robert could speak. During that time he was in a daze as Timothy the bailiff and Alice welcomed him back. Alice folded him in her strong arms and almost crushed him in consolation, and shed a tear for his father. Timothy assured him that the family possessions were safely hidden or in the castle. Robert could scarcely take the facts in, but promised to seek them later to find out more.

Rachel then led him into the residence and to Rebecca's room where the pain of the bad news was softened by the sight of the boy his father had not lived to see. They spent only a few minutes together, but Robert watched with Peter while his sister fed his little nephew. He marvelled at the calm peaceful joy on her face at the fulfilment of her womanhood. This continuity of life helped Robert to accept his father's death, especially when he learned the new baby's name.

After a few minutes Robert roused himself from his silent introspection, and his mind turned to the other urgent things that he must do. He silently asked his father to forgive his rushing on. He turned to Rachel, whose hand he was painfully but unconsciously gripping. She had been gazing earnestly at his face, understanding the pain within him, while trying not to show the pain in her hand.

'I must see your mother, Rachel, my love. I must reassure her that your father is well. Where is she? Can you show me?'

'Yes, but before that I must have a look at your wounds,' Rachel pleaded. 'Please let me look at them in case they need any of my ointments to ease them.'

Robert crossed the room to be away from the birth bed, and tried to take off his shirt, wincing as he raised his left arm. Rachel's hands smoothed over his shoulder and gently eased the torn and stained clothing away from his skin, exposing his brown well-muscled torso. His skin tingled as her cool soothing hands touched him.

The entry wound had sealed over, but still looked red and swollen, though there was no sign of inflammation that might presage deep-seated infection. She gasped when she turned him round to look at the long wound where the bolt had come out at the front of the shoulder. The wound looked healthy enough, but it had ripped its way through the muscle and skin, and she paled to think of the pain he must have suffered during the long treks of the last few days. She ran her fingers lightly over the raised flesh, and peered closely at it, both front and back.

Peter came across and peered at the wound, sucking his lips in, and shaking his head.

'It's all right. The barber cauterised it well with a red-hot iron,' said Robert firmly. 'It's only a bit stiff, and as it's the left arm I don't need to use it that much for fighting, or for eating,' he added with a grin.

24 August 1377

'Just raise your arm up sideways,' Rachel retorted with pursed lips.

Robert tried to lift his arm with it outstretched, but grunted when it reached about waist height, and he had to let it fall back down to his side.

'I thought so. There is still damage to the muscles. It needs time to repair. It looks as if it is mending well, but I think I have the ingredients to make an ointment that will help it. You should rest it and support it in a sling. While you speak to my mother I'll prepare some liniment that should help the muscle to mend, and make it easier to move your arm.'

After he had put on a clean shirt that Peter found for him, and with his arm in a crude sling, Rachel took his other hand and led him down the corridor to her mother's room, faithfully followed by the small shadow of Harold.

Robert entered the room, feeling ashamed of his dirty and unkempt appearance. He didn't think that he was likely to impress the woman he hoped would eventually be his mother-in-law. Isabel de Kingston was sitting with her hands folded in her lap, but twisting a handkerchief round her fingers. The tension showed on her face, and there were dark circles beneath her eyes.

Her eyes lit up when she saw Robert, guessing immediately who he was. She sprang up and embraced him, then held him at arm's length and inspected him. The smile on her face indicated approval; obviously she had accepted him as Rachel's chosen man. She drew Robert across to a chair and sat and held his hand firmly between both of hers. Though the lines of worry weighed heavily on her face, she smiled again, relieved that she at last had the prospect of firm information about her lord.

There was not a great deal that Robert could say, except to reassure her that de Kingston was well and cheerful, and that he was being well treated. He described the camp, the French commanders and the food, trying to give her an insight into the relatively comfortable conditions and the tolerant captors. The strain on her face gradually eased, and she began to quietly weep with relief in Rachel's arms.

After a few minutes Robert excused himself. He left Rachel with her mother and went to the chapel where his father's rough

Evening

coffin stood in front of the altar. It was cool, quiet and peaceful there, away from the bustle and noise outside. There was no one else to disturb his solemn prayers; he didn't see Harold stealthily creep in and stand at the back of the chapel.

Previously Robert had never obtained any relief through prayer. Though he had gone to church because it was expected of him, it had never meant much. But this time he felt that someone was hearing him, listening to his entreaties for the peaceful rest of the soul of his father. A calm peace welled up inside him and for the first time in his life he could believe in, as well as feel, the presence of God. He felt tears prickling his eyes and a great lump of anguish hurt his chest. His shoulders bowed and the tension of the last few days, and the stress of his wound found relief in a series of sobs. Tears coursed down his cheeks. Harold stood silently, praying as well as he knew.

It was not long before a repeated polite cough made Robert wipe his eyes, rise from his knees and turn. Sir Hugh was standing inside the door, his hands crossed in front of his chest, looking care-worn and sorrowful. Almost apologetically he asked Robert to excuse him for requesting so soon that he meet with the other lords to give an account of what had happened when he was captive of the French forces, why he had been released, and what he knew of their plans. Robert was obliged to tear himself away from his contemplation, mentally promising that he would return as soon as he could. On the way out he saw Harold, and for the first time recognised him as the lad he had saved at Yarmouth. Crouching down he took the lad in a firm hug and ruffled his hair. Then, with his hand on the lad's shoulder, he followed Sir Hugh outside into the bright and windy sunset, with Harold gazing admiringly at him.

A few minutes later Robert sat in the great hall of the castle, leaning wearily on the table, drinking and eating the frugal meal that was all that rationing of the provisions would allow. He was surrounded by the other lords and was relating to them all he had seen and experienced while in French hands. As he ate, he quickly recounted his capture and the march to Nieuport. Most of his account was an assessment of the French numbers, as far as he could estimate them, their disposition and arms, and the threats

24 August 1377

that they were making. Sir Hugh was dismayed to hear that there were possibly as many as 6,000 French, and to have it confirmed that the East Wight had also been attacked. Though he was aware that the French fleet was moored in the Medine, he didn't know how many ships there were in total. Despite the show of strength impressed on them by the daily routine parading round the castle, the garrison had not realised the real numbers of enemy they were up against. They were horrified to learn that there were simultaneous invasions occurring elsewhere along the English coast. That would mean the prospect of relief from the mainland was slim; the troops there would be busy on several other fronts.

When Robert got to the hanging of the burgesses in retribution for the lack of progress on the ransom demands, their dismay increased. They had not grasped the full meaning of de Beauvais' speech and hearing directly from an eyewitness brought the event home in full measure. Robert was sure that the French commander's intention was to shorten the ransom discussions by letting them have a first-hand account of the hangings, as well as an understanding of the impact that the forthcoming use of the siege weapon would have.

'What is this thing the French are building that they call a trebuchet?' asked de Gorges.

Once Robert had described the mechanical sling, everyone realised what a threat it was. None of them had ever seen one in action, but they realised they *had* heard of it. It had once been known as the 'warwolf', and had been used by Edward I in the siege of Stirling Castle during the wars against the Scots. That seemingly impregnable castle had been forced to surrender within a matter of days under a hail of huge stones fired by the dreadful siege engine.

At this new explanation the looks of despair lengthened, as the lords came to understand the vulnerability of their position. It had been obvious that the French could starve out the defenders if they were prepared to continue the siege for long enough, and the only consolation had been that the attackers did not know how poor the defence was nor how short their supplies. Now it looked as if their fate could be decided within a few days.

John Urrey jumped to his feet in agitation. 'I think that we ought to surrender straight away, and throw ourselves on their mercy.'

'But how do you know that they will show mercy?' someone else interjected. 'Look at the way they hanged the poor burgesses. At least we can delay until the machine is ready to fire. Perhaps it won't work well enough, or assistance will come from the mainland. And if the weather worsens the French may withdraw.' There were murmurs of assent from several of the others.

'I have an alternative plan,' said Robert, 'one which de Kingston and I discussed at length. It is risky, but it may work.'

It was growing dark outside and candles were brought in, illuminating the expectant faces around the table. The flames flickered in the blustery wind that had begun to howl around the castle and moan through the passageways. After the food and the anticlimax of his release Robert felt tiredness creeping over him, and he had to fight to stifle his yawns. He haltingly revealed the desperate plan that he and de Kingston had talked about and refined during the hours following the hangings in the town, when their fury at the invaders was at its height. The crucial element of the plan was surprise. If it were to misfire the plight of the defenders would be almost untenable. It was based on the apparent complacence of the French, who had not encountered very much in the way of resistance to their invasion; though they had been careful to start with, they had become lax in their alertness and were now not setting much in the way of guards, nor anticipating any sort of trouble or retaliation.

'The idea is to catch the French unawares, when their forces are divided and not expecting attack,' said Robert. 'You know where the roads divide at the bottom of the hill, one going to the west gate of the town, and the other round to the south. Well, the one to the south leads to the French encampment. They take that way every night and morning to come up here to carry out their ritual parade. It's a sunken lane, very narrow, with thick undergrowth on either side. They can't use outriders and can only march three abreast in the lane. We could ambush them there. Archers hidden in the undergrowth on either side along the lane, attacking simultaneously, would hit them so hard they wouldn't

24 August 1377

know what was happening until it was too late. Within a few seconds at least half of the force could be out of action, and with luck even more of them. Any horsemen wouldn't be able to get along the lane to help, and couldn't get into the woods to fight back. Even if some escaped back to the camp, assistance would take many tens of minutes to come from the camp or the town. By that time we would be back in the castle.'

'What if they have changed their routine?' asked Peter.

'It has been the same ever since they have been here, but if there are differences then the signal to attack needn't be given and we can let them pass. The critical thing is that the attack must be well disciplined so that the head of the column is well past the ambush point before the attack. Otherwise their rearguard will not be trapped, but could circle round and trap us before we can get back to the castle. They have always come with about 200 or so men. Marching three abreast, the column would extend about half a furlong. We would need enough men on either side of the lane to cover the whole of that length, and to kill or injure half of them in the first flight of arrows. The second flight should hit half of the rest before they could regroup and retaliate.'

'How many men would that need, Robert?' asked Sir Hugh.

'I think that about a hundred on our side would be all that we would need to cover the length,' he replied. 'That would give one every two yards or so. Any more than that and there would not be enough cover and there would be the risk of being seen.'

'That's all very well, Robert,' said John Urrey, 'but we barely have that many men in the castle to release for such a risky enterprise. We must ensure that we have enough left to defend the castle if anything goes wrong. If all those men were lost or couldn't get back into the castle, we couldn't stop a full attack with scaling ladders on the walls and the gatehouse at the same time. I think it's too risky.'

'I agree that there is a risk, but I like the idea,' said de Gorges. 'But we would need to silence the patrols that are always watching us at the gates. They will give the alarm if we try anything unusual, and then it would be us who would be ambushed. They change guard every time the others come up from the main camp to do their circuits of the castle and the engineers arrive and leave.

Have you seen how, night and morning for the hour or so before their relief comes, the men are not out patrolling around the castle walls, but are sitting by their fire in the woods outside the main gates talking, and in the morning many are still sleeping? If we sent out men by the postern gate we could surprise them and either kill or capture them. But every one of them would have to be taken, or the warning could be given to the French. If they weren't, we would have to abort the ambush and then in future the French would be suspicious and come another way or bring more men. We only have one chance. If we try it, and are unsuccessful, the French will give us no quarter at all. But that is what they are proposing anyway, unless we give in!'

'If we can successfully silence the sentries the ambush could go ahead. If not, we would have to abort it, but we would end up with some hostages of our own to bargain with. I think it is worth the risk,' said Sir Hugh. 'But de Kingston's life is at stake. They will kill him in retribution. We must try to rescue him if at all possible.'

'We thought of that eventuality when we discussed the plan,' interjected Robert. 'Both of us were adamant that our fate was not to be considered as important against the possible defeat of the French, should the possibility of an ambush ever arise. We were quite prepared to die if the Island and our families could be spared. If we can silence the patrol, it would be possible to set fire to the trebuchet, or damage it enough that it would take several days to repair. That would give us more time.'

'Excellent!' said Sir Hugh. 'We must do it tonight. The wind will give us good cover. We cannot wait until tomorrow. We must move quickly, because we need to be in place along the lane at least half an hour before the Noddies come. That means we would have to leave the castle a good hour before dawn, and have the guards dealt with and out of the way before then.

'I will need to lead the ambushing party and Sir Theobald should stay in charge at the castle.' He said to de Gorges, 'You have fought the French before, so you know how to deal with them.' He was alluding to de Gorges' successful defence of the Island against French invaders some fifteen years before, when they had been driven back to their ships after a considerable battle near St Helen's in the eastern Wight.

24 August 1377

'You will have to come too, Robert. You have seen the road and thought out the best place for the ambush, and the way that it can be most effective.'

'Just you try and stop me,' retorted Robert. 'I saw them hang the burgesses. I must take revenge for that.'

'Excellent!' said de Gorges, leaning forward, charged with excitement. 'We will need our best men, those who can be trusted to obey orders, and be quiet and still until the word is given; those who will fight to the death if necessary. Luckily all our men are Island born and bred. They can sneak up on a coney without it knowing, and outsmart the deer in the woods. This is their island. They will fight and die, if necessary, for freedom and their families. All they want is the chance.'

'We only have one chance,' said Sir Hugh. 'If we fail we may lose the castle and our lives. If that were the case the French might bring in reinforcements and stay over the winter. Once we are into the autumn storms it would be difficult for those from the mainland to force them out and recover the island.'

'Sir Hugh,' broke in Peter, 'please excuse me speaking my mind but I think it would be rash for you to lead the party to attack the guards. It should be left to some of the younger fighters. You are too important to be wounded and incapacitated in a small, dangerous skirmish. If it were to fail, you would be needed to organise the defence of the castle.'

Sir Hugh frowned and thought before speaking. 'Very well! Yes, I see your point. I agree. I am old and not light and quick on my feet these days. I should leave it to some of the young bloods with courage and strength.' Then, looking pointedly at Peter, he said, 'You can lead the first stage then.' It was obvious that he thought it an opportunity for Peter, rather than a punishment for speaking out.

Then, looking round the table at the eight assembled lords, he told them to each pick twenty of their best men for the ambush and have them assemble in the courtyard in an hour's time so that they could be instructed in the plan and could prepare their weapons. 'But be sure that there is no noise or sound of unusual activity. The French outside must believe that all is normal.'

★

After Robert had washed and dressed in fresh garments he had fetched from Alice, he returned to the de Kingstons' room. He entered with a spring in his step, feeling a new man now he was clean and fed. Lady Isabel had already gone to bed, to sleep the soundest she had for several nights. Rachel had finished preparing the ointment and was sitting talking quietly to Harold. He was lying on the floor, his head resting on his hands, gazing at her with admiration while she told him a story. He had never had stories told to him before, as his parents had never had the time, the knowledge or the ability. He was enthralled.

As Robert entered Rachel brought the story to an end, and Harold transferred his gaze to Robert who had sat beside him.

'Take your shirt off, Robert, and I'll rub in some of this,' Rachel said, picking up a bowl of evil-looking, vile-smelling grease. While she started to rub the ointment into the areas around the wounds, Robert told her of the plan to outwit the French. Harold was wide-eyed and excited at the idea, but Rachel was afraid; afraid of Robert going back into danger, afraid that this time he might not come back. But she kept her fears hidden and succeeded in keeping her face clear of any concern. She knew that he had to go, that it was his duty and that he would still go whatever she said. She loved him all the more for his sense of responsibility and the personal sacrifice he was making to help others. Anyway, she was also worried about her father who was still in the hands of the enemy. What would happen to him if the ambush were to succeed? If they didn't manage to free him at the same time the French would almost certainly take immediate vengeance on him.

Robert sensed the reason for her unease and explained that her father had considered this possibility when they were discussing the plan before Robert was released. He had suggested the ambush should go ahead anyway, and was prepared to sacrifice himself if necessary to ensure victory for the Islanders. In fact, they had both felt the same. Robert had said that he would want de Kingston to do precisely the same as he was doing if their roles had been reversed.

24 August 1377

'If they follow their normal pattern, they will bring him along to display during their circuit of the castle. If so, we may be able to rescue him during the ambush,' said Robert.

'I pray to God that it shall be that way, and that you will return safely to me. I don't want you harmed again, now that you have survived capture once.'

Rachel gently massaged the soothing grease into the wound; Robert could feel the stiffness easing and the nagging pain lessening. He worked his shoulder a couple of times and found he could now raise his elbow as high as his ear. His eyes were closing with weariness and he yawned cavernously. Rachel signed to Harold that he should leave them alone, and she gently shooed him out of the door and back to his bed with the servants.

She took Robert by the hand. 'That is enough for now, my love. You will need some sleep before you venture out to the ambush. Why don't you sleep here? I will wake you in time.' She kissed him softly, and drew him down onto a pile of rugs and skins in a corner of the chamber. Putting her fingers on his lips to stop further kisses, she laid his head on her lap. Soothing his ruffled hair, she softly crooned to him, so that he could snatch a few hours of well-earned rest. He fell asleep almost immediately with the taste of her warm kisses still on his lips. She watched over him with love in her heart.

25 August 1377

Dawn

The knight approached him with drawn sword. Robert fought to raise his own, but his arm felt heavy. He even had to use his weak left arm to help raise the tip of the sword to waist height. An archer by his side gripped his arm, preventing him raising it any further. Even though he fought as hard as he could, he failed to get his defence raised in time. Desperation flooded through him as the Frenchman gave a hollow, sneering laugh and drew back his sword for a lunge. Robert awoke with a start to find his arm being shaken by Rachel. He had been struggling and grunting in his sleep in the throes of a nightmare. Her face showed the concern she had at how long it had taken to bring him out of it. Beside her stood one of Sir Hugh's squires.

'Sire, the raiding party is assembling at the postern gate and are preparing to attack the Noddies. Sir Hugh is asking for you to be there while the instructions are being issued, just in case there is any more that you can remember that may be important before they leave.'

'I will come at once,' Robert said as he clambered to his feet.

After a quick farewell to Rachel he hurried down the stairs after the squire. He was not part of the group setting out to attack the guards and disable the trebuchet because his presence was deemed to be more useful for the ambush. As soon as the troops on guard outside were disposed of, and the way was clear, the ambush party would immediately need to set out to the sunken lane.

The postern gate was on the northern side of the castle, set low at the bottom of the moat around the keep. There a silent group of about fifty men-at-arms stood quietly, some resting on their drawn swords, others whispering softly to each other. The large form of Michael Apse appeared to tower above the others,

25 August 1377

but he stood alone with a look of subdued excitement on his face. He was itching to get into the fray.

It was dark, and was still windy and warm. The men were all dressed in dark leather cotes, on top of short chain-mail haubergeon, and with leather-covered helmets protecting their heads. All metal parts were covered with mud so as not to shine in the light from the sky, and many had also smeared their faces. Armed with short swords and bucklers, they were prepared for close hand-to-hand fighting. There were also some others who were more lightly clad to help catch any invaders who might flee.

Sir Hugh acknowledged Robert when he appeared and turned towards the men. They ceased talking so that he could quietly address them. Peter de Heyno, who was to lead them, stood by his side.

'We depend on you men to silence the guards. Our lookouts in the gatehouse say that the Noddies are all at their shelters. They will give warning if the guards move. You should have surprise on your side provided you maintain silence. Silence is imperative. No one can be allowed to escape to warn the other Noddies at Nieuport. There will be ten men posted on the road down from the castle. If any do escape in the dark, they are bound to take the road rather than going through the woods. This will form a second line of defence, but make sure that you don't take the road and fall into that trap yourselves. Once the guards are silenced and we have been told, the next phase of the ambush can go ahead. Once dawn has broken and the ambush mounted, you can burn the timber. Do what you can to destroy the siege engine. That may be difficult because it is all green wood, and it may just create smoke. Peter de Heyno here is your leader. I wish you all God's luck. The safety of the Island depends on you.'

'There will be no survivors if they do escape,' Peter said with determination to Sir Hugh. He gestured towards the men, 'Every one of you has lost something to the French marauders. All we have been wanting is a chance to get even. Now is that chance.' Then, turning to the support party who were to man the road, he gave some necessary instructions. 'If we do not trap them all I will give a double owl hoot so that you know to expect someone running on the way to the town. When we get them all I will give

Dawn

a bark like a dog fox. You all know those sounds. Get ready to open the postern!'

'God be with you, Peter,' said Sir Hugh as he clapped him on the shoulder. 'The rest of the ambush party will await your signal.'

Peter and Robert embraced, and whispered 'God be with you' to each other as the postern gate was unbarred. The huge wooden bars were lifted out of the stone sockets on either side as quietly as possible, and the gate swung back without a squeak on hinges specially greased with goose fat. The men filed silently through. The gate closed briefly behind them and then opened again to let the second group of ten men through, those who were going to guard the escape route down the road.

The postern gate opened on to a narrow raised pathway that crossed the moat to the cleared ground around the castle. The thorn bushes were thick in the moat on either side, but were trimmed down so that anyone using the path would be exposed to fire from the battlements above. The group stood for a moment close against the castle wall in the darkness, while Peter ran like a ghost silently across the bare ground towards the trees. There was a brief pause while everyone waited to hear whether an alarm would be raised. All was quiet. Happily, the French troops were not paying full attention to their duties. Following a wave from Peter, one by one the rest crossed to the surrounding trees. The moon was on the wane, but the darkness was intense when the moon was covered by cloud. All the men had very good nightsight, and the darkness was a comfort rather than a hindrance. They were used to poaching the lords' conies and pheasants in the darkest nights of hungry winters, to creeping silently through the crackling twigs and rustling leaves of autumn woods, and snatching sleeping birds from the frozen branches. All they hoped was that the French were not there to see them, but were still in their camp by the main gates. No signal was given by lookouts spying from the slits in the gatehouse walls that anything unusual had occurred. All was quiet; the invaders were still unsuspecting and the attack could continue.

Once in the trees they split into two groups. The first group moved slightly down the hill, and then around to the west, to

25 August 1377

ascend on the far side and outflank the French column by coming in from the side away from the castle. The second group waited for a while for the others to reach their objective before, at a signal from Peter, they started creeping up the hill directly parallel to the road. The rustling of the night wind in the trees covered the small sounds they made. An owl hooted mournfully in the woods across the valley. A loud and unearthly scream nearby made everyone jump and started hearts beating even faster but it was only a vixen calling for a mate – a sound to make the hairs rise on the back of the neck. Peter was afraid that this frightening noise would set the French on edge, and make them alert and wakeful. They edged along with even greater caution; the moon shone fitfully through a gap in the clouds, which were rushing past on the brisk wind.

It was only about a furlong through the trees to the spot where the French guard platoon was camped. They had several lean-to shelters at the edge of the woods and beside the trebuchet, where they would have a clear view of the castle main gate, and the road leading up to it. The postern gate was not in their sight. With the trees behind them, the soldiers could come and go with ease, and there were ample supplies of wood to hand to feed the cooking fire and to keep off the chill of the night and the heavy dewy damp of the early summer mornings.

There was enough moonlight for the creeping Islanders to see a few yards, keep in touch with each other and avoid the intervening trees. The first flush of dawn was still a couple of hours away.

Peter gestured for the party to stop. They could not have been more than a few yards away from the enemy. They stood silently, holding their breath and with their mouths open, in order to hear better. Their straining ears detected no sounds from the encampment. All at once the rustling noise of a brief movement came, but then silence. The noise was not repeated. Either a guard had moved to ease his position, or perhaps a sleeper had stirred in his dreams.

Peter decided that they could wait no longer and had to take their chance; further delay might mean detection. At a sign from him the Islanders fanned out to form a semicircle in the trees, but they froze when there was a sudden crack, followed by a muffled curse. A dry twig had broken under a foot. The noise sounded deafening to the nervous attackers, but there was no call of alarm, no rush of the watchman to grab arms and defend themselves.

After a couple of minutes' waiting with bated breath, the steady advance resumed. Several attackers crept along the edge of the wood, still undercover, able, if necessary, to rush into the open to cut off that escape route. To the left, across the clear ground the walls of the castle rose sheer and dark, just visible silhouetted against the paler sky. All was quiet within the castle, though Peter was sure that invisible watchers would be at every window and loophole. Beyond the camp the two trunks forming the uprights of the trebuchet peered over the surrounding trees, sinister and overbearing, capped now with the crossbeam and the throwing arm in place.

Once he was sure the outflanking group had sufficient time to get into position, Peter cupped his hands and blew one soft owl hoot, the pre-arranged signal for attack. Quickly, but still quietly, they advanced towards their foes. Peter could see the figure of one guard standing leaning against a tree, vaguely outlined against the night sky. His head was drooping, his chin resting on his chest – obviously not expecting trouble – he didn't even have a helmet on. Sounds of gentle snores came from his sleeping comrades in the shelters. Noise of a sudden scuffle and a half-throttled coughing came from the other side of the camp. The guard, now more than half-awake, started to move towards the noise, struggling to unsheath his sword. Luckily, and unexpectedly, he didn't call out. Suddenly the huge grey shape of Michael Apse rose, like a wraith, from the ground in front of him, and thrust a short sword to the hilt upwards through his belly and into his chest, at the same time clasping a hand over his mouth to suppress the dying scream. The dead man was lowered gently to the ground. Now, the Islanders rushed into the shelters, ruthlessly hacking and thrusting with their swords. The French were completely surprised and stood no chance, their screams quickly silenced. Many were cut down before they could reach their arms to defend themselves. Others fell to their knees crying for mercy, their hands over their heads.

25 August 1377

In a minute or two, which seemed only seconds, it was all over. Peter walked around congratulating the men and making a count of the captured, wounded and dead French. He knew, by comparison with numbers counted previously from the battlements, how many there should be. There was one missing! He swore an oath and ordered the men to spread out again to find the missing soldier, who could well be hiding nearby, waiting to escape and raise the alarm in the French camp. The circle widened until a triumphant whispered call revealed discovery of the man hiding in a bush. He was brought into the camp still trying to tie the belt around his waist to stop his breeches falling down. Obviously before the attack he had been answering the call of nature and had been unable to escape with his breeches about his ankles. That made a full count of the French: ten dead, sixteen wounded and twenty captured.

Relieved that the foray had been a total success, Peter cupped his hands to his mouth and gave the agreed signal, the bark of a dog fox. Faintly from the castle came muffled cheers, quickly suppressed.

'Back to the postern gate with the captives, and take care to guard them well,' ordered Peter. 'We will leave the trebuchet for later. Others will come back and deal with that once the ambush has been mounted.'

He doubted the French would even contemplate trying to escape. Many were shivering with shock at the suddenness of the attack and the deaths of so many of their friends. They didn't want the same fate to befall them, and realised their best future lay with ensuring the goodwill of the Islanders and the possibility of being exchanged as hostages. The wounded were helped or carried by their compatriots and the procession slowly returned to the postern gate, leaving the dead lying where they had fallen. At the postern gate the guard, having watched them cross the grass outside, opened it at the first knock. Once inside everyone was jubilant. Sir Hugh clapped a widely smiling Peter on the back with satisfaction, and Robert embraced him too, relieved that he was safe again. The first step of their plan had succeeded.

The captives were questioned, but could reveal nothing, as they knew nothing. They were simple soldiers doing as they were instructed, and their officer had been killed. They were all relieved to be taken captive rather than being killed, as they might well have been; such were the rules of war. It was not expected that ordinary men would be captured and ransomed or used as hostages. That privilege was normally kept for the knights, whose families and friends could be relied upon to find considerable fortunes as ransom. Back in their own ranks they could expect little mercy for having been surprised and defeated, but fair exchange would regain them some honour. Now they would be put to work in the treadmill at the well.

The Islanders dispersed quickly. Some of them headed for the well to wash their heads, hot and sweaty from inside their helmets, and their hands from the blood. Others went to relieve themselves, the excitement and tension having filled their bladders. All fetched their bows and had a well-earned drink and a quick bite to eat. But within minutes they all reassembled ready to set out again for the ambush. This time they were joined by many more, to make up a total force of about 150, as many as could be spared from the castle defences. Their departure had to be carefully timed. To arrive too early would leave the men waiting at the ambush keyed up for too long. If they got stiff their concentration would lapse. Arrive too late, and they might not get into position in time.

Robert's plan was to set out in plenty of time, and to travel not directly down the road, which might lead to an encounter with a French patrol, but along one of the side tracks through the woods; a rather roundabout way, longer but safer. They could then rest near to the ambush point before moving into position at the appropriate time. The total distance was only about a mile, and so a start an hour before dawn had been agreed upon.

Peter and Robert divided the force between them. The men would have to be on opposite sides of the lane, and communication was easier through the trees along the lane rather than across it. Peter was to be near one end of the ambush, and Robert near the other. All the men, including the two leaders, were armed with longbows and swords, their faces and all metal work covered with mud. Peter was in overall charge, once he had agreed with Robert the place of the ambush and the timing of the

25 August 1377

attack. In the event of unforeseen trouble it was up to Peter to make the decision whether to break off the engagement and retreat to the castle.

While they were away a third group would sally forth to the trebuchet and attempt to destroy or disable it. Again, however, timing would be rather crucial, for any sign of smoke, or too much noise would alert the French before the ambush, and too much delay might curtail what they might achieve. They might only have a few brief minutes to do their worst.

On the signal the postern gate opened, and the troops started to file through. Just as Robert was about to move, there was a touch on his arm. Rachel had appeared from the darkness under the walls. She had obviously been watching and waiting her opportunity, not wanting to intrude upon the soldiering and the preparations. Her blue eyes were unusually dark and soulful in the night and her normally shapely mouth was drawn into a tense, tight line. Her bosom heaved as her breathing came quickly.

'Robert, my love! Please wear this favour for me. Let it be a sign to the Lord, of my love, and of the prayers I will be saying for your safe return.' She tied a kerchief round his arm, and the scent from it wafted to his nostrils. She pressed her warm body urgently against his and raised her lips to his. It was only a moment, that kiss, but within it they exchanged a deep understanding of their urgent passion for each other and of their desire for the future together. With it their minds were content. Come what may, they knew profound and everlasting love, the depths of which had no restraint, nor needed any questions.

He held her at arm's length for a second and looked deeply into her eyes. Despite their worries and concerns for each other, the slow smile that spread across his face was immediately mirrored in hers, shining from the shared light within. 'I will return this favour when we marry, my dearest. I pray it will be soon, and with all our foes vanquished.'

Robert abruptly turned to cover the rising lump in his throat, and without a backward glance followed Peter through the gateway to join the men now assembled outside. The two of them went to the head of the column, and Robert led them to a narrow deer track almost obscured by thick undergrowth. It wound gradually round the hill and down towards the town and would bring them to the sunken lane from the south, rather than from the south-west. The clouds had largely dispersed, the wind had temporarily moderated and the first trilling of birds heralding the day came from the wooded valley below. The light of dawn was growing in the eastern sky, and the remnant of the moon was high enough to give them light to see their way. They marched in single file, tense and silent, with swords drawn and bows across their backs, each man trying to be quieter than his neighbour. They picked their steps so as to avoid snapping dry twigs or tripping on stumps or in coney scratchings. Their legs rapidly became soaked from the wet undergrowth.

When Robert judged they were less than a furlong or so from the lane he whispered for them to halt, so that they could rest for ten minutes before moving on. The message passed back down the line. The men sat down, and some lay with their eyes closed, trying to relax. But the atmosphere was charged with tension as everyone stretched their senses to the limit to catch any noise, any bird alarm call, or other warning that their foes might be early in approaching. However, not many distant sounds could filter through the trees to their resting place. All sounds were lost in the rustling of the wind in the trees. The white knuckles gradually relaxed, and the butterflies in the stomach settled down.

Second by second, more and more could be seen clearly and in detail. First it was just the nearest neighbour, then a tree trunk, the man beyond, then one more.

Robert and Peter moved around the relaxing men, reminding them not to shoot before the signal, and to avoid hitting John de Kingston, should he be with the party. He would be easily distinguished in the rapidly approaching dawn by his shock of white hair. When Robert gave the signal for the men to move into position there were several whispered blessings between friends and relatives.

It was only a few steps through the trees and they were on the brink of the hollow way, looking down into the lane and the trampled leaf mould and mud of its floor. The hollow was about five or six feet deep, and about eight feet wide at the bottom, though it was twice that width at the top. The sides were crumbly

25 August 1377

earth festooned with ferns and ivy, and burrowed by rodents. Overhead the trees met, adding to the gloom. The track rose slightly to the right, where the French were due to come from.

Where they crossed would need to be the furthest point that the French would be allowed to reach. Robert jumped down into the hollow, landing with a thump muffled by the soft leaves. He then beckoned that his half of the men should follow him, and help each other up the far bank to minimise damage to it. When they were all across he covered over their footprints with leaves, and he held out his bow so that someone could pull him up the bank.

Care was taken that no other marks were made further along the track in case they alerted the enemy. The men then spread out on either side along the banks, spaced every two or three yards, and far enough back not to be seen when they were squatting down. Luckily there was moderately thick undergrowth of ferns and brambles reaching about two or three feet high, that would help provide a good screen. The boles of some trees were even large enough for a man to hide behind, and the thick foliage provided deep shadow. Altogether, the ambushers should be virtually invisible.

Robert had chosen a straight section of the track about a hundred yards long below a bend. If the same routine as before was followed, the mounted knights would be at the head, hemmed in and unable to help further back. He calculated that the back of the column would not be able to see what was happening at the van, and yet the ambushers would be able to see each other satisfactorily to signal. Robert was near where they had crossed, and would be able to make a sign when the marching column reached him. He could see where Peter was crouching behind a large tree far down the other side near the bend, and Peter could see the path beyond the bend, to where the tail end of the column was likely to be. He would be able to see the strength of the French force, judge whether there was any need to abort the ambush. He would also see how many men escaped the hail of arrows to run back and raise the alarm at the French camp.

All the men prepared themselves for the fray. They stuck their swords in the ground, near enough at hand to be easily seized.

Dawn

They unslung and strung their bows and nocked arrows into their strings, sticking a further two or three in the ground beside them. Then crouching down or kneeling to make themselves invisible to mounted men riding on the track, and in as relaxed a way as possible, they waited.

The steady breeze rustled and rattled in the treetops, but close to the forest floor the rain-damp earthy smell of the woods was sweet to the nostrils. Ears strained for sounds of the enemy. There was little birdsong in their part of the woods, but the final strains of the late summer dawn chorus could be heard further away. Did the birds sense that blood would soon be shed? It was almost as if the whole world held its breath.

Robert was glad for the wind, as it would cover any sounds the men might make as they eased their cramped positions. From where he was he could just make out the top of Peter's head where he knelt behind a tree, but he could see none of the men he knew were on the other side of the track. He could only see the nearest three on his side, one of them being the broad back of Michael Apse. Their camouflage was complete. All was now in the hands of the gods. He rested his hand against the rough bark of the ash tree beside him, taking comfort from its solidity and feel of permanence. He thought of Rachel.

Suddenly the clattering alarm call of a blackbird came from along the track towards the camp. Everyone drew a deep breath, crossed themselves and muttered a Hail Mary, for the testing time had come. The die was cast, to fall as it may. Then came the sound of marching, the regular thump of feet evenly placed on the soft earth, together with the clink of armour and the snuffling of horses. Initially muffled by the foliage, gradually the sounds became louder.

Robert could feel his heart pounding, almost in time with the beat of the footsteps. His excitement was building up and the adrenaline began flowing, but his mouth felt peculiarly dry. He cautiously peeped through the foliage and saw Peter holding his hand up in the lee of the tree, his fingers and thumb forming an ecstatic circle. The hand was quickly withdrawn just as the leaders came into sight round the bend. Robert caught sight of the first horse and then crouched even lower to be out of sight.

25 August 1377

Nevertheless he could see the steady progress of the French band between the leaves and branches.

At the head of the column were about a dozen mounted lords and their squires. Because the track was so narrow they had to ride in single file. The low sweeping branches forced the riders to carry their lances at rest across the saddles. Even so, they had to take care that the tips didn't foul the undergrowth on either side. At the head was the Duke de Beauvais, his long hair poking out from beneath his helmet, and his beard sticking stubbornly forward. He was looking weary and somewhat listless. Perhaps the strain of the past few days of continual activity and little sleep had had an effect on his judgement. Why else would they be so careless to the possibilities of attack? Behind him came the swarthy and scowling de Mortagne, perhaps the source of most of that strain, followed by the other riders on less well-apparelled steeds. To Robert's relief, amongst them was de Kingston, bareheaded and with his head held high, his white streak of hair showing brightly. His eyes flicked to and fro as he surreptitiously scanned the undergrowth for the attack that he half-expected, but he took care to appear relaxed and diffident. The mass of archers followed behind them, two abreast, talking quietly to each other, or humming softly one of their marching tunes. Their swords were sheathed and crossbows were not drawn. It would take each archer a good half a minute to crank the handle to draw the crossbow before inserting and firing the bolt; they were totally unprepared. It looked as if fortune was indeed smiling on the Islanders that day.

Robert wanted to make sure that de Kingston was beyond the line of fire before he gave the signal to attack, but that meant the two enemy chiefs would also be well beyond the main flight of arrows. He decided to aim for de Mortagne himself: Robert saw him as being the cause of most of the harm coming to the Island. He let the last of the horses get just past him, gave a signal to Peter, and with a shout leapt to his feet. At the same time he drew his bow to about half-stretch – no more was necessary at such close quarters, and let the arrow go. Around him the whole phalanx of Island archers erupted from the undergrowth with bloodcurdling shouts and screams and loosed a withering hail of arrows. The arrows were directed down into the hollow way so that none would endanger those on the other side of the lane. Only a few yards between the bow and the enemy meant that most found their mark, though some bounced off the iron helmets. Screams of terror and pain filled the air, many falling where they stood. Before the men were down, the archers quickly nocked a second arrow into their bows, and some were successful in loosing them off and finding further victims.

The startled Frenchmen looked to right and left with fear and horror on their faces, not knowing which way to turn for safety. The quicker minded held up their shields with one hand, threw down their bows and tried to unsheath their swords. Within the sunken track, as men went down with screams and curses, they fell against each other and brought down even more. Others tried to keep their feet as they struggled to reach their attackers.

Unfortunately, de Mortagne's horse shied when Robert leapt to his feet; his arrow glanced off the man's metal armour and ricocheted into the trees beyond. The horseman immediately spurred on, driving de Beauvais' mount before him, and cantered on up the track to a wider part, where they turned and dismounted. De Kingston also spurred his mount forward with a look of eager joy on his face, thinking he might be able to get away, but he was stopped by the two French leaders before him, as well as the melee of squires which followed him.

About half of the column was down, wounded or dead after the first flight of arrows. They were writhing on the ground. Blood was spurting from where arrows stuck through men's necks, chests and limbs. The screams of the wounded men and some injured horses were ear-splitting, and set the rooks cawing frantically in the trees.

Once the initial shock was over, the French started to regroup. Some struggled up the steep sides of the hollow way in front of the archers, who threw their bows aside to grab their swords and renew the attack in a different fashion. But not all the banks could be climbed, so archers not being attacked went to help repel the scrambling French elsewhere. Shouts and curses came from further along the track showing that battle was hot and strong there too.

25 August 1377

A man-at-arms struggled up the bank in front of Robert, his feet slipping on the slope. Robert snatched his sword from its earthy scabbard, and swung it at the man's head. Thorny brambles grabbed at his legs so that he, too, was off balance and the blade struck the man's helmet, denting it, but not penetrating the thick iron. The blow knocked the man sideways and he fell back to the bottom of the track, only to be trodden on by the next climber. Robert quickly changed his footing and was well balanced and ready for the next assailant. A thrust and a parry followed by a cut across the neck sent the man backwards screaming, with blood spurting like a pulsating fountain from his jugular. This was a memory that would haunt Robert for many future nights.

Robert glanced around. To his left he could see Michael Apse roaring like a bull and hacking at two Frenchmen who had managed to clamber up a gentler part of the bank. For the most part the Islanders stood along the top of the steep bank, and were virtually unassailable. Only on some short sections had their foes managed to clamber up. Other invaders began to flee along the track, rather than face their foes directly. As soon as this happened some of the Islanders forgot their orders and their common sense, in the heat of the moment, and began to descend the bank to chase them. Robert bellowed at them to stay where they were. From the corner of his eye he could see the dismounted French lords and squires striding back into the fray, as fast as their armour would allow; their long swords and armour made them fearsome opponents. They tried to force their way through the melee, shouting, striking right and left with the flat of their swords to drive their men back into some disciplined order. But they too found it difficult to keep their feet, tripping on the bodies in the track and, because of the weight of armour, had to struggle to regain their feet. They were overwhelmed by the press of their own men trying to escape, and began to be forced backwards themselves.

Some of the Islanders now picked up their bows anew, since they couldn't get to use their swords any more, and began to send more arrows into the struggling mass below, as well as towards the French leaders. It was obvious that things had not gone quite so well at the other end of the track. There, many of the Frenchmen had forced their way up the track sides to thrash about in hand-to-hand combat in the undergrowth and to best the attackers.

The tail of the column extended beyond the hidden archers and a solid body of fresh troops now clambered out of the track beyond the bend, and approached through the trees to come to the aid of their fellows. Unsure of the strength of the opposing ambushers, they were careful and slow. While the French hesitated, Peter decided that the main objective had been achieved and signalled his aide to blow the horn for a retreat to the castle. It was better to make a tactical withdrawal now, before they took too many casualties and before further French reinforcements came from the camp, who must have been alerted by the noise.

Suddenly, out of the corner of his eye, Robert saw a man swinging a sword at him from his left. He dodged, but was not quite quick enough. The sword tip swished past his ear, and was deflected by the brim of his helmet, but nevertheless it dealt him a long cut across the brow, just breaking the skin. Robert was dazed by the blow, but stepped backwards to avoid a second swing. Unknowingly on the edge of the bank, he slipped and fell down into the track, his fall being broken by a body. All the breath was knocked out of him, but he struggled to his feet, trying to find a firm footing. His assailant slithered down in front of him, swinging his sword anew for what he thought would be the final cut. Robert stumbled but managed to dodge and moved in closer, while the man was still recovering his balance from the desperate swing. Inside the man's defence he thrust his sword with all the power of his shoulder into the man's chest. His attacker was lifted off his feet and slumped backwards against the bank, pulling Robert with him, and during the struggle to free the sword, Robert became covered in his opponent's blood. He turned quickly and clambered up the opposite bank, so that he could get back to the castle along the track they had come down.

Wherever they could break away the Islanders had melted into the trees. Some of the wounded were helped by their comrades. Others, a small handful, had to be left, eventually to be dispatched by the French. The French were loath to follow too quickly, as

25 August 1377

they had little confidence after the shock of the ambush, and their leadership was still too disorganised to marshal them to effectively counter-attack. Had it registered in Robert's buzzing head, however, he would have heard de Mortagne's loud voice trying to rally his troops to chase the disappearing Islanders.

Before he also turned to go, Robert strived to see what had happened to de Kingston. He couldn't see the captive directly so he sneaked away from the track, circling round to where the French lords had left their mounts. By dodging from tree to tree he managed to get close enough to see de Kingston also dismounted, but with a squire on either side with drawn swords. They were obviously guarding the hostage with their lives, though they anxiously peered down the track at the melee, rather than watching the prisoner.

Robert thought the odds were favourable of rescuing him, as de Kingston himself would probably help by disarming one of the men. Just as he gathered himself to attack, de Beauvais and de Mortagne reappeared from along the track, together with three or four other knights. The odds were now absolutely impossible.

Cursing under his breath Robert turned and started carefully retreating up the hill through the undergrowth. He could hear crashing noises away to his left as the more confident French started to chase the attackers, so he moved to the right, which was towards Caresbrooke. He was confident that the other ambushers were now well on their way to the castle, and that he was one of the last away. At least they should be all well ahead of the pursuing French. He had little alternative to taking a long way round to the castle, as he couldn't risk now using the direct track, in case there were French scouts advancing rapidly along it, trying to cut off the retreating Islanders.

The blood from his cut brow was troubling him. It was running into his eyes and he kept on having to brush it away. He paused, his head turning one way and another to try to work out where the enemy were, so that he could avoid them. Shouts and crashing sounds seemed to be coming now from all quarters. He pushed on trying to avoid the pathways and ended up enmeshed in a thicker part of the undergrowth. This slowed him down, because he had to step over low-lying brambles, which seem designed to trip the unwary, and he had to avoid dead twigs that might crack under his weight. Despite the noise going on around him, he still wanted to make as little noise as possible. With relief he saw that he only had a few more yards to go to a clearer patch, only to see a movement out of the corner of his eye.

A Frenchman in half-armour and with drawn sword had just stepped out of the shadow under the trees into the clearing. Robert froze, hoping that he had not been seen, but to no avail. With a whoop of joy the Frenchman leapt forward to try to catch Robert before he was clear of the clinging thorns. Now that silence was to no avail, Robert swiped at the last of the thorny tendrils with his sword and jumped into the clearing in time to meet the swinging sword of his opponent. Robert was desperate to get away quickly, before further enemies appeared, and while he could still reach the castle. Forgetting the niceties of swordsmanship he forced the man back by the sheer strength of his swinging sword. Right to left, left to right, his wide horizontal swings were blocked. The clash of blades echoed around, and Robert's grunts at each stroke showed his urgency. The Frenchman gave foot by foot and, because of the helmet covering most of his face, he became unsure of his footing. He could not take his eyes off Robert's face, because that was the only way of anticipating Robert's next thrust, and yet he could not see where he was about to tread.

Robert could see a fairly large branch, about four inches in diameter, lying on the ground behind the man. If only he could force the Frenchman to step back against it! He renewed the violence of his attack and pushed forward. His opponent gave way, stepped back and his heel was almost against the branch. One small step more and his foot would be snagged. Robert had to wipe the blood from his eyes with his left hand, and his opponent surged forward with glee. Robert, his vision now temporarily cleared, renewed his attack and forced the man back again – back to the branch. The Frenchman could now feel it pressing behind his heel and he couldn't take a step back. He was forced to glance down as he tried to keep his balance. It was then that Robert took his advantage, stepping closer and thrusting his sword straight at the man's body. It cut through the surcoat, but

25 August 1377

slid off the chain mail beneath, failing to penetrate. But the force of the blow pushed the man over. He tripped backwards over the branch, twisting as he fell, trying to keep his sword aloft to protect himself. As he hit the ground his helmet flew off and his face was revealed.

Robert stood over him, and raised his sword to deliver the fatal blow, catching a glimpse of the favour Rachel had tied on his arm as he did so. A look of abject terror came into the man's eyes, and Robert, blood once more clouding his eyes, could almost see a mirror image of himself as he had been only a few years before. The man was hardly out of his youth, still with only a faint shadow of a beard. He could have a long and happy life, if only...

The fire went out of Robert's soul and he lowered his sword, feeling tired and dispirited. He had at the last moment realised that his assailant was none other than Charles, the young squire who had been his companion on the long march from Francheville those few days before. Similarly, the lad had not realised till then who his bloody adversary was either.

In French Robert said to the lad, 'Be thou well, my young friend. I have no quarrel with you. I give you your life, use it to good benefit!' With that he turned and ran off up a faint path out of the clearing that led in the direction of the castle.

The sounds of their conflict had drawn more soldiers in, and another one stood in Robert's way. Robert felt weary and drained of energy. If he stood and fought, the delay would allow even more of the enemy to come near. He didn't want to have to fight again, or he would never get to the castle. He chose to flee, and ducked into the undergrowth and weaved through the trees beside the path, with the second soldier in close pursuit. A branch tore across his face, opening the cut on his forehead anew. The sap stung in the wound and the blood trickled down into his eyes. The red fog half-blinded him and he stumbled into more trees, gasping frantically for breath, and almost sobbing now with fear. Nevertheless, the pursuer dropped further behind and became nervous of outrunning his compatriots and becoming trapped among the fleeing enemy. He eventually stopped, shouting to his comrades to rally to him and help catch one of the damned English. Frantically brushing the blood from his eyes Robert ran on, not knowing precisely where he was, but realising that going uphill must lead to the castle.

There were more sounds behind him, shouting and the noise of horses crashing through the woods. The French, their spirits returning, were bent on revenge, and no quarter would be offered. His head ached, and his shoulder had begun to throb again, but at least the blood had ceased to flow into his eyes. Brambles clutched at his legs, slowing him down and threatening to trip him up. He looked quickly over his shoulder, glimpsing movement further down the path. There was a shout of triumph. He had been seen and the chase was on again in earnest.

It was going to be a close thing, whether he got to the castle first, or whether the French would catch up with him. Robert knew that there would be no mercy this time. Once it was known that he had taken part in the ambush, despite the leniency of de Beauvais, he would be sure to be killed, and de Kingston too would have the same fate, ransom or no ransom. He twisted and turned through the trees in a desperate attempt to evade his pursuers, going as fast up the hill as he could. Breath was coming in gasps through his open mouth, and his heart was pounding. His knees felt like they were turning to jelly and sweat trickled unnoticed down between his shoulder blades and streaked the blood on his face. Fear drove him on.

The woods suddenly thinned and before him the tall grey walls appeared, tipped with early morning sun. With relief he broke out into the open grassy sward surrounding the castle, and ran straight towards it, shouting to the archers on the walls to give him covering fire. Behind him several soldiers burst from the woods, but stopped when they saw they could not go further without the likelihood of getting an arrow from the battlements. Robert ran round the castle, luckily going the right way towards the postern gate. He stumbled across the entryway spanning the moat and reached the foot of the walls, the protecting arrows hissing overhead from the battlements towards the wood going unheard. He stumbled towards the gate, keeping well in the shadows close to the bottom of the wall, but he was still very exposed. A bolt shattered against the wall just in front of him, and several others embedded in the

25 August 1377

grass behind him. The Castilian crossbowmen had arrived on the scene.

He was in range of their crossbows, and the archers were leaning against the trees to steady their aim at the weaving, stumbling runner. Just another few yards and he would be in reach of the gate. Head down, he was panting, and his chest was heaving. Tiredness was making him shake and his legs wobble. When he reached the gate he raised his fist to pound upon it, for it had been closed some while before, after the other ambushers had returned. It seemed an age that he stood there waiting for the guard to respond, even though the gate opened under his raised fist – they had been watching his erratic sprint and shouting him encouragement. Waves of blackness threatened to envelop him. He felt a cold sweat breaking out on his forehead and around his nose, and all he wanted to do was to lie down and rest. He was sliding down a slippery slope into a black void. He slid down the door in a dead faint as it opened, just as another bolt buried itself deep in the woodwork where he had been only an instant before.

25 August 1377

Morning

Once the ambushing party had left the castle, a further score of men sallied forth with axes, horses, lamps, and kindling, to do as much damage as they could to the trebuchet. They were the older men and some of the stronger youths, those not fit for fighting, but who still wanted to play their part. They would have to be careful, for they could not make any noise that would warn the approaching French that something untoward was happening, though the wind was still making plenty of noise. They would have to be quick, or they might get caught after the ambush; consequently, they had carefully prepared tasks. Some assembled near the machine and started coupling the horses to the larger timbers to drag them away. Others collected the wood chippings lying around the site, piled them up at the base of the two massive uprights, and prepared a fire, to be lit as soon as the sounds of fighting could be heard. Since the wood was largely green, armfuls of dry grass and tallow were to be added to help it to burn.

After what seemed to be an interminable wait, the shouts and screams of the ambush came clearly through the morning air. The signal was given to light the fires. A bundle of dry grass was thrust into the candle lamp, and when it was well alight the flames were applied to the heap of kindling round the uprights of the trebuchet. The fire did not catch. One man took off his jerkin and fanned the smouldering kindling, trying to entice it into catching flame properly. After a minute or so a flame grew and spread, but produced heavy smoke rather than burning.

The horses were whipped up to drag some of the tree trunks away, and wedges were hammered into others to try to split them and make them useless. The big stones that had been brought up as ammunition were rolled across the clear grass and into the moat, where they could not be reached by the enemy.

25 August 1377

Everyone worked frantically for the few brief minutes until the lookout on the battlements called for them to return, because the first of the ambush party could be seen returning. The whole party was safely back inside the castle by the time the fleeing ambushers arrived. They then joined with the others on the battlements to count their friends back, and prepare to repulse any attack the French may try to make. Unfortunately, the fires had barely scorched the main frame of the trebuchet, and the other damage could probably be put right in a few hours.

★

Robert didn't see the postern gate open nor did he feel hasty hands drag him into the castle. The heavy door slammed to behind him. Peter and Sir Hugh appeared at the gate just as it closed behind Robert's slack form. They leant over him with relief, though they worried at the amount of blood matted in his hair and covering his face; they could not see a wound that could account for so much.

Peter had not seen Robert fall and, in the heat of the battle and the ensuing rush back to the castle, he had assumed that Robert had got away and was at the castle before him. He had been aghast to learn that Robert was not there already, waiting for him. He had questioned the other men closely, but no one was sure what had happened in the confusion and didn't know what had become of Robert either – they had all been too busy looking after themselves. Michael Apse could remember glimpsing him fighting with a tall Frenchman, but the next time he had looked, Robert was not there. As a consequence Peter had begun to worry that Robert had been killed, or had been injured and recaptured and killed.

Rachel had been convinced that Robert would return, though doubts had begun to arise when the flood of returning Islanders had diminished to a trickle, and then had stopped. She had been determined not to shed a tear, even though she had been driven to resolutely pace up and down to maintain a semblance of calm, occasionally peering anxiously over the parapet. Only the twisted handkerchief in her hands betrayed her inner turmoil. When

Morning

Robert had finally appeared from the trees and staggered towards the haven of the castle walls, she had shouted encouragement with the others. Her heart had leapt at the sight of him and she flinched every time a bolt was released towards him. Now he was back safely she quickly wiped away the tear before she pushed through the soldiers surrounding the postern gate, elbowed between Peter and Sir Hugh, and took charge.

She ordered some of the men to carry Robert into the dwelling house and up to the chamber where his father had lain not long before, hoping that this coincidence would not be prophetic. The small shadow of Harold followed them, dodging around and between the adults, to hover silently in a corner.

Robert was pale and still unconscious. Blood covered his face and stained his light brown hair; it had smeared widely over his hands and arms and down his clothing. However, a close look, together with judicious mopping with water applied with part of an old sheet, showed that the damage was not as bad as it appeared. She could see that some of the blood must have come from someone else and not just the cut on his forehead, which, though not deep, was a long one. Normally such a wound would have been of little consequence, but the loss of blood was added to the loss that he had suffered from the wound in his shoulder. She knew that time, good food and rest were the best cure for that problem, but that luxury was not available.

Robert was feeling warm and comfortable, softly floating in a dream world. He could feel the heat of sunlight on his body, and his spirit was peaceful, almost elated. It was rather like his memories of childhood in the arms of his mother. The sunny feeling gradually faded but he became aware of soft hands smoothing his face, and water mixed with wine filling his mouth and spilling, trickling down his chest. He swallowed and coughed, choking. A voice whispered near his ear, and crooned a gentle cradle song, calling him back to consciousness. His eyelids flickered and with an effort he forced them open against the heavy weight of tiredness pressing them closed. Directly in his vision were the sky-blue eyes of the loveliest woman he had ever seen, eyes tinged with concern and relief. His lips formed a question, but it wasn't an angel he had seen: he was alive. The angel was

25 August 1377

his Rachel; he remembered her now, and instinctively pulled her face down for a long kiss.

Soon he was struggling to sit up, despite Rachel's protestations. He took a long draught from the jug, dipped a piece of bread into it and crammed it into his mouth, wiping his fingers on his breeches. His memory was still cloudy, and he felt that he was clawing at a thick wall of mist inside his head that covered something he should be worrying about. Suddenly the mist started to clear; he remembered his fight with the Frenchman Charles. He puzzled over what had happened before that. As his mind slowly cleared he remembered the ambush, and everything came flooding back. Relieved of the confusion, he asked what had happened to the rest of the ambushers, whether they had returned safely, and how many were missing. Rachel knew little of the final outcome, except that most of the men had come back full of excitement at the way in which the column had been completely surprised and routed. Though she wasn't aware of any being killed or captured, Robert was sure there must have been some casualties.

'Robert, can you remember whether my father was there? Was he hurt?' Rachel asked.

He paused, groping for information within his memories. Then his vision of her father came clear. 'He was with the van of the Frenchmen, and they escaped without any loss, as far as I can remember. I did try to rescue him, but there were too many Noddies around him,' he said sorrowfully. 'I had to leave him there. I'm sure he is safe.'

He felt dismayed that he had let her down in not having done more. But she chided him for being silly because he had done so much and come back safely. She was overjoyed that her father was still apparently fit and well, hadn't been wounded, and remained alive for another day.

Robert swung his legs over the edge of the bed, saying that he must report to Sir Hugh, as he was the second-in-command of the raiding troop, and it was his duty. Rachel insisted on him staying while she cleaned him up. She gently washed his face clear of the accumulated blood and, leaning him over the bowl, poured water over his head to clean his hair.

Morning

Harold had found some clothes to replace Robert's torn and bloodied ones. Robert, with help, managed to put them on. He had another drink of water mixed with wine and this made him feel less sick and brought some colour back to his wan cheeks. After a few minutes Rachel helped him to his feet, where he stood dizzy and swaying, happily holding on to her for support. He took a few shaky steps to the door, feeling stronger and more confident with each step. Outside, a squire was waiting and took over helping him with a hand hovering near his elbow, though Robert scowled at the attention and kept shrugging the hand off. Rachel gave him a brief kiss and went to tell her mother the news of her father.

Robert, closely followed by Harold, joined Sir Hugh and the other lords as they stood on the battlements. There were frequent volleys of bolts rattling against the walls and soaring across into the courtyard. Largely ineffectual volleys of arrows were fired in reply.

Peter rushed over and embraced his brother-in-law, and the others all applauded his reappearance in apparent good health. Sir Hugh pumped his hand energetically. They had been watching the crossbowmen standing in the shelter of the surrounding woods, who had been watching them in return. The sun had risen well above the horizon and its rays shone westwards from the castle gatehouse, directly into the eyes of the besiegers. There was no sign yet of an attack being prepared, nor of the customary parade and show of strength. More likely than not, the French leaders were recovering from the shock of the ambush, and discussing what to do next. They probably hadn't thought the defenders had either the resources or the courage to mount such an attack.

A head count had revealed that of the 150 who had set out from the castle, 115 had returned virtually unscathed, and twenty more had been wounded. It was possible that some of the remainder had been captured, but the loss of fifteen men seemed a high price to pay, when considered as a proportion of the small number of defenders. The lords were speculating on how many of the French marauders had been killed. Peter had questioned the men as to how many each had dispatched or wounded They

25 August 1377

all had a good memory of the impact of the first volley, but thereafter the fighting had been too confused for numbers to be anything but guessed at. Peter estimated that at least 200 Frenchmen had been killed or badly wounded. This meant that the column must have been larger than normal – they had been lucky to get away so lightly with their skirmish.

'That should be a good lesson to the invaders and upset their morale. But it will make them more cautious in future. We won't be able to catch them like that again,' said Peter.

But Sir Hugh was more concerned about the retribution that might be exacted on the people of Nieuport and against anyone else they may have captured. He thought that the French would now give no quarter to the Islanders. However, it was the general opinion that John de Kingston would still be considered worth more alive as a hostage for ransom than dead.

'Sir Hugh,' said Peter, 'I have an idea. There will only be one opportunity, but it might work. We've all noticed that the French, during their parades around the castle, always stayed out of longbow range. But by the gatehouse they occasionally come within the range of a crossbow. They probably think that we don't possess a crossbow, as it isn't a customary English weapon; in fact, I think mine is probably the only one on the Island. I could shoot from one of the upper loopholes, where they wouldn't see me, and aim to hit their commander. There would be a chance for only one shot. If I succeed then we would really have an advantage. If not, we'd have lost nothing. Of course it would rely on them approaching in the way they have done before. They may be more cautious now, and adopt different tactics, but they may want to act in the same way to make us think that the ambush hasn't affected them. What do you think? Is it worth a try?'

Sir Hugh looked thoughtful for a moment and stroked his long moustaches. Then he said. 'I agree. If you could hit their leader, they might be more willing to negotiate a withdrawal. Go and prepare your crossbow. If they resume their routine and make out the ambush has not affected them, they may appear at any time now. I leave it to you to choose the best place and time to shoot, but don't violate the white flag of truce should they show it.'

'They've always circled the castle twice before they've showed the truce flag for negotiation, so there should be plenty of time for a good shot – if we are lucky!' replied Peter.

Leaving the others on the battlements watching the French, Peter hurried down the steps to the courtyard and ran across to the room where his belongings had been stored. He took the prized crossbow from the box in which it had been so carefully kept beneath the bed that Robert had only just left. As he took it from the enfolding cloths, the silver embossing glinted in the light that filtered through the window. It looked as if fire was playing along the bow, giving it life.

Peter felt the customary thrill at the touch of the smooth wooden stock and the cool metal. As always, he felt that the weapon was alive and eager to work, but today was different: it was as if the bow realised it had reached its day of destiny. Peter spoke to it softly as he took out the finely fletched bolts, one of which would soon rest in the slot on its back, to be dispatched to the target by the sinews of the taut string. He eyed along each bolt in turn to check that he was choosing the straightest and best balanced, the one that would fly true and quick. Through his whispers he tried to instil in the bow some measure of the importance of the task they were taking on. It could be the make or break chance for the Island; one opportunity to strike at the heart of the enemy. In the silent room he had the distinct impression that the bow was listening, had heard and understood.

He picked up the handle to span the bowstring, and stuck it in his belt, and he cradled the bow and two of the best bolts in the crook of his arm. Then, with a light step and excitement in his heart, Peter left the chamber and climbed back up the steps to the battlements to see what was happening without.

'The Noddies are gathering in the trees over there,' said Sir Hugh, pointing. Peter peered through an embrasure and could see the mass of men gradually forming up into a column. It looked very much as if they were intending to go through their daily ritual of trying to intimidate the defenders by marching round the walls, but on this occasion the defenders were buoyed up by their recent success and jeered and catcalled.

The two leaders, well mounted on their chaparisoned steeds

25 August 1377

came forward to take the van, and the squires fell in behind them. Amongst them the broad figure of de Kingston was visible, sitting astride a chestnut palfrey, obviously still unharmed. The body of archers, in divisions, followed, being encouraged by the men-at-arms, but the spring had gone out of their step; their shoulders were slumped and their heads were down. An attempt by some to sing a marching song to buck the men up, straighten their backs and put a spring in their stride, was not initially successful. But a few persistent vocalists managed to keep going, and the singing eventually spread. As it did so the pace of the marching feet became more regular, the heads went up and defiance crept back into their voices and into their bearing.

'It seems as if you will have an opportunity to try your idea, my lad,' said Sir Hugh turning to Peter. 'Away with you to a good vantage point, and may St Sebastian direct your bolts.' Sir Hugh then resumed his gloomy watch over the marching column and the French engineers who were busy at the trebuchet, repairing the damage and continuing its construction. He thought, a little despairingly, that it couldn't be more than a few hours before it would be ready to fire.

Peter turned to Robert. 'Do you feel up to helping me, Robert? I will need someone to act as lookout and tell me what is happening while I prepare.'

'Of course I will help, and may God also help us,' Robert replied, and together they hurried down the steps. Robert beckoned to Harold to come with them, and Peter gave him a cloth and the bolts to carry.

'Where do you intend to go?' Robert asked.

'I thought about the south side of the gatehouse,' Peter suggested. 'It sticks well out, and the riders come closest to the castle there. The sun will still be in their faces if they look towards the castle, but it will outline them well and give us a good view.'

'And they will be relatively relaxed, having got back into their routine again,' chimed in Robert. 'That was just where I was thinking of. Excellent! I cannot think of anywhere better.'

They made their way through the gatehouse door into the gloom of the spiral stairway within. They climbed up the worn steps and into the chamber on the left. It was a small room, long, thin and curved. It was being used by some of the garrison troops, and was full of their bedding and belongings, smelling of old sweat and unwashed feet, stale and musty. The room was lit by a small archer's slit that was cut in the outside wall. It was shaped like a cross, each arm ending as a circular hole about four inches wide, and was set in a triangular recess that penetrated about three quarters of the thickness of the wall. In each recess was a stone platform for an archer to stand on, elevated about one foot above the floor. The centre of the window was then about shoulder level, and a long bow would fit nicely within the height of the recess, with a minimum of the archer exposed.

Peering out, the two friends could see the tail end of the procession just passing out of sight to their left on the first circuit round the walls. They would have about ten minutes or so to prepare before the head of the column reappeared from the right, and they must hope that there would be a second circuit, otherwise the idea would not work.

Peter held up the crossbow to the slit, but because of the narrowness of the recess in the wall he was not able to rest the crossbow on the sill – the bow was too wide. The position clearly was designed for the longbow.

'You will have to help steady my aim,' said Peter. 'If you bend down, I can rest the bow on your shoulder. Do you think you can stay still enough?'

'Only if you think your aim is good enough,' retorted Robert with a grin. 'Don't blame me if you miss!'

Peter rested the end of the bow on the floor and turned the handle to crank the bowstring back and draw the bow. The string nocked back over the trigger mechanism. He took one of the bolts from Harold, checked it instinctively for straightness and put it in the groove on top of the shaft. When all was set, he held the bow up, and snuggled the stock into his shoulder. Satisfied with his preparations, he lowered the bow and wiped his hands, which had suddenly gone very clammy, on the cloth.

Robert peered out of the slit, but could see nothing bar the greensward and the sunny green woods of his beloved Island. The blue sky was patterned with wispy veils of thin white cloud,

25 August 1377

presaging more windy weather to come. The swell of the hazy downs stretched away to the west, towards the manor estates of which he was now lord. With God's good grace he would soon be able to take Rachel as his wife home to the house of his youth, provided that it still stood unravaged, or at least was habitable, he reminded himself with a curse.

A trumpet sounded, making them all jump. Robert stood to the window, where he could hear the steady tramp of many feet. By looking round the corner he could see the heads of the leading horses. He withdrew quickly to avoid being seen, signalled to Peter to get ready, and as their eyes met they simultaneously crossed themselves. Robert then turned and crouched down by bending his head and hunching his shoulders. Peter turned him round slightly to be nice and square, ready for the bow. Harold clambered into the recess, and on tiptoe peeped out of the bottom end of the loophole.

'Down a bit,' Peter demanded, and Robert hunched slightly lower with his hands on his knees bracing a firm triangle. 'That's good. Hold it there, and don't move.'

Robert could feel the pressure of the bow on his back increase as Peter aimed, and he heard the tension in Peter's voice. He breathed very gently so as not to move too much, and tried to relax his muscles to stop his knees beginning to tremble. By turning his head a bit he could just see out of the corner of his eye what was happening.

'Tell me when you are going to fire, so that I can hold my breath,' he said quietly.

He could hear Peter behind him and feel his breath on his ear. They could both see the leaders coming into view. Their pennants were fluttering bravely in the breeze and the horses were plodding quietly along. All that was needed now to spoil the plan was for them to get skittish and start prancing. Peter judged the speed of the horses and the range for the shot at de Beauvais, who was on the side nearest to the castle. De Mortagne was on his right and half-hidden by the Frenchman. His horse started, as if sensing the danger, and Peter cursed under his breath. His finger wavered on the trigger.

'Get ready,' he said quietly to Robert. He would have to shoot within a few seconds, or the chance would be lost. He concentrated anew and squeezed lightly on the trigger. Just another two paces…

'Now!' he said as a warning to Robert. He squeezed again more firmly, the bow twanged and the bolt sped towards its mark.

Robert felt the crossbow bounce on his back as it fired. Peter snatched the bow away, and both straightened up and peered out of the loophole. They lost sight of the bolt against the background of the moving trees. But Harold jumped for joy and shouted, 'You've hit him!'

For a few seconds everything carried on as before, and both of them thought that the bolt had missed, and Harold was wrong. But then de Beauvais clutched his chest, leaned sideways and slowly slid from the saddle. De Mortagne started and leant over to catch his leader, but the weight of man and the armour was too much and he too started slipping from his saddle. De Mortagne shouted a warning to the rest of the column. Squires jumped from their mounts and rushed to help him. They eased de Beauvais free from his stirrups and carried him towards the shelter of the trees.

A shout of exhilaration and triumph went up from the battlements above, followed by a flight of arrows, many of which fell short. This was met by a ragged volley of crossbow fire from the French and Castilian archers, who had realised what had happened, before they retreated to the protection of the trees. Their bolts rattled harmlessly against the walls, with only a few reaching the parapet or soaring over into the courtyard, and raising a chorus of derision. The tail end of the column was confused by the turmoil ahead and stopped, until ordered into the trees also.

Robert thumped Peter on the back, saying, 'You did it! What a shot! You did it! That will be a shot to boast about to your son when he can draw a bow.'

'We did it together. I couldn't have done it alone. You and Harold helped too,' stated Peter modestly. 'Let's go to the battlements so that we can follow what happens now.'

Despite his jubilation, Robert had a great sense of sadness for the man whom he had come to respect and in a way admire

25 August 1377

during their encounters of the last week. Then he remembered the hangings in the square at Nieuport, and was pleased that the French had been deprived of their commander, although it wasn't clear whether he was dead or just badly wounded.

On the castle battlements the other lords, the men-at-arms and the archers, all common men of the Wight, had been crouching behind the merlons and peeping out of the embrasures on either side. A few of their womenfolk were there, more by mistake than design, as war was not considered women's work. It wasn't clear at what point the bolt was shot, but as soon as the Duke de Beauvais was seen to fall to the ground everyone jumped up, shouting with glee.

Sir Hugh beamed a great smile and banged his gloved fist down on the stonework. 'We have knocked down the kingpin of the invasion. Without his leadership the rest should have little hope of taking this castle before we get help from the mainland. Peter de Heyno has really turned the tables on them today!'

Robert and Peter came bounding up the steps to be met with congratulations, handshakes and embraces. Rachel rushed forward and threw herself into Robert's arms. They held each other tightly before Robert, taking her hands in his, led the way to the nearest embrasure. He gestured towards the west and said, 'This land will be the heritage of our children, and our children's children, God willing.'

Rachel looked tearfully into his eyes and nodded her agreement. She was too overcome to trust her voice.

Before any more could be said, a voice shouted, 'A truce flag! The Noddies wish to parley.'

There at the edge of the trees a group of dismounted knights was congregating. A white pennant fluttered overhead at the tip of a lance. De Mortagne was in the centre of the group, surrounded by half a dozen knights and squires. Sir Hugh shouted that the defenders should hold their fire and await further orders. When it was clear that the defenders were watching, the group moved forward a dozen paces, then stopped, unsheathed their swords and stuck them in the ground and leant their shields against them. At a word from de Mortagne they moved forward across the cleared sward, their armour clinking and their surcoats waving around their legs. When they reached about halfway, they stopped and shouted a demand for a face-to-face meeting with the captain of the castle and the other lords, there on the grass between their two forces.

What could they be up to now? What were they going to propose? Could they be trusted to honour the flag of truce after the shock of the ambush and the attack on their leader?

25 August 1377

Forenoon

Sir Hugh stoked his beard in his customary thoughtful way. He had to accept the demand for parley. He had no choice. He called to one of the sentries to wave an acknowledgement to the French. Then he turned to the lords gathered around him.

His gaunt face looked even more haggard as he selected half a dozen of them, including de Gorges and Peter, to accompany him. After a little thought, Sir Hugh included Robert, since he knew both of the leaders, as well as some of the other French knights, and could translate. One by one they descended the steep stone steps to the gates. As they didn't know what the French were going to say, they could not discuss and agree any sort of strategy. Sir Hugh, as captain of the castle would have to take the lead if any quick decisions were needed, but the others would have to be consulted if there were major proposals.

Several guards struggled with the great baulk of timber that barred the heavy oak doors at the inner end of the gatehouse passage. It was slid sideways into one of the recesses into which the ends fitted, and lifted over the retaining brackets on the gates. One of the heavy iron-bound gates could then open. This gave access to the portcullis that barred the passage to the outer gatehouse. The portcullis was raised to head height so that they could scramble underneath. At Sir Hugh's signal two guards stepped to the winch and started to lower the drawbridge. The chains squeaked and groaned over the pulleys, and the massive timbers shuddered and creaked as it settled towards the abutments on the other side of the moat.

Before they passed through the gates, Sir Hugh gave orders that a number of archers should line the battlements, ready armed. If there was any sort of treachery they were to shoot irrespective of the risk of killing their own knights. He thought it highly likely the French lords had given precisely the same instructions to their men.

In the gateway a mass of men stood behind the lords in case a rush was made by the French to penetrate into the castle and to give the impression that there were many more defenders in the castle than there actually were.

Sir Hugh stepped on to the drawbridge and, with a flourish, removed his helmet and unsheathed his sword, handing them to one of the defenders behind. In clear view of the enemy, the others all followed suit. Despite this show they were not entirely unarmed; they retained their poignards, or daggers, hidden either in the loose parts of their cote-hardi or in their tunics. If it became necessary, they would have some defence in hand-to-hand fighting. They assumed, rightly, that the French would have taken the same precautions.

A man-at-arms preceded them with a banner held high displaying the cross of Saint George. Sir Hugh followed him, and behind came the others, two by two, with Robert striding alongside Peter. Their heads were high; although they were the besieged, they were no longer the underdogs. They would now be able to negotiate from a position of relative superiority. The battlements behind them were lined with archers, as well as some women and children. All were silent with the tension of what could be an historic occasion, a confrontation that they might live to tell their grandchildren about in the long winter evenings in the years to come. Robert felt a mixture of elation and apprehension. This could be the final throw in the game.

The man-at-arms stopped about half a dozen paces from the French knights, and moved to one side to allow Sir Hugh and the six others to come face to face. The two groups of antagonists surveyed each other, taking a measure of the spirit and demeanour of those opposite. The two leaders moved to within a couple of paces of each other, with the rest of the knights on either side of them, forming two rough semicircles.

The contrast between the leaders could not have been greater. The tall, gaunt and austere Sir Hugh had composed his face into a calm serenity. With his beard lifting gently in the wind he faced the younger and more solidly built de Mortagne – as tall as Sir

25 August 1377

Hugh, but darker-skinned and with a scowl on his face. The red cross on his surcoat lent him an air of flamboyant brutality.

Opposite Robert was a short knight with a scarred face. Robert remembered having seen him several times before in charge of one of the Castilian divisions. His black eyes showed only hostility as they stared at each other unblinkingly.

The French and Castilians were differently arrayed. The latter were more colourful and quite recognisable by their black hair and darker skins. Their style of armour was more elaborate, with fluting – to deflect arrows and lances – and embossed stylised decorations. The French were more plainly attired, with flat-plate armour, more like the English style. Unusually, the armour was dull and showing signs of red rust in places – obviously there had not been time during the invasion to give it a regular clean and polish. None had swords or other weapons in view, and several played nervously with their empty scabbards, clearly feeling vulnerable without them.

In contrast, the English were a motley collection, some with old-style pieces of armour, or the hauberk, the long coat of chain mail, or the shorter version, the haubergeon. Others wore quilted leather actons or gambesons. They were dirty and, like Robert, had blood about their clothes. Although they were not as impressively arrayed and disciplined as the French, they made up for it in their pride and looks of determination and resolve.

De Mortagne stood rock-like, straddle-legged, with his hands on his hips. He looked steadily along the English ranks assessing each man in turn until his gaze lighted on Robert. With a scowl and a quick motion of his hand and his head he gestured for Robert to step forward towards him. With an apologetic glance at Sir Hugh, Robert moved up to the right hand of the Castilian.

De Mortagne looked directly at Robert and spoke to him in French. 'So, my young lord, you have recovered, and it looks as if you have been involved in the ambush of my men. I always thought it was rash of de Beauvais to have returned you to your people. His faith that you would help to avoid bloodshed was stupidity indeed. But he has now paid the price of his foolishness.

'This man is obviously your leader.' He gestured to Sir Hugh, who could only guess at what was being said, as his French was not at all good.

'Comte de Mortagne, this is the captain of the castle, Sir Hugh Tyrril,' said Robert in French, indicating each in turn. Then in English he said, 'Sir Hugh, this is Count de Mortagne, leader of the Castilian battalion.

De Mortagne continued to speak in French, but now to Sir Hugh. 'Sir Tyrril, you and your Islanders have put up a stout resistance to our forces and by a cowardly stroke have killed our commander, the Duc de Beauvais. But this is a minor setback. It is obviously only a matter of time before we will starve you into submission. We have all the food and supplies of the towns, and we will happily wait and watch you get hungrier and thinner while we feast. Our archers can ensure that your battlements will not be safe places to walk, and no one would be able to escape. The stomachs of your women and children will ache from hunger. The babies will cry from want of milk. I'm sure you would not want to see them suffer and starve.

'However, this will not happen, for we have the trebuchet.' He turned and gestured to where the tall timbers towered. 'You have tried to damage it, but to no avail – the damage is insignificant. Within a day we will have it working, and a rain of stones will soon breach the castle walls. Many of your people will be killed, but in the end we will take the castle, and will give no quarter. All your protestations will be in vain. We will take your money, your valuables and we will take the finest of your women back to France with us. But it needn't be so if you don't wish it.'

Sir Hugh was able to understand the meaning of what was said, even though he didn't follow every word. Nevertheless, Robert translated, giving him and the other lords more time to think.

'Monsieur le Comte,' Sir Hugh replied, 'you underestimate the magnitude of the castle supplies and the strength and determination of the defenders. We have more than enough food and drink to dine royally until the armies come from the mainland to our aid. Do not forget that they know that you have invaded. They have seen the fires, and many of our people have

25 August 1377

fled to the mainland. You may be assured that right now they will be mustering an army big enough to destroy you in open battle; it might even be embarking at this moment to sail here. You will not be able to prevent them landing, especially with us at your backs waiting for the opportunity to ambush you again. To linger and hope to starve us into submission would be inadvisable – the autumn storms are already overdue. Your trebuchet is untested and our walls are thick. It would take much more time than you think to breach the walls, and it is obvious that you do not have enough stones of size to fire. Should you breach the walls, you would still have to capture the castle: not an easy task, and one which would be very costly to you. I advise you to withdraw to your boats and sail back to France before you become trapped by the autumn storms and the wrath of England.'

Robert translated into French this time, but de Mortagne had also understood the gist of what was said.

'We have your Lord de Kingston.' He waved his arm and called for de Kingston to be brought forward. De Kingston was easily distinguishable to all by the white streak in his hair. With a guard on either arm he strode out from the mass of the French army, trying to maintain as much dignity as he could, but now looking tired and old. He looked at Sir Hugh, nodded and smiled wanly. He then glanced at Robert and gave him a surreptitious wink that revealed that though his body was weary, his spirit was unbowed.

De Mortagne continued, building up to the real bargaining. 'I am willing to either ransom or execute this man. And there are many of your people still in the town and in the countryside. My troops have been angered by the ambush. They have lost their friends and comrades; they want revenge for that and for the death of their lord, the Duc de Beauvais. Without some reward, some compensation, I'm not sure that I will be able to stop them wasting your land. They will be very pleased to hunt your people down and kill them, burn their houses and their crops. I only have to say the word, and hell will visit this island. Or I can give them some other reward: I can buy them off with English money. The choice is yours.'

'How can the choice be ours? What choice is there?' demanded Sir Hugh. 'You will never take the castle, but the rest of the Island is in your hands.'

De Mortagne smiled grimly, stepping forward half a pace so that he and Sir Hugh were almost nose to nose. 'We have already made an offer to ransom this Lord de Kingston for 5,000 marks. You have refused this offer. To this we have added the lives and the homes of all your people. If you pay this ransom we will leave the Island, and not do any further damage. If not, the consequences will be on your conscience, and we will still return next year to finish you all off!'

Sir Hugh held up a hand and stepped back from the confrontation to consider the demands. He turned to Peter and the other lords and whispered, 'To pay the ransom may be the only way of getting them to leave before he exacts even more retribution. If we do not pay, our people outside the castle will be tortured and killed and there will be little that we can do to stop them. I think that we have to bow to the inevitable.' There were general murmurs of assent.

Then he turned to de Mortagne. 'We agree to pay a ransom, as you demand, but there are not 2,000 marks on the Island. Ours is a poor island and can only pay 1,000 marks; that is all that we have. There may be other small sums that people have hidden in their houses, or buried in hiding places. It would take many days of searching to find it, and much of it you have probably already found anyway. It is likely that you have already loaded onto your ships the equivalent of a thousand marks. I cannot offer more!' He held out his open hands and shrugged his shoulders in emphasis.

De Mortagne frowned and raised his eyes, looking over the heads of the opposing knights at the ramparts of the castle, and at the cross of Saint George flying above the keep. Heads filled the embrasures and banners fluttered bravely at the flagpoles. He was weighing up his chances of reducing the garrison quickly, before further disasters should befall his men. Perhaps he was not relishing the decision that previously would not have been his: the choice between returning to France with honour and some booty, or the risk of being cut off and never reaching his home shore. To many, being second-in-command is frustrating and unsatisfactory, decisions made by the leader are wrong and good advice is never heeded. Then, he reaches the position of ultimate

25 August 1377

authority, it is realised that decisions can never be clear cut, things are never black and white, and determination wavers.

De Mortagne was a bad sailor and was not looking forward anyway to the long sea voyage home; to think about doing it when storms turned the waters to stomach-churning waves was hard to contemplate. How could he manage to fulfil the demands required by the oath of allegiance to his king, the principles of chivalry and also save face before the determined, ragged group before him? The breeze ruffled his black, shiny hair. It seemed to help him make up his mind. He looked sideways to the knights on either side of him, gaining support from their passive faces.

'Very well,' he said, 'we accept this ransom, but under a number of conditions. First, you have struck down our commander, the Duc de Beauvais. We will be unable to carry his body back to France, but we require that you recognise his honour and valour by giving him a ceremonial funeral befitting his status.

'Second, if we should return within a year you will not resist us, and will pay the rest of the ransom. We will bury our dead and prepare to embark. You will have the ransom money here tomorrow morning at this hour, and we will then exchange your knight de Kingston. We will leave on the tide by noon, providing the wind is fair.' He looked at the sky, as if praying that the weather would be good to them, and not trap them on the Island any longer.

Robert's heart leapt as he heard these words, and smiles creased the faces of the Islanders as he translated. Sir Hugh moved forward, removing the gauntlet on his right hand. He held out his hand towards the Frenchman to seal agreement and, with only slight hesitation, it was grasped in return. His left hand then moved to grip the Frenchman's right elbow as if reinforcing the emotion of the moment. De Mortagne did not go so far as to embrace Sir Hugh, as he would have done another Frenchman, but he returned the two-handed salutation. Both groups of knights relaxed and let out pent-up breaths. Each knight moved towards his opposite number and all shook hands in relief. A babble of speech broke out. Even though one half did not know what the other half were saying, there was common understanding.

On the castle battlements the archers and the common people started to cheer, even though they didn't know precisely what they were cheering for. All they could see was that the warfare must be over, and some sort of agreement had been reached. Under the trees the assembled French and Castilian soldiers cheered likewise. Everyone felt that it was their side that had gained the victory, and were happy.

Sir Hugh, with a grim smile, stepped back and said, 'It is the unfortunate consequence of war that there are always those who get hurt, or killed. There are those who lose their husbands, sons or lovers. We have all lost. We will remember the burgesses at Nieuport, just as well as we will remember your warriors in the ambush. We are all pawns in the games that our liege lords play. We are at their mercy. May God bless us and forgive us our sins.'

Robert translated this homily, and there was a general chorus of 'amens' at the end; many crossed themselves.

'Let us carry your Duke de Beauvais to rest in our chapel,' Sir Hugh continued. 'Perhaps a party of your men will carry him and accompany us there. We will guarantee their safety.'

Peter called to the castle for two men to bring out a stretcher for the dead commander, and a hurdle was brought out at the run to the place in the trees where the duke's body lay. De Beauvais lay as if asleep, only marred by the stain of blood down the side of his tunic where the bolt had by mischance found the gap between his armour plates. In death he looked at peace, with the lines of strain gone and his face not yet drawn by cooling and the shrinking still to occur within. The noble commander was lifted onto the stretcher and his body covered with the oriflamme banner, the ancient banner of France. This plain red flag with golden flames seemed to be strangely appropriate, more so than the fleur-de-lys flag commonly used by the king and nobles. His ornate helmet with its flowing plumes was placed on his chest, and his bejewelled sword lay by his side.

Two pairs of the French knights took hold of the ends of the stretcher, displacing the two archers who had brought it from the castle. Then, with Sir Hugh leading and de Mortagne pacing

25 August 1377

slowly behind, they moved towards the gates of the castle that now opened fully to receive them. The other knights formed up as a line of honour on either side, Englishman facing Frenchman, eyeing each other rather warily. It was almost as if de Beauvais was running the gauntlet of both friends and foes to reach his resting place. Silence fell over both castle and woods as everyone honoured the dead man. At the castle gates some of the French knights stopped to ensure the gates remained open for their new commander. The rest went inside, and in the cool of the chapel laid the stretcher beside the bier of Robert's father. De Mortagne went down on his knee and bowed his head in a silent prayer, and the knights stood with bowed heads and their hands clasped, whispering their own prayers. Crossing himself, de Mortagne rose and turned to leave, followed by the bearers.

Outside the chapel de Mortagne stood in the courtyard and looked around the inside of the castle walls with interest. He saw the thin line of bowmen standing at the battlements. He saw the throng of hushed women and children crowding round the courtyard between the piles of belongings and the tethered animals. Many times he had seen the insides of castles captured after sieges. Then conditions had been much worse, the defendants racked with starvation and hardly able to stand, plagued with disease, and infested with vermin. Caresbrooke was still in good heart, but after a few weeks of siege conditions it also would have been in a similar awful state. He shrugged his shoulders with resignation, and breathed a soft *'C'est la vie!'*

His eye alighted on Robert, who was standing to one side with his hand resting on Harold's shoulder, the lad having run joyfully to his side as soon as Robert had come through the gate. De Mortagne moved across to stand before the weary young man. He looked Robert searchingly in the face, then said, 'You are an honourable man and a worthy foe. Had you been French, and if we had more like you, we would have regained our lands of Gascony and Normandy years ago, and rid ourselves of the pestilential English. Still, it will happen yet,' he said with assurance.

His gaze shifted to Harold. 'I assume that this boy is the one you rescued at Eremue.' Then, on impulse, he pulled a ring from his finger and held it out to Robert. 'Take this! The young man, Charles, whose life you spared in the woods this morning, is the son of my sister. A life for a life, a ransom for a ransom!'

The heavy gold ring, set with a large blue jewel, lay shining in his hand. Flabbergasted, Robert could only stutter a few words of thanks, bowing low, as courtesy demanded. 'Lord you are exceeding gracious.' He took the ring and slid it onto the little finger of his left hand, as he would a signet ring.

De Mortagne looked him deep in the eyes, gave a slight inclination of his head, turned abruptly on his heels and strode out through the gates to meet his waiting knights and face his army. The gates closed behind him.

25–26 August 1377

For the rest of the day the castle gates remained firmly closed and watchful guards patrolled the walls in case of tricks. The woods outside appeared to be deserted, though it was suspected that there would be spies lurking, posted to give warning should the defenders launch an attack. The lookout at the top of the keep reported much activity in the neighbourhood of Nieuport. Messengers were seen setting out along the road towards the west, probably carrying news and orders to the garrisons at Francheville and Yarmouth. Troops moved backwards and forwards to the wharves with carts and laden horses, obviously taking food, and goods pillaged from the towns and hamlets to be loaded on the ships moored on the river. The procession seemed endless, and the speculation was that there would be nothing left on the Island. Since the campsite could not be seen, it was not clear whether everything had been moved, or not. Presumably, also the dead men from the ambush were being buried, as fresh graves were eventually found on the site of the camp.

Sir Hugh had gone into the armoury where the money was kept and had carefully counted out what was there. There was not enough, and he told the lords that they would have to pay their shares to make up the ransom money needed. Each then went to where they had hidden their wealth and, not without much regret, produced what they had to. A large box was found for the gold and silver coins, and when it was all assembled it was carefully counted out and checked. The box was then locked and placed just inside the gates, guarded by a couple of men – not that anyone would attempt to steal it. A crowd of Islanders stood looking at the box, thinking of what might be done with the money, and how they had all worked and sweated to raise the rents and taxes which it comprised. There was little else they could do until the French left and they could freely walk outside and return to their homes.

Sir Hugh and de Gorges were already beginning to think about how the rebuilding of the Island could be carried out, and of the problems involved. There were bound to be shortages of food, as the harvesting of the corn was long overdue – that is, if the marauders had left any of the crops standing. It would be necessary to import grain, and possibly also meat from the mainland. There might even be a shortage of boats to fetch it, if the French had destroyed or taken them. Fishing might also be curtailed. It was going to be a hungry winter. Representations would have to be made to the King to ensure that burden of taxes was relieved, and assistance made available to relieve hardship. Many of the dwellings would have been destroyed, so it would be a cold winter too. Strictly these worries were the job of de Gorges as Warden of the Island. It was he who had the responsibility of ensuring the health and welfare of the King's subjects on the Island. Sir Hugh's job was limited to defence of the castle and of the Island, but the job of one could not be done in isolation from the other.

After the events of the past few days, Robert had felt completely drained of energy. Rachel gave him a special draught that she had prepared and persuaded him to lie down for a while, knowing full well that the potion would send him to sleep for many hours. While he slept Harold sat and watched over him.

In the early evening Robert awoke after about eight hours' sleep, feeling totally refreshed and ravenously hungry. Luckily he was in time for the meal that had been prepared for the lords and their families, to be eaten together in the great hall. Sir Hugh welcomed them all rather formally, and they sat at the long tables chattering with relief, sharing memories and speculating on the conditions they might find at their homes. Everyone ate well that night, because there was no need for rationing now the siege was lifted. They wondered what supplies would be available outside the castle once the French had gone. Was everything pillaged or destroyed? Would there be enough for the winter? But in the mood of celebration these worries were pushed into the background, and hunger was dispelled for the moment.

After the meal Robert had a relaxed evening with Rachel, talking with Peter and Rebecca, and Rachel's mother. Rachel had sent Harold off to eat with Timothy, but Isabel had joined their group at the meal. They had comforted her, for she had been very tearful and worried about her husband, who was still a hostage with the French, even though he should be returning safely the next forenoon. Later she was well diverted by watching Rebecca's little son fed and washed. A contented little baby, he was happy being fed every four hours, and slept the rest of the time. The lines of strain on Isabel's face began to disappear and a smile touched her eyes and her mouth as she watched, and listened to them talk. Peter was anticipating the day when his son could be taken hunting and hawking, but Rebecca chided him for wanting the baby to grow up too quickly.

'Plenty of time for that after he has tired of playing with his brothers and sisters,' she said laughing. Peter smiled with anticipation. He, in turn, teased Robert and Rachel about their future prospects as parents, much to their embarrassment.

Rachel and Robert held hands and joined in with the banter as well as having to endure it, considering their real desire was to be alone together. Rachel whispered to Robert, reminding him of their time in the fisherman's cave. They gazed into each other's eyes, remembering those heady days of eager anticipation before the worry of invasion.

Claiming a headache, Isabel retired to bed and told the two lovers to go and walk the battlements. They walked around happily and sat in one of the embrasures, oblivious to other people. The sun was sinking over the downs to the west, with golden rays shooting between the clouds, turning the sky to a cascade of colour: yellow, gold, red, crimson, violet and blue, gradually becoming darker and darker. The long shadows of the woods crept across the greensward, and the mists began to rise in the valley as the warmth of the day dissipated. The birdsong slowly dwindled as they settled for sleep and the nocturnal animals began their stealthy foraging. A sense of peace settled over the Island for the first time in five days. Robert could hardly believe that, such a short time ago, life had been so different; five days had changed their lives and all those around them. Would they ever be able to remember life as it was before the invasion?

25–26 August 1377

The effects of Rachel's potion began to wear off, and tiredness and stiffness in his wounds began to make Robert lapse into longer and longer silences. He had to force his eyelids open by an effort of willpower. Rachel eventually made him another special draught of herbs to ease his soreness and help him to sleep anew. Within minutes of taking it, Robert was fast asleep. He didn't wake until the sun was well over the horizon, and he was amazed to find his soreness gone and his head clear of any after-effects of the blow. He even had to feel the scab on the wound on his forehead to be sure that his memory of the previous day's conflict was correct.

It must have been about prime when the lookout shouted that a column of marchers was leaving the town on the road towards the castle, and the call was echoed round the castle by many voices. From the keep it was possible to see the banners flying and the horses prancing. They estimated at least 500 men-at-arms and archers were coming, together with knights and their squires. Obviously those left behind were still busily engaged in loading the last of the goods onto the ships, and scouring the town and the campsite for other valuable items.

Among the waiting garrison speculation was strong as to whether the column, when it reached the castle, would complete their customary two circuits. Wagers were even laid on it – not that anyone now had any money to honour the bets.

The lords gathered on the battlements on the north side of the castle, between the postern gate and the main gatehouse. They watched the army come up the track through the trees and out onto the greensward close to the walls. All swords were sheathed, and bows were slung over shoulders – impossible to use quickly. Contrary to previous occasions, one or two men started singing, tentatively at first, but when no reprimand was forthcoming, the song spread along the ranks and the volume increased. It was obviously a triumphal song celebrating victory and success. The occasion was just like a ceremonial display, and it seemed as if the Frenchmen felt they were marching home.

As the column moved westwards towards the gate, the defenders walked around the walls, keeping pace with them. Every window, loophole and vantage point was occupied by men, women and children, none of them wanting to miss any part of the next few minutes.

Contrary to the hopes of many, and the delight of others, the column didn't carry on round, but stopped in front of the gates and executed a left turn to face the castle. The mounted knights were in the centre of a wall of men, three deep, that stretched for almost a furlong. The knights dismounted and grouped together round de Montagne, who was distinguishable by the magnificent blue cape that covered his armour, displacing his customary red cross. He thrust the cape back with a sweeping gesture, and said something to a squire on his right who broke out the white truce flag. The broad figure of de Kingston was brought forward, and they looked expectantly towards the firmly closed castle gates.

Sir Hugh, who had been passively watching all this, said 'Good! Their intentions seem to be to honour the agreement of yesterday. Let us go out.' He descended to the courtyard, followed by Peter, Robert and the other lords. At a sign the main gates were thrown open, the portcullis was raised, and the drawbridge creaked as it was lowered. Two men picked up the chest of money and, staggering, joined the column marching out to the truce meeting. Their footsteps drummed on the wood of the drawbridge and echoed back from the grey walls behind them, mingling with the murmuring of the apprehensive watchers.

The group came to a halt in front of the French knights. The chest was put down in front of Sir Hugh, who stepped forward and opened the lid. The early morning sunlight glinted on the contents, gold and silver coin, with a few pieces of jewellery, goblets and other valuable trinkets. He gestured to the chest with his open right hand.

'This is the ransom of 1,000 marks, you have demanded. We do not have it all in coin, but have included all the valuables we have. This should make up its equivalent. Additionally, we have a number of soldiers captured yesterday before the ambush. They are to be released. With this ransom you have agreed to release Lord de Kingston and quit the Island. Do you still honour this pledge?'

'We agreed to your offer yesterday, and do not intend to change it and ask for more,' replied de Mortagne haughtily, offended at the implication that they might have reneged on the bargain. 'As we agreed, we exchange your knight de Kingston.'

He gestured for de Kingston to come forward from his place between his guards in the ranks and join those of the Islanders. Sir Hugh signalled for the French hostages to be released, and they ran waving from the castle to join their colleagues. Then two French squires came forward, picked up the chest, carried it over to one of the horses, and slung it across the saddle in a net.

De Mortagne gave a salute and a bow. 'You will have seen we have readied the ships and will embark forthwith. The other towns have been evacuated already, but you must give us safe passage until we depart. I bid you *adieu*, until the next time! Remember not to oppose us if we return.' He abruptly turned to his horse and mounted.

While he gathered up his reins Sir Hugh replied, 'If you do return, we will be waiting to greet you, and no doubt we will be better prepared.'

No more could be said and de Mortagne began trotting down the line of his men. His knights scrambled for their mounts and went to follow him. A chorus of cheers broke out from the French, and this was countered by cheers from the castle. The whole line of French and Castilians turned and followed their leader down the road towards Nieuport, obviously glad to be on their way home. Sir Hugh and the others watched them go, and as they watched the Islanders flooded from the castle gates, some dancing with relief and joy that they could return to some semblance of normal life. Others were keen to go back to their homes as soon as they could to find out what damage had been done, to rescue livestock, gather the remnants of the harvest and start rebuilding their lives. Many also wanted to find out what had become of their friends and relations who had not appeared at the castle.

Isabel appeared in the throng with Rachel and Harold close behind. She immediately went over to her husband gazing into his face as she curtseyed. He took her hand and, smiling, wrapped her in his arms in a display of emotion that took her very much by surprise. After a long minute, with Rachel and Robert watching the reunion with pleasure, de Kingston turned to his daughter

25–26 August 1377

and embraced her as well. He stood back with tears of joy in his eyes.

'I know that you have a yearning to marry this young man.' He grasped Robert's forearm. 'I know that he is a man worthy of you and I will be proud to have him as a son. I think that we had better arrange the wedding quickly! Then, if those French return, I will not be responsible for looking after you, as well as your mother.' His eyes were twinkling as he embraced Robert in turn. 'I trust you agree.'

'Yes, of course, sire!' answered a flabbergasted Robert, who had not expected to have his heart's desire granted so easily. Harold jumped up and down in delight.

Together the five started walking towards the castle, arms linked, with Harold proudly striding beside Robert. De Kingston winked at Robert as the women started to discuss the wedding arrangements. Suddenly a shout went up from the castle walls. 'The Noddies have set fire to Nieuport! I can see smoke and flames.'

There was a stampede back into the castle, and up to the walls, for it was only from that height that the town could be seen beyond the woods. It was true: a pall of smoke was rising from the town and blowing away to the north-east. Initially the smoke was grey, but then it turned darker and the red glow of flames appeared at its base as the fires took hold and grew. There was nothing that they could do but stand and watch. They could not go down and hope to put the flames out – the French were still there and may have been hoping to catch them. Some of the women started weeping at the destruction of their homes, and the men cursed the French for breaking their promises. Robert was sure that it must either have been started accidentally or by some wayward soldiers; de Mortagne and his troops could hardly have got back to the town in time to start it purposely. So they all stood and watched until they saw the sails raised on the ships moored in the Medine. One by one the ships started to move down the river in the afternoon breeze, their pennants fluttering.

When they were well down the river towards Shamblord, Sir Hugh agreed with those who were demanding an immediate armed expedition to Nieuport. The risk of meeting any opposition was small now. Within half an hour 200 of the castle defenders, including Robert and de Kingston, were at the edge of the town where they encountered the inhabitants standing forlornly watching. They said that some of the enemy soldiers had gone round setting light to the houses after the majority had left. The town was still burning fiercely, though many of the houses had collapsed into heaps of glowing embers. The heat shimmered and kept back those who tried to get close. A vast column of smoke rose into the air, and was beginning to create its own wind, sucking the heat upwards, fanning the flames anew. All they could do was to stand and watch.

The elation of victory left the people as they watched their town burn, the men grim and cursing, the women in tears. They felt utter dejection and turned away, intending to return when the fires had at last died down, and when hope for the future had grown again. Then they would feel able to rake through the ruins and find what they could of their possessions, and start to rebuild their homes and their lives. Even those who did not live in Nieuport had their lives inextricably linked with the town's markets, the fairs, and the merchants. They would have had family, relations or friends living there. It was as if the heart of the Island had ceased to beat. Some of them cried until there were no more tears to flow.

Before they returned to the castle, they walked up the well-worn track to the area where the French camp had been. Most of the empty shelters were still standing and dogs scavenged round them. Rubbish and abandoned loot lay everywhere. As some of the cooking fires were still smouldering a number of men started to poke the fires to life and pile on them the remnants of the French occupation, almost as if they were trying to erase all signs of the hated enemy. The shelters were left standing; they might still be needed. All the useful goods were put on one side for communal distribution later. Outside the camp there was a large area of mounds of freshly turned earth, each one having a crudely fashioned cross, and some with names scratched on them. These were the graves of the Frenchmen killed in the ambush. Many of the Islanders went round gloatingly counting them, to compare with the number of their own who had been lost.

25–26 August 1377

After a few days, when the fires had burnt themselves out, and the embers had cooled, they were able to penetrate the ruins of the town. The fire had consumed everything except the church of St Thomas, which was the only building left standing, mainly because it was built of stone, rather than wattle, wood and thatch. Many townsfolk had been killed in the blaze, but how many they would never know. Quite a number of young women were never accounted for or seen again. Whether they had been abducted and taken to France, or simply killed in the fever of departure, would be unknown by all but the good Lord. All sorts of sins had been obliterated from the view of man by the fire. It could only be hoped that there would be some divine retribution for their suffering.

28 August 1377

Two days after the French had departed, the Island was in a ferment of recovery. Search parties had been sent out to all parts of the Island to tell those who had been hiding in the woods and caves that the threat was over and they could return to their homes. An inventory was underway of the damage that had been caused, and an accounting of the food stocks and other essentials for living that remained. Theobald de Gorges was determined that everyone should work together and pool their remaining food, crops and workmanship to rebuild houses. One of the first jobs was recovering the released and strayed animals. The lords of the manors took the lead in organising this communal work, and everyone joined in.

As the reports came in, it was apparent that the French had not occupied the whole of the Island. The second force that had landed near St Helen's had burned Brading and Nunwell. But the high downs running east to west had formed a fairly effective barrier against the French, except where the river valleys broke through. The invaders had not penetrated further south than Arreton, and there were many families in small villages such as Godshill, Shorwell, Apse and Nyweton who were totally unaffected by the French invaders. As far as they were able, they rallied round to help their friends and relations. However, there were many families who abandoned any hope of rebuilding their lives on the Island and were preparing to go across to the mainland.

Immediately the French had left, Michael Apse had been sent to the de Kingston house and estates and quickly returned saying that they were untouched, as were those of Peter de Heyno at Stenbury. Consequently, the de Kingstons and the de Heynos returned to the comforts of their homes.

After saying farewell to Rachel and to Rebecca, with promises to visit them within a couple of days, Robert and Harold had set

28 August 1377

out on Bess for Affeton. William, Alice the other servants and Timothy followed with the cart containing their possessions, together with the coffin containing Sir Roger's body. They found the manor house ransacked and partly burned. Luckily the thunderstorm had wetted the thatch sufficiently to prevent the flames taking too strong a hold. One end of the house was untouched by fire, though virtually all the furniture was gone. There was enough roof left to keep them dry while rebuilding was carried out and the outbuildings had survived, with only the stock and stores of food and drink missing. Robert was thankful that it was not worse. All could be repaired or rebuilt before the worst of the winter, though it would be a hungry time until the next summer.

Immediately Alice bustled about and, with Harold's help, set to organising the kitchen, and preparing some sort of meal from what remained. William and Timothy recovered the valuables from the carp pond, and the tapestries from the tree behind the stables. Then Timothy went across the causeway to the church to see if the vicar was there, with instructions to arrange the interment of Sir Roger.

The church of All Saints had been burned and the roof had collapsed into the nave, but the tower still stood. John King, the vicar, had not long before returned from his hiding place in the south. He had many calls on his time, with many burials to arrange. Nevertheless, Sir Roger's burial was agreed for the following day. Robert chose the site of the grave in the shadow of one of the dark-green yew trees in the churchyard where the badgers scratched. From beneath those ancient trees Yarmouth could be seen down the river, and it was warm and peaceful with rooks cawing softly in the background.

The following day at a brief, moving funeral, with only the local people and the manor villeins present, they laid the old man to rest in a position overlooking the land and the river that he had loved so well. Then, leaving instructions with Timothy for organising the local peasants and villeins, Robert set out again for Caresbrooke. There were still some tasks to be completed; the ceremonial burial of the Duke de Beauvais was to be the following day, and further organisation of the recovery of the Island was needed.

28 August 1377

The church of St Thomas in Nieuport had escaped the conflagration that swept the town, but the smoke and the smell of burning was still strong, and the door could scarcely be reached through the stinking debris of the fire. As well as being a burial, the service was also to be a thanksgiving for deliverance from the invasion, and prayers in supplication for attacks not to be repeated. Consequently, the Duke's burial would take place at the abbey of Quarr. It had been untouched by the French, and the abbey church was the only one left that could accommodate everyone.

As he galloped along the track over the downs Robert thought on how much had happened since he had covered the same route only six weeks or so before. He was now the lord of the manor, was betrothed to the prettiest girl on the Island; he was to be married as soon as it could be arranged and he had a perfect little nephew. Despite the trauma of the intervening weeks, the sun was warm on his back and the shadows pranced onwards before him as he galloped. The Island – his island – would still survive as a haven of peace and happiness. The future looked quite exciting as well as satisfying. He felt that he had had enough adventures to last the rest of his life. No more would he want to go to the wars over the seas; he would remain on the Island, raise and look after his family and act as protector to his peasants.

Harold's parents had not been found, and it had to be presumed that they had been killed. Robert resolved to take the boy as a page, so that he would eventually grow to be a squire, and a staunch right hand to his lord.

Robert did marry his lovely Rachel. They had a son, Richard, who in the fullness of time succeeded him as lord of the manor of Affeton. He, as Sir Richard de Affeton, was eventually buried in the same churchyard as his parents and his grandfather before him. All these centuries later the family is still commemorated in All Saints Church at Freshwater, by Affeton Chapel. In it there is a fifteenth-century sepulchral recess dedicated to Sir Richard, and there is a plaque to Sir Roger de Affeton, lord of the manor in the reign of Edward III. Adjacent is a third memorial showing an unnamed man in knightly dress and a woman, side by side.

Historical Note

After Edward III died on 21 June 1377 there were extensive French raids on the English south coast.

On 21 August 1377 the Isle of Wight was attacked by the 'Noddies', and reputedly taken by craft rather than force. Yarmouth, Francheville, Nieuport (today Newport) and Brading were burned, together with smaller villages such as Freshwater and Nunwell, the invaders penetrating as far south as Arreton. In Yarmouth the town and one of the two churches were destroyed, while in Newport the church of St Thomas was the only building to survive. Both towns took many years to recover; no one lived in Newport for at least two years after the invasion. Francheville (now Newtown) never recovered its former importance.

There were supposed to have been 7,099 inhabitants of the Island at the time, and folklore suggests 6,000 invaders, comprised of both French and their Castilian allies. The invaders hung the burgesses (bailiffs) of Newport and besieged Carisbrooke (then Caresbrooke) Castle. To intimidate those besieged, the French made two circuits of the castle night and morning, but one morning they were ambushed in a lane on their way to the castle, and many were killed. The lane was then known as Deadman's Lane, later to be renamed Trafalgar Road. Their bodies were buried at the French camp, which became known as Noddies' Hill, later corrupted to Nodehill.

During one of the circuits round the castle, Peter de Heyno, Lord of Stenbury, a noted bowman, shot and killed the French leader with his crossbow from the gatehouse.

Finally, the French withdrew after extracting a ransom of 1,000 marks from the Islanders, together with a promise not to resist should the French come back the following year. The funeral of the French commander was held in Quarr Abbey.

There was a three-day market held at Francheville on 22 June, the Feast of St Mary Magdalene. This was one of the largest

Historical Note

annual fairs on the Island. By edict it would have included archery and other competitive events.

In the Afton Chapel of the church of All Saints at Freshwater there are two tombstones, which probably had inset brasses, but now only the matrices survive. One is 'The supposed monument of Sir Roger de Affeton, Lord of the Manor in the reign of Edward III'. The other is unmarked. One shows a knight and his lady, the other a single knight. The slabs lay formerly in the floor in front of a sepulchral recess, which was in the south wall of the chapel. Traditionally this recess is thought to have been the fifteenth-century tomb of Sir Richard de Affeton. When this tomb was opened in the eighteenth century, it was found to contain a skeleton with its head placed between its legs, suggesting Sir Richard had been executed. In the Compton Chapel on the north of the chancel is a brass memorial 'Probably to Adam de Compton in the reign of Richard II'. To the right of the head is a scroll inscribed: *'Por mes petches merci prie'*.

The timing of the various events during the invasion is conjectural, as are the relationships of the characters. The lords of the manors and their roles in defence of the Island are known. Robert de Affeton was a real person, but nothing is known of the women. The names of the French leaders have had to be invented, and the rest of the action is imaginary. While every attempt has been made to ensure the supporting facts are correct, the author is solely responsible for any mistakes, misunderstandings or other errors in this account.

Printed in the United Kingdom
by Lightning Source UK Ltd.
126179UK00001B/19-33/A